TESSA'S TRUST

THE ANNA ALBERTINI FILES

❧

REBECCA ZANETTI

RAZ INK LLC

This one is for Karlina Zanetti, one of the strongest, sweetest, and smartest people I've ever met. Even though I work with words, it's difficult to find the right ones to describe how wonderful I think you are and how proud I am to be your mom. From the first time I saw you on a sonogram to now while you're in college forging your own path, I've been in awe of you.
I hope you know how very much I love you.

NOTE FROM THE AUTHOR

Howdy everyone! Thank you for so much support for his new series of mine. Sometimes, as an author, you have to write something a little different. This series is that for me.

I've loved the emails and FB notes about this series, and I'm happy to keep writing about Anna and her family. Sometimes we need a little bit of humor, right? This is a side note for the family with a full romance, which was fun to write.

Also, I am a lawyer, and I might live in a small town, but this is in **no way** autobiographical. It turns out that the name Albertini is a distant family name of my relatives, which is pretty cool. However, the story is all made up. The characters are all fictional and so are the towns and counties (like usual). Also, the law is correct. :)

I hope you like Anna's world as much as I do!

Also, to stay up to date with releases, free content, and tons of contests, follow me on Bookbub, Facebook, the FB Rebel Street Team, and definitely subscribe to my newsletter for FREE BOOKS!

Also, I like to pair up with other bestselling authors to cross promote and give away books in our newsletters, so I will be giving away copies of my friends' books coming up. Just go to my website (RebeccaZanetti.com) to sign up for my newsletter.

XO

Rebecca

ACKNOWLEDGMENTS

Thank you to:

Big Tone, for always being supportive and having a great sense of humor, and to Gabe and Karlina for being such great kids who give me plenty of ideas to write about;

Chelle Olson of Literally Addicted to Detail for the in depth edits;

Asha Hossain of Asha Hossain Designs, LLC for the truly excellent cover;

Stella Bloom for the perfectly pitched narration for the audio books;

Caitlin Blasdell, for being my insightful and cheerful agent;

Anissa Beatty, for your hard work as you try to keep me organized and for being such a fantastic leader for Rebecca's Rebels (my FB street team);

Thanks to Rebels Madison Fairbanks, Suzi Zuber, Kimberly Frost, Heather Frost, Asmaa Qayyum, Jessica Mobbs, and Leanna Feazel, for their excellent insights;

Thank you to Writer Space and Fresh Fiction PR for all the hard work;

Thank you also to my constant support system: Gail and Jim English, Kathy and Herb Zanetti, Debbie and Travis Smith, Stephanie and Don West, Jessica and Jonah Namson, Chelli and Jason Younker, Cathie and Bruce Bailey, Liz and Steve Berry, and Jillian and Benji Stein.

CHAPTER 1

I ignored the worried looks of the two lawyers in the dusty space and signed my name with a flourish, careful not to press too hard since the contract perched precariously on an overturned wooden barrel that had once held whiskey. *Contessa Carmelina Albertini.* It was difficult, but I fought the urge to dot the last *i* with a heart. This was a dream come true, and I had worked my butt off for longer than I wanted to admit to get here.

Sadie Brando signed right after I did, her gnarled hand moving slowly across the paper as she no doubt fought both arthritis and a slight tremble.

Her lawyer, who also happened to be her younger brother, shook his head. Even though it was the day after Christmas and he'd been called in unexpectedly, he wore a blue suit with a red power tie. "Sadie," he said again.

"Shush." She lifted her other hand. "It's done, Jonathan. Mind your business, young man. Tessa and I have been dickering about this place for the last two months. We just needed you here to make sure it was official."

Jonathan was about eighty with thick gray hair, dark blue eyes, and slightly stooped shoulders. He had come over from Billings just for the day and no doubt hadn't expected this.

I wanted to be sympathetic, but I was too happy to finally be getting this place. I'd paid a pretty penny for it, but it was worth it.

My lawyer shook her head. I trusted her implicitly, even though she wore leggings covered in drunken ducks, a ripped University of Idaho sweatshirt, and her hair in a ponytail. When I'd asked her to drive over the mountain pass and meet me here, I hadn't exactly told her why. She was my younger sister, and I had known she'd want to sign as a witness. She'd come the second I called, even though it was the day after Christmas and she'd been holed up with her sexy Irishman, who, quite frankly, I figured was difficult to leave.

Anna reached for the papers. "Let me at least read the contract."

Sadie shook her head. "Don't need you to read it. We just needed two witnesses and figured lawyers would be good."

Anna narrowed her eyes. "You don't need witnesses to this type of contract." She frowned at Jonathon and somehow managed to look more beautiful than ever. "I'm uncomfortable having my sister sign a contract I haven't read."

"We had an agreement," Sadie said, waiting for Jonathan to sign as a witness—which he did after sighing loudly. Then she jutted out her chin. "Anna? You have to sign your legal name."

"Are you sure about this?" Anna asked, her gaze direct on me.

"Yes, Anna," I said. "Trust me in that I've read over the contract and I'd love to have you as a witness. Believe me, I want this."

She bit her lip the way she did when she was concerned. She was a couple of inches shorter than me and didn't take after either our Italian or Irish sides in the looks department with her grayish-green eyes and auburn hair.

I, on the other hand, was all Irish—reddish-blond hair, green eyes, and skin that burned at midnight. I wished I could tan like my sisters did.

"I do trust you but still want to read this," Anna said.

Sadie glanced at her overlarge watch. "It's now or never."

"Please, Anna?" I asked. "I already signed it, so I'm bound."

Unlike Jonathan, Anna kept from sighing when she took the pen and signed her full legal name, *Anna Fiona Albertini*. We came from Irish and Italian stock, so all three of us girls had both an Irish and an Italian name.

Our older sister, Donatella Tiffany, was a realtor and would help me record the deed when she returned from a girls' trip to Napa Valley. She'd left earlier that morning after the holiday revelry had concluded.

Sadie smiled, showing worn dentures. "That's better." She turned to me, spat into her brown-spotted hand, and held it out. I did the same, and we shook. It was kind of gross, but Sadie was ninety years old, and I figured that was how they'd done it back in the day.

The building was older than she was by at least twenty years, and now it was mine. I looked around the wide space at the old bar against the corner and the new wood paneling on the far wall. The vast space would make the perfect restaurant.

I kept from wiping my hand on my jeans when we'd finished.

Sadie did the same. "I'm glad you'll be moving in upstairs since we I renovated it all before selling. It's a beautiful space."

I absolutely couldn't wait. "You did an amazing job, although my old furniture won't do it justice." I grinned. "Hopefully I can get some new furnishings as soon as possible."

The door burst open and a man barreled inside, his face ruddy and his brown hair standing on end. "Aunt Sadie? You cannot sell this place. It's mine."

Sadie sighed. "Tessa, Anna, meet my nephew, Rudy."

Huh. The name fit his red face. "Hello," I murmured. Who the heck was Rudy? Everybody knew everybody in the small town, and I did not know this guy. He had to be around thirty, and was tall and lean with blond hair that bristled. Actually bristled.

Sadie cracked her gnarled knuckles. "Rudy's dad was my younger brother, George. Georgie died about fifty years ago, and we just found out about Rudy a few months ago."

Rudy glowered.

"It's done," Sadie said.

Anna peered over my shoulder at the contract again. "Where did you get a hundred and fifty thousand dollars in cash, Tessa?" she murmured.

I just smiled. "Doesn't matter." Her eyebrow lifted, and I knew there would be a lot of questioning later. "This place is amazing." Finally, I could start the life I wanted.

Sadie nodded, the thin skin of her neck jiggling. She was probably about five feet tall and had her gray hair in tight curls. Her blue eyes were faded and almost translucent. She could see well enough, and she had the hearing of a bat, which I knew from experience after negotiating with her the last couple of months. "This is a good place, honey. It served me well." She patted my arm. "If you run illegal gambling out of the back again, watch out for the FBI. When they raided us in eighty-nine, it was a real pain in the ass."

Jonathan smacked his palm against his forehead. "Crap, Sadie, we don't talk about that."

"Eh, everybody knows about it," Sadie said. "My profits sure took a hit for a while, though, I've got to tell you." For our signing day, she'd worn a lovely green linen dress that hung on her wiry frame and reached the floor. I was pretty sure it was supposed to be knee-length, but on her, it was longer than her thick gray wool coat. "Okay, we're set. Don't forget what you promised, Tessa."

"I couldn't if I wanted to," I admitted.

She cackled and slid her arm through her brother's. "Come on. You're taking me to breakfast."

Jonathan looked at me, glanced at the contract, and then shook his head. "All right, sister." He barely glanced at Rudy. "You're not in the will, kid. Get over it."

Rudy glared, narrowing bright blue eyes at me. "We'll see about that." He turned on a polished loafer and stomped out.

Sadie snorted. "What a dork. He actually thinks he owns the place already."

Anna stiffened. "Why would he think that?"

My stomach clenched. "Yeah. Why?"

Sadie shrugged. "Heck if I know. He doesn't, so don't worry."

Jonathan then glanced at the iron sign hanging on the far wall. The hammered metal held an engraved high-heel shoe and text that said *Silver Sadie's*. "Are we taking the sign?"

"Nope," Sadie said. "That was part of the deal."

"I want the sign," I admitted. The thing had character and had hung there for probably over a century. Sadie had been named for her great-aunt Sadie, and it was rumored that the first Sadie had run alcohol when it was illegal.

I didn't doubt there had also been some prostitution at the beginning of the century when the mines were flush. But for as far back as anybody remembered, the place was a bar with a gambling den in the back, one the FBI had shut down in 1989. I noticed there were still poker tables back there, but I had plans for that space that didn't involve gambling.

Sadie and her brother left, leaving Anna and me to look around the large, vacant place.

"You just bought a restaurant," my sister said, frowning.

Even if she couldn't see the potential of the wide-open space, I could. It had been gutted in a fire about a year ago. Sadie had tried to repair it but decided she would live out the rest of her years without worrying about the place. She was a tough negotiator, as I could attest from the contract. I had no idea what she planned to do with my hundred and fifty thousand dollars, but hopefully, she'd keep it from the cranky and newly found Rudy. This place was well worth the money. It was in a two-story brick building, and I was going to live above the restaurant as I got it going.

Anna shook her head and reached for the contract. "I don't

mind you having me here signing things, but don't you think I should've read this first?"

"You just signed as a witness. You're not obligated or anything," I said as something scurried in the far background. I shivered. I really needed to clean out the entire first floor. Thus, I'd worn old jeans and a white T-shirt to get right to work today, even though it was snowing wildly outside.

"Okay." Anna reached for the contract and flipped through it. "This is good. The agreement for the deed is good." She paused. "What the...?"

I knew what she had found. "It's okay. It's not a big deal."

She looked up, her grayish-green eyes wide. "Are you kidding me?"

"It's not a big deal," I repeated, heat climbing into my face.

She shook her head. "You agreed to go on a date with each of her nephews within one week of signing this contract? I didn't even know Bobbo was still around."

"They're her great-nephews. Rudy is *not* included in the deal, whoever the heck he is." I kicked a brick out of my way. "She really wants one of them to marry and carry on the Brando name since her brother never did. I told her I wasn't looking for romance, and it was just one date each."

To be honest, I didn't think Bobbo was around either, but I was about to find out, considering Sadie had arranged for us to meet for dinner in a few hours. I told Sadie that I hadn't dressed for a dinner date, but she said I looked fine and that I shouldn't appear as if I were trying too hard.

I didn't want to try at all. I'd given up on romance after a disastrous time with a jerk of an ex-boyfriend. He'd ended up getting murdered, and even though I didn't think anybody deserved that, nobody really missed the guy.

"Huh," Anna said. "What else did you agree...?" She stopped mid-sentence. "Oh."

I shifted uncomfortably. "That's the other reason you're here."

Anna had a penchant for solving crimes. She was a big-shot lawyer in the city—or what constituted a city in my small northern Idaho life—and when helping out clients, she usually solved a crime or two.

Tendrils of her shiny brown hair fell out of her ponytail. "Tessa, Lenny Johnson was murdered nine months ago. It's still an active case."

"I know," I said, my shoulders hunching until I remembered to straighten them. Lenny Johnson had been a vagabond and drunk in our small town. His body had been found in the cellar of Silver Sadie's. I needed Nana O'Shea to perform a sage cleansing down there as soon as possible. "I promised her we'd do our best to figure out who killed him."

"We?" Anna's eyebrows rose.

Yeah, Sadie was no dummy. She knew the Albertini girls stuck together, and that if I signed the contract, Anna would help me. "Sure. You solve crimes all the time."

"I'm a lawyer," she muttered, looking more like a teenager headed out for a sleepover.

"I know," I said. "All I did was say I'd *try* to solve it. As you can read in the contract, I was sure not to promise." Because, honestly, I'd never solved a crime in my life. I hadn't even gone to college. Not that you had to go to college to solve crimes, but my sister had a law degree, which meant she'd been to college for seven years and knew a lot more about crime than I did.

"I didn't know you were going to buy a restaurant in Silverville," she murmured.

We had both grown up in the small Idaho mining community and then moved over the pass to the bigger metropolis of Timber City, where she worked as a lawyer, and I had waitressed at Smiley's Diner until, well…next month, after I trained two servers to take my spot. But I knew if I opened a restaurant, I wanted to be closer to home. And something about Silver Sadie's called to me.

Women had owned it from the beginning, and I was talking probably from 1890 until today. Strong women fighting upstream and making their dreams come true. I wanted the place, and now, it was mine. To keep it, all I had to do was go on a date with three guys I barely knew and solve a murder.

What could possibly go wrong?

CHAPTER 2

I had just finished mucking out what had been the bar area when my phone rang. I looked toward the windows and the vast blizzard spinning snow around outside and shivered. Had I found enough space for my tables? I wasn't sure. I may have been a little exuberant when I purchased them the month before.

"Hello?" I said absently, wiping dust off my jeans. At least I'd flipped my white T-shirt inside out before moving items around.

"Tessa, it's Nonna. I heard you just bought Silver Sadie's."

I jolted and looked toward the expansive windows again. Nope, nobody was out in the blistering weather. The snow bombarded the area, covering the icy sidewalk. "That was quick."

She chuckled. "This is Silverville. When did you sign the papers?"

"About two hours ago."

"Huh, I must be losing my touch," she murmured. "Why didn't you say anything?"

I chewed on my lip. "I wanted to do it myself, Nonna," I said. "It's not that I didn't trust anybody, I just..."

"I get it." A slight Italian accent came through the phone.

9

"That's fine. Tell me you at least had your sister look at the contract."

I turned my head and sneezed. Man, this place was dusty.

"Anna signed as a witness." There was no need to go into more detail than that.

"Oh, good." She sighed. "That Sadie, she can be a shyster, you know."

I cleared my throat. "Yeah, I know." I sneezed again.

"Bless you, sweetheart," she said. "Well, what can I do to help? If I recall, that place needs some work."

I loved my nonna. She looked like Sophia Loren, acted like the queen of England on a mission, and loved us with all her heart. She was fully Italian and often kept a wooden spoon in her purse in case she needed to smack somebody.

"I think I'm good for now. I have a date with Bobbo Brando tonight."

She sighed. "Don't tell me; it was part of your contract?"

I grinned. "Yeah. Sadie wants me to go on a date with each of her great-nephews. It's not a big deal. We're just having dinner at McCloskey's, and then I'll head back over the pass."

"McCloskey's for a date?" she murmured. "That's not exactly romantic."

"Good," I burst out. "This is contractual. I'm not interested in Bobbo. I haven't seen the guy in what? Ten years, at least."

"Oh, I see him all the time," Nonna said. "He is too old for you, though. What is he, like thirty-five?"

"I think so." Bobbo had been a high school football star when I was still in elementary school—a huge linebacker. "I just remember he seemed like a large kid."

"Oh, yeah. He's a big farmer now. He's got quite a few acres, and I heard he broke up with his fiancée not too long ago. Apparently, the woman had quite a temper," she said, the beeping of a microwave coming over the line. "I don't think he's Italian."

So much for Bobbo, then. I turned my head and sneezed again, searching for a Kleenex in my purse.

"Bless you," she said. "Obviously, we need to clean that place."

"Obviously," I agreed. "I'm working on it now, but I don't want to get too dusty before dinner. Besides, isn't Brando an Italian name?"

"Huh," she said thoughtfully. "I don't know, but I don't see you living on a farm."

The woman definitely knew me. "No, I think I'd rather be here in town."

Calling Silverville a town might be a little silly, considering it was two blocks of businesses and a county courthouse. But still, I didn't want to be way out in the middle of nowhere. Not that I was interested in Bobbo. I didn't know the guy but maybe we'd have a nice dinner.

Nonna cleared her throat. "After dinner with Bobbo, why don't you stay the night here? The roads are only going to get worse, and I don't think the snow's supposed to stop all night."

"I'll think about it. I need to start packing my apartment and was planning to do that tomorrow."

"You can't do that all by yourself," Nonna said. "I assume you're moving to the second floor of your new building? Those steps aren't easy to navigate while carrying boxes. We used to have rummage sales up there once in a while, and I remember nearly tripping a few times."

She wasn't wrong. "I know," I said. "But my lease is up tomorrow, and I have to be out by Monday."

"Oh, my. All right. I'll get your cousins on it. They'll come help you."

I wanted to protest, but frankly, I needed the help. "Okay, great, Nonna. Thank you."

Nobody could say no to Nonna, so at least that was taken care of. I hadn't done it on purpose, but things were falling into place nicely.

"All right. Call me after your date and tell me if you're heading over the pass so I can worry the whole time or if you're going to stay with us for the night. I have huckleberry pie."

"I'll be over after my date," I murmured. She knew I couldn't resist huckleberry pie, and the guilt trip worked as planned.

"Oh, that's good. What a smart decision. All right. Have a lovely date." She hung up. About six months ago, she'd stopped saying goodbye and just ended every call like some executive from New York. I think she fancied herself the chess master of us all, so it greatly amused me. So long as none of my cousins started picking up the habit, I thought it was kind of sweet.

Sighing, I turned back to the building's interior and wondered what to do with the stacks of extra lumber in the far corner. Maybe one of my cousins needed it for a project or something.

I worked quietly for another couple of hours, creating piles of items to keep, stuff to throw away, and building supplies that somebody in the family might want.

Glancing at my watch, I gasped. Oh, crap, I had to run. I looked at the windows to make sure nobody was outside, and darkness had already fallen, then tore my shirt up and over my head before pulling it back down, making sure it wasn't too dusty. It looked all right.

I finger-combed my hair and grabbed some colored lip gloss from my purse before dusting off my jeans and hurriedly putting on my boots. After pulling on a heavy coat and gloves, I hustled outside into the billowing weather, forced back a foot by the freezing wind. Man, it was cold. I ducked my chin into my coat and started to jog across the now-snowy sidewalk the two blocks to McCloskey's.

Bobbo was waiting outside, his hands in his pockets and his body huddled with no coat.

"Hi," I said.

"Hi," he echoed. "It's freezing. Come inside."

I'd forgotten how big he was. He was at least six foot eight with shoulders broader than a Buick. Well, maybe not that wide, but he was big. I wasn't a tall girl, but I was taller than both Anna and Donna, so I'd always felt that being five foot six had some height. Apparently not.

"Here, let me take your coat." Bobbo had a deep voice.

For our date, he'd worn clean overalls and a blue-and-white-checked flannel. He had thick brown hair and matching beard, and his eyes were a cornflower blue. Crinkles extended from them, showing he smiled often.

"Thanks." I let him take my coat and then made sure my jeans were brushed free of dirt.

"Thanks for doing this," he said. "I guess your biological clock is ticking?"

I paused and then coughed before clearing my throat. "No. No ticking. No clock."

"Oh." He looked mildly disappointed. "All right."

He slapped a name tag sticker above my heart. I looked down. "Tessa Albertini?"

"Yeah." He stuck his name tag on his chest.

I looked over to see tables lined up and people milling around with drinks in their hands. "What's going on?"

"It's speed dating," Bobbo said. "I figured I'd kill two birds with one stone."

My mouth gaped, and I quickly shut it. "We have a date to speed date?"

"Sure." He lifted a shoulder. "To be honest, I didn't remember you from when we were kids, but I know you Albertini girls cause a ruckus."

"Hey," I said, instantly protesting not only my innocence but also my sister's. Just one. Anna. Donna never got into trouble. "That's not true."

"Dead bodies keep piling up around your sister's place over in Timber City," he murmured. "I don't like dead bodies."

I brushed the hair away from my face, knowing the snow

would make it a mass of curls whether I liked it or not. I often didn't because curls turned frizzy, but at this point, I didn't care much. "That wasn't Anna's fault."

"It's never Anna's fault," he rumbled. "But wasn't a dead body found in your apartment? The guy you used to date?"

I winced. "Yeah." Danny Pucci, my last disastrous boyfriend, had been found in my apartment. "But Krissy Walker killed him. I didn't." She'd tried to frame me, and she was now in prison.

"So they say," Bobbo said, scratching his beard.

"Fair enough." At least I didn't have to get through a whole dinner of small talk with Bobbo. This was the price of owning my little slice of a future, and it was worth it. "How long ago did you break up with your fiancée?"

He gulped. "You checked me out, huh? It was a couple of months ago. Louise took one of my credit cards as well as my debit card and spent a fortune, saying we needed new furniture. I need food for the animals and like my home the way it is right now." His sigh moved his entire chest. "If I had stayed with her, I'd be bankrupt by now."

It wasn't any of my business, and I should stick to that. Business. "Real quick, tell me about Rudy."

Bobbo rolled his eyes. "Guy showed up a few months ago with a birth certificate that showed he was the son of Aunt Sadie's youngest brother, who left at eighteen, never looked back, and apparently died young. Rudy does look a bit like the family, but he waltzed in acting like we all owed him something. We don't."

"So there's no chance he owns any part of Sadie's restaurant?" I wasn't a moron and thus had paid for a title search. It was clear.

Bobbo shook his head. "Not that I know of." He winked. "You ready for our speed date of dates?"

Sure. Why not? "Okay. How do we do this thing?"

"We'll start together," he said. "And then, if things go well, maybe we'll end up together."

Yeah, that wouldn't happen. "Do we just pick a table?"

"Sure. You want a drink first?"

"Yes," I said. "I definitely want a drink first."

We ambled up to the bar. He ordered a lager stout while I requested a glass of prosecco. I wanted to tell the bartender to leave the bottle, but I figured that probably wasn't proper, though *proper* was quickly fleeing.

A rustle sounded by the door, and I turned, my heart stopping. "Nonna, what are you doing here?" I hurried toward her just as I noticed Gerty Basanelli behind her. My heart started to sink into the pit of my stomach. No. What were they doing?

"Hello," Nonna said, walking the rest of the way inside and unwrapping her scarf. "I heard there was speed dating going on here."

"Yes, Nonna, but you're married. Happily, I might add," I said dryly. What was the woman up to now?

Gerty giggled next to her. Whereas my nonna was tall with dark hair tinged with gray, Gerty was a tiny little thing with curled white hair and a button nose. They were an odd couple but the best of friends.

"Why are you two here?" I asked again.

The door opened, and everything became all too clear. Nick Basanelli walked in, wiping snow off his broad shoulders. "Grams?" he asked. "Where's your car? You said you had a flat."

Heat flared in my face, and honestly, if the proverbial floor could open, I would dive in headfirst.

His gaze caught mine and then flicked to Bobbo before returning full force to me, his eyes bourbon brown, piercing, and intelligent. "What's going on?"

"Oh, there you are." Sally Franks hustled up from a table I hadn't noticed near the door. She pressed a sticker to Nick's chest. "We're so happy to have you here. I sent out a call that you'd be at the tables, and we're having the best turnout ever." She patted the sticker and hummed happily. Sally was recently divorced, around forty, and rumored to be looking for a new man.

Nick took a step away from her, looked down at the name tag, at his grandma, at me, and then back to Gerty. "What is going on? You said you had a flat tire."

"Oh, that." Gerty waved it away. "I had that taken care of, but I thought you should try this speed dating. I didn't want Tessa to have to do it alone."

His gaze flicked to me again. Nick Basanelli was well over six feet of raw Italian muscle. He was sleek and strong, one of the smartest people I'd ever known, and more ambitious than a wide receiver ten yards from goal. His hair was black, his eyes a tawny brown, and his bone structure all Italian. In other words, he was fucking gorgeous, and the guy probably knew it.

"You're speed dating?" he asked.

I lifted a shoulder.

"Yes, and she's not alone," Bobbo said, dropping a beefy arm over my shoulders.

I staggered under the sudden weight, tightening my hold on my champagne glass.

Nick cocked his head. I couldn't really think of a good explanation, so I didn't say anything. Sometimes, that was the best move. Nick leaned toward his grandmother. "Grams, I'm not speed dating."

"The heck you aren't," she said. "I called earlier with a credit card. I paid your fifty dollars. You wouldn't disappoint your grandma, would you?"

I couldn't help the smile twitching my lips. At least I wasn't alone in this. Plus, considering he'd had me arrested for murder late last year, I was ready for some payback.

CHAPTER 3

arrow tables were bracketed by an orange leather bench running the length of the far wall, opposite well-crafted wooden chairs. Apparently, the women were to sit on the luxurious bench, and the men would take the chairs and then move every ten minutes. I liked that idea, so I settled in with my glass of Prosecco and snuggled my butt against the plush leather.

Bobbo spilled out of the chair across from me. He tugged on an overall strap. "Is there something going on between you and Nick Basanelli?"

I cast a guilty look down the long rows of tables to see Nick seated across from Sally. Huh. I wondered how she'd managed that. The woman was preening and twirling a lock of her bottle-blond hair.

"No," I said shortly. "Our grandmothers have been trying to fix us up since before the holidays, but there is definitely nothing going on between Nick Basanelli and me."

I'd go to the grave before admitting I found him intriguing, but I was female, and I had a pulse, so it probably wouldn't shock anybody. We didn't fit, and there was no question about that. He'd been a football stud in high school. He'd gone on to play in college before becoming a hero in the military, and now, he was a prosecuting attorney. I had no doubt that his future held higher offices, whereas I was a small-town girl who worked in a diner. It was sweet that our grandmas thought we'd make a good match, but we didn't.

"Hey," Bobbo said. "Where'd you go?"

"Sorry. I was in my head."

That was rare. Usually, Anna was in her head, and I was the one drawing her out, but Nick Basanelli did that to me, and that was just life. "So, tell me about your farm." I focused on my three-minute date.

"Oh." Bobbo leaned forward. "I own thirty head, a bunch of chickens, and now have diversified into raising alpacas."

I blinked. "Alpacas?"

"You bet," he said. "They have a minimal negative environmental impact, and they're a lot of fun to have around. I've chosen wisely when it comes to the different colors of fur."

I didn't think I'd ever seen a real alpaca up close. "Well, that's nice," I acknowledged. "How long have you been speed dating?"

"They do it every other month here at McCloskey's. I've been a few times, but I haven't found my soulmate. I usually end up with somebody for the night or weekend, though." He waggled his eyebrows. "Looking down this line, I've seen and talked to most of the people. Not that gal three down, though."

I leaned forward to peruse the long length of the many tables. "Whoa. That's Kelsey Walker," I murmured.

He jerked his head. "Walker? As in the gal who killed Danny Pucci?"

"That's her sister." If I remembered right, she'd attempted to help remove a bomb from my sister's leg and then stayed with Anna, even as the ATF guys were trying to dismantle the explosive. "She's a nice person. You should talk to her."

"Huh. She's pretty."

She was pretty. All the Walker girls were. She was blond with crystal-blue eyes. I'd heard she'd had a rough time of it. In fact, she dated Danny after I did, so I *knew* she had a rough time of it. That was one of the reasons her sister had killed the bastard.

"I guess I should just lay it out there." Bobbo stretched his mammoth arms. "You want to come home with me tonight?"

I lifted my glass and took a deep drink of the bubbles. "Nope."

"Huh." His jowls moved, and he scratched his beard. It must be a nervous habit. "Was it because I brought you speed dating for our date?"

"Sure." I drank half my prosecco in two gulps. "Also..." I might as well give him the truth. "I don't think you can really meet somebody based on a contract."

"Sure, you can," Bobbo said. "A lot of people have arranged marriages. It's rare not to. We're the odd ones here in this country."

The man had a point. "I guess that's true."

"Now will you come home with me?" Bobbo patted his stomach. "I'll give you a good time and cook you a great breakfast in the morning."

I was a sucker for a good breakfast, but not that much. "I appreciate it, Bobbo, but I'm not going home with you."

"I wonder if I could change your mind," he said thoughtfully. The buzzer went off, and relief flowed through me. "All right." Bobbo shoved his chair back. The thing almost fell over, but he caught it. "I'm not done yet," he told me. "I'm coming back."

I just smiled. It was warm in the bar, and the champagne was already going to my head, so there was no doubt I was staying with Nonna tonight. "My grandmother is right over there," I said. "She'd throw a fit if I went home with some man on the first date."

Which, incidentally, was something I had never done. Out of the three of us girls, for some reason, I'd been thought of as the wild one until recently. I didn't know why. I was a free spirit, but I rarely dated, and I worked all the time.

Maybe it was because Donna was automatically type-A, the

eldest and hugely successful. Then Anna, my younger sister, had been lost for quite a while—but that was another story. So, I guessed people just put me into a slot. The important thing to remember was that I could do what I wanted with it.

Nick side-stepped Bobbo and pulled out the chair to sit.

"You skipped several people," I murmured dryly.

"I don't care. You're the reason I'm in this mess." Nick settled in, looking sexy in a black button-down shirt and faded jeans.

I smiled. I kind of *was* the reason he was in this mess. "You can't blame me for what our grandmothers planned." We'd been fairly successful in avoiding their matchmaking attempts these last few months. They'd even put us on a charity board before the holidays, but neither of us had made a meeting. We'd both been working.

Bobbo glared at Nick and winked at me. "I'll be back." He moved down to sit across from Kelsey Walker.

Apparently, there wasn't any sort of seating order at McCloskey's. I'd seen speed dating on television and thought the moving party had to shift to the next table. Apparently not. I scrutinized Nick. "Well?"

"Well, what?" he muttered.

"You're supposed to charm me."

He cocked his head, looking way too handsome under the soft lights above the tables. "I'm supposed to charm you?"

"Yeah. You think you can?"

"A challenge? Oh, baby, if I wanted to charm you, your socks would be off," he retorted instantly.

I chuckled. That was one thing about Nick. He was quick with a comeback. He was probably amazing in court.

"What are you doing on this side of the pass anyway?" I asked.

"It's the day after Christmas," he said. "I went snowmobiling with my brothers and returned to the family home just in time to catch my grandmother's call. You know, about her flat tire."

"Oh, that. I've heard there's a flat tire bandit going around town," I murmured. "They must have gotten Gerty."

Nick just watched me, reminding me of a hawk about to dive hard on scurrying prey. "Are you still mad at me?"

I swallowed. While I understood he'd only been doing his job, the guy had issued my arrest warrant, probably instinctively knowing I didn't do it. "Yes."

"Can't blame you." Man, his voice was smooth. Like good whiskey poured over ice. "But I had a job to do, and I knew your lawyer would take care of you. I couldn't appear to give you favoritism."

I didn't want to be fair about that, but I did understand. Plus, my sister had informed me that Nick had also worked behind the scenes, around the clock, to find out who had really killed my ex. I had a feeling he'd wanted the killer to be Aiden Devlin, my sister's beau. Apparently, Nick was still irritated that Aiden had hidden his affiliation with the ATF while undercover. "I don't want to talk about old news," I finally said.

"Fair enough. Why are you in town?"

I lost my smile and reached for my prosecco again. I was proud of what I'd accomplished, but even so, my voice softened just a little when I spoke. "I bought Silver Sadie's." Then I looked down at my glass.

He was quiet for a moment. "Wow."

I looked up. "Would you care to expound on that statement?"

"That's impressive," he said. "People have been trying to get Sadie to sell for years."

"It took me months," I admitted. "We've been negotiating for quite a while." I gestured down the line of tables toward Bobbo. "Hence date number one."

Nick's grin reached his eyes. "You have to go on more dates with Bobbo?"

"Oh, no. Just one with Bobbo, but then his other two brothers, as well."

The look of amusement slid out of Nick's eyes. "You're not going on a date with Eddie."

Eddie was the middle great-nephew, and I didn't know much about him.

"I am. It's in the contract," I said.

Nick leaned forward, a muscle ticking in his jaw. "Your sister let you sign a contract that forces you to go on a date with Eddie Brando?"

I reared up, and even my ears heated. "My sister didn't *let* me do anything. I read the contract. I understood it. I was happy with it, and I signed it."

Nick's chin lowered. "You are not going on a date with Eddie Brando."

"Listen, Nick," I said, "I'm sure you're used to being all bossy with everybody in your office, but I'm not in your world. I don't work for you, and you're not going to tell me what to do."

Pretty much nothing in the world could have stopped me from going on a date with Eddie Brando at that point.

"You're as unreasonable as your sister," he muttered.

"Don't you talk about my sister like that." Heat raced through my veins.

True, Anna had made some miscalculations when working for Nick that had ended with her getting fired, but she was happier than happy could be owning her own law firm. "She was the best lawyer you've ever had in your office."

"Yeah, she was," he said quietly. "And she let her personal life cloud her judgment."

Was that a direct hit? It felt like it. My foot tensed.

"You kick me, and we're going to have a problem." His gaze turned piercing.

I stilled. When Basanelli issued a threat, it came across clean. I had to respect that. Also, I had barely moved my foot. How did he know I wanted to kick him? "My guess is most women want to kick you," I retorted.

"It's possible, but I strongly recommend you don't." Then he just waited, watching me patiently. It was almost a dare.

Maybe that was how I earned the *wild* moniker. I could never refuse a dare. So, I kicked him. It was just with my snow boot, which wasn't even a little pointy and glanced off his shin. Even so, it pushed his chair back a little bit.

Then I waited. Oh, the bubbly had most certainly gone to my head.

One of his dark eyebrows rose, and then his lids lowered to half-mast. He was fully Italian, and I'd expected something... more. Was I disappointed? Maybe. I didn't want Nick to be a guy I could push around. Not that it mattered what kind of guy he was, but still.

"You're all talk," I said.

"What makes you say that?" His voice was velvet over steel, and an unwilling tremble ticked down my spine.

"I kicked you," I said unnecessarily.

His chin lifted just enough to give him a predatory look. "I'm well aware you just made the colossal mistake of kicking me in the middle of McCloskey's. I meant every word I said. You will regret it." He crossed his arms, flexing pretty impressive chest muscles, and his smile sent butterflies winging through my stomach...mainly because it wasn't a smile. What was that look? "You didn't think I'd make you regret it right here, right now, did you?"

I kind of had. I figured he'd snap at me or stomp away. "Yes." I forced a smile.

"Oh, no, baby," he said so softly I leaned forward to hear him better. "I'm the most patient man you'll ever meet. I have no problem biding my time."

I lost the smile.

CHAPTER 4

The buzzer rang before I could think of anything to say to Nick, which was probably a good thing because I most likely would've challenged him, and right now, I felt more off-centered than I had in a long time.

With a slow, sardonic smile, he pushed away from the table, stood, and walked down to sit across from Kelsey Walker. A surprising spurt of jealousy ripped through me that I quickly quashed.

The rest of the evening proceeded quietly and calmly as I met a couple of new people but mainly spoke with men I'd known from high school. To be honest, by the end of the evening, I'd had a good time, but I certainly hadn't made any romantic connections. I'd also had my prosecco glass refilled a few times, and when I stood, the room tilted. Smiling, I beat Bobbo to my coat, even though he was trying to take it from the hook.

"I've got it," I said.

"That's okay." He wrenched it easily from my hands. "Turn around."

Unable to come up with an argument, I turned and let him

assist me with the wool jacket. "Thanks." I pivoted and quickly buttoned it up myself.

"You bet. You coming home with me?"

"I most certainly am not." I patted his beefy arm. "But I had a good time tonight, Bobbo. I have to say, I might try speed dating again someday." Not that I was looking for a man, but the activity had beat staying home and watching reruns while eating ice cream, which was my normal Friday night.

He scratched his beard, his brows drawing down, and his blue eyes looking like that cute cat's from the old *Shrek* movies. "Alrighty, then. You got a safe ride home?"

"I do," I said. "My grandma's here."

"Good." With that, he shoved both hands into the pockets of his overalls and strolled out the door. Wind and snow blew in until he shut it. I turned and walked over to where Nonna and Gerty sat at a table with two empty bottles of merlot in front of them.

"Ruh roh," I murmured. "I can't drive. Can you?"

They both shook their heads and then giggled. Wonderful. It looked like I was in charge. "All right, I'll call Papa to come pick us up."

"That's not necessary." Gerty hiccupped. "Nicolo," she yelled.

My heart sank. "No, really. That's—"

"Yes, Grams?" Nick suddenly spoke over my right shoulder.

Heat flushed my back, even though I wore a heavy coat.

"It looks like we all need a ride home. You can drop Elda and me off and then take Tessa over the pass. I believe she has to put her apartment together tomorrow. I mean, you're going to help her move, right?"

Oh, no. I was not being maneuvered like this. Not tonight. "Nope, that's okay," I said before Nick could say a word. "All of my cousins are coming to help me pack and move. Honestly, we have a full house already."

"That's good," Nick said dryly. "I'm in trial this week, Grams. I really do need to get back to work."

"Huh." Gerty looked crestfallen. "Well, maybe you two can have a nice chat over the pass."

Nope. There were huckleberries in my immediate future. I'd earned them. "I'm staying at my nonna's house tonight," I said smoothly. "She promised me huckleberry pie."

Nonna stood and wavered slightly, looking regal. "Oh, I forgot to tell you. I gave that pie to your cousin, Vince. Gosh darn it. And really, I have a lot to do tomorrow. You can stay next time, Tessa."

I narrowed my eyes at her. She'd been quite worried about me going across the pass before.

Nick's sigh was heavy behind me. "All right, let's get going, ladies. The storm's only getting worse."

Somehow, and I had to give him credit for it, he managed to bundle all three of us into his SUV. He must not have had anything to drink because he maneuvered through the storm easily and dropped Nonna off first before taking Gerty home. Finally, it was just the two of us in the warm and quiet vehicle.

"Do you think they'll ever give up?" I asked, wishing I hadn't drunk so much prosecco. I needed to be on my game when dealing with Nick.

"They will never give up...unless you want to marry Bobbo."

I laughed. "I think he might have offered, but we're not a good match. However, maybe he found true love tonight." We drove by my new building, and I cocked my head. "There's a light on inside Sadie's. I didn't leave one on."

Nick slowed down and parked at the icy curb. "Are you sure?"

I bit my lip. "Not really, but I want to make sure they're off." Had I forgotten in my haste to get to my odd date? I jumped out of the vehicle before he could respond and then hurried through the blasting snow to unlock the door and walk inside.

The place smelled like the wood polish I had used earlier, and a sense of warmth and belonging filled me. I really loved this place. I carefully stepped over to the light switch at the end of the bar and then paused, noting that the door to the stairs leading to the basement was open. "I know I shut and locked that."

Nick came up behind me and looked down the rickety wooden stairs, snow falling off his dark hair. "Are you sure?"

"Yeah, I am," I said. "I didn't want to drop anything or fall, and I left it shut all day." Plus, and I would never admit this to anybody, but it was a little creepy considering Lenny had been killed down there—a crime I was supposed to solve. "I'll go check it out."

A firm hand on my elbow drew me back. "*I'll* check it out," he said. "Stay here." Squaring his shoulders, he pushed the door open farther and started down the wooden steps.

Oh, heck no. This was my place. I wasn't ashamed to admit that I stayed behind him as he maneuvered all the way to the damp basement. When an ex-soldier with a hard body wanted to step in front of danger, I wasn't a dumb girl. His shoulders nicely blocked my view of the brick wall downstairs. He turned the corner and muttered something I couldn't quite make out.

"What?" I pushed to his side and stared into what should have been an empty cellar. In the middle of the room lay Rudy Brando with a six-inch knife handle protruding from his chest. Blood pooled on the floor around him, and his eyes were wide-open in death.

"Aw, crap," I muttered.

* * *

IF SHERIFF FRANCO had a first name, I didn't know it. He'd been sheriff for my entire life, and I only happened to know his last name because it was stitched across his softball uniform, a game he still played, even though he was in his eighties. He had thick white hair and normally wore faded jeans and a battered cowboy hat he'd had for as long as I could remember.

My soon-to-be cousin-in-law, Heather, had bet me about his age, thinking he was only sixty, yet you merely had to stare into the man's eyes to know that he'd lived at least eight decades.

Some of them looked to have been hard.

I sat across from the sheriff in his office. Pictures of his softball team, his grandkids, and the Seattle Seahawks covered the walls around us, except for a wide window behind him that faced the blistering storm on Main Street. He'd been questioning me for over an hour, and I'd stuck firm to my story because it was the truth.

"Are you sure you don't want an attorney?" he asked again.

"I don't," I said. "I trust you, Sheriff. I know you'll figure out who killed Rudy."

The sheriff nodded. "I appreciate that, but again, I think you should get a lawyer."

I sighed. Anna had returned over the pass hours ago and was no doubt in bed. It had to be about two in the morning. I was thankful that Nick had dropped off Nonna so she didn't have to deal with this tonight. Upon finding the body, we had, of course, called the sheriff, who had taken both Nick and me to the station.

"Is Nick still here?" I asked.

"Yes." The sheriff ran his hand through his thick, white hair. His hat hung on the coat rack near the door, along with his sherpa-lined jacket. "I've questioned him a few times, as well, and he stuck to the same story you have. That you both found the body."

"Exactly," I said. "And we were both at speed dating at McCloskey's all night, so obviously, neither of us killed that guy."

"We don't know how long he's been dead," the sheriff said softly.

I winced. I'd been the only person in the bar all day. "Rudy didn't come back after he stormed away."

"Well, that's one story," the sheriff muttered, his faded green eyes looking tired.

A sharp knock sounded on the door, and then Nick poked his head in. "Sheriff, I'm done. I'm heading home, and I'm taking Tessa with me."

I jolted. This was getting stranger and stranger. Nick was a prosecuting attorney, and he sometimes worked in our county, as well.

"I guess you're disqualified from trying to put me away this time," I said dryly, attempting a joke.

He didn't smile. "I'm well aware of that. Come on, Tessa, let's go. If you're not going to arrest her, Sheriff, then I'm taking her home."

I could admit that I shouldn't like Nick Basanelli attempting to protect me, yet it felt pretty good. It'd been a long time since anybody outside the family tried to shelter me. I would never begrudge Anna any sort of safety in this life, considering she'd been kidnapped for a few harrowing hours in our youth, but it did feel like I spent a lot of time trying to shield her. I tried not to warm too much to Nick because it could never happen. Even so, I smiled. "I am tired." I stood.

"Is there anything else, Sheriff?" Nick asked, his eyes narrowed.

I exhaled slowly. What did he know that I'd missed?

"Yeah." The sheriff opened a desk drawer and pulled out a baggie filled with some sort of paper. "There's this."

I leaned closer. "I don't know what that is."

"It's a quitclaim deed for Silver Sadie's, made out from Sadie to Rudy, the dead man," the sheriff said quietly.

I shook my head. "She gave me a deed this morning. There can't be another one."

"Here it is." The sheriff tapped the plastic. "It was dated six months ago."

Nick swore under his breath in Italian.

I looked over my shoulder at him. "What does that mean?"

He shook his head. "If his deed was signed before yours, even if it wasn't recorded, he would've had a valid claim to the property."

I gulped and nearly fell back onto the chair. "But I paid Sadie a hundred and fifty thousand dollars. Cash."

The sheriff's bushy white eyebrows rose. "Cash? Where did you get that kind of money?"

I threw my hands up into the air, my temper finally exploding. "What do you mean where did I get it? I've been working my ass off in diners since I was fourteen years old. You get tipped in cash."

"Good lord," Nick muttered. "Where have you kept it?"

I glared at him. "I'm not a moron. I have a safety deposit box." I'd finally had enough to pay Sadie, and I did. I was actually pretty proud of the fact. "Have you gotten ahold of her yet?" I asked the sheriff.

He shook his head. "I called several times and sent a deputy out to her place, but she's not there."

A pit started to form in my stomach, and yet even now, I trusted Sadie. "We shook hands," I murmured.

Nick's gaze hardened. "You shook hands?"

"Yes," I blurted. "That still counts with some people." I believed with my whole heart that it had counted with Sadie. "I don't know what happened earlier, and I don't know what happened with Rudy, but he did not have a valid deed to that restaurant."

"It's right here." The sheriff pointed to it again.

None of this made any sense. "Take another look," I argued. "Because I don't believe Sadie double-crossed me."

"Then where is she?" Nick asked, obviously tired of waiting by the door. He strolled forward and grasped my arm, gently pulling me away from the sheriff's desk. "Is Tessa under arrest?"

"No," the sheriff said. "Although I searched Rudy's place and found notes about Tessa's different interactions with Sadie in a very detailed notebook. It looks like he'd been following you for a while, and it's possible he spoke with you?"

Even I had to admit I had a pretty good motive for killing Rudy. "I didn't know Rudy existed until he barged into Silver Sadie's right after I signed the contract. I have no clue where Rudy was even staying."

"We're keeping that confidential for now," the sheriff said.

Nick's eyebrows rose. "You sure got a quick search warrant, didn't you?"

"I did," the sheriff countered. "Got the judge up, got the papers signed, and sent the deputies out."

"Where'd they find the deed?" Nick asked. "Was it just sitting right on the table for you to find easily?"

The sheriff shook his head. "I don't have to share any information with you at the moment, Basanelli. You might want to remember that you work for the state."

"Actually, I'm a witness in this case," Nick said smoothly. "And I don't work for any of you right now. Come on, Tessa."

He slipped an arm around my shoulders and propelled me out of the room. I went, my mind reeling. Just how screwed up had my life become where the guy who'd tried to prosecute me mere months before was now attempting to protect me?

"This is unbelievable," I muttered.

Nick scoffed. "I think you're a lot more like Anna than any of us realized."

I sighed. Even though I absolutely adored my younger sister, that was not a compliment. Trouble followed her wherever she went.

CHAPTER 5

We drove behind a snowplow for several miles through the mountain pass, the harsh wind blowing snow sideways against Nick's SUV. The interior of the vehicle was warm, and I snuggled into the heated seat, trying not to notice how well he drove. After a while, he finally passed the snowplow and kept the Jeep steady on the icy road, maneuvering almost gracefully through the storm.

Everything he did, he seemed to do well.

His hands were big and broad on the steering wheel, and he'd shoved his long-sleeved shirt up to reveal sinewy forearms. The windshield wipers kept a steady rhythm against the weather as he drove, cocooning us from the frozen tundra and lending a feeling of intimacy to the cab.

I was warm and sleepy, yet even so, I tried to study him from beneath my lashes. In profile, his features were sharp and cut. Even in the darkness, I saw the tawny glow of his eyes as he watched the road.

"Did you have fun at speed dating tonight?" he asked.

"I did," I admitted, hiding a yawn. "Until we found the dead body."

Part of me was still in shock about that, and another part had settled into the warmth of the vehicle and the sleepiness from the prosecco as my mind tried to ignore the reality of finding Rudy's body. Who could've killed him like that? Why was he in my basement? I just couldn't figure out what had gone so horribly wrong.

Nick glanced at me and then turned back to the road as we twisted around the mountain. "You had no idea about that quit-claim deed?"

"No," I said honestly. "Also, I don't think Sadie would've lied to me."

Nick lifted a shoulder. "I have no idea if she did or not."

My hackles rose. "I may not have a million degrees like you do, but I can read people. She was telling me the truth." In fact, reading people was one of my skills, and I'd learned it from my Nana O'Shea. In the olden days, people would've thought her touched. But these days, I just figured she could interpret facial expressions and body language better than a trained FBI agent.

Nick glanced at me longer this time. "What's that about, Contessa?"

"Don't call me that." It was rare that anybody used my full name. It didn't fit me.

"The name suits you."

I jerked upright. "Contessa? It's an elite British royalty type of name. Some modern-day princess with multiple doctorates."

"Huh." He switched the beams to low in order to see better through the catapulting snow. "I see it as the name of a stunning redhead with Irish eyes, ones that can spit fire or warm with intrigue."

I blinked. "Stop being nice."

His chuckle warmed me in all sorts of impossible places. "Nobody ever accuses me of being nice. That's funny." He sped up. "What's your glitch with doctorates? Some of the dumbest people I know are lawyers."

I snorted and caught myself. "Too easy," I murmured. If I had a glitch because I'd decided not to attend college, then that was on me. Sometimes, I looked at Anna with all her education and felt like I should've done more. But all I'd ever wanted was to run my own restaurant, and I'd figured out the fastest path to take. I was happy. "You're not a dumb lawyer," I said. "Rumor has it you're one of the best in a trial."

"You're sweet, too." He turned the final corner, and Timber City with Lilac Lake came into view. "I'm not looking for a relationship, Contessa, but I would like a date for the New Year's Eve party at the Elks Lodge. Full disclosure? It's my grams' birthday wish."

His honesty was greatly appreciated, and I had always adored his grams. But playing make-believe for even one night with him could lead to a disaster. Yeah, he was hot and sexy, but there was no way he was staying around, and I was setting down roots. Deep.

And even though I was the wild sister, I never gave my heart away quickly. I was even slower to give my trust. I'd learned that lesson the hard way, and I'd take it to my grave. It was time to focus on reality and not silly daydreams. "We need a copy of the deed found on Rudy's body."

Nick nodded. "I'll see if I can get one so we can compare it to other documents Sadie signed. The weirder part is, why can't we find her? It's the middle of the night. She should've been home when the sheriff called on her."

"I don't know." I'd been thinking the same thing and hoped she was all right. "I did give her a hundred and fifty thousand dollars in cash and didn't ask what she planned to do with it."

"She probably didn't take it to the bank," Nick said, shaking his head.

I rubbed my eyes. "No, she probably didn't."

Sadie didn't seem the type to trust banks. However, she was a smart lady, so I figured she had a plan. I hoped she was all right. The idea that something had happened to the older woman yanked me out of my warm fog. "I take it the sheriff couldn't find her brother, either?"

"Nope," Nick said. "He even called a buddy somewhere to track their phones. They're both turned off."

Now that didn't sound good. At all. "We have to find her."

"The sheriff will find her." Nick turned away from the lake and into Timber City, where I lived. "Don't go playing private detective like your sister has done several times."

I wanted to defend her, but it was a miracle she was still standing. So, I just looked out the window and tried to make out the buildings through the storm. "Do you know anything about Lenny Johnson's murder? It's odd that his body was also found in the basement." Maybe there was a psychotic ghost killing folks down there. I shivered, even though I didn't believe in ghosts.

"No. It's a local murder, so their local prosecutor would have been involved. I'll give him a call tomorrow and get the details, just so we know." He reached over and took my hand. "I'll make sure you're safe, Tess."

Heat flashed up my arm and sizzled through my entire body. My heart rate picked up, and my lungs stuttered. "That's kind, but I can take care of myself." My voice came out breathy, so I freed my hand. "It's okay, Nick. Don't worry." A sense of loss filtered through me as he put his hand back on the steering wheel, so I looked out the window again and not at his hard body.

Timber City was about fifty minutes from Silverville and had about fifty thousand residents. It used to be a small forest-industry town. Now, it was all about tourism with the lakes, mountains, and golf courses. I lived above Smiley's Diner, where I had worked for years.

Nick pulled through the archways to town and drove down Main Street to park right outside the diner. Holiday lights still sparkled from every streetlight and many of the businesses, now barely glowing through the angry blizzard. He shut off the engine and turned to look at me, big and broad in the small cab.

Heat infused my face. "What?"

"You still haven't agreed to go out with me on New Year's," he rumbled, his voice low and velvety soft in the sudden quiet.

I could admit that a part of me wanted to agree. I figured it'd be a lot of fun to go out with Nick Basanelli. He was intriguing and looked good in everything from gym shorts to power suits.

"We just don't work." I fumbled for the door handle.

"How do you know we don't work?" His voice licked across my skin.

"Because I'm not a moron." I opened the door, and the frigid air instantly slammed into me. Wincing, I slid out onto the sidewalk while holding the door so I didn't fall on my face. The concrete was extremely icy, and it didn't look like anybody had scattered any salt for at least the last several hours. "Thanks for the ride," I said, waving and then shutting the door.

His door instantly opened, and he came around the vehicle before I could blink. "Oh, I don't think so."

I paused and looked up—way up—into his face. While I was a good five foot six, he had significant height on me. "What?" I asked.

"I'm not letting you go in there alone. Didn't you find a dead body here one time, too?" He shook his head.

Yeah, but that wasn't my fault. "I'm a big girl, Nick."

He brushed my hair back from my face and then cupped my jaw, his thumb sliding across my cheek. Tingles spread from his touch, and I fought to remain immobile and not move against his hard and no doubt very warm body. "I promised my grams, and I shouldn't have, but I would also love to spend New Year's Eve with you, Contessa." He leaned in, and I caught my breath.

"I'll think about it." My gaze dropped to his mouth, and a riot broke out in my veins. Oh, I looked Irish through and through, but I was half-Italian, and that half wanted to find a Mediterranean beach somewhere and get naked with Basanelli for a weekend…or five. "I'm surprised your grams wants me."

"Why?" His thumb was driving me crazy, still moving on my face.

I ignored the shiver that overtook my spine, moving right down to my tingling private parts. "I look all Irish." No doubt his grams wanted him with an Italian woman, just like mine wanted me with an Italian man. So far, out of us three, Anna was with an Irishman, so Nonna was upping her game.

"Baby, you're more than enough Italian." He grinned. "You'd better be careful. Our grandmothers are a force."

I leaned into his touch, unable to stop myself. "Maybe you're the one who should show caution, Basanelli. If I wanted, I'd have you prepared to live in Silverville your entire life prosecuting jaywalking crimes." Yeah, I said it to scare him while also keeping my mind rooted in reality.

"For you? It might be worth it." He leaned in and kissed my forehead, marking me for all time. Just with one little kiss.

I stepped back. "Thanks for the ride. I can handle it from here." Yeah, my voice was breathy again, but it was cold out.

"Right. Not happening." He released me and walked toward the side of the diner to a barely there doorway, which he opened. "Come on, Contessa." He reached for my hand, sending traitorous butterflies up my arm.

"Nick, I don't need an escort upstairs." Rolling my eyes, I allowed him to pull me inside, up the steps, and down the hallway to one of two apartments. Then, I paused. My door was partially open.

He nudged me behind him, releasing my hand. "Did you leave this open?"

"No." My shoulders slumped. This night was insane.

The last time I had walked into a partially open apartment, my ex-boyfriend was dead on the floor. This could not be happening again. Nick gently nudged the door open and then flipped on a light. He whistled.

"What?" I asked, unable to keep from crowding closer to look inside.

My apartment had been torn apart. Drawers were emptied, cushions were slashed, and the couch had even been flipped on its side. I gasped and almost stumbled back. "What in the world?" I started to go inside.

"Wait." Nick drew me back. "Stay here."

Squaring his shoulders, he walked through the mess, obviously trying to avoid stepping on broken items, then searched the one bedroom and bathroom before checking out the kitchen and returning. "Nobody's here. But the entire place is a disaster."

"Why?" I asked.

"I don't know. Let's take a quick look to see if anything's missing before we call the police."

That was a good idea. I did as he instructed and looked through everything but couldn't identify anything missing. Even my jewelry, such that it was, was safe, albeit scattered across my bedroom floor. "Nothing's gone."

Nick stood in the kitchen, staring at the old, battered, dingy white refrigerator that had come with the apartment.

"What?" I stepped to his side, crunching broken glass from a picture frame.

"Is that blood?" he asked, looking at the handle.

I tried to peer closer. There *were* red marks on the handle. "I don't know."

Nick shook his head, reached for a paper towel, and gingerly used the other side of the handle to open it. We both looked inside the fridge to see a six-inch, dangerous-looking knife covered in blood. The handle was brown and curved at the end, just like the one protruding from Rudy's chest.

"Damn it," Nick muttered.

CHAPTER 6

Almost midnight and for the second time that evening, Nick and I were separated at a police station and interviewed—this time in the bigger city and a larger conference room. I sat across from Detective Grant Pierce with a crappy but steaming mug of coffee in front of me.

Pierce was one of Timber City's finest. He had darkish blond hair and piercing green eyes that matched his name. I'd always thought that was interesting. He often worked with my sister, and by the irritated glint in his eye, he wasn't happy to be working with another Albertini.

"Why are you here, anyway?" I finally asked after he'd finished his questioning. "Don't you deal with homicides?"

"Normally," he muttered. "But when the Albertini name is mentioned, they call me in for some reason." He didn't sound too happy about it.

"Well, I didn't recognize the knife, and I don't understand why it was in my fridge," I said for what had to be the thousandth time. "Yes, it looked a lot like the one protruding from Rudy Brando's chest, but I can't say for sure." They both had dark wooden handles with hooks on the ends. That was all I knew. "It's not my knife, it's not a knife I've ever seen before today, and it most certainly isn't one the diner uses."

Pierce shook his head. "All right. I've already called Sheriff Franco in Silverville, and we're going to send both weapons to the state crime lab. We'll see what's going on."

I bit my lip. "You don't think there's another body out there, do you?" If so, why leave the knife in my fridge?

"I hope not," Pierce said. "I'd love it if this case stayed in the other county. I'm swamped right now." He stood. "Come on, I've already interviewed Basanelli. He's waiting to take you...well, somewhere."

I didn't think Pierce cared where I went.

He walked me outside. "Do you have somewhere to go?" All right, scratch that. Maybe he did care.

He was tall and lean with a swimmer's body. And if I remembered right, he had a killer smile. I hadn't seen it in a while, but I wasn't usually around Detective Pierce. I thought he'd asked my sister Anna out once, but they'd never made it, and she told me a while back that she was pretty sure he was glad they hadn't gone on that date. Now, she was safely living with Aiden, her one true love.

So, Pierce would have to look elsewhere, although rumor had it he wasn't looking anywhere near the Albertini women.

I couldn't blame him. We did seem to have a plethora of dead bodies showing up. As a homicide detective, that probably didn't sit well with him.

Nick waited at the end of the hall, somehow not appearing as exhausted as I felt. In fact, he looked slightly dangerous. It wasn't the clothing or even his expression...it was just the man. Not for the first time, I wondered what he'd done in the Marines besides being in the JAG Corps. From what I'd heard through scuttlebutt, he didn't talk about those times. They most certainly weren't my business. So, I kept my thoughts to myself as I reached him. "Is she good?" he asked Pierce.

"Yeah, you're both good. She can't go back to her place, though. It's a crime scene." It was a fact he'd already informed me of. At the moment, I didn't *want* to go back there. It was a huge mess, and I didn't want to deal with it.

"Thanks, Detective Pierce," I said, zipping my coat and turning to jog down the stairs to the main entrance of the Timber City Police Department. Nick opened the door for me, and we both ducked our heads against the keening wind as we ran to his Jeep and jumped inside.

"Where to?" He started the ignition and began driving across the snowy parking lot.

I considered my options. Anna's little bungalow had been blown up the week before, and she was currently living in Aiden's new and sparsely furnished cabin that was still, at this point, a fixer-upper. Plus, they were living in new domestic bliss, and I didn't want to intrude. I had a lot of cousins around town, but most of them had small apartments, and a lot of my family resided in Silverville; no way were we driving the pass again tonight.

There was only one choice. "Just take me to Donna's." I wasn't surprised when Nick automatically turned the car, somehow knowing where my sister lived. Basanelli seemed to know everything.

"Should you call her and tell her we're coming?" he asked, flicking the windshield wipers up faster.

"Oh, she's not in town. She left this morning, but she'll be back in a couple of days." However, I had a key to her place, so it wasn't a big deal.

He engaged his blinker and turned, driving away from Donna's neighborhood.

"Where are you going?" I looked out the back window. Maybe Nick *didn't* know where she lived.

"You're not staying at Donna's by yourself tonight," he murmured, driving away from town and toward the smaller and even quainter Tamarack Lake.

My heart zinged sharply against my rib cage. "I'm not staying with you." Nope. No way. I was only human, and I needed to be smart.

"Why not? You've stayed with me before." He easily slowed to drive over several thick chunks of ice that looked as if they had fallen from a nearby tree.

I gulped. "Yeah, but that was when Anna was staying there." My sister had had a bad reaction to some brownies and ended up at Nick's house just in time to throw up in his potted plant. She then became paranoid and called me, and I had stayed the night with her to keep her calm. I didn't like remembering that night, but Nick had been a sweetheart. He'd braided her hair, took care of her, and then cooked us both breakfast.

Anna had gotten a twinkle in her eye the next morning, and I couldn't prove it, but I think she had then enlisted Nonna to help with her matchmaking scheme. If I proved my theory, I would make her pay. Revenge was a religion in my family, but so far, I couldn't truly prove her guilt. Everybody around us seemed to be trying to matchmake, and it just wasn't working.

"I really don't think I should stay at your place."

"That's unfortunate." He reached the lake road and wound around the southern shore. "Because I'm not driving you back over the pass, and I'm not leaving you alone. So, it's either my place or Devlin's. And I don't even think they have a bed yet, do they?"

"I think they have a bed," I said softly, though I wasn't sure if Anna and Aiden had a bed or not. They had been staying in Anna's place until it blew up. The good news was that the bad guy bomber had been caught, was now dead, and nobody was after Anna any longer—at least not this week. "Nick, I'm fine."

"I'm so glad." He parked at one of the luxury condos overlooking Tamarack Lake and turned off the vehicle. "Come on, Tessa. I have a spare room."

I was too tired to argue. "You're bossy," I grumbled, opening the door and once again stepping into the freezing night.

"You have no idea. And I still owe you one. Don't forget." He gestured for me to go ahead of him.

I stumbled and then righted myself before climbing the stairs and sliding to one of the heavy metal doors that protected the high-end condominiums.

He unlocked and opened it, and I stepped inside his ultra-modern apartment with its wood floors, marble countertops, and a shocking number of books piled on and spilling out of book-shelves to the side of the living room. A wide, two-story window looked out at the quiet and dark lake, with only a few twinkling lights across the way.

I turned to face him as he shut the door. "I realize you owe me one, and I'd like to get it over with." I held out my leg. "Go ahead. Kick me."

His smile, if there was a way to describe it, would be with the word *devastating*. "I'm not going to kick you."

"You don't seem like a kicker." I put my foot down. "I just thought I'd give it a shot."

"If I wanted a shot, I'd take it," he said. And with that, he moved in, straight at me.

Interest flared through my entire body, hot and bright. "Whoa." I held up a hand.

His gaze dropped to my mouth, and I swore to the saints, my lips started to tingle. "One kiss."

Man, I wanted that. Badly. "Contrary to popular opinion, I'm not that wild," I murmured.

He paused, cocking his head, and that bourbon-lit gaze lifted to meet mine. "You're not wild at all."

I stilled, my eyebrows rising on their own. "I'm the wild one."

If anything, his focus softened even more. "Right, you are. The wild one always works two shifts every day, visits her family over a dangerous mountain pass at least once a week, and goes to church regularly. Yeah. You're *wild*."

"Triple shifts," I retorted. "And God and I are tight." I wasn't sure I liked how well he saw me. Actually, *me*. "I'm not your type."

His smile was slow. "I have a type?"

"Yeah." My chin lifted. "Another Type-A and very ambitious woman who wants to rise in the ranks like you do."

"You're not Type-A?"

It hit me then. He was truly enjoying this conversation. Not just as a way to get me into bed, but in a slow and languorous way that I couldn't read. Not completely. "No. Donna is."

"You can't both be?" He moved even closer and brushed my hair over my shoulder. "I'd say working toward a goal as hard as you have, like your restaurant, is all Type-A, Contessa." The drawl of my name rolled through me as if he'd kissed every inch of my skin.

Naturally, I took a step back. "Maybe, but I'm also a hometown girl. Not leaving."

That caught his attention. "Very good point."

There was no doubt in the universe that Nick Basanelli was leaving...probably to Boise in the governor's office or even Washington, DC, in Congress. Or the US Senate. Who knew? "Sometimes, it's easier to break the world into reality," I said. "I try to live there."

After dating the now-deceased Danny Pucci, I'd learned to stop daydreaming about what could be. I liked what actually was, and I kept my imagination at bay by remembering that salient fact.

Nick surprised me by chuckling, and the humor reached his eyes. "Ah, sweetheart. You're a dreamer, whether you like it or not."

I did not. "I'm not the fling type, Basanelli." Right or wrong, missing out or not, I knew myself. Plus, a sense of vulnerability wandered through me, brought out completely by the sexy Italian, and since I wasn't a complete moron, I wanted to protect my heart. "So, friends?" I held out a hand.

He took it, his fingers warm and strong around mine. "Yeah. Friends."

Being the realist I wanted to be, I ignored the instant pang in my heart. "Good."

CHAPTER 7

*A*fter a good night of sleep, I wore my dusty jeans down the stairs to Nick's kitchen, touched that he had left a long-sleeve T-shirt with the JAG Corps logo outside my door. The well-worn and soft material hung to my thighs and smelled like laundry detergent with a hint of male. The shirt was too big, and I couldn't explain it, but something girly in me rejoiced at the difference in our sizes. He made me feel feminine, and I liked that, although I had been truthful when I said we should just be friends.

"Morning," I said, walking through the kitchen and stopping at the windows to gaze at the gorgeous view.

Wandering streaks of pink and gold meandered across the sky as the early sun glimmered off the ice-and-snow-covered lake. The ice appeared thick enough to walk across and perhaps fish, but I didn't see any evidence of shacks out there. The clouds were already barreling in from the west, but for now, the silent world was beautiful in the morning light.

"Morning." Nick pulled what looked like a casserole out of the oven, bright pink mitts on his hands.

"Cute," I murmured, accepting the cup of coffee he nudged across the counter with an elbow.

"Thanks. They were my grandma's." He placed the steaming dish onto a wooden hot pad with a faded Italian flag decorating the center. "Full disclosure, she made the casserole, too."

The concoction smelled delicious as cheese bubbled up through scrambled eggs. The moment was way too charming and intimate, and I had the urge to run back upstairs and grab my boots. Instead, I took a drink of the coffee and then sucked in a breath, turning my head to the side and coughing. "Oh, holy Mary," I sputtered.

He winced. "Too strong?"

"Too strong?" My eyebrows hit my hairline. "This is motor oil, Nick."

"Sorry." He didn't look sorry. He looked amused. I had to admit, a tousled-haired Basanelli looked good in a threadbare green shirt, faded jeans, and bare feet. Way too good.

I glanced at my watch. "Don't you have to get to work?"

"Yeah," he said. "I was going to change clothes after we had breakfast."

That was sweet. This whole friend thing would be a lot easier if he didn't look good enough to tackle to the floor and kiss. "I thought you were in trial this week."

"I am. Today's just prep. We have voir dire tomorrow." He dished up two plates, and his phone buzzed on the counter. He glanced at the face. "Oh, excuse me. I have to grab this."

"No problem," I said. "I'll finish the rest." I wandered around the counter and opened a few drawers before finding utensils.

A knock sounded on his door. He looked up and gestured with his chin toward it as he started rambling on about depositions and motions in limine.

I knew what a deposition was, but the limine thing was beyond me, so I just nodded and wandered over to open the door, where I stopped, shocked. I had to blink twice.

"Hi." Jolene Sullivan took a step back, her wide blue gaze instantly turning calculating.

"Hi," I said, not knowing what else to say.

Jolene Sullivan was a thorn in my family's side. She'd slept with my sister Donna's prom date back in high school. She'd dated Aiden Devlin, who was now living with Anna. While both of those situations were in the past, and I could easily forgive them since we had all grown up, she was now working as a reporter in town and seemed to have made it her life's mission to go after Anna and attack her in the paper. In addition, Jolene had slept with my cousin Quint and used him to get more information on Anna in a move that was too recent to forgive.

So, I smiled. "Can I help you with something?"

Her gaze raked me from head to toe, taking in what was obviously Nick's shirt and my messy hair. "It looks like you've been helped enough."

It was bait, and I didn't rise to it. Why in the world was the reporter on Nick's front stoop? He wasn't dumb enough to be dating her, was he? The woman would not go away. This morning, in the freezing cold, she wore green yoga pants and a loose shirt, and she had a massive blue mug in her hand.

I leaned over and peered into the empty cup. "Are you looking for loose change?"

She pushed past me into Nick's apartment. "Hey, please tell me you have coffee." She seemed more than comfortable wandering through his living room to the kitchen as if she'd been there before. Many times.

He finished his conversation and disconnected, turning to look at her. "Of course, I have coffee. I always have coffee." He gestured toward a nearly full pot on the counter.

"Once again, you're my hero." She headed directly toward the coffee pot. "I'm out again."

I looked from one to the other, curious.

"I live two condos down," she answered, apparently noting my expression before pouring herself a full cup.

She took a deep gulp and smiled, pink filtering through her

still-flawless skin. She was blond with pretty and rather sharp blue eyes, and I imagined that we might have been friends if she didn't enjoy being such a complete violation of the sisterhood—or rather, my sister. Jolene definitely wanted to hurt Anna, which made me want to toss the reporter out on her ass.

Instead, I leaned against the counter and tried to sip the overly strong coffee. By the pleasure wandering across Jolene's face, she actually did like the sludge.

She took another deep drink and then smiled at Nick. "Was that call about your trial tomorrow?"

"You know the rules." He reached for his mug and drank the contents in two gulps.

Nope. I didn't like that they had rules. Not at all. "Rules?" I asked, trying to avoid taking another drink, even though the cup was warm in my hand.

Jolene rolled her eyes. "Yes. Since we live in the same complex, we have an agreement that there's no business on the premises; otherwise, Nick won't even talk to me."

"Smart guy," I murmured, unable to keep myself from taking another sip. The thick liquid meandered down my throat to smash into my stomach. Ugh.

She smiled widely. "So, this is sweet." She looked back and forth between us, her gaze even more calculating. "Didn't he arrest you last month for murder?"

Jolene knew very well that Nick had arrested me on suspicion of murder. "I believe that's business and against the…ah…rules," I said evenly. Then, because I could sometimes be a brat, I smiled even wider. "You know, Jolene, I really liked that article you did on the dog pound last week regarding some of their funds going missing after the fundraiser."

Her head jerked enough to show surprise. "You did?"

"Yeah. I thought it was well-written." Truth be told, I had liked it. It was well-written, and maybe a compliment or two would throw her off her game. I enjoyed the thought, especially since she probably believed I wanted to deck her for messing with my sister. Which I did.

"I was proud of that piece." She lowered her chin, holding her mug against her lips as if in thought.

I smiled. "I also liked the article you wrote about the new veteran's hospital opening in Timber City. I thought your turn of phrase was very clever, and you did a good job of bringing out the humanity of the organizers."

She blinked as if not quite sure how to respond. Considering she'd been coming after my family for the last several months, I didn't blame her. However, the articles really were good, so why not say so? Maybe she'd spend more of her time writing such things instead of harassing my sister.

"That's nice of you to say," she said grudgingly.

"Oh, I'm a peach," I agreed.

Nick turned to pour himself more coffee, but not before I caught a hint of a smile on his full lips.

Should I like the fact that I amused him? Probably not, but I did.

"All right." Jolene moved with her extra-large cup toward the door. "Nick, I'll be at your office later today."

"I'll take that as a warning," he said mildly.

She laughed, and the sound was musical. "You can take it any way you like, but I want to know more about the trial tomorrow." Reaching the door, she paused. "I'm looking forward to tonight. Pick me up at seven."

"I'll be there," he said.

I didn't care. Nope. Not at all.

She opened the door, and frigid air wafted in. "Sure you don't want to talk about the trial? I heard you lost a witness."

"No comment, and if you ask again, no more coffee for you." He reached for a full plate of food.

"That's all right. I'll get my information elsewhere." She turned and winked at me. "I can't wait to see how you factor in—you Albertinis always make good copy."

With that last parting shot, she exited the condo and shut the door quietly. "I hope I don't factor in," I murmured.

"Amen to that." Nick glanced at the food. "For now, let's eat."

We sat. "Did you neglect to invite Jolene to breakfast because I'm here?" There wasn't a doubt in my mind that Nick's manners were as good as his Italian grams wanted.

"She doesn't eat before noon," Nick said around a mouthful of casserole. "Some type of intermittent fasting."

Nope. I didn't care that he knew that much about her, and as I looked at my overflowing plate, I didn't have even one insecure thought about my thighs. Not a one. "You have a date with her tonight?" I was just curious...and concerned for his sanity.

"No. Every year after Christmas, the press and the justice offices have an after-holiday party. Somebody started it decades ago to keep things congenial, and Jolene asked for a ride. We live at the same place." He shrugged, his five o'clock shadow giving him a roguish look.

"How convenient." Although I hadn't sensed any kind of romantic vibe earlier, if I were being honest with myself. Were they even friends? As far as I knew, Jolene hadn't screwed Nick over yet. "Well, just watch your back. She'll do anything for a story."

"I'm aware," he said dryly.

Nick's phone pretty much started blowing up, and he read the screen as we ate quietly. The food was delicious. I looked at my quiet phone. That's what happened when people knew you needed help moving. They often didn't call. However, I also believed my family would arrive to help me out later today.

Nick looked up from one of his texts. "Detective Pierce just texted that your apartment has been cleared. It's all yours."

"Oh, good." I shot off texts to all my cousins, letting them know that if they were available, they could help out.

"I don't like that the knife was left in your fridge. Does the family know yet?" Nick asked.

If they did, my phone would likely be buzzing right off the table. "No, and I don't see why they should." It was impossible they wouldn't find out about the murder in my new building over in Silverville, but I might have a day or so of reprieve. Sheriff Franco wasn't one to talk much, although he did have two deputies.

We ate in silence for a while, and it was too comfortable for my peace of mind. Even so, I let myself enjoy the moment until my phone rang. I sighed and lifted it to my ear. "Hi, Nonna. I made it home safely last night. I should have texted you."

"Well, that's quite all right," she said. "I heard you spent the night with Nick Basanelli." She sounded entirely too thrilled with the situation. I sat back. So, she knew where I was at the moment but had no clue about the murder or the extra knife found in my fridge. How in the world?

And then I sighed. "Jolene," I muttered. She must've called her family in Silverville the second she'd left with her coffee.

I was no doubt on her radar big time now.

CHAPTER 8

ℕick dropped me off at my apartment on his way to work. Today, the hotshot lawyer had dressed down in black slacks and a golf shirt—since he was prepping for trial the next day, apparently. "What's your trial about anyway?" I asked.

"The case started as a timber trespass," he said. "Couple of neighbors fighting. One guy stole another guy's trees. Things got physical. They got in a fight. So, yes, it's also a battery."

"That sounds like a normal Saturday," I murmured.

Nick chuckled. "Yeah, it's a misdemeanor case, but my office is busy, so I said I'd take it."

"Who's the witness you lost?"

He shook his head. "I didn't lose a witness. The defendant's brother is on a bender, but he'll show up for trial. I'm not worried about it. Jolene was just fishing for a story earlier."

"That seems to be her thing," I muttered.

It had started to snow again, but this time, light, fluffy flakes dotted the windshield. He flipped on the wipers and continued down Main Street to stop in front of the diner. I sighed. My cousin Rory stood outside, leaning against the wall near my door.

"You called Rory in?" Nick asked mildly.

"Nonna called Rory." I pushed to open the door. Rory was one of the six Albertini brothers, and he and I had always gotten along well—probably because I didn't ask questions about his life that he didn't want to answer.

I hurried across the sidewalk and leaned way up to kiss his whiskered cheek. "Rory, I didn't know you were in town."

"Yet here I am." Rory looked over my head at Nick. I couldn't gauge his expression, but it was one of those male ones that made me want to kick him in the knee. "Basanelli," Rory said calmly.

"Hi, Rory." Nick jumped out of his vehicle. "How's life?"

"Pretty good." Rory was about six foot four with thick, dark hair and piercing blue eyes. Nobody in the family really knew what he did for a living except that he left town often, and when he was home, he often worked for the Forest Service, or took odd jobs, kind of goofing off. He had an intensity to him that I'd always enjoyed, but right now, I didn't need anybody defending my honor.

"Knock it off." I punched him lightly in the gut, noting there was no give. Rory was solid muscle and even had that tough-guy neck thing going for him.

He slowly dropped his gaze to mine and then looked at Nick again. "It's a little early for a house call. Where have you been?"

"None of your business." I pushed him, not surprised when he didn't move. I looked over my shoulder. "Thanks for the ride, Nick. I appreciate it."

Nick shook his head. "Rory, you need to know—"

"I already know," Rory said quietly.

I jolted. "What do you mean?"

"I've already seen the apartment. Called Detective Pierce and found out what was going on." Rory still watched Nick. "Heard about the dead body in Silverville, as well."

My mouth gaped. "How? Hey, wait a minute. How'd you get into my apartment? I locked it."

He didn't bother answering me. Man, he had some wicked

skills that I didn't understand. We had pretty much decided he worked for either Homeland Security or the CIA as some sort of spy or operative or whatever, and we knew not to ask questions because he wouldn't answer them, so it probably wasn't a surprise that he'd broken into my place.

I was somewhat taken aback that Detective Pierce had spoken so freely, though. "I didn't know you and Grant were close."

"We get along just fine," Rory said. "Are you staying to help today, Basanelli?"

"No." Amusement tilted Nick's lips. "I have trial prep, but it was really nice seeing you again, Albertini." Then, with a wink at me, he jumped back into his SUV and drove slowly away from the curb.

Rory shook his head. "What are you doing? That guy's not going to settle down."

I wanted to stomp my foot, but I also didn't want to act like a two-year-old. "I didn't ask him to settle down. Mind your own damn business." With that very perfect response, I pushed him back. This time, he let me.

I opened the outside door just as a truck rumbled down the street and slid to a stop right in front of the diner. I paused and looked to see a 1970 Chevy with hay mingled with snow in the bed.

"Hey there," Bobbo said, jumping out. The truck actually jerked when he lifted his bulk out and slammed the door.

I blinked. "Bobbo, what are you doing here?"

His smile was wide. Today, he wore a black pair of overalls with a white-and-lime-green-checked shirt beneath it. "Your nonna called. Said you needed help moving and wanted me to come."

I swallowed. "She did?" She knew I wasn't interested in Bobbo.

"Yeah. Said to make sure I dropped by and told Basanelli that I got this." Bobbo shook his head, and snow flew off his thick hair. "He wasn't at the office yet, so I just left a note. Can you believe it?" He jerked his head at Rory. "It's almost eight in the morning, and the guy's not at work. I mean, come on. I've been up since four."

"Me, too." Rory looked at me, then Bobbo, then me again.

I shook my head. "Nonna." That was all I said.

"Fantastic," Rory muttered.

Bobbo scrubbed both hands down his beefy face. "I heard about Rudy. I didn't know the guy, but it sucks that he was killed at Sadie's old place. I'm sure you didn't do it, Tessa."

"Um, thanks." Did anybody think I'd killed him? "I don't suppose you know where Sadie is at the moment?" I asked.

Bobbo shook his head. "No clue. I've called and she doesn't answer, but that's not rare for her. I'm not worried." His wide smile spread across his face. "What do you need me to do here?"

Rory turned toward me. "My brothers will be here soon, and Anna and Devlin are on their way, as well. We've got three trucks coming, and we'll have you moved within a couple of hours. Although, from the looks of things, one of those trucks will have to go right to the dump."

I bit my lip. "I know."

"Who do you think trashed your apartment?" Rory asked.

"I have no idea," I said. "It must have something to do with Rudy Brando's murder, and the only reason I say that..." I trailed off.

"Is because the knives looked the same," Rory finished.

"Yep." Detective Grant had apparently told him everything. Rory had a way with people that others didn't because I knew for a fact that Grant Pierce didn't share information unless it was pretty much tortured out of him.

Bobbo smacked his hands together, not looking cold in the slightest, even though it was well below zero. "I don't want to hear a thing about knives or murders, so please leave me out of that. However, your nonna said you might want to come home with me tonight, and that plan still works just fine with me." He clapped his hands again, the sound gleeful.

"No." I noted Rory's quick flash of amusement. "I'm not going home with you, Bobbo." But then I had an idea, which was pretty darn good. "Let's get started, and then we'll talk."

We tromped inside and walked up to my apartment. Maneuvering in, I was caught again by the damage. Whoever had broken in had been in quite the frenzy.

"Whoa," Bobbo said, bumping into me from behind and nearly tossing me across the room. Rory easily caught me and set me to the side.

"Did you do this?" Bobbo asked.

"No."

"Oh, good." Relief filtered across his beefy face. "I thought you were messy. I can't stand messy."

"Somebody else did this." Irritation and a hint of fear ticked through me as I studied the deep knife gouges in my old sofa.

Bobbo shook his head. "Trouble sure does seem to follow you Albertini women."

As much as I wanted to argue, I couldn't. Footsteps echoed, and then Anna and Aiden walked inside. Aiden whistled, and Anna's eyes widened. "Wow," she whispered. "Rory told me what had happened, but still." She looked around at the tufts of cotton all over the floor. "What do you think they were looking for?"

"I have no idea," I said. "I also don't know why they left me a knife in the fridge."

"Oh, that was a threat." Devlin's very slight Irish lilt emerged with his words.

His gaze met Rory's. They shook hands and did some weird half-hug guy thing before Aiden shook Bobbo's hand. "Somebody's threatening you, Tessa. You're going to have to stay with us."

I slowly turned my head to look at the Irishman. He might be six and a half feet of raw muscle and danger, but he was Anna's problem, not mine. "I can handle myself. Thank you." My voice was cool.

His flash of a smile irritated me even more.

"You're coming home with me," Rory ordered. "After you explain what you were doing with Basanelli all night."

"It's not your concern." My temper was about to make an appearance.

Bobbo took a step back. "You stayed with Basanelli last night?"

"It's nobody's business." I threw up my arms. Nothing had happened, but again, I wasn't a two-year-old, and they could all back off.

Curiosity lit my sister's grayish-green eyes, but she wisely kept silent. Oh, I knew she'd get the whole truth out of me later, but right now, we were as united as could be. She was my sister, after all.

My cousin Quint, Rory's brother, strode into the apartment, looked around, and whistled. "Whoa, Rory, you weren't kidding. This is bad." His hands were full of boxes. "Heather has a cold, so she stayed at home, but she said if we needed help to give her a call. I think we can have this done in a couple of hours."

I took a box, nodded at my sister, and pointed her to the bedroom. "We'll start in there. You guys start in here."

"Okey-doke," Bobbo said. "Although I would like to hear about Basanelli later. If you're coming home with me tonight, I don't think you should be staying with him."

"I am not going home with you!" I stomped through the small apartment to the bedroom. Anna almost kept from chuckling as she followed me. Rolling my eyes, I took my phone from my back pocket and quickly sent a text.

One of the nice things about being from a small town was that everybody had everybody's number—or if they didn't, they knew who to call. I waited, and when the answering text from my nonna came in, I took note of the number she sent me and instantly sent another message.

"What are you up to?" Anna asked.

"Just going for some good karma," I admitted, sitting and starting to unravel my jewelry from the thick carpet.

Anna looked around. "I'll take your dresser, or what's left of it. At least I'll try to gather clothes into piles."

"Thanks."

"Basanelli?" She began sorting my Ugg socks, which I loved.

I picked a silver charm out of the carpet. "Brought me home, saw the mess, and took me to his condo. I slept in the guest room, and we decided to be friends because he's leaving town, and I am not."

Anna nodded. "If you say so."

I did. We worked quietly for about half an hour until another knock sounded on the door. More family members arrived, and soon all the furniture was out of the apartment. It really didn't take long at all, and my cousins left to deliver furniture either to the dump or my new place in the valley.

After we'd cleared the bedroom, I headed to the kitchen, trying to gather whatever dishes hadn't been broken, just as a more timid knock came from the door. "Open that, would you, Bobbo?" I called out.

He was just finishing wiping down some scuffs on the baseboard. There was a chance I'd get my deposit back, considering all the damage had been to my belongings.

"Sure." He reached up and opened the door before stiffening. "Oh, uh, hi." He fumbled to his feet and towered over Kelsey Walker.

She blushed a bright pink and then looked around the now-empty room at Anna, Aiden, Rory, Bobbo, and me.

"Oh, good. Kelsey, I'm glad you're here," I said, running over and patting her arm. "Thank you for coming to help."

She bit her lip. "I came as soon as I could, but it looks like you're almost done."

I swallowed. "Yeah, I am, and I was going to take everybody

out to lunch, but something's come up." I opened my eyes as if I had just come up with the best idea ever. "Bobbo, do you mind taking Kelsey to lunch? I feel terrible that she made the drive for nothing, and I really do need to get over the pass before my cousins put everything in the wrong place." I was only half-kidding about that.

Bobbo straightened even more and stared into Kelsey's pretty blue eyes. "I'd love a luncheon date."

Kelsey faltered and then stared way up at him. "You own that farm, right?"

"I do. I have alpacas," he said. "They're the best animal for the environment, you know?"

She gasped. "I've never seen an alpaca."

My heart started to warm. This was a good idea. Anna cut me a look and then rolled her eyes. I didn't care. Sometimes, an Irish gal just knew things. I'd inherited the gift from Nana O'Shea. She occasionally knew things, and so did I. "I really appreciate it." I reached into my back pocket for a card. "Here. It's for Smiley's Diner. I have a lot of coupons."

"Oh, we don't need a coupon," Bobbo said gallantly, holding out his beefy arm for Kelsey. "Let's go eat at The Clumsy Penguin. I've heard they've got a great lunch soup."

"The Clumsy Penguin?" Her smile was cute and lit up her whole face. "I love that place."

It was a fantastic idea. The Penguin was a charming bar and restaurant that sat at the edge of Lilac Lake, which made for a romantic background.

"Are you sure?" Bobbo asked me, his eyes quizzical yet also full of hope.

"I'm positive," I said. "You guys go have fun."

His smile was wide. He looked huge next to the petite Kelsey Walker, but considering her sister was in jail, and the rest of her family didn't seem too kind because of it, she could probably use some cover. Bobbo could handle that. Besides, they made a somewhat cute couple. A little odd, but in my experience, the odder the couple, the happier they were.

"All right, let's go." He gestured her out. "If you need any more help, Tessa, let me know."

"You've got it," I said cheerfully. The room seemed bigger once he'd left.

Anna shook her head. "You have always been such a matchmaker."

"I have?"

"Yeah. Always."

Rory snorted. "You have. You even matched up Uncle Brett, remember?"

"Well, yeah, but he and my second-grade teacher were perfect together. They've been married for decades now."

"Uh-huh." Rory shook his head. "All right, we have everything. Let's drive over to the valley."

"Okay," I said. "My car's still over there. I need to get it."

"We're going to argue about where you're staying," Rory muttered.

I rolled my eyes. "I know." To be honest, I wasn't sure what was going on. Somebody had obviously tried to scare me, and everything inside me knew it was about Silver Sadie's, but it didn't make a bit of sense.

We headed outside, where the storm had increased in force just as Nick pulled to a stop and jumped out of his Jeep. "Hey, I was hoping to ask you some questions about that knife."

"I thought you were in trial prep." My abdomen heated in a truly annoying way just from how smoothly he moved his muscled body.

"We finished early and don't start again 'til tomorrow," Nick said. "I've been thinking about the knife in your fridge, and it doesn't make any sense. I called the lab."

"Was the blood Rudy Brando's?" I held my breath as awaited the answer.

"Don't know yet," Nick said. "We don't have any results yet." All of a sudden, he stiffened.

"What?" I asked. Had I said something wrong?

A truck came roaring down the icy road, slipping and sliding.

"Get down!" Rory yelled.

Everything that happened next was too fast to track.

Nick tackled me. Aiden tackled Anna, and Rory somehow seemed to tackle everybody. We hit the snow-covered sidewalk just as gunfire sprayed the top of the building and then the pavement by the vehicles. Pain ricocheted through my knees and face from the icy ground. We were all silent for a minute, and then everybody leaped to their feet.

"What the hell?" Aiden snapped.

Rory made to run after the truck, but it zoomed around a corner. He looked at the three vehicles at the curb with their tires flat. "Damn it."

I shook my head and looked up to see a smattering of bullet holes at the very top of the building that were barely noticeable. We wouldn't even think of fixing them until spring. Thank goodness the diner windows hadn't been hit.

Nick grabbed his phone and called it in, giving an eerily accurate description of the battered white truck. "Did anybody see the shooter?" he asked, his voice low with command.

"Guy was wearing all black, including a ski mask," Rory said roughly.

"Definitely male," Anna murmured.

I swallowed. I looked up at Nick.

His pupils had constricted, and tension rolled off him. "Are you okay? Did I tackle you too hard?"

I wiped snow off my face. "No. I'm fine."

"Come on, inside." Rory opened the door to the diner, where a multitude of people had their noses pressed to the glass. I gulped. The shooter had aimed for the vehicles and just the doorway to the apartments.

"Oh, he's gone," Aiden said grimly.

All three of them looked at me as Anna put an arm around my waist. I had a feeling the shooter had been aiming at me, but then again, the four people around me all had dangerous jobs.

What in the world had just happened?

CHAPTER 9

The coffee at the police station in Timber City was much better than the sludge Nick had tried to give me earlier in the day. We'd each been questioned separately, and now Detective Pierce had put us all in the same large conference room. His green eyes were still sharp, but tired lines extended from them. We'd been questioned for nearly two hours, and he was just repeating himself at this point.

Everyone around me was involved in law enforcement in one way or another, and they seemed fine with that. It must be an acceptable method for interviewing suspects.

"Does anybody know who the shooter was aiming at?" he asked, scribbling in a notebook. None of us answered.

He looked up. "Rory?"

"Not me," Rory said.

"Why is that?" Anna asked from my side. She and Nick flanked me, and I thought it was interesting that Nick had chosen to sit next to me instead of letting Rory do so. His presence was comforting and intriguing. For some reason, I felt both shielded and on alert.

Anna sighed and leaned over me to look at our cousin. "We all know you have some mysterious job. How do you know the bullets weren't meant for you?"

Rory kept his gaze on the detective. "I'm not saying I have a mysterious job, but if I did, and if somebody within that world wanted me dead, I'd be dead, and it wouldn't be done on a busy street with witnesses."

A chill clacked down my back, and I fought a shiver.

"Not that I have a weird job," Rory drawled. "I work when I want, and play when I want."

Detective Pierce's jaw tightened. "We'll return to you later. For now, how about you, Basanelli? I know you're involved in a couple of trials right now, and didn't you put away one of the Morrison brothers a week or so ago?"

"Yes," Nick said. "A few threats were made as they carted Felix away."

Pierce jotted more notes on his paper. "I'll do a follow-up on that, but I need you to send over a list of anybody else who might want you dead." He turned his attention to Aiden. "Is there anything interesting going on with your ATF unit at the moment that could lead to an assassination attempt?"

Aiden shook his head. "Nothing viable right now, but I'll take a look through past cases. The shooter was sloppy. He should have hit at least one of us."

"Maybe he only meant to scare us," Anna said softly.

Pierce turned his attention to her. "Who wants you dead these days?"

I reared up, but she patted my arm. "I don't think anybody. My last few cases have been pretty tame." She sounded slightly perturbed by that.

Aiden shifted his weight on the leather chair. It was a slight movement, but menace emanated from him. "That's a good thing."

Finally, Grant focused on me. "The shooting occurred outside your place of residence, where a bloody knife was found. It's a good chance you were the target, Tessa. You know that, right?"

I nodded. However, it was just as plausible that it was one of the people around me. I didn't like the coincidence, though, nor did anyone else. I was accustomed to staying in the background, and I didn't like feeling so exposed. At all.

Pierce looked at his watch. "All right. The crime scene techs should be finished with the area soon, and I'm having the neighborhood canvased. Your vehicles were cleared an hour ago. We haven't found the truck or any hint of the shooter."

Aiden sighed. "The guy hit all our tires."

The scent of Nick's musky cologne, nature-y and wild, somehow grounded me.

He cleared his throat. "I already texted my brother. He had them towed to his garage. They should be fixed and delivered here by the time we're done." Nick had two brothers, and one was a mechanic that everyone in both Timber City and Silverville used. He was the best.

"Thanks," Rory said.

"Sure. What else do we know?" Nick asked Pierce.

Pierce flipped his notebook shut. "From what we can tell so far, the shooter drove toward Lilac Lake and then took the south road, which means he could be anywhere. We'll keep looking for him, but in the meantime, Tessa could use some protection." He shook his head. "I don't have anybody I can put on you right now. We're stretched too thin."

"We've got her." Rory's usual smile was gone.

For the first time, I saw the dangerous man he hid behind his easygoing façade. What exactly did he do for the government, anyway?

"All right," Pierce said. "Everybody keep me informed. I'll let you know if we find anything with the ballistics."

I was feeling way out of my element. "Any news on the knife found in my fridge?"

"Not yet. The crime lab is behind, and we won't have anything for a bit. We did run all prints found in your apartment. Nobody popped. My guess is that the person who tore up your place wore gloves. Well, person or persons," Pierce said. "Have you thought about what they were searching for?"

I hadn't thought of much else. "I have no idea. I'm broke after paying Sadie. They didn't take my valuables, and it's not like I have a safe or anything." Or secrets. I'd never been a secretive person.

"All right. Keep thinking and let me know if you come up with anything." Pierce hid a yawn. "I'll call Sheriff Franco tomorrow and see if his investigation is going anywhere. I'll also call in a favor at the lab to see if the blood on the two knives matches."

That would be so weird.

Aiden looked at Nick. "Any news on Sadie or Jonathan Brando?"

Nick shook his head. "Sheriff Franco said he'd text me with updates. So far, nothing."

My throat went dry. I hoped Sadie was all right.

We all stood and walked back outside, and even I scouted the area as if looking for threats. The lazily falling snow masked whatever danger was out there. Our vehicles were already parked near the snowy curb.

"Your brother was quick," Rory said. "Make sure to thank him."

Nick nodded and crouched to study a couple of bullet holes above his left rear tire. "They dug out the evidence." He sighed. "The shooter was aiming for tires and the building. Was it to scare or harm?"

Nobody had an answer.

Anna tugged on my jacket. "You'll have to stay with us."

I shook my head. "You guys don't even have an extra room or a bed." In fact, if I remembered right, Aiden's new cabin didn't have decent insulation yet. "I'll stay at Donna's. Or better yet, I'll stay at my new apartment in Silverville."

"Above where the dead body was found?" Anna asked, her eyebrows rising. "I don't think so."

I couldn't quite grasp that somebody was trying to hurt me, but if that were the case, I didn't want to stay with my parents or grandparents. I didn't want to put them in danger.

"You're staying with me," Rory murmured. "And I'm not arguing about it."

As cousins went, he was usually pretty mellow, but right now, he was ticking me off. However, I also wasn't an idiot. "That's fine," I said primly. It made sense to remain in pairs, at least until I figured out what was going on. I looked at Nick, who had been quiet through my exchange with my family.

"You could have been the target," I said. "It's entirely possible this whole thing is a coincidence and not tied to whatever's going on with Silver Sadie's."

He nodded. "Agreed. I have had a few threats. I will look into them."

"All right, good enough." Aiden bundled Anna against his side. "It's getting late. We're headed home. If you need help arranging furniture tomorrow, let us know."

"I thought you had to work that case in Nevada?" Anna looked up at him.

His gaze flicked to me and then moved back to her, blue and dangerous. "I'm going to send in the team. For now, I'm staying here."

Anna blushed, and I thought it was kind of sweet. It was also kind that Aiden Devlin would put his life on hold for whatever was happening right now.

I hugged my sister before she jumped into the truck, and then they slowly drove away in his large black truck. A smattering of bullet holes marred the rear door, and I had no doubt he'd have it taken care of in no time. Aiden seemed to love his truck.

I looked at my cousin. "All right. How about we drive over the pass and at least make sure everybody put my furniture in the right places? Then we can argue about whether we're going to stay at my new apartment or at your cabin."

Rory had a place near the river that he stayed at when he came home. "Oh, we're staying at the cabin," he muttered.

I rolled my eyes.

"Call me if you hear anything." Nick's gaze was warm on me. "I'm glad you're okay."

"Thanks," I said, feeling breathless. He'd taken me right to the ground and covered me with his large body. "I mean it, Nick. I appreciate how quickly you moved to protect me."

Rory's phone buzzed, and he lifted it to his ear. "What? When? Now? I'm on my way." He put the phone down and started toward his silver truck and then paused, looking at me. "Shit."

"What's wrong?" I asked.

He shook his head. "It's Serenity. There's a problem."

Serenity was Rory's ex-fiancée, who had dumped him after finding out that he hadn't been exactly honest with her about his job. In true Rory fashion, he'd first given her until Christmas—then extended that to New Year's Day—to get over it so they could work on their relationship.

My stomach dropped. I'd always really liked Serenity. "Is she okay?"

"I don't think so," he muttered, clearly at a loss for what to do.

"It's fine," I said. "Go. If she needs your help, go. I'll be fine."

"I've got her," Nick murmured.

Rory paused and looked from one of us to the other. He met Nick's gaze squarely. "You sure?"

"Yeah," Nick said. "She's safe. I'll make sure of it."

"Hey," I objected. "I can keep myself safe." Even as I said the words, I felt like an idiot. Rory was some government operative, and Nick was an ex-soldier, who was both brilliant and incredibly quick. They had skills I couldn't even imagine. "But I appreciate the ride home," I finished lamely.

Rory leaned down and kissed my cheek. "Stay safe, and if you need me, call. I'll have my phone on." With that, he jumped into his damaged truck and drove off.

Nick scanned the area again and then walked over to his Jeep. "Hop up, Princess," he instructed. "It looks like you're mine for now."

CHAPTER 10

*J*uddled into the heated seat as Nick drove away from the cheerful Christmas lights downtown and maneuvered the on-ramp onto I-90. He texted with one hand while keeping an eye on the storm.

"I wouldn't think you'd break the law by texting and driving," I murmured, stretching my feet to the heat blowing from the vents.

"You're right. I'm wrong." He placed the phone on the console beside us.

Surprise filtered through me. "Wow. An Italian male who admits when he's wrong."

He snorted. "I shouldn't have been texting. I was just making sure Jolene understood that I wasn't attending the get-together tonight."

I smacked my hand against my head. "I forgot about that. I'm sorry. Why don't you just drop me off?" Not that I wanted him having a great time with the stunning Jolene, but he wasn't mine to worry about—a status that had been my idea, actually. "It's okay. I can find another way across the pass."

"No," he said. "I don't know how or why, but we seem to be in this together. Besides, news of the attempted shooting will be all over town, and the last place I want to be is at a dinner with the media."

I rubbed an aching spot on my jaw that would probably bruise from my face smacking the ice when Nick saved my life. While I definitely appreciated it, I didn't love him acting like one of my overprotective cousins. The whole alpha-male type wasn't for me, and I could definitely see those characteristics in Nick Basanelli. "We're just friends, Nick."

"I know." He cut a quick glance my way before refocusing on the wide-open road. "But I'm still not going to leave you alone while you're in danger."

I actually could take care of myself, but I didn't want to argue at the moment. So, I turned my attention and thoughts back to the dead guy we'd found in my basement. "I wish we knew where Sadie was. I'm worried about her."

"So am I. The woman walked out of your new restaurant with a hundred and fifty thousand in cash and is now missing. I have contacts looking for her, but so far…nothing." He sped up to pass a logging truck.

The windshield wipers were rhythmic against the window as they pushed away the snow, and I felt my eyelids becoming heavy. Darkness had fallen at least a couple of hours before, and it had already been a long day.

My stomach rumbled, and I tried to remember the last time I had eaten.

Nick's profile was strong in the shadows. "We'll grab something to eat when we get to Silverville."

"I'm surprised you're okay taking me across the pass," I said. "I know you have trial tomorrow." I was starting to feel guilty about the entire situation. It wasn't fair that Nick was covering my back when he needed to do his job.

"It's okay. I'll drive back over in the morning." He sped up, and snow smashed into the windshield. "I've done it a million times before."

I paused. "No. Unless, I mean, why would you stay with one of your brothers?"

"I'm not. I'm staying with you."

I gulped and tried really hard not to react. Yep. Definite alpha-male move that I would have to squash. Hard and fast. "You're not staying with me."

He didn't answer. I wasn't really up for an argument, but I could get there if necessary. His phone buzzed, and he flicked a button on the dash. "Basanelli."

"Hey, Nicolo, it's Uncle Bay."

"Thanks for calling, Bay," Nick said. "I know your duty as the county coroner is to report to the police, but I appreciate the call this quickly. What do you have for me?"

"Well, I finished the autopsy on Rudy Brando about an hour ago and sent the information to Sheriff Franco. Do you want the medical jargon or just the straight results?"

"Give it to me straight," Nick said. "I don't need the medical crap."

I appreciated that fact and held my breath as I waited to hear more about the victim found in my newly purchased basement.

Bay cleared his throat. "The victim died from a stab wound to the heart." Bay sneezed twice before continuing. "It was one clean and fast strike, and the angle shows that either the killer was taller by quite a bit, or Brando was on his back, and the killer struck down—which is more likely. He died instantly."

"Anything else of interest?" Nick asked.

I couldn't help it; I started to tremble. Keeping casual about it, I held my hands out to the vents and let them warm from the heat.

"Not really," Bay said. "I could tell you that he had shrimp for lunch, and based on the report from the crime scene techs, was killed right where you found him."

Nick switched his headlights to lower beams to combat the storm. "What about time of death?"

"I can give you a three or four-hour spread, but that's about it."

I blinked. "Can't you get more exact than that?"

"Who the hell's there?" Bay snapped. "This is official. Well, kind of."

"Oh, it's Tessa Albertini," Nick said. "Sorry. I should have told you she was in the car. But considering we found the deceased in her building, she'd have the information anyway."

"Yeah, once she got a lawyer," Bay sputtered. "But, anyway, I can only give you three or four hours—from around three to seven pm date of death. There's no way to tell beyond that in this situation."

My stomach lurched. I was definitely alone at my building for part of that time. Darn it.

"All right. Thanks, Bay," Nick said. "I'll talk to you tomorrow." He clicked off.

I swallowed. "Doesn't your Uncle Bay work in Timber City?"

"Yeah, he's the coroner and medical examiner." Nick slowed down as a truck passed.

"Why didn't the coroner in Silverville conduct the autopsy?" I asked.

Nick glanced in the rearview mirror. The lights from the vehicle behind us were bright enough to reflect against the glass and illuminated his face, illustrating his sharp bone structure.

"Gem County doesn't have a medical examiner or a forensic pathologist," he said. "Coroners don't even need to have a medical license."

"Oh, I didn't know that. I thought every county had a coroner who did autopsies."

"No, we're lucky in Timber City," he admitted. "All northern Idaho counties used to send suspicious deaths to Spokane for autopsy. Uncle Bay changed that when he moved back to Idaho a decade ago after traveling the world in the service."

Maybe I should take a class in civics at the community college. "Yet another thing I didn't know."

"That makes sense." Nick grinned. "Most people don't know

74

that county coroners don't usually conduct autopsies, so don't feel bad. I only know because I deal with murder half the time. Or at least some of the time."

I hadn't really thought about it, but Nick's job was actually dangerous.

The truck behind us got closer.

"What is that jerk doing?" Nick pulled into the right lane and slowed down. "He can pass me if he's in such a hurry."

I didn't pay much attention. I was still trying to figure out why I thought every county in the world had a coroner who did autopsies. Maybe I'd been watching too many police procedurals on TV.

Nick's hands tightened on the steering wheel. He looked over his shoulder.

"What's going on?" I sat up straighter in my seat.

"I'm not sure."

I looked around. There were trees, ice berms, and a lot of snow on my side of the SUV, and cement dividers on his. We were just starting to descend through the mountain pass, and the roads were icy, the snow falling hard. "Nick?" I asked.

Just then, the vehicle behind us smashed into the rear of the Jeep. We jerked forward, and the seat belt cinched hard against my chest. Pain blasted through my rib cage, and I gasped.

"What the hell?" Nick grabbed the wheel and fought the ice. I yelped and planted a hand on the window. The vehicle spun and went off the side of the road, smashing against a tree.

My head jerked back and forth, and I sucked in air, my ears ringing. I looked wildly around. No other vehicles were coming either way right now.

"Get down!" In one smooth motion, Nick released my seat belt, grabbed my neck, and shoved my chest to my knees. Pain flared in my back, but I didn't move, my heart thundering.

He opened the console, and I caught the glint of a gun out of the corner of my eye.

"Wait," I protested.

"Stay here." He stopped the engine and ducked down. I turned my head to see the entire interior of the vehicle awash with light. Whoever had pushed us off the road was right behind us with their high beams pointed at the Jeep.

Nick partially levered up, turned, and pointed. "Cover your ears."

I did so instantly. Two shots rang out, jolting my entire body, and then darkness descended. The remaining glass from Nick's back window clattered into the back seat. Whoa. Nick had just fired through the vehicle.

With the darkness came silence. Hard and heavy.

Nick opened his door and dropped out, rolling once across the ice. I gasped and scrambled over to watch, reaching into my bag for my weapon. We were all armed. After Anna's frightening experience as a child, we all knew how to shoot and were more than ready to protect ourselves.

I kept low and fell to the ground in case Nick needed backup. Icy shards bit into my knees. I crouched, pointing my gun at the darkened form of the truck behind us. I couldn't see anybody, but as my eyes adjusted to the darkness, I could tell that the passenger-side door was open. Whoever had hit us had gotten out that way.

Graceful and smooth, Nick kept low as he hurried toward the back of his Jeep and pivoted, heading straight for the passenger-side door of the other vehicle, all animal grace.

I saw a flash of fire and heard the sound of a gun firing a second later. Nick dove to the ground, and then faster than I could track, got up and tackled the shooter with an impact that echoed through the storm.

They barreled into the forest. Snow and ice fell from boughs, and the sound of grunts and punches echoed back. I couldn't breathe. I could barely think. My legs shook, but I stood and hurried toward the truck, my gun pointed inside it. It was empty.

A man yelled from the tree line, and then there was silence. The wind blasted me, and I had to wipe snow from my eyes. My heart pounded wildly, and I could barely breathe. But I put my back to the empty truck and slid along the side and then across the grill, pointing my weapon toward the trees.

"Nick?" I called out.

"I'm fine."

Gratitude nearly buckled my knees. "Are you sure?" I fumbled for my cell phone to hold up. I pressed the flashlight icon and nearly fell in relief as I saw him walking out between two snow-laden pine trees, dragging a figure by the collar.

I lifted the light to see Nick's face. There was blood on his lip, swelling on his cheek, and fury in his tawny eyes.

I slid to the side. "Who is it?"

Nick twisted his shoulders and tossed a half-conscious man against the grill of the white truck. The guy groaned and fell to the ice.

"It's Ozzie Morrison," Nick snapped.

I lowered my weapon. "Morrison?" And then I looked at the truck, shining my flashlight on it. It was the white one the shooter earlier had driven so quickly past the diner. "The brother of the guy you convicted? So this *is* about you?" I should be ashamed to admit that a little bit of relief flew through me.

"Apparently, so." Nick pulled his phone from his back pocket, looking dangerous and pretty much invincible in the swirling snow.

It was a totally inappropriate moment for me to catch my breath at how sexy and deadly Basanelli could be after kicking the butt of a man who'd tried to hurt us.

I didn't know Ozzie Morrison, but he looked like about two hundred and fifty pounds of solid, beefy muscle. It must have been a good fight, and Nick had won. Parts of me warmed inappropriately.

Nick quickly called Sheriff Franco and reported the events of the evening.

Ozzie started to stir, and almost casually, Nick kicked him in the jaw. Ozzie's head thunked back against the grill of his truck, and he slumped unconscious again.

"Asshole," Nick muttered.

I couldn't help it. Or maybe I didn't want to. My hand shaking, I made sure my safety was engaged and then shoved my gun into the back of my waistband. Without letting myself think about it, I jumped forward and planted one on Nick's mouth.

He took over the kiss almost instantly, using just the force of his lips.

Nick Basanelli knew exactly how to kiss. The air around us was freezing, but his lips were hot, his tongue volcanic.

I moved into him, no longer caring about the guy on the ground. Desire skittered through me, zinging down to my abdomen. Basanelli was a hard man; I had known that already.

But against him, body to body, his mouth taking mine? He was hard everywhere. Head to toe.

Sirens echoed in the distance.

I stilled and then took a step back, surprised that he'd captured me with only his mouth.

What in the heck had I just done?

CHAPTER 11

A frantic call from Smiley's Diner had me out of my comfortable bed at my parents' house at six in the morning. Darn it.

The previous night, Nick and I had checked out my new place above the restaurant after reaching town and being interviewed once again by Sheriff Franco. Afterward, I'd decided to stay with my folks for the night.

My cousins had done an all right job of placing what furniture I had left, but I hadn't wanted to stay alone until the sheriff discovered who'd killed Rudy Brando, and I sure wasn't letting Nick sleep over after that kiss.

Yeah, things got silent, tension-filled, and awkward between us afterward. Mainly because I just wanted to kiss him again.

I slowly drew on clothes, my mind filled with the feeling of his steel-hard body. So not good. I'd felt fine staying with my folks since the shooter had been after Nick and not me. My gut feeling was that Rudy's murder had nothing to do with me, except for that darned quitclaim deed. It had to be fake. I hoped.

Man, I was tired. I paused in brushing my hair to dial the diner.

"Smiley," Mert Smiley answered, his tone brusque.

"Hey. It's Tessa. Are you sure you need me today?" I engaged the speaker button so I could lean toward the mirror and apply mascara without taking out an eye. "I have the next couple of days off before training the new workers."

Mert growled. A true growl. The guy was around seventy and built like a linebacker, and contrary to his name, he was a grump. "One waitress has a sick kid, and the other some sort of personal problem. I'm swamped here already. People are tired of leftovers after Christmas and want food. Be here in fifteen minutes."

"I'm over the pass." I was more than used to Mert's moods. "I'll be there for the brunch rush in a couple of hours. You've already handled the early morning crowd—and you owe me." I clicked off before his temper could explode because I just wasn't in the mood.

I shoved everything I'd need for the day into my overlarge bag and quietly crept into the kitchen, where my dad had already left on a pot of coffee. He had no doubt headed to the mine a couple of hours ago to start his shift, and my mom was still asleep.

I poured myself a large travel mug, snatched a plate with croissants, and then headed out to my car, which one of my cousins had delivered to my folks' house at some point. While a large family was often meddling and in your face, they sure came in handy, and I did appreciate them. I didn't even know which cousin had done it, but I thought it was sweet.

My Nissan Rogue drove perfectly on the winter roads.

Taking a chance, I popped by the sheriff's office, which was located in an old brick building in the middle of town. I walked inside and waved at the deputy behind the desk, who was answering a call about what sounded like a missing dog. I went right by him and down the long hallway past cabinets to the sheriff's office.

"Hey, Sheriff Franco." I moved inside. The place smelled like papers and Old Spice. "I brought you some of my mom's croissants." I'd figured she wouldn't mind since she had made so many. I handed over the plate.

The sheriff looked up, his grizzly eyebrows rising. "Excellent. I was going to run down and grab something to eat at the little hotel, but this is better. How you feeling after your ordeal last night?"

"I'm fine," I said.

The sheriff looked me over. "You've got a bruise on your chin."

"I know. That's from when the shooter tried to take out Nick in Timber City. I hit the ground pretty hard." Truth be told, despite Nick tackling me and then our car accident the night before, I was feeling all right. My body was a little sore, but it was nothing I couldn't handle.

I took a seat. "Do you have any news on the Rudy Brando murder?"

"Nope," the sheriff said cheerfully, or as cheerful as Franco ever got. He reached for a croissant and shoved half of it into his mouth, peering behind me as if to make sure neither of his deputies knew there were snacks close by.

"So far, all I got on Rudy is that he was an insurance salesman from Denver with three ex-wives who want nothing to do with him. He found out about the long deceased George Brando being his father six months ago and apparently started contacting all the members of the Brando family he could find."

"Does he have any sort of record?" I wished I'd kept one of the croissants.

The sheriff eyed me shrewdly and then nudged the plate closer. "You can have one. You brought them."

"Thanks." I took one of the crumbly treats and tore off a piece.

"No record that I could find so far, but I have to say, the three ex-wives hated his guts. Said the guy hid money and lied in their divorces. One of the women claimed he cleaned her out since she hadn't made him sign a prenup."

I winced. "Is there any chance any of them have been to Idaho?"

"Not that they've said. I have a couple of buddies in Denver and asked them to discreetly investigate the three ex-wives—more specifically to trace their movements over the last week. My friends are all retired law enforcement and excited about the project."

It didn't surprise me that the sheriff had friends everywhere. He was that kind of guy, and he'd always reminded me of Sam Elliott. Who wouldn't want to be friends with Sam Elliott? "Have you had any luck finding Sadie or Jonathan?" I held my breath as I awaited the answer.

"Not yet. I had acquaintances checking with the airlines, and they didn't fly anywhere. And so far, none of her neighbors know anything. I've contacted his colleagues and friends over in Montana, and all they know is that he was coming to spend the holidays with his sister. It's really quite the mystery. I hate murders in this town. We get one every few years, and it just irritates the crap out of me."

I nodded. "No kidding. For the record, I really had no idea about the quitclaim deed from Sadie to Rudy, and I don't think it's authentic."

"I sent it to the tech lab in Boise, along with samples of Sadie's writing that we found in her cottage. Guess we have some new handwriting analysis expert. I swear, everyone is moving to Idaho from the big cities." The sheriff took another croissant.

That was true, and hopefully, it would make my new restaurant successful. "I hope the deed was fake," I said fervently.

"They'll be able to tell us if she signed it or not. Sadie was a trustworthy gal, except for all the gambling, so my gut instinct is with you, Tessa. If it turns out it's valid, then he owned the place," the sheriff said. "But let's not borrow trouble. We'll figure it out when we know."

I rubbed the bruise on my aching jaw and took another bite of the delicious croissant. I was a decent cook and a pretty good baker, but I still wasn't up to my mother's level. Like my younger sister, I loved to bake. Donna, on the other hand, could burn water and went through pots and pans like most people did water filters.

I cleared my throat and tried to think of a decent segue to my next question but came up empty. So, I just asked it outright. "Where are you on the Lenny Johnson murder?"

The sheriff scoffed. "Yeah, I heard about that clause in the contract you signed."

Of course, he had. There were no secrets in Silverville. "You'll help me out?"

"No." The sheriff leaned back in his chair. "I don't want you snooping around and getting into more trouble. I have enough to deal with when your sister does it."

"Hey, that's not fair. I should be able to get into as much trouble as Anna does," I protested, finishing off my croissant.

The sheriff looked at me for a while. "You know that's true. She does take up a lot of the oxygen in the family, doesn't she?"

I sat back, surprised and oddly warmed that somebody actually saw me. "No, Anna is a sweetheart. She's smart, she works hard, and she'd do anything for, well...anybody," I admitted.

He steepled his fingers beneath his chin. "Yeah, but she's often everyone's focus, and I get it. Being kidnapped as a kid and going through that ordeal definitely made us all protective of her."

I nodded. It had been a rough three hours. Although her kidnapper hadn't had time to truly hurt her, the ordeal had been terrifying. And then Aiden, as a sixteen-year-old, had rushed in and rescued her before anything truly bad could happen. Even so, we all shielded her as much as possible, even though she didn't want it. Plus, she was the baby in the family, so it was probably normal.

"So you're going to let me help with this?" I asked hopefully, changing my angle with him.

The sheriff shook his head. "No, but I will tell you what I have because it ain't much."

Hey, it was a start.

"As you know, Lenny Johnson was a vagabond who just did odd jobs in town for the last thirty years. He had a drinking problem, and it tortured him," the sheriff said.

"I know." He was a decent guy, but he also could be found drunk in an alley. I knew many people in town had rescued him from freezing to death through the years. "Was he originally from Silverville?"

"Spokane. He grew up there and actually played football for Shadle High. He seemed to have wandered the country and was unhomed a few times before finally ending up here thirty years ago and taking odd jobs," the sheriff said. "Never married. Didn't have kids. Only family members were his parents, who died years ago."

That was sad. I knew of several people in town who had tried to help Lenny throughout the years, but he seemed so lost he didn't want help—or maybe it was the alcohol. I never knew. "He did spend a lot of time in your jail cell, didn't he?" I murmured.

The sheriff nodded. "Yeah, especially on cold nights. I'd make sure to go and find him and hold him for the night so he could stay warm. The church took him in a lot, as well. He was a decent guy. He just drank too much. Didn't cause any problems. Worked when he could. But, you know, the alcohol ruled him."

"I know," I said. "Did he have any ties to Sadie?"

"Rumor had it Lenny and Sadie might've dated in high school and flirted throughout the decades," the sheriff said. "I have no idea why he was found dead in her basement, except maybe he snuck in there for a night or two. He often broke into local buildings for shelter."

"But who would kill him, and why?" I asked.

"No clue. So far, I got nothing," the sheriff said. "I think that clause in your contract is silly, and now that you've questioned me about it, I'd say you fulfilled the requirements."

Yet, I hadn't. I'd promised to really try, and I wasn't done yet. Plus, and I couldn't help it, I was curious. Why had Lenny been in Sadie's basement? More importantly, why would anybody want him dead?

"Don't you think the fact that two dead bodies were found in the same spot is more than just a coincidence?" I asked.

"Not really," the sheriff said. "Like I said, Lenny was known to break into buildings all over town if he wanted to stay warm, and anybody could have followed him in and killed him. As for Rudy Brando, somebody's making a statement to you, though I haven't figured out what or why. Or perhaps they're making a statement to Sadie. That whole murder could have everything to do with her and nothing to do with you or even the building," he mused.

I bit my lip. "Were there any other similarities between Lenny's and Rudy's murders, besides them both being stabbed?"

"No. Different knives, different placement of the bodies. And Lenny was actually stabbed several times—in the throat, slashed in the thigh, and elsewhere. It was a bloody mess. We never found the murder weapon, but the crime lab identified the cuts as being from a hunting knife with a serrated edge. Much different than those other two knives."

Oh, I hadn't known that fact. "You've kept that a secret."

"I don't tell everybody everything," the sheriff said. "But I don't mind telling you."

It warmed me that he trusted me.

"Especially since you're now off this case," he uttered sternly.

It reminded me of when he'd coached my fourth-grade softball team, and we'd been goofing off instead of practicing. While the sheriff was a softie, he was also the sheriff when he had to issue an order.

"I appreciate your help," I said. "Would you please let me know as soon as you find Sadie? I'm worried about her."

"Of course, I will."

Deputy McCracken poked his head in the door. He was about five years younger than me, with thick blond hair and odd green eyes. He'd always seemed like a nice guy, and our families were well acquainted, but I didn't know him well.

"Hey, there's a lady here to see you," he said.

"Seems to be my day for ladies." The sheriff unobtrusively took the plate of croissants and pulled it toward himself so nobody else could reach it. "Send her in. Tessa, drive carefully today. There's another storm coming."

"Thanks," I said, standing and recognizing an invitation to leave when I heard one.

A woman walked inside, and I didn't recognize her.

"Hello, Sheriff," she said, her gaze cutting to me before she looked back at him. She had to be in her late thirties, with frosted blond hair and sharp brown eyes. Her blue outfit was high-end, and her jewelry sparkled with diamonds.

"How can I help you?" The sheriff rose to his feet.

"Well, for starters, you can tell me who killed my husband. I'm Marilyn Brando. Rudy and I have been married for a year and a half." She tugged a piece of paper out of her purse. "He was in town to take possession of a building we purchased. Here's a copy of the quitclaim deed that he sent to me right before he was murdered."

She looked me square in the eye. "I'm the new owner of the building, and you're on notice to remove your belongings immediately."

CHAPTER 12

I called my sister the instant I left the sheriff's office, my body now aching from the crash and the tackling the day before. For some reason, I was hurting worse after the mental body blow from Rudy Brando's wife, and I was sure it was psychological.

"Hey, what's up?" Anna answered instantly. I gave her the rundown and then waited for my brilliant lawyer to fix all of it. "Well, crap," she muttered. "Wait a minute. You said that Sheriff Franco reported that Brando had three ex-wives. He didn't mention *this* wife?"

Hope flared in my chest. "No," I said. "Is that significant?"

"Probably not," Anna said. "No doubt Franco has only been in touch with people in Denver. It's entirely possible Rudy Brando got married in a different state, and Franco just hadn't discovered it yet. I'm sure he's interviewing the woman now and will have full details." She sighed. "Did you get a good look at her deed?"

"No. It just looked like a regular deed. She handed it to the sheriff, and then he asked me to leave." I got into my Nissan and brushed snow off my hair.

"Crap. Do you have a copy of your deed?"

I gulped. "Yeah." I had tons of stuff in my bag. "Why?"

"Go to the courthouse right now and record it. I didn't even think of that, especially since Rudy is dead and can't record his now. I also didn't think it was a big deal because we all trust Sadie."

I jumped out of my car. "I'm right next to the courthouse. Why is that so important?" The wind slapped me, and I ducked my head to combat it, hurrying toward the courthouse's marble steps. The place had been built when the mines were flush, so it was elaborate, to say the least. "Anna?"

"Idaho is a notice-race state, which means the first to record pretty much wins. It's a race to provide notice, in other words. You provide notice by recording a deed."

I slipped on the icy steps, caught my balance, and walked inside the ultra-warm building. The recorder's office was to the right, and I moved inside. "Just a sec. I'm here."

"Okay, well, it's all right. We'll figure this out," Anna said, the sound of clothing rustling in the background. "Keep me on hold."

I hustled up to the counter, handing over the deed. Craig Panzini had worked in the office for a couple of decades. He was around forty, bald, and rarely smiled. "I need to record this."

"Sure." He went through the motions, and then all was good.

Yelling came from my phone, and I took it from my pocket to hold to my ear. "What?"

"Ask him if anybody else has recorded a deed for that property lately." Anna huffed.

I did. Craig gave me a look and then flipped through an old-fashioned ledger on the desk. "Hmm," he said, pursing his lips. "A deed was recorded they day before yesterday first thing in the morning. I was out, so Lila must've handled it."

My heart sank. "Don't tell me. Rudy Brando was the recorded owner."

"Yep."

He'd done it just hours before I signed the contract, received my deed, and then later found him dead. "I need a copy of that."

"All right." He sighed as if it were all too much but made me a copy anyway.

I thanked him and hustled outside, fighting tears. "I can't believe this."

Anna coughed. "We'll find out if his deed is authentic or not."

"But if it is, they own the building, right?" I asked.

Silence ticked over the line for a moment. "Well, yeah. I think so. You conducted a title search and had a good faith belief that the title was clean when you signed, so you definitely have cause for action against Sadie but not really against Rudy if his deed is valid."

"I gave Sadie a hundred and fifty thousand dollars cash," I burst out, jumping into my Rogue and starting my engine. How stupid was I? There was no way to get it back. "But I did a title search." How could somebody just refuse to record a deed? It wasn't fair. That money could be long gone.

"I understand," Anna said. "Take a deep breath." It was odd for my sister to be calming me down, it was usually the opposite. But I did what she said and took a deep breath.

"Okay. Right now, don't worry about it," Anna said. "You have the place locked up, and Marilyn Brando doesn't have keys, right?"

"I have no idea," I said.

Anna loudly exhaled. "All right. Call McDerny's Hardware store right now and have them go change all the locks. If this thing ends up in litigation, the court will probably issue a temporary order where nobody can use the building until the conclusion of the case. But at least your stuff will be safe."

"Okay," I murmured. I couldn't believe this. I had saved for years to compile that amount of money, and now that time and effort could all be down the drain. I had to figure this out. "Anna, we need to find Sadie."

"I know. I'll come over and help you now."

I couldn't do anything until we found the woman. "No, wait. Don't you have court today?" I thought she'd mentioned that she had a stupid trial between Christmas and New Year's that was irritating her.

"I do, but I can ask my partner to handle it."

"No, no, don't do that. There's nothing to do right now," I said. "The sheriff is on it, and we all have work to do. I'm coming back over the pass."

"Do you need a place to stay tonight?" she asked. "I know you gave up your apartment."

It was a kind offer, but no way. "Thanks, but I'll stay with Donna. She should be home later this afternoon." I smiled. "Last thing I want is to watch you and Aiden Devlin flirt."

"We don't flirt."

"Oh, you flirt," I countered. "He is smooth about it, and you're just dorky."

She laughed, probably because it was true. "All right. Call me when you're over here. Maybe we can grab lunch," she said. "Love you."

"Love you, too." I hung up and turned the heat on full blast. I didn't have to be across the pass for a few hours, and my mind was absolutely reeling. So I drove down to the local coffee shop— well, the *only* coffee shop.

I noted several big rigs in the parking lot. Perfect. Jumping out, I smoothed my hair and then strode inside, instantly assailed by the smell of coffee and burnt toast.

Sunshine Eats had been a staple in town for years, and I had no intention of truly competing with it. Oh, I'd offer a breakfast menu for tourists, but I would be geared more toward the lunch and dinner crowds. At least in my head, I would be. *If* I ever got to open the restaurant.

Freddy Sunshine smiled from behind the counter. "Hey, Tessa. Find any dead bodies lately?"

I shook my head. Freddy was actually Freddy Junior and was only a year older than me. His family had owned the small diner for a century. We'd been pals in high school and then had stayed in touch. He was a decent guy who had married Franny Abernacky, and they were working on their seventh kid. It was impossible not to like Freddy.

"No, but the day's young," I murmured, glancing around to see who was in the area. The mah-jongg and bridge players wouldn't show up until later in the afternoon, but the old political crowd— and I mean old—sat over in the far corner. They were a mixture of men and women who'd been involved in politics in the area for decades, and they met early to talk about the day and drink the too-strong coffee.

Today, there were only three of them, and I headed their way. "Hi."

"Hey, Tessa," Mrs. Canterbury said. She had been a librarian in my grade school before retiring twenty years ago. She had to be at least ninety and didn't look a day over a hundred.

"Hi, Mrs. C," I said. "I came to ask you folks if you knew anything about Sadie or Jonathan or where they might be."

The three senior citizens shook their heads.

The other two were men who used to work in local business or government. Bert Grizzly, a former mayor, rubbed his thick jowls. "No, and it's quite concerning. They just disappeared. We haven't heard a thing."

Mrs. Canterbury sighed. "However, did you know that Sadie had taken in a tenant at her cottage?"

"No." I perked up. "The sheriff didn't mention that to me."

"It's probably a big clue," Mrs. C said, her faded blue eyes widening. "What do you think? Should we check it out?"

Oh, no. Definitely not. I did not want her help. "Actually, I think we should let the sheriff do his job," I advised. "Do we know anything about the tenant?" There were no secrets in Silverville, so I was surprised I hadn't heard anything.

"No," Mrs. Canterbury said. "I only know what I do because I saw a vehicle going to and from her place every few days or so. I used my binoculars, but all I could see was that the person in the truck was a woman. I never saw the truck around town, though, so my guess is they were working either in Montana or over in Timber City."

I looked at the other members of the gossip crew. "Does anybody else know anything about this?"

They all shook their heads.

"No," Timmy Phillips, another eighty-year-old and a retired banker, cast a wary glance at Mrs. C. "Sometimes, you imagine things. I think it's because you're such a good writer." He hastened to say the last bit.

"I don't imagine things. I know I saw that vehicle on more than one occasion," she protested. "I saw it at least twice."

I fought the urge to smack my head. That could have been anybody. It might have been a delivery person. Since we were so rural, the bigger shipping companies often contracted jobs out, and sometimes people just used their cars.

"What about Lenny?" I asked. "Does anybody else think it's strange two bodies were found in that basement?"

"Many people wanted Lenny dead," Timmy muttered. "He owed everybody money, and even though we all kind of loved him, he turned into a mean drunk sometimes."

That was true. I'd always thought he was a sweet man, but I'd never really seen him late at night at a bar, and I'd heard he caused more than one ruckus through the years. "Did he have a problem with anyone in particular?" I had no idea what I was doing as an investigator, but curiosity often led to decent results.

"Well, he and Sadie had a dustup," Timmy said thoughtfully.

I nearly sat down. "This is news. Does the sheriff know?"

"Of course, the sheriff knows. You can't expect him to tell you his whole case." Mrs. Canterbury shook her head sadly. "Come on, Tessa."

Truth be told, I had expected him to tell me everything.

"You're a suspect," Timmy said, his gaze filled with what might've been respect. "We all know about the quitclaim deed Sadie signed over to Rudy."

"Huh?" I didn't really feel like a suspect. "You know I wouldn't kill anybody."

"Oh, I don't know..." Mrs. Canterbury pushed her thick glasses back up her nose. "People do strange things when pushed to their limit. Have you been pushed to your limit lately?"

"Not yet." I was certainly getting there, however. "What was the problem between Sadie and Lenny?"

"They dated in high school, you know," she mentioned.

The sheriff had mentioned that, but high school for them was a long time ago. I grabbed a chair and flopped onto it. "Do you have any more details?"

"Oh, yes. Sadie grew up over in Burke, and she met Lenny at a football game when Burke played Shadle. I mean, they were hot and heavy from what I've heard. I, of course, grew up in the city here, in Silverville," Mrs. Canterbury said.

Yeah, the *big city*. I bit my lip. "I don't think Sadie's strong enough to stab somebody like that. I mean, she's tough, but physically, that would've been quite the ordeal," I murmured.

"Her brother has the strength," Timmy murmured.

"Jonathan?" I asked, stunned. I just couldn't see him getting bloody.

"Oh, yeah. Jonathan and Lenny hated each other." Bert seemed as if he didn't want to be left out of the discussion.

"Really?" I said, leaning forward, unable to help myself. This was good gossip. "Why?"

"It was always a mystery," Mrs. Canterbury said softly, looking around as if eavesdropping ears were in every direction. But the diner was vacant. "They went way back, too. I'm sure it had something to do with a girl. Things always do, right?"

"Either that or money," I muttered.

Mrs. Canterbury reached out and patted my hand. "Lenny was kind of an asshat, Tessa. I wouldn't worry about his murder. I think you've probably done all you need to do to fulfill your duties under your contract to buy Silver Sadie's and the building."

I sighed. "You've heard all about the contract, too?"

"Everybody's heard about the contract," Timmy said. "You can't seriously be going on a date with all three of the Brando nephews."

"I kind of have to," I said. Maybe, if I owned the building at this point—which I wasn't sure about. However, there had been a week time limit in that contract, so I would stick to it. After that, I wasn't sure. There had to be a way to prove that I owned the building legally, and Anna would figure it out. I was sure of it.

I glanced at my watch. "Oh, I'm sorry, I have to get going. Thank you for your help. You've all been wonderful."

They all smiled, and Mrs. Canterbury leaned forward again. "If I find out anything else, I'll call you."

"Thanks, Mrs. C. I really appreciate it." My mind reeling, I exited the diner and sat in my vehicle for a few minutes.

I could head over the pass, or I could scout around a little bit more. After making a quick call to the hardware store for somebody to change all the locks on the building, I decided to channel my sister and do something I shouldn't. Taking a deep breath, I started down Main Street and then turned away from the river road toward an even more rural area outside of town. I might as well check out Sadie's house.

The sheriff texted me on the way, and I read his message as I drove. Apparently Marilyn Brando had a solid alibi for her husband's murder since she'd been on a plane headed our way. Darn it. Sheriff Franco had tracked that one down very fast. I could only hope he'd find the real murderer as quickly.

After several miles of driving on the windy backwoods road, careful of black ice, I noticed a car behind me. When I sped up, it did the same, and when I slowed, it kept perfect pace.

My heart hammered against my rib cage.

I was being followed.

CHAPTER 13

I took several deep breaths to calm myself and reached for my phone on the other seat, pulling it toward me and glancing down. Darn it. I was too far down the river road and didn't have service.

Okay, I could handle this. My hands shook as I tried to calm myself into dealing with the moment. I was armed, and I knew this road like the back of my hand. I squinted into the rearview mirror to try to make out the vehicle. It was gray and pretty nondescript. Through the snowy day, it was difficult to tell more than that, and I wasn't an expert on cars anyway.

I took the next turn slowly, carefully, and then sped up around the corner when I was out of sight. Within seconds, the car turned the corner, as well. I slowed down, forcing it to do the same, and then I waited. There was a turnoff about half a mile ahead that led to a campground.

My options were to either drive into the deserted campground and wait with my gun, or try to flip around on the ice and head right at the car. I didn't know if the occupant was armed. I didn't think that was my best option, so I drove cautiously, and at the last second, turned down the unplowed road toward the campground. It was winter, and nobody would be around.

I punched the gas, slid on the ice, and fought the thick snow, but I barreled down the road and then took a sharp left at the first camping spot. I spun around and then yelped as my car kept spinning. Finally, I came to a stop.

I instantly opened the door and jumped out, sinking to my thighs in the snow. Pulling my gun from my purse, I kicked through the powder as best I could and positioned myself behind a massive spruce tree.

Then I waited. I could hear the car behind me struggling against the thick snow, which had been part of my plan.

Finally, the vehicle pulled in behind me and rolled to a stop. The lights were on, and snow nearly covered the windshield. I steadied my aim and pointed it at the driver's side, waiting. The car remained still for a moment, and then both doors opened.

Fear scissored down my spine, and I stepped slightly to the right of the tree for a better view. Could I really shoot somebody? I never had, and I wasn't sure.

Two hands wrapped around the top of the window of the open driver's side door, and it took me a second to realize there were pink-painted nails. A woman levered up, poking only her head out.

"Tessa," she yelled.

Oh, holy crap. I instantly flicked the safety back on my Smith & Wesson Ladysmith and dropped my hand. "Nonna?" I asked incredulously, kicking my way through the snow and out from behind the tree.

"Oh, hello, dear. What in the world are you doing back there?" she asked.

I just stared at her, stunned. There were no words. For a second, there were no thoughts. And then I shoved the gun into the back of my waistband, not wanting to scare her. "Who's in the car with you?" I asked, unable to think of anything else to say.

"Oh, it's me, dear." Georgiana Lambertini levered her impressive bulk over the top of the passenger-side door while still keeping most of her body inside.

My heart sank, not slow but fast, right to my abdomen. "Wait a minute. What are you two doing?" I moved toward their rumbling vehicle.

Nonna smiled. A silk scarf covered her hair, while wide Audrey Hepburn-style sunglasses hid her beautiful eyes. As I neared her, I could tell she wore an overlarge trench coat that had to belong to my grandfather.

"Nonna, what are you doing?" I asked again, my legs freezing, considering the snow was almost up to my waist.

"Well, we were tailing you," she said honestly. "I don't know if you knew this, but Georgiana, Thelma, and I have started our own private detective agency."

Oh, God. I had to fight throwing up. Anna had told me they were talking about this, but I hadn't truly believed it was true.

Georgiana nodded. She had dyed her hair light pink. I wasn't sure if she'd been going for streaks or not, but it curled to her shoulders and contrasted nicely with the papery white hue of her face. "We're pretty tough," she yelled out.

I kept my cool and breathed through my nose. "Where's Thelma?" She and Georgiana shared a home in a retirement community in Timber City. I had to know where all three of them were before I could figure out what to do.

"Oh, she's back at headquarters, also known as our duplex," Georgiana said. "She's fighting a cold, and we thought she should avoid being in the field, as they say."

I couldn't believe this. It was beyond reality right now, and my life already belonged in a strange world only meant for Netflix thrillers. "Whose car?" I pointed to the nondescript gray sedan. I still couldn't tell what kind of car it was.

Georgiana smiled. "It's our work vehicle. It's easier to track people in."

My nonna usually drove a maroon Buick that I would've recognized instantly, so I could not fault their logic. "Why are you following me?" I pinched the bridge of my nose.

"We figured you were trying to solve Sadie's disappearance or one of the two murders," Nonna said cheerfully. "You need our help, honey. And you know it."

I didn't know what to do. To be honest, I had been greatly amused when the elderly ladies had tried to help Anna with cases. I hadn't anticipated the heavy weight of responsibility that instantly slammed down on my shoulders. I couldn't let any of them get hurt.

"We take it you're going out to Sadie's place?" Nonna asked.

"I can't afford a private detective," I said weakly. "I'm so sorry."

Georgiana partially fell back into the car. "Oh, that's okay, honey. We can exchange services."

"Services?" I whispered, my voice barely strong enough to rise above the wind.

"You're opening a restaurant at some point," Nonna said. "We'll just take food in exchange for our work."

Well, I would've fed my grandmother for free anyway, so there wasn't a way to argue about that. Still, I studied the closed campground. It was December, so nobody would be around for months until the snow melted. "I'm not sure you can get that vehicle back out of here," I said. While my Rogue had snow tires and some heft, their tread looked pretty flimsy.

"Oh, don't you worry. I've been driving in the snow for eons," Nonna said. "Okay, we'll lead the way because you seem to be having a little trouble with your speed."

Without waiting for an answer, both women ducked back into their vehicle, and my nonna hit reverse. The car hissed and thumped several times on the way back to the road leading to the camping area, but they made it that far.

Sighing, I climbed back into my Rogue, put my purse and gun on the passenger seat, and turned the heat on full blast. I was soaking wet from the waist down, and plenty of snow had landed on my shoulders, as well. Muttering to myself, I followed them sedately out of the campground, noting my grandmother getting stuck several times but managing to use the gas and brake pedals to get herself out of trouble.

To be honest, she was a pretty good driver in the snow. We made it out to the main road, which was vacant of other cars, and I followed them for several more miles until they turned down a long drive that looked as if it hadn't been plowed in several days. At least the snow wasn't as deep as it had been at the campground. We reached Sadie's quiet and dark cabin, and I pulled up alongside my nonna.

She was out of her vehicle first with her hefty handbag over her shoulder. She patted it. "Don't worry. I have both my wooden spoon and my Smith & Wesson, sweetie. We can handle any trouble that arises."

Oh, this was a disaster. Worse yet, Sadie lived outside of cell service, which was something I could barely imagine. There was no way to call for help unless I hit the 9-1-1 emergency button, and frankly, I didn't know if even that worked out here. It probably did, but I didn't think we were in danger. Plus, I wanted to snoop around and didn't want the sheriff stopping us.

"All right, but if anybody sees anything suspicious or gets even a hint of danger, we're out of here," I ordered the ladies.

"Sure thing." Georgiana forced herself from the vehicle.

For this rendezvous, she had worn bright pink ski pants, a lime green puffer jacket zipped up to her neck, and a pink and green scarf that somehow tied the entire outfit together. She kicked her way through the snow to the front door. At least it was only high enough to reach our knees.

"Wait, wait, wait. Let me go first." I brushed past them both in case some idiot fired a shotgun from inside. I knocked on the door. Nothing.

Sadie's cabin was a one-story A-frame with a wraparound porch that probably sported lots of chairs during the summer. During the winter, it held only snow.

I moved to the side to look inside a window and saw only darkness. Nonna tried the front door. It was locked.

"I'll go around back," I said.

"We'll cover the front." Nonna tugged her wooden spoon from her purse. It was a formidable weapon. I'd seen her smack everyone from errant grandchildren to a judge on the ear with it, and it always earned results.

"Good idea," I murmured, walking around the porch. I truly appreciated that the porch wrapped around the entire property. It was brilliant, and considering there were eaves, it kept a lot of the snow, if not all of it, off the deck. Of course, the bottom was iced over, so I carefully picked my way around to the back that faced a slow-moving, ice-crusted creek.

Bear Creek was a small tributary off a couple of larger rivers, and not many people lived this way, so the eerie silence didn't scare me. Nope. Not a bit.

The back deck was filled with snow, and I had to push my way through it, freezing my legs once again. I pulled open the rickety screen door and knocked on the back door.

Nothing.

Expansive windows looked out toward the lake, and I peered in them, cupping my eyes to look inside. Just darkness. I could make out living room furniture next to a kitchen, but that was it. The place was cold and silent and felt empty.

I tried the back door again, trying to determine how strong the lock was. It didn't give. That figured. It made sense that Sadie would have some strong security.

Glass shattered somewhere around the house, and I jumped. What in the world? Ducking my head, I started running around the deck and slipped, going down hard. I caught myself with my hand, which went through the snow to hit ice. Pain flared up my arm.

"Damn it," I muttered, pushing myself up and trying to wipe some of the snow off my jeans. I then opted for a more sedate pace around to the front to see Nonna and Georgiana standing in front of a small window to the left of the door.

Georgiana shook her head. "A bird flew right into that window." She brushed glass off her handbag.

I lowered my head. There was no way a bird flew into the window. "Georgiana, did you break that window?"

"Of course not." She drew up to her full height. "Right?"

Nonna swallowed. She was a wild woman, but one thing I knew about my nonna was that she did not lie. She did, however, hold her wooden spoon ahead of her.

"Nonna?" I asked.

She just swallowed and pressed her lips together.

"Well," Georgiana said, "I mean, the window's broken. Shouldn't we at least look inside?"

I wanted to fault her logic, I really did, but I also wanted to own my restaurant, and I was really worried about Sadie. I should never have given her that much cash, but it had been her biggest demand in signing the contract. A little voice whispered in the back of my mind that someone who wanted to take the money and run, maybe because they'd already sold the property, would want cash, but I couldn't believe that of Sadie.

"I'll go in," Nonna said.

"No, no, no, no." I held up my hand. "I will go in." I couldn't believe I was doing this since I'd never actually committed a crime.

I took off my jacket and made sure all the glass was out of the way. The window was higher than expected, so I had to reach up and pull myself in. I tried to keep my balance, but the angle was awkward, and I fell inside, landing with a thump on a hard, wooden floor.

"Ugh." I groaned as my shoulder protested. My body had taken way too much battering the last couple of days.

"You okay?" my nonna asked, her hands curling over the windowsill as she looked over.

I rose. "Yes, I think I'm all right."

"I'm coming in," Nonna said.

"No, no, no, no," I argued more forcefully. "You two, keep watch. We're breaking the law here."

"No, we're not," Georgiana retorted. "We're worried about Sadie, and we're doing a wellness check."

As far as I knew, only police officers could do those, but I wasn't going to argue with her. Instead, I pulled my fairly useless phone from my back pocket and turned on the flashlight. Sadie's place was pristinely clean, but a light layer of dust had settled. There were no dishes out, and nothing was out of the ordinary in the living room. The kitchen abutted that room, so I hurried over and looked in her fridge. There was no milk, no cheese, nothing to rot.

"No perishables," I called out.

"Ooh, that means she meant to leave," Nonna said.

"Well, maybe," Georgiana yelled back.

That had been my thinking, as well.

I crossed the living room to go into the bedroom, which was small with a queen-sized bed. A beautiful hand-crocheted purple and white coverlet covered the bed, which was neatly made. There was one dresser and one small closet. I hurried to the dresser to find normal clothing for a woman Sadie's age. The closet was also full. However, I saw no suitcases anywhere. Had she just gone on a short trip?

I checked out the bathroom, and again, it looked as if somebody lived here. There was no evidence that she'd left. However, I often took day trips or even weekend trips, and my apartment looked the same. "There's nothing here," I said upon returning to the living room.

"No signs of a struggle?" Georgiana called out.

"None." I had a thought and hurried back into the kitchen, flipping on the light switch. No lights came on.

"Electricity's out," I relayed.

"Well, the storm has been pretty bad. Electricity is out up at the river, too," Nonna yelled.

I turned on the faucet. The water was still working, so Sadie hadn't turned that off. When a homeowner left Silverville for any length of time in the winter, they always turned off the water to prevent the cold from bursting a pipe. So, either Sadie hadn't been planning to leave, or she'd only thought to be gone for a couple of days. Maybe she'd return any minute. I bit my lip and then looked around.

There was no knife block on the counter.

Not that it mattered. Not everyone kept one.

I moved closer to the fridge to see pictures upon pictures hung there. Some photos were at least twenty years old and faded, while a couple looked as if they'd been taken at a town festival just last summer.

There was a cute one of Sadie and her brother smiling in the kitchen, surrounded by Christmas platters.

Awareness cascaded down my spine, and my shoulders went back. I moved closer to peer at the picture, pushing the flashlight closer. Behind Jonathan, on the very counter next to me, was a knife block. The knives looked exactly like the ones found in Rudy's body and in my refrigerator.

Yet another thing Sheriff Franco hadn't told me.

This was getting weirder and weirder. If Sadie or Jonathan had killed Rudy Brando, then why in the world would they leave one of Sadie's knives in his chest? Unless they had just panicked, which made sense. But why would they have left the matching one in my fridge? It didn't make any sense. Had somebody stolen her knives? I didn't get it.

"Ca-caw, ca-caw." The almost wild-bird sound came through the window.

I snagged the pictures off the fridge, shoved them into my pocket, and turned. "What?"

"It's our signal," Georgiana yelled. "A car's coming. Get out here, Tessa. We have to run. Now!"

CHAPTER 14

I ran toward the window, belatedly wondering where I'd left my fingerprints. If this were a crime scene, which I didn't think it was, I should have been smart enough to wear gloves. Sheriff Franco had said he'd already searched the place, but even so, this was probably one of the stupidest things I'd ever done. I made it to the window, and Nonna's hands reached in to pull me her way.

"I've got it." I planted both hands on the sill and all but catapulted myself free.

I flew out, and my grandmother yelled, jumping out of the way. I kept going, hitting the icy deck with my hands and somersaulting over to come up standing.

"Whoa," Georgiana murmured. "Respect."

"Thanks," I said. "Come on."

It was too late. The truck they'd heard had already stopped behind our vehicles, and it took me two seconds to recognize the driver. "Oh, no."

"What's going on?" Nonna reared up, her spoon in front of her, and then she was all smiles. "Nicolo Basanelli, how kind of you to come check on us," she said.

I jerked my head toward her. "Did you tell him we were coming out here?" I asked through clenched teeth.

"Of course not." She leveled me with a look. "When we break and enter, we try to keep it between us. Right, Georgiana?"

"It's the detectives' code," she said, brightening up the entire day with her fluorescent outfit.

Nick stepped from the vehicle and looked at all three of us.

I swore I wasn't a mind reader, but everything in me said he wanted to get right back in that truth and drive away. "New truck?" I asked.

"Just bought it off my brother," he said mildly, looking at the assembled group. I couldn't blame him for wanting to get away from us. Instead, and very much to his credit, he walked past the vehicles and up the stairs to the porch, his gaze taking in the window. "Anybody care to explain?"

"It was a bird." Georgiana patted her chest and fluttered her eyelashes. "Came out of nowhere. So frightening. We were just sitting here trying to figure out how we could help our good friend Sadie with this problem."

I felt heat rise from my chest, move up my neck, and into my face. I couldn't help it. I blushed so hard it hurt. With my fair skin and my slightly reddish hair, I was sure I looked ridiculous.

Nick turned that formidable focus on me. "Anything you want to tell me, Contessa?"

"Aw, isn't that sweet of him to use her full name?" Nonna whispered.

I really wanted to leave, just walk away, but this was my grandmother, and I couldn't. "I have absolutely nothing I want to tell you," I said honestly, right from my heart.

Nick wasn't a police officer, but he was a prosecuting attorney, and I thought that made him an officer of the court or something like that. Anna had mentioned that to me before. He was probably duty bound to report a break-in if he had proof of one.

I held my ground and tried to step slightly in front of my grandmother. "I think maybe you shouldn't be here," I said.

"Huh." He moved beyond me and peered inside the broken window. "At least the so-called bird hit from the outside and sprayed glass inside." He looked over his shoulder at me, his brown eyes intense. "Did you cut yourself?"

"Of course not." Nonna patted his shoulder. "How would she cut herself? She wasn't anywhere near the window when the terrible tragedy occurred."

Nick looked across the snow-covered porch. "Where's the bird?"

"He flew away," Georgiana said. "Well, he fell back, hopped a few times, and then flew away. I think it was a robin."

"I would say owl," Nonna added.

I just kept silent. There was nothing to say. Then a thought hit me. "Wait a minute. What are you doing all the way out here?"

Nobody lived out this way, or at least hardly anybody did. Most of the residents resided along the major river and lived to the west. We were far south right now.

"Looking for you," he muttered.

"Isn't that sweet?" Nonna said. "Nicolo, how did you know she was out here?"

That was a good question.

Nick shook his head. "I stopped by the county recorder's office because I had a thought about the deeds, and they told me you'd just been there. Then I stopped by Sunshine Eats, and they told me that you had just been there. Mrs. C saw you head this way, and I just had a bad feeling, Contessa."

"Well, now." Nonna smiled at him, beaming. "It's as if the two of you are on the same wavelength. How lovely."

I was getting a headache. The pain crawled from the base of my neck into my skull. There was no question about it. "We should probably get going." I turned to look at the window.

Although considering we'd broken the window, I couldn't just leave it. More bad weather was on its way, and it wasn't fair to Sadie.

Nick shook his head. "I'll tear out the carpet in the back of my truck, and we can use it to cover the window."

"Oh, no, we can't let you do that," Georgiana said.

"It's all right," Nick said wryly. "My brother chose a bright purple for some reason, and I was going to get it replaced anyway."

Nonna clapped her hands together. "Well, isn't that a wonderful idea?"

"I'll assist you." I gave in gracefully. The poor guy was only trying to protect us, even though he no doubt regretted his decision to follow me to Sadie's house.

I helped him tear out the carpet, and we managed to attach it well enough to protect the window and the inside.

"Should we leave a note?" Nonna asked.

"That's not a bad idea." I headed back to my car for a notepad. I left a quick note, explained about the bird, and said that if she had any questions to call me. Then I added that I needed her to call me anyway.

We opened part of the flap, threw the note in the window, and then refastened it.

"Well, then," Nonna said. "We should probably get going. Nicolo, will you be a love and take Tessa to lunch? I know she missed breakfast, and it's well after lunchtime. Do you mind?"

"Not in the slightest," Nick answered. "Your granddaughter and I need to talk." His voice was a low rumble that affected me in inappropriate places, but even so, there was a hint of a threat in it. I couldn't blame him. He'd just helped us cover up a crime and could get into trouble.

I would have to play nice, at least for the moment. "I'll meet you back in town," I said.

"I'll follow both of your cars to make sure you get there safely." He held out his arms to assist both of the seniors across the icy porch and to their car.

"Thanks, Nick," Nonna murmured. "You are a true darling."

"You have no idea," Nick muttered.

* * *

NORDELIANO'S WAS LOCATED one street over from the sheriff's office and had been a Silverville staple for as long as anybody remembered. The food was authentic Italian, and they poured the house red with every meal, whether you wanted the wine or not. I had never thought the place romantic until I sat across from Basanelli near a roaring fireplace with candles flickering on the table.

Mrs. Nordeliano was a friend of my nonna's, and she'd made sure we had the one secluded table to ourselves.

I munched on a breadstick, somewhat preoccupied with the fact that I'd committed a crime earlier today. Breaking and entering or perhaps petit theft, considering I'd taken the photographs off Sadie's fridge.

"I can't believe you broke into Sadie's home," Nick said, reaching for his third breadstick. Where did he put the carbs? The guy's stomach was flatter than an ice rink, and I'd bet my last dollar his abs were ripped. Like actually ripped and not airbrushed.

"I didn't." I may have jumped through the open window, but I wasn't the one who broke it.

He sipped his wine, just watching me.

I watched him right back, although my face soon heated with that painful blush again. "Shouldn't you be in trial?"

"The defense made a motion for continuance, and since nobody wanted to be in trial during the holiday season, we all agreed." He shrugged. "Nobody wants to work between Christmas and New Year's Day."

Crap. "Just a sec." I tugged my phone from my purse and sent off a quick text to Mert Smiley, telling him that something had come up and I wouldn't be able to make it today. Yeah, I was too cowardly to call the guy. He could have quite the temper, and right now, I'd just yell back at him. Then I promised I'd be there first thing tomorrow morning. Hopefully, that appeased him enough that he wouldn't have a coronary.

Mrs. Nordeliano delivered our meals herself, smiling widely. She was around seventy but looked fifty with her olive-toned skin and dark hair cut in a bob. "It's so nice to see you two together finally."

The fragrant smell of lasagna mellowed me out. "It was kind of Nick to finally ask me to lunch," I agreed, more than happy to toss his butt under the bus.

His chin lowered in a clear warning. "I've been asking you out forever. It took your nonna pushing you to say yes."

Good to know that Nick had no trouble rolling me under that bus with him.

Mrs. Nordeliano beamed. "I heard you were fighting the inevitable. Darn young'uns." She smacked Nick on the shoulder with a loud clap. "Call out if you need more wine." Then she bustled off, leaving us with truly brilliant pasta.

"Did you find anything in Sadie's place?" Nick asked mildly after sampling his butternut squash ravioli.

I swallowed. "Hypothetically, if I had been inside Sadie's home without her permission, then I might have—hypothetically—found a picture showing evidence that the murder weapon found in Rudy's chest and the knife in my fridge came from her kitchen."

Nick stiffened. "No kidding?"

I nodded. "I take it Sheriff Franco neglected to inform you of that fact, as well?"

Nick took another bite of his lunch. "Yeah. Can't blame him, though. I'm a witness on this one, not a prosecutor. He shouldn't share anything with us unless he's also fishing for information, which I'm sure is his plan."

"I had a good motive to kill Rudy Brando," I mused after taking a drink of my wine. It tasted like a merlot, which was pretty good.

"That's true, but why would you do it in your own building?" Nick shook his head. "Or put the other knife in your fridge?"

I didn't have a clue. "To throw off the authorities?"

"Was the entire knife block missing?"

I nodded. "Yeah. I just saw a picture of it. I mean, if I'd been there, I would've just..." I gave up and tugged the photos from my bag, handing the relevant one to Nick. "Would you somehow believe that we found this outside her place in the snow?"

The word he muttered wasn't one his grandmother would appreciate. Even so, he took the picture and studied it. "Yep. Same knives."

I'd examine the rest of the pictures later when he wasn't around. I cleared my throat. "You never said why you were looking for me to the point where you followed us out to Bear Creek."

He placed the picture on the white tablecloth and lifted his chin. "I wanted to talk to you. A search of Ozzie Morrison's truck unearthed both a copy of the charging documents for his brother...and a picture of you."

My head jerked. "Huh?"

Nick nodded. "Yeah. It was a printout. No words and no direction." He reached into his back pocket and drew out a folded piece of paper, handing it over.

I unfolded it to see a grainy picture of me taken last week when I was waitressing at Smiley's. I was wearing a Christmas apron and had reindeer antlers on. "This was for a kids' party. Several local preschools came by for holiday pancakes." The photograph had been taken through the window, and I hadn't even noticed. The pasta suddenly tasted like dust. "I don't understand what this means."

Nick reclaimed the paper, his warm hand brushing mine. "Best guess? Apparently, Ozzie wanted to shoot at us both."

CHAPTER 15

"Can you die from sexual tension?" I asked my sister Donna as I finished moving my clothes into her spare bedroom later that afternoon, the phone pressed to my ear.

She chuckled, sounding slightly inebriated. "I don't think so. You could probably get a heart attack or something."

I smiled and walked into her kitchen to look for a cabernet in her wine cabinet. She always had the good stuff.

"Are you sure you don't want me to come home?" she asked again.

"No, really, stay and have fun."

She and a few of her friends had decided to extend their wine tour trip from Napa Valley to hit the wineries in Walla Walla for a few days.

"Thanks for letting me crash at your place," I said.

"Of course," she said. "You're welcome to stay for as long as you want. Please tell me you're not in actual danger."

I carefully opened the wine, trying to be quiet about it. She hadn't exactly said I could take the good stuff, but it was Donna, and she usually didn't mind. "As far as I can tell, I'm fine," I told her. "Nick said Ozzie is in jail and won't be getting out anytime soon, so we have time to figure out why he targeted both Nick and me. I think it had something to do with Nick's trial because the brother was put away."

"But why would Ozzie have your picture?" Donna asked.

I poured myself a generous glass. "I have no idea. Basanelli is looking into it, and so long as the shooter stays in jail, I'm not horribly worried about it."

Perhaps I should be concerned, but I wasn't feeling it. I didn't think I was in any danger at the moment, which was probably naïve. However, everything that had gone down at Silver Sadie's seemed to have more to do with Sadie and her building than me.

And being shot at by a guy whose brother Nick had put away surely had to do with Nick's job. It was rumored we were dating, so maybe that explained the photo of me. I suddenly had definite sympathy for Anna, who often found herself in situations like these.

Maybe none of it was her fault.

Donna cleared her throat. "So, if Rudy Brando recorded his deed first, he legally owns the building. Or at least he did, correct?"

I bit my lip. "That's my understanding from Anna. My recourse would be to sue Sadie for the money back, but we're not entirely sure the deed is authentic. We're trying to figure that out now. It could be that Rudy and his so-called wife are trying to commit fraud." That was my hope. The question remained as to who had killed Rudy. It just didn't make sense that they'd stabbed him and left that deed for the sheriff to find. Unless the wife had done it.

"Hmm," I murmured.

"Nope," Donna said loudly. "Do not become Anna. Do not go investigating your own case. Let the authorities take care of it, for the love of all that is holy and good. Please."

I laughed, I couldn't help it. "I'm not going to turn into an amateur sleuth like Anna, I promise."

"All right," Donna capitulated. "Engage the burglar alarm and stay safe. Are you packing?"

"Of course," I said. The compact nine-millimeter was my favorite and fit in any purse. We'd trained since we were young with weapons, so I knew what I was doing and could protect myself if necessary.

She snorted. Whatever wine they were drinking was getting to her, and I was happy she'd made time to have fun. "All right, you know where the safe is if you need anything. Love you."

"Love you, too." I ended the call and took a deep drink of the wine. The Merlot was dry with a smooth aftertaste, and I hummed happily. Donna's wine collection was something to admire, and it was kind that she shared.

I wandered over to her comfortable sofa and flicked on the TV. I should probably start thinking about dinner, but right now, just having a nice glass of wine seemed good enough.

Nick and I had been entirely too cozy at our luncheon, and I wanted to believe that I didn't enjoy his bossy side. But considering he had only wanted to protect me, I figured I shouldn't lie to myself, and I needed to stop thinking about Basanelli and his fine body.

My phone buzzed, and I answered it absently. "Hello?"

"Hi, is this Tessa?" a male voice asked.

"Sure." I dropped my feet from the coffee table to the floor. "Who is this?"

Shuffling sounded, and the beep, beep, beep of a door before it was shut came over the line.

"Hey, it's Eddie Brando. I had a message from my aunt Sadie that you and I were supposed to go out this week. Are you looking for some sort of arranged marriage or something? Because I've got to tell you, that's not my thing."

I had wondered which of the two remaining Brando brothers would call first. It was nice they wanted to make their great-aunt happy, even though she'd disappeared. "No, I'm definitely not looking for an arranged marriage. I think your aunt just wants one of you boys to get married while she's still alive. I'm not looking for marriage at all, Eddie. I've got to be honest with you."

His chuckle sounded relieved. "Oh, good. Neither am I. Sorry. I've been hitched twice before, and it just didn't work out. However, I did promise my aunt that I'd go to dinner, and I'm here in town for the day. What do you say?"

"I'm in town, too. Dinner's fine. Where do you want to go?" The sooner we got this over with, the better.

"I was thinking we should try out the Crème de la Crepe. They opened right before Christmas over on Cedar Street."

Surprise kept me immobile for a moment. The last place I would've expected Eddie Brando to want to meet was at the new French restaurant in town. "I was thinking something more casual," I admitted.

"Let's live a little. Plus, we're talking Timber City. Even French is casual."

He wasn't wrong. "All right. I'll meet you around six?" I'd have to change out of my jeans.

"Sounds great."

"Hey, Eddie?" I asked. "Do you have any idea where your aunt Sadie is?" I had tried to find Eddie's number earlier to question him but couldn't find it. It was a good thing he'd called me.

Eddie snorted. "I have no clue. I've been trying to call her for days, and I've got nothing. My brother has, too."

I perked up. "I need his number, too. Do you mind sending that to me?"

"Not at all. I'll forward it to you right now."

That did beg the question: "How did you get my number anyway?"

"Aunt Sadie sent it to me, of course."

Yeah, that made sense. I had no idea if I owned the property or not, but I planned to stick to the rules of the contract until I found out. I only had a week to go on a date with each of the guys. Plus, meeting Eddie would give me a good chance to question him about where Sadie or Jonathan might have gone. I didn't know much about Jonathan except that he lived in Montana, was an attorney, and wasn't married.

Since Eddie seemed to be in a sharing mood, I decided to push my luck. "Eddie, do you know anybody who would've wanted your cousin Rudy dead?"

Eddie snorted. "That dude wasn't my cousin. I don't know who he was, but I think he was full of crap. Oh, hey, Tess, I gotta go. I'll meet you in an hour." He clicked off.

Didn't anybody say goodbye any longer? I rubbed my chin. This was getting weirder and weirder. A ding sounded, and the contact information for Hank Brando flashed across my screen. Well, I knew many people didn't like Eddie, but so far, he'd been decent, and he'd come through.

I quickly dialed Hank's number and reached his voicemail.

"Hi, Hank, it's Tessa Albertini. I promised your great-aunt that we would go on a date this week. I assume you already know about that. Also, I'm looking for her. Would you give me a call when you get a chance? Thanks." I clicked off.

If I were completely honest with myself, I had to admit that I wouldn't mind going on a date with Hank. He was a semi-professional snowmobiler, and the guy wasn't bad to look at. He was actually a couple of years younger than me, closer to Anna's age, but I remembered him being pretty handsome in high school. Either way, it would give me another line on finding Sadie and my money.

I finished the glass of wine and then stood, wondering what I should wear to dinner to meet Eddie. This was more of a contractual obligation than a date, and the last I heard, the guy was a little slimy, although he'd seemed pretty decent on the phone. I decided to go with black slacks and a pink cashmere sweater that I borrowed from Donna.

My phone buzzed again, and I looked down to see a text from

Nick. My heart started to beat faster, and I cursed myself. I had to get over this little crush I had on him. It just wasn't going to work out. And then I read the text.

Nick: *I hope you're staying safe tonight. Let the authorities do their jobs.*

I rolled my eyes. It was a little disconcerting how well he already knew me. So I decided to shoot off a quick reply:

Me: *Don't worry about it. I'm just watching movies.*

Nick: *Why don't I believe you?*

Me: *Because you're a prosecutor and suspicion comes easily to you?*

Nick: *Huh. More likely, I understand the Albertini need to solve crimes and get into trouble.*

That reminded me...

Me: *Hey. Didn't you have a crush on my sister?*

I believed he'd kissed her once when inebriated, and that should cool my interest in him, right?

Nick: *No. At first glance, there might've been some interest, but it quickly cooled when we became friends. I have since discovered that my taste goes much more toward an Irish rose, who works hard and hopes big.*

I gulped. Was Basanelli flirting with me? I thought we'd agreed to be friends, but this was as alive as I'd felt all year—maybe longer. I hadn't had good luck with men, and Basanelli was definitely a heartbreaker. But I couldn't help it. I texted him back.

Me: *Are you flirting with me?*

Nick: *Yes.*

Desire winged through me, which was nuts since we were only texting. Even so, this was more fun than I'd had in way too long.

Me: *We decided to be friends. Different life paths, remember?*

Then, dork that I was, I held my breath, waiting for a response.

Nick: *I've decided that I forge my own life path. Right now, you seem to be as much trouble as your sister, but I like you.*

Nick Basanelli had said the softer l-word to me. I was such a complete dork.

Me: *I'm starting to think you like trouble.*

Nick: *There's enough truth in that statement that it keeps me up at night. Thoughts of you do, as well.*

It was the sweetest thought he'd ever shared with me. I swallowed, noting my body was full-on alert and ready to rumble. That kiss had stayed with me, and I couldn't help but wonder what an entire night with Nick would be like. Probably life-changing.

Me: *What's your plan, then?*

It was a risky question.

Nick: *I'll let you know when I figure it out. For now, you stay safe. I mean it.*

I'd never been good at taking orders from anybody. Even so, I knew what he said came from a good place, even if his bossy execution didn't sit well with me. And he was actually flirting on purpose.

I sat back, bemused. It was time to banish thoughts of the hot Italian and figure out my life. Yeah, I'd lied to him, but why worry the guy? I was fairly safe right now, and I really needed to find Sadie and that money. It was my life savings, and if it turned out I didn't own the building, I had to figure something else out. But I'd be crushed.

However, right now, my only goal was finding the woman.

CHAPTER 16

I had my doubts Timber City was big enough for an authentic French restaurant like Crème de la Crepe. They'd kept it fairly casual, however, which had been smart.

I arrived before Eddie, and a smoothly moving woman in a form-fitting black cocktail dress showed me to my table, which was at the far end of the restaurant and in a nice, secluded area.

Trying to be different instead of going for the normal fireplace found in most of our establishments, the Crème de la Crepe owner had opted for a vast and bubbly aquarium in the wall that featured beautiful and vibrant fish, floating around peacefully. It actually gave me a sense of calmness, and I could understand why they'd chosen that for decor, although I didn't see anything French about it.

I put my back to it so I could watch the door. I didn't recognize many people in the small dining area; most of them must have been tourists in town for winter sports.

Eddie soon entered, wiping snow off his head. He looked pretty much like I remembered. He wore a blue button-down shirt open halfway down his chest, and a dark brown corduroy jacket over jeans. His thin hair was slicked back, and he had two black earrings in his ears. A gold necklace hung into what could only be called a copious amount of chest hair.

He was sparsely shaven, and his eyebrows appeared as if they'd been tattooed on, because they were much thicker than his hair. They looked a little unnatural. Although that chest was hairy, so who knew?

He winked at the hostess and maneuvered between tables to reach me. "Well, Tessa Albertini, didn't you grow up nice?"

I wasn't sure whether I should stand or not, so I didn't. "Hi, Eddie. It's good to see you." I kept my hand around my water glass.

He pulled back the chair opposite me and dropped onto it. "So, what's the truth about this whole situation?" This close, he smelled like a combination of cheap cologne and cigarette smoke.

"I think you know the deal," I said. "Your aunt wanted me to go on a date with each of you, and Bobbo and I already met up."

Eddie threw back his head and laughed. "I heard he took you speed dating. Tell me that isn't true."

I couldn't help an unwilling smile. "It is true, and we actually had a pretty good time." Plus, I might've found a romance for Bobbo and Kelsey, so I was taking the night as a win.

Eddie reached for his water glass and drank half of it down. "Don't tell me something is up between you and Bobbo."

I shook my head. "No, I did have a good time, and he's a nice guy, but that was our one and only date." I didn't mention that I had set Bobbo up with Kelsey Walker. I didn't know why. It felt like Eddie would probably prank his brother and mess things up. If Kelsey could find some happiness out on that alpaca farm, I was all for it.

"I'm surprised Bobbo went out with you," Eddie admitted, twirling his dinner knife on the pristine white tablecloth.

I sat back, slightly affronted. "Why is that?"

Eddie reached out a hand to pat mine, ignoring the fact that I was still holding my water glass. "No, no, no. I don't mean anything insulting. It's just that he and his fiancée recently broke up, and I thought he'd become a hermit. Poor guy. He really liked her, but man, that chick." His voice trailed off.

"What about her?" I asked. Hopefully, I hadn't gotten Kelsey into another disastrous situation.

Eddie shook his head, and not one strand of hair moved. I didn't know what kind of gel he'd used to plaster the few remaining strands he had to his head, but it was clearly industrial strength. "Let's not talk about them. They're nuts."

I didn't think that was very nice, but all I had to do was get through a dinner, and we'd be good.

The door opened, and my gaze flicked quickly to the snow blustering in. Something jittered in my heart. It was stupid and I knew it, but when Nick Basanelli walked in with Jolene Sullivan, I swore to the saints all I wanted to do was chuck my glass of water at his head.

His gaze caught mine. He looked at Eddie, and his jaw tightened. Then the jerk put his hand at the small of Jolene's back and pointed to a table off to the side. I could not believe it. He was on an actual date with Jolene Sullivan? So much for staying away from the press. The slash of betrayal I felt didn't make a lick of sense, but even so, I'd learned to accept my feelings.

So I turned my full-wattage smile on Eddie. "What are you up to these days, Eddie?"

He sat back as if stunned for a moment. His gaze roamed my face. "Well, I work for Northern Electricity as an electrician. We mainly service residential homes. Don't do much commercial. I figured you at least knew what I did for a living."

I shook my head. "I don't know much about you. Your aunt wasn't generous with the information about the family." Or the fact that she was taking all my money and then disappearing.

"Oh." Eddie sat back and proceeded to tell me pretty much everything about himself, from the time he scored the winning soccer goal in high school to his failed marriage to a chick, as he put it, who was dumber than a box of rocks, to his current profession. We managed to order food in between, and I had to admit, the boeuf Bourguignon was delicious. Unfortunately, the company wasn't great.

"So," he said when we'd finally finished eating, "this was a lot more fun than I expected. You want to go out again?"

I so did not want to go out again. I had watched Nick and Jolene from the corner of my eye during their entire dinner, and they seemed to have a pleasant time talking, but there was no touching, and from what I could tell, no flirting. I was starting to feel a little silly about my earlier jealousy, which didn't make sense anyway. "I don't think so, Eddie. I appreciate it, but I'm really busy with opening my restaurant—hopefully."

He snorted. "Yeah, about that. Dude, sorry about Rudy being dead."

We'd avoided the topic for the entire dinner, mainly because Eddie had insisted upon it. However, I took the opening now. "I'm shocked, too. You mentioned that you didn't think he was your relative."

Eddie lifted his shoulder. "He could be. I mean, he did look like the family. It's just, you know, Great-uncle George died across the country and hadn't kept in touch with any family. He never told anybody he had a kid. So, who really cares, right?"

At the moment, I did, because the guy had been found dead on my floor. "You don't think Sadie would've sold him the property and then tried to sell it again to me, do you?" I asked, finishing the one glass of wine I'd allowed myself with dinner.

Eddie rubbed his flabby jaw. "I don't know. Sadie was always out to make a quick buck, but I never knew her to be a liar. Well, except she did hold illegal gambling parties in her back room."

For some reason, and I couldn't explain why, that seemed different than lying to my face and shaking my hand. "Do you have any idea where she is?"

"I don't," Eddie said. "If I had to guess, and if she was fleeing, I think she would've gone to Jonathan's place over in Montana. But surely the authorities have checked there."

I nodded. "Yeah, they definitely checked there, and Jonathan can't be found either."

"Well." Eddie's gaze dropped to my breasts for what had to be the fiftieth time during dinner. "If you had a hundred and fifty grand in cash, and yeah, I heard all about it... Everybody knows. Where would you go?"

I hadn't really thought of it like that. "I'd go to the bank," I muttered.

Eddie shook his head. "Nah, not Sadie. She'd probably hide the money, but then she'd reappear. So, the question is, why? Do you think she knew something about Rudy? Do you think she skipped town with your money on purpose?"

"Well, you know her better than I do."

"Not really," Eddie said. "We've never been close. I think she just requested these dates to find someone to carry on the Brando name. I always liked her. She was a mean old broad, but..."

I shifted uncomfortably in my chair. "Why are you talking about her in the past tense?" This had taken a turn I didn't want to follow. "I'm sure she's still alive. God, I hope she's still alive." I meant every word.

Eddie whistled. "Who knows? That's a lot of money. People have killed for a lot less."

"Yeah, but who knew about it?" I asked quietly.

"Everybody," Eddie answered. "There aren't any secrets in that town. I don't even live in Silverville, and I heard about it. Sadie told the family she was selling."

That surprised me. I'd figured she would've kept it under wraps. "What do you mean she told the family?"

Eddie wiped sauce off his chin with his shirt, although his napkin was still in his lap. "Well, okay. To be fair, she told Hank, and then he told me. I guess maybe that's not the whole family."

The quiet bubbling of the fish tank behind me was starting to lose its calming effect. "Sadie told Hank?"

"Yeah." Eddie rolled his eyes. "She adores Hank. If I had to guess, this plan of you dating all three of us was a setup. I bet she wanted me and Bobbo to put on a bad face so you fell for Hank. I mean, let's be honest. He is the golden boy."

I had to find Hank. If Sadie had confided in him about the sale, then perhaps he knew where she was. As far as I knew, Nick hadn't been able to find him, and neither had Sheriff Franco. I needed to try harder. "This was a nice dinner, Eddie. Thank you."

"No problem. You're not my type, so don't feel bad. I like more of the bad girl," he said. "We're splitting the tab, right?"

It was good to know he didn't consider me a bad girl, although I could probably kick his ass if necessary. Our folks had taught us to fight after Anna's early abduction. However, I nodded. "Absolutely." Of course, we were paying separately.

The door opened, and cold air wafted in, I felt it even across the expanse. We probably had snow for quite a while longer, so the chill didn't faze me, but I looked up to see a woman with curly black hair dressed in jeans and a white puffer coat looking around the area. I wasn't sure why, but my instincts started to hum. Her gaze caught mine. She lowered her chin and stormed across the restaurant.

"Oh, crap," I muttered. "Eddie?" I asked.

He turned to look and then groaned. "Oh, shit."

I put my napkin on the table, noting Nick stiffen across the way.

"You bitch!" she yelled, coming up to me.

"All right," I said calmly. "I need more than that. Eddie, is this your, I don't know, girlfriend?"

"No, I'm not his girlfriend." The woman grabbed my water glass and slammed it down on the table, breaking it. Glass shattered and landed on the floor.

"Holy crap." I pushed away from the table. "Who are you?" I

asked as Nick instantly stood over by his table. Jolene already had her phone out of her purse, glee on her face as she pointed the camera at me.

The woman shook her head. "I'm Louise Transkei. Bobbo's fiancée. You went out with him the other day."

"Ah, crap. How did you find me?" I knew it was an odd thing to ask at this point, but people were finding me way too easily these days.

Eddie had the grace to blanch. "I may have posted on Facebook that you and I were hooking up tonight."

I couldn't believe it. This guy was a complete moron.

"Listen," I said to the woman, "Bobbo and I went on one date. That's it. It's over. I heard you were broken up, and I really don't care. It was only a contractual obligation."

"Ha. I heard you went home with him." She came closer.

"Listen, knock it off, or you're going to get hurt." I had no idea if I could harm her or not, but I had been in a bar fight with an ATF agent not too long ago because of my sister, and I had held my own. Not that I wanted to get into a fight again.

"Oh, yeah?" Louise lunged for me, and I took the tackle, letting my chair fall over. We landed hard, and I rolled, landing on top of her and punching her in the jaw.

She hit back, her nails clawing toward my neck.

I saw red and pulled my arm back but was rapidly hauled off her and pushed behind Nick.

Eddie ambled over and assisted a struggling Louise to her feet, shoving her toward his seat.

She shrieked and yanked a gun from her purse. "You don't understand. I'm willing to fight for my man."

Nick pushed me farther behind him, and I stepped to his side to keep him from getting shot. "You can have your man," I said, putting a hand up. I couldn't get to my gun, and the last thing I wanted was a shootout.

She hissed. "You deserve everything you get." The gun waved wildly in the air, and then she fired.

I jumped and instinctively covered my head.

Louise looked at the gun as if shocked and then tossed it to the floor.

A loud crack came from behind me. Water swooshed out and blew me across the table into Eddie. We fell to the floor. I didn't know how he moved so quickly, but Nick suddenly had Louise on her belly on the floor, his belt wrapped around her hands behind her back. And he did it faster than I could breathe.

"Oh, my God. The fish!" I yelled. I rolled over and started grabbing them. "We need water." A quick glance confirmed that the bullet had taken out the top half of the aquarium. There was enough left in the tank on the bottom that if I got all the fish back in there, they should be okay. "Help, Eddie!" I yelled.

Eddie stood and slipped on the water, falling down. I hoped he didn't hurt any of the fish. I grabbed a purple one and tossed it into the tank, and then one by one, started throwing every flopping body I could reach over the jagged glass and into the water. There was definitely enough water in there that they'd be okay if we could get to them in time.

I saw an orange Nemo-type fish squirming on a nearby table and grabbed it, tossing it easily across the room. I yelled at the other patrons, "Get the fish!"

Everyone scrambled at once, chairs falling, tables pushed aside, as both waitresses ran out to also save the animals.

They were slimy and squirmy, but I managed to save three more.

Sirens soon trilled outside, and I wanted to finish before the police arrived and dragged us all away.

Nick just looked at me as if it were all insane. "There's one by your left ankle!" I bellowed. Keeping one knee on Louise's back, he reached over, snagged the flopping fish, and lobbed it over his shoulder. It flew neatly between the broken glass into the bottom of the tank and then swam away.

I searched around frantically and then calmed, soaking wet from head to toe. "Okay, I think we got them all."

One of the waitresses shook her head. "Wow, this is the wrong night for the owner to take the evening off. Are you sure you don't see any more fish?" She leaned down to stare at the wet wooden floor beneath a table.

"I don't think so." I wiped water off my face. Rivulets still dripped from my hair onto Donna's cashmere sweater, which was now ruined.

"Here I was worried about my next article." Jolene snapped pictures as fast as she could with her phone.

I sighed. Great. I really was turning into my sister.

CHAPTER 17

For the *wild* Albertini sister, I had to admit, this was the first time I'd sat inside a jail cell. The police had been quick to secure both Louise and me, considering we'd been in a fight.

The arresting officer was a cute man named Bud, whom my sister had gotten shot a time or two. He'd only sighed as he escorted me to the vehicle and then the station. The guy was built like a solid pine tree but seemed sweet, putting down a blanket in the car since I was soaking wet.

So far, all I'd done was sit in the holding cell. I hadn't truly been arrested or fingerprinted. I was waiting to call my sister until I actually needed a lawyer.

Detective Grant Pierce had merely shaken his head at me and instantly provided me with some warm clothing before questioning me, which I appreciated. Right now, I wore blue sweats and a matching top with a Timber City Police Department logo on it. My hair was back in a ponytail and drying nicely, if with a mass of curls that I couldn't get rid of.

A tough-looking redhead with very curly hair sat across from me in the cell. She wore a camo tank top, tight jeans, and pretty cool black boots. The benches we sat on were hard and cold, and the floor was dirty and scuffed. It wasn't horrible, but it wasn't great.

The police had taken Louise somewhere else, and I didn't know if she was being questioned, arrested since she had fired a gun, or if they just put her in a different holding cell to keep us apart.

"What are you in for?" the redhead asked.

I chuckled. I couldn't help it. "That's the most cliché thing I've ever heard."

She grinned, somehow making her look even tougher. "I know, but it's boring in here, and we might as well talk."

The woman wasn't wrong. I fluffed my ponytail and tried to squeeze more water out of my hair. "I got in a fight that ended up with a very expensive fish tank being blown up. However, it wasn't my fault."

"Did the fish die?"

I didn't know why, but I instantly liked the woman since she was worried about the fish. "No, we got them all back in the tank. The owner will have to fix it, but I think we saved all of them."

She grinned. "That's a good thing. I'm Roxy Smith."

"Tessa Albertini," I said. "It's my first time here."

"Oh, not mine," Roxy admitted.

I checked out her tank top. "Did you have a jacket? It's pretty cold out there."

She nodded. "I did, but they took it as evidence."

I bit my lip. I was really curious, but I also didn't know holding cell etiquette. Was it okay to ask detailed questions? My gut said it wasn't.

She snorted. "You are new at this. I got in a fight, and there was blood on the coat. But, actually, like you, it wasn't my fault."

"What happened?" I might as well pass the time and make a new friend.

"We were protesting the county commissioner's refusal to

allow us to expand Bernie's Outfitting on the south side of the lake. There's no reason. There wasn't a bad environmental impact or anything, but all of a sudden, they're anti-growth."

I thought I'd read something about that in the paper. "How far do you want to expand?"

"Just about twenty feet to the south. Not even close to the lake." She shook her head. "I know we can appeal, and maybe they just didn't understand the plans, but we thought we'd stage a minor protest. I mean, why not? It's Christmas season. We were just having fun."

I scratched my chin. "Then why the fight?"

"Oh, it actually had nothing to do with the expansion. My ex-boyfriend's new wife decided to show up with a couple of her friends, and things got ugly."

I shook my head. "Why are people fighting all of a sudden? What happened to the good old days when we just argued, sent letters or, I don't know, ignored each other?"

She rubbed her impressive biceps. "I don't know, but I kicked her ass, so I ended up here."

I could believe it. The muscles in her arms were surprisingly cut. "You must work out."

"I do. I do CrossFit at least once a day."

That was impressive. I tried it once and thought I was going to die. "Sorry about your ex."

"The jackass was a jerk. The guy was a Lordes member. Have you heard of them? They're a motorcycle club, or at least they used to be. They're disbanded now."

Oh, I knew way more about the Lordes than I wanted to. Aiden had been undercover with them for a while. "I think I've heard of them. They're no longer around, are they?"

She stretched out her legs. "I guess some of the members are still around, and somehow this chick won't leave me alone."

I nodded. "I get it. I mean, I don't understand any of it, but I'm sorry that happened to you."

"Thank you. Man, I wish I could find somebody good to date. You know? A stable and friendly man who just wants to hang out and maybe hit the bowling alley once in a while."

"That makes sense to me," I said. She seemed tough and sweet at the same time. In fact, the more I thought about it, Eddie had tried to help me save all those fish. He'd fallen several times, but he had made sure not to squash any, and he'd even picked one out of a lady's hair.

I cleared my throat. "You know, I know a guy you might like to meet." Maybe if this whole restaurant thing didn't work out for me, I could start a matchmaking business.

"Yeah, what's he like?"

I described Eddie in great detail, not leaving anything out or putting a rosy blush on the guy, but pointing out that he was gainfully employed. "He could use some fashion help, and maybe some manscaping." I was assuming the last.

"Huh. You know, it's been a long time since I dated a guy with a regular job," Roxy said.

"Let me give you his number." I didn't have my phone. Did I leave it at the restaurant? I was well known for losing my phone, but at the moment, I hadn't thought about it. "Okay, I don't have my phone. I will get you his number. Where are you staying?"

"I live over on the north side in the 10th Street Apartments," Roxy offered.

That was not an area of town I loved. "Okay." We were silent for a few moments, and the chill in the room slithered to my cold skin beneath the thick sweats. "If you had over a hundred thousand dollars in cash, where would you go?"

She scrutinized me, her blue eyes shrewd. "It depends."

I rested my head against the brick wall. "On what?"

"What I had going on in my life. If all was good, I'd take it to a bank, buy a house, and then start a business." She leaned forward, her bare elbows on her jeans. "If I was afraid of somebody or didn't get the money legally, I'd run with it."

"Where?"

She pursed her lips. "Mexico or Canada? Or maybe a big city where I could just get lost?"

Sadie wasn't in a big city, I was sure. I also didn't see her crossing the border into Mexico with that much money, but parts of Canada were similar to our hometown. "Then what?"

"Heck if I know. Depends on how long I wanted to stay hidden or who was after me."

That was a fairly decent analysis. "What if all was good, you weren't scared, but you still disappeared?"

Her smile made her appear younger, possibly even sweeter. "Then I'd go to Vegas. How about you?"

My smile felt rueful. "I'd open a business and work my butt off, more than likely pushing away any chance of a great romance." I sighed. "One that wouldn't work with my life choices, unfortunately."

The far door opened and Bud moved toward us, walking gracefully even with his muscled bulk. Man, I hoped I was being released, although I almost felt bad leaving Roxy. We'd kind of bonded. I wondered if that was normal for this type of thing.

"All right, you're both being set free." Bud opened the door.

I jerked. "We are?"

"Yeah. We spoke to the other people involved, and no one's pressing charges. Tessa, in your case, it sounds like it was self-defense anyway, so I don't think anybody wants to take it further. Nick didn't make the decision—somebody in his office did. He had to be shielded from this."

Roxy pulled her legs toward her. "You're seriously hot. Are you single?"

"No, Ms. Smith." Bud cleared his throat. "We've had several witnesses describe what happened with you, and even though you definitely won the fight, it sounds like you were also defending yourself. Alice decided not to prosecute or have you arrested at this time."

"Hot damn." Roxy stood, reached for my hand, and yanked me to my feet. "Looks like we both had a good night. Maybe you're my good luck friend."

"I don't know, my luck hasn't been all that great lately." In fact, it had been downright dismal.

We left the jail cell and headed up the stairs to the police department's main level. Eddie waited on a bench with my phone in his hand. He was still wet, but somehow the outfit looked better on him wet than it had dry.

"Hey." He handed over the phone. "I found this in a pool of water. I'm not sure it'll still work."

"Thanks," I said.

Roxy tilted her head and studied him. He looked right back at her. They both had that rough-but-possibly-cool thing going. I introduced him quickly. "Eddie, Roxy needs a ride home. Do you mind?"

He faltered. "Not at all, but what about you?"

Oh, I definitely wasn't going home with Eddie. Before I could answer, Nick emerged from an office to the right. "I've got her, Eddie. She's coming home with me."

Roxy turned and eyed him up and down. "If I had to guess, this would be the hottie who doesn't work with your life choices?"

"Yep." I shook my phone, only to watch water drop onto the floor.

"Girl, I'd change my life choices," Roxy drawled. Then she winked at Eddie. "I don't know about you, but I need a drink. A big one."

Eddie gallantly held out an arm covered in wet and curdling corduroy. "It's on me." They walked almost gleefully out of the station.

I looked up at Nick's implacable face. "I don't—"

"Nope. You're coming with me, Albertini. I'm done with this." Without waiting for a reply, he ducked his head, and I flew over his shoulder to land hard, barely keeping my face from smacking his lower back as he started walking toward the outside door. Oh, he did not. Shock kept me immobile for several seconds.

"Hey," Detective Grant Pierce called from the top of the staircase.

I planted a hand on Nick's butt and forced my body up to look at Pierce with Nick's arm banded across my legs to keep me in place. Had I ever been over anybody's shoulder before?

"What?" Nick asked, not turning around.

Grant's green eyes scanned us both. "You sure you know what you're doing?"

"God, I hope so," Nick growled.

Grant set his stance. "Tessa? Do you want me to interfere?"

Oh, I didn't need another of these tough guys saving me. "No, but keep this in mind when you find his body later," I snapped, flopping back down. "This is war, Basanelli."

"About damn time." He started moving again. Soon, we were outside in the cold.

"Put me down," I hissed.

His chuckle rippled through me as if I'd taken a gulp of heated wine. "Oh, no. We're going to get a couple of things straight, and you'll stay where I put you until we do."

Yep. There would definitely be a dead body.

CHAPTER 18

I gave Nick the silent treatment in the truck, although he gave it right back to me. He'd dumped me in—rather gently, to be honest—and then secured my seat belt. I kept my cool and gave absolutely no indication that he smelled like a god, or that his caveman routine had kind of turned me on. Okay. It totally turned me on.

It shouldn't have.

We often gave Anna a hard time because she liked Aiden's bossy side. She'd tried to explain once that she found it sexy and that, somehow, he made her feel safe. I'd figured that was all because he'd saved her from a monster in her childhood.

Now, I wasn't so sure. I could've had Basanelli arrested right then and there at the station for tossing me over his shoulder. Instead, I'd refused help and threatened him. The ease with which he'd carried me was impressive because I was no lightweight. My stomach was all fluttery, and I could relate to Anna. For the first time, I understood.

I did not want to understand.

We were almost to Donna's house when I deigned to speak.

"Your asshole move of carrying me out of the station will be all over town by tomorrow."

He easily maneuvered the vehicle around an icy bend. "Baby, it's all over town right now. I can feel the cell phones dinging in every direction, right back to Silverville."

I groaned. He wasn't wrong. "What in the world were you thinking?"

He pulled into Donna's drive and surveyed the quiet Craftsman-style cottage. "I was thinking that I didn't like you out on a date with Eddie Brando." He turned and looked at me, switching off the ignition. "I was thinking that I really didn't like a woman pointing a gun at you." He cocked his head, his gaze slashing across my face. "And I was thinking that you lied to me." His irritation swelled in the vehicle, heating the air.

"Oh." I unbuckled my belt and opened the door, jumping out into the frigid air. As a comeback, it sucked. But I had lied to him.

He followed suit and waited until I crossed in front of the vehicle. "We need to get a couple of things straight."

I shivered. With my hasty exit, I'd neglected to retrieve my wet clothing from the police. "Not tonight." I headed past him and moved to the keypad that would open the garage door.

"Huh." He followed me, blocking the blistering wind with his body. "Where is Donna?"

I flipped open the protective cover and punched in the code, waiting until the garage door lumbered up. "She's not here." I didn't want to lie to him again.

"Where is she?" The persistent jackass followed me through her empty garage to the door to the kitchen and then inside.

"None of your business." Once inside Donna's cheery yellow kitchen, I turned to face him. Then I couldn't look at him any longer. Basanelli was just too damn sexy standing there, all masculine in such a feminine place. His black hair had curled beneath his ears, and his eyes were a mellow bourbon color. His lips were firm, and now I knew what they felt like.

In fact, after kissing him the other day and then being hauled over his shoulder, I knew what most of his body felt like. Hard and strong. So, I turned away, stomped to the island, and poured two glasses of the excellent cabernet. "What is it you wanted to discuss?"

He prowled forward and accepted one, tipping it back and swallowing the entire thing down before placing the glass deliberately back on the granite counter.

All right. So maybe he wasn't as in control as I'd thought. The idea gave me courage, and I took several deep gulps of my wine before pouring more for us both. Yeah, I knew exactly what I was doing. "Donna is still out of town."

He reached for his glass, swirling the liquid. "So you lied to me twice."

A chill skittered down my spine. "Like I said, my life is not your business." Then I tipped back my second glass of wine.

He did the same in an odd dance that was making breathing difficult. Even the way his throat moved when he swallowed was masculine. Sexy. "I want you to give us a chance."

The words jolted me into fumbling to place my glass safely back on the granite. "No."

"Why not?"

"We're too different, and we want contrasting lives," I said lamely. "And you're just too much, Nick." I had to be honest with him.

My luck with men had sucked so far, and I'd been taken over by a strong personality in my last relationship that had ended with him punching me and stealing my car. Oh, I hadn't stayed with him after that, but I should've gotten out faster than I had. The guy was an asshole. Nick was not, but he was still just too much. "I don't want to give up my dreams to follow yours."

He cocked his head and reached for me across the kitchen island, easily lifting me up and across.

I completely lost the ability to breathe as I ended up sitting on the cool surface with my knees on either side of his hips.

He leaned in. "I'm not asking you to marry me, Contessa. We don't have to worry about dreams right now, if ever. But there's something here, and I don't want to always wonder. Do you?"

"One night," I blurted out, my mouth way ahead of my brain. "Just one night." So I'd never wonder. So I could replay it in my mind when he was a famous senator, and I was happy with my diner...or diners. My plans to expand beyond Silverville were mine alone, and I'd never shared them with anybody. "All right?"

His chin lifted, and his eyes glittered with an expression that slammed heat into my abdomen. "If you think I'm too much of a gentleman to accept that offer, you've read me wrong." Then he kissed me.

Deep.

The kiss on the side of the road had been nothing compared to this one. Hard and fast, he took me under, all passion and Italian fire. I clutched his shirt and drew him closer, tired of fighting myself. Of forcing myself to do nothing but work, forgoing all pleasure just because I didn't want to get hurt.

The pain might be worth it this time when he left. Or when I did.

We had this one night.

Nick wrapped an arm around my waist and lifted me from the counter, his mouth still busy ruining me for any other man. I murmured and ran my fingers through his thick hair, tugging lightly. Then he started toward the nearest open doorway.

"No. That way," I whispered against his mouth, pointing.

He pivoted and walked through Donna's living room to the guest room, stepping inside and kicking the door shut with one foot. All while kissing me senseless. Placing me on the bed, he released my mouth and tugged my shirt over my head. His hands slid over my breasts, and his mouth nipped my jawline before kissing up to nibble my ear.

My bra released and flew through the air.

Then his hands were on me, followed by his mouth. Nick was all heat and fire, hands and mouth. Somehow, my sweats were gone, and his clothes were soon somewhere else, as well. He pushed me back onto the bed and trailed his fingers down my body, finding me more than wet and ready.

His mouth was on me then, my legs over his shoulders.

Nick knew exactly what to do with the female body. The rumors about him from high school were true. Beyond true.

His hands were everywhere, as were his mouth and his heated breath. A small whisper in the back of my brain hinted that this was a bad idea, but it was way too late for logic. The orgasm of all orgasms waited for me, and I wanted it.

The climax roared in hot and fast, just from his mouth, but he didn't stop. Before I knew it, I was climbing again, my brain turning to mush. Only after a second climax did he move back up my body, paying attention to every inch. There wasn't a place on me he didn't caress, lick, or kiss. It was too much, yet not nearly enough.

I had no idea where the condom came from, but it was suddenly on him, and then he was pushing inside me.

Wow. This was happening. I grabbed his strong face and yanked him down for another kiss, desperation a new feeling. He was wild and fast, not holding back, and I wrapped my legs around his hips, wanting to take all of him. There was a lot to Basanelli, and I soon tipped over into another orgasm. My third, which was crazy.

Nobody had three orgasms in one night.

As it turned out, neither did I. We made it to five before he gently nudged me beneath the covers, wrapped his hard body around mine, and followed me into dreamland.

CHAPTER 19

I woke naturally at five in the morning, accustomed to getting to the diner early. It took me a few moments to remember where I was, and then I jolted, realizing there was a strong arm banded around my waist and a very heated and bare chest against my back. What in the world had I done? My body was sore in a way that I rather enjoyed, but my mind started spinning as fast as it could.

So many thoughts went through my brain that I had to stop, slow down, and take a deep breath. Okay. I'd said it would be one night, and it had been a fantastic night; Nick had taken advantage of every second.

My heart pitter-pattered, and I knew that was bad. I also realized it probably would have happened no matter what. Basanelli was a guy a girl wanted to keep, but he wasn't mine, and I didn't think he could be. Although after the previous night, I *did* entertain the thought of changing that reality, but I didn't want to change him.

He was pretty great the way he was.

After his antics at the police station, sleeping with him had been a mistake. I didn't want to encourage that type of behavior. Yeah, it had been sexy, but that wasn't a fact he needed to know. If he ever tried to carry me out of somewhere again, I had no choice but to take out his kidneys. As soon as he woke up, I would explain that to him.

He breathed softly against my neck, his body relaxed and still hard as a rock.

I heard a shuffling sound outside the bedroom and frowned. Had the storm gotten that loud? What was going on? Then the door opened.

I jumped, and a woman shrieked. Then, faster than I could track, Basanelli was out of the bed, between me and the door, rushing the interloper.

"Whoa, whoa, whoa." My older sister backed away.

I sat up, clenching the bedclothes to my chest. "Donna?"

Donna flicked on the light, looked at me, looked at a very naked and well-endowed Nick Basanelli, and burst into laughter. She laughed so hard, tears streamed down her face. "Oh, my God," she said, backing away, her eyes going wherever they wanted, which was right down Nick's impressive body.

"Damn it." Nick reached for the hand-crocheted blanket at the end of the bed and wrapped it around his trim hips. "I thought you were in Walla Walla."

Hmm. I must have told him that the night before.

"I was." A pretty blush flitted across her face. While I took after the Irish side of our family, Donna was all Italian with thick black hair, dark eyes, and ruby-red lips. Even this early in the morning, obviously caught off guard, she was stunning. "When did this start?" she asked, seemingly having no problem standing there with a half-naked Nick Basanelli.

"Donna, can you give us a moment?" I asked, my voice cracking.

"It looks like you had more than a moment." She looked at my chin and upper chest. "That's quite the whisker burn up there, sister." And then, because Donna was a decent person, she turned, shut the door, and disappeared.

I buried my face in my hands and peeked at him through my fingers.

Nick turned around, looking tall and broad and slightly pissed off. "Are you okay?" he asked, surprising me.

"I think I might have had a heart attack," I admitted, putting my hand on my chest. Yep. There was definitely whisker burn there.

His gaze dropped to my hand, and his eyes flared.

"Oh, no, you don't." I pulled the covers closer to my neck. "We're done."

"We might be done for today," he murmured softly. In the morning light, Basanelli was all male with tousled dark hair, lazy brown eyes, and sharply cut muscles.

I pushed my wild hair out of my face. "Hey, we didn't exactly get to the talking last night." There had been a lot of movement, plenty of moaning, and some whispering, but there certainly hadn't been any talking. "What exactly did you want to speak with me about?"

Basanelli stood in the middle of the room, seeming more than comfortable with the thin blanket around his hips riding low. "I thought it might be a good idea if you talked to Ozzie Morrison about his reasons for shooting at us. I've spoken with him, and so did Pierce. The guy definitely wanted to shoot at me, but more to scare me. However, he wouldn't tell us why he had your picture."

"You want me to go talk to the guy in jail?"

"With protection there," Nick said. "Or at least through the glass. All my research on him shows he's a family guy who was only defending his brother. It's too bad his sibling's a criminal. I thought maybe you could talk to him, but we'll keep you safe. You don't have to go if you don't want to."

"Oh, I definitely want to get some answers." I wanted to know why that guy had my picture more than anything.

Nick nodded. "All right. I'll arrange the meeting for later today, and we'll keep you covered. There's a story there I don't understand. My hope is the rumor was going around that we were dating, and that's why he had the picture. Because he was looking for you to find me. I want to make sure you're not in any danger."

The words warmed me, and I tried to look tough. "I appreciate it, Nick, but no—"

He held up a broad hand. "We're not doing that."

I pulled my knees up, careful to keep myself covered, although he'd not only seen everything the night before, he'd touched and kissed every inch of me. "We're not doing what?"

"We're not doing the whole I-can-take-care-of-myself-and-I-know-what-I'm-doing bullshit." It was rare to hear Basanelli swear, and it caught me off guard.

It kept me silent for a moment. "Wait—"

"Nope," he said. "We're not doing that. If you're going to talk to someone who shot at us, you'll be covered, and that's final."

I wasn't loving his caveman routine as much this morning as I had the night before, but even so, I wouldn't go talk to some shooter without protection, anyway. My brain worked just fine, and my sense of preservation was strong.

His phone buzzed, and he looked around and picked his jeans off the floor to pull it out. Watching me, he put it to his ear. "Basanelli." His expression didn't change. "What are you talking about? When? Damn it. Are you kidding me? All right. No, I got it. Thanks." He clicked off.

"Was that about me?" I sure hoped it wasn't.

"No." His grin softened the hard lines of his face. "A junior prosecutor hit a deer this morning on the way to our office. He's got a misdemeanor trial this morning. I need to go cover it."

"Is he all right?" I asked.

"Yeah, he's fine. He's busted up a little bit and has a concussion. The case is in misdemeanor court, so it should only take a day."

Nick glanced at his watch. "I do need to go familiarize myself with the case this morning."

"Why was your prosecutor going to work at five in the morning?"

Nick shrugged and muscles across his chest flexed nicely. "He's new. It's one of his first trials. He was overeager, wanted to get there, and...I don't know, read the law. I admire the commitment, but he's a kid I hired from down south. Obviously, he doesn't know how to drive in the snow."

"That's not fair," I murmured. "We've all avoided a deer before, and a lot of us have hit them. Maybe the deer hit him."

"I'm not mad at the kid," Nick said. "You don't have to defend him. He's not a fish." Amusement danced in his eyes.

I shared his smile. "We did save all those fish." I took that as a win.

He sobered. "Tell me you're not dating Eddie Brando again."

"Oh, no. That was a one-time deal," I agreed. "I still have one date to go on with Hank, and then that's it."

Nick scratched the whiskers across his jaw. "I don't know how I feel about you going on a date after last night."

"I don't blame you," I said cheerfully. "But it's in the contract, and I'm doing it."

"What about this morning? Please tell me you're going to hang out here with Donna."

I wished. "I would tell you that, but I also promised not to lie to you, remember?" It had been between the second and third orgasms last night, and he'd wrung that promise out of me a little too easily.

"Oh, I remember what you moaned." His voice was low and sexy.

I rolled my eyes. "I told Smiley I'd help at the diner today. I'm supposed to train two of the new servers. He's having trouble with them."

"Okay," Nick said, surprising me.

I narrowed my gaze at him. "What?"

"Nothing."

Oh, no. This honesty went both ways. "Tell me."

"I have Bud on you all day," he said. "I made the request last night."

I sat back. "You have police protection on me? Do you really think I'm in danger?"

"I have no idea," he said. "But I'm going to make sure nothing happens to you. Pierce said he could spare Bud for at least the next couple of days."

Didn't Bud have a choice? "What did Bud say?" I asked, well aware that he'd gotten hurt more than once trying to protect my sister.

"He seemed all right with it," Nick said thoughtfully. "For some reason, he seems to think you're not as trouble-prone as Anna. I think he just doesn't know you yet."

That was actually a fair statement.

"What time should I be at the station to speak with Ozzie Morrison?" I asked.

"I'll text you and let you know. My guess is around four this afternoon. It may take me that long to get this trial out of the way. I don't know the details yet." He dropped the blanket as if completely unconcerned with his nudity, which I couldn't blame him for. I mean, who would be if they looked like that?

He pulled on his jeans and T-shirt and ruffled his hair. "I need to head to my place and change for court." Eyeing me, he moved forward and put a knee on the bed, leaning down to kiss me on the nose. "We're not done here, Contessa." With that, he walked out of the room. As he left, most of the tension went with him.

I could not believe I had slept with Nick Basanelli.

I heard the front door close, counted to three, and then my sister was in the room with two cups of coffee.

"Here." She held out a mug. "You are telling me everything."

I gratefully took the cup and then did exactly that. She was my older sister and I trusted her. I left out nothing in the retelling of the best sex of my entire life.

"Wow," she said when I wound down. "You know, he had quite the reputation back in high school years ago. But you never know if those things are true."

"Oh, they're true." I took another sip. "Everything you've ever heard, take it and multiply it by ten."

Her eyes gleamed. "What are you going to do about it now?"

"Nothing." I took another deep drink of coffee. "It was one night."

Her smile reminded me of our mom. It was sweet and slightly sardonic. "You are so full of it," she said. "You have stars in your eyes."

"I do not." I finished the coffee. "I may have whisker burn on my chest, but there are no stars in my eyes or flutterings in my heart."

"If you say so," she said.

Enough about me. I concentrated on her. "Hey, what are you doing home?"

"You sounded off on the phone. So I waited until I could sober up and then drove home in case you needed me." She eyed the disarray of the blankets on the bed. "I guess you didn't."

CHAPTER 20

⚜

$\mathcal{I}$ reached the diner around six in the morning after taking a quick shower and borrowing jeans and a sweater from my sister, who'd taken me to retrieve my Rogue from the French restaurant on her way to work. The second I walked inside Smiley's, a harried-looking Mert Smiley tossed an apron at me over the counter.

"It's about time you got here," he yelled.

"Knock it off, Mert." I quickly tied the apron around my waist. "I could leave in a second, and you know it."

Harrumph, was the sound he made as he shoved open the door to the kitchen and disappeared.

Man, it was odd, but I'd really missed the old guy.

The apron already held a notebook and pencil, so I hurried to the far booth and started taking orders. He'd been correct that most people didn't want to cook between Christmas and New Year's, and work was steady.

One of the new servers took the other half of the diner, and I noted she did a pretty good job. I gave her tips a few times, but she'd obviously waitressed before, and she would be a good replacement. We still needed at least one, maybe even two more servers, but we could handle it.

Bud remained out of sight in the very back of the diner, covering my back and drinking way too much coffee. I forced eggs on him early and then a club sandwich later on.

I worked steadily through the early crowd and then into the regular breakfast crowd. Soon, the brunch crowd started to slow down.

Tips were pretty good, so most folks must have had a good holiday. I started wondering what I'd do with my cash this time. I was completely empty after buying Silver Sadie's, but I had plans. Someday, I'd expand and move, maybe into Timber City. But that was a long way off.

I carried several plates of pancakes to the far back booth and then walked to the one nearest the door, flipping over a page in the notebook. "Hi, can I help...?" I paused and looked at the woman waiting for me. Somehow, I kept my expression stoic. "What can I get you?"

Marilyn Brando sat in the booth, looking as regal as any queen. Today, emeralds dripped from her ears and matched a gorgeous emerald and diamond choker secured around her thin neck. She wore a blue cashmere sweater with what appeared to be linen pants. Who wore linen pants in the middle of winter? I shook my head. I could understand if she were at home entertaining, but she was out and about, and there was a freaking blizzard going on.

"I wanted to talk to you," she said. Her frosted blond hair was piled on the top of her head, and her sharp, brown eyes were heavily mascaraed.

I looked around. Things had slowed down, and I hadn't taken a break all morning. I nodded to the other server, whose name was Loretta but went by Tito. I hadn't figured out why yet, and I hadn't had a chance to ask her. "Tito, can you cover?"

"You bet," she said. She was around forty with bright red hair that matched her lipstick. She moved efficiently and had done a good job all morning.

"Thanks." I slid across from Marilyn and put down the notepad. "I know we only saw each other for a few moments the other day," I said softly, "but I wanted to tell you I'm sorry for your loss. I didn't know your husband, but I imagine it's very difficult being without him."

Her gaze narrowed, and she tapped sharpened, red nails on the table. "He was an ass," she said. "I didn't kill him, but I ain't sorry he's dead."

The *ain't* surprised me. It didn't go with the cashmere and emeralds. "Why are you here?" I asked.

"I thought we could reach an agreement. I don't want to own that old building. How about you buy it from me? I understand the going rate was a hundred and fifty thousand."

"Sure," I said. "Find the cash I gave Sadie, and it's all yours." I shook my head. "Do you really think I have more than that?" I looked down at my ketchup-stained sweater, thanks to a bottle that had overflowed. "Honestly."

She studied me. "Maybe we can make another arrangement. Like, perhaps you can make payments."

I cocked my head. "Lady, I'm not giving you anything. We don't even know if your deed is genuine."

"Oh, it is." Her eyes gleamed.

"How long have you been married to Rudy?" I asked, searching her eyes. I wasn't as good at reading facial expressions as my mom, but I wasn't bad either.

"We've been married for a year and a half," Marilyn said. "He kind of swept me off my feet."

Interesting. Apparently, the ride hadn't lasted long. "Well, that's sweet," I said. "He has three ex-wives who said he stole their money." I glanced at her jewelry. "You obviously have some."

"I do, and I also have an ironclad prenup." Her smile showed perfectly straight teeth. "Like I said, he swept me off my feet, but I still kept my brain."

Good for her. "When did he acquire the quitclaim deed from Sadie?" I asked.

Marilyn shrugged. "I don't know. I guess it was about six months ago. He approached her, told her all about his life, and they kind of bonded."

"It's interesting that nobody else bonded with him."

"That's not true. Nobody *wanted* to get to know him," Marilyn insisted. "The other three great-nephews didn't want anything to do with the poor guy. Well, except for the one. The famous one."

"What famous one?" I asked, smiling when Tito placed a glass of water in front of me. "Thanks."

"Sure thing." She moved on.

I took a big drink. I hadn't had enough water this morning, but we'd been busy. As I sat, I realized how sore my body was from playing with Nick all night. I couldn't help but smile.

"That's quite the smile," Marilyn said.

"You have no idea," I agreed. "So, I guess the famous brother would be Hank?" The guy was a good snowmobiler and even had sponsors, but I didn't know that I would call him *famous*.

"Yeah, they met up a couple times. He was a nice guy. Much nicer than the other two."

That didn't make a lot of sense. "Why did Sadie hand over her property to a guy she barely knew?" I wasn't giving in on the quitclaim deed because I still believed Sadie had been honest with me. Still, I might as well get all the information I could.

Marilyn swallowed. "I don't know. I think she felt bad that Rudy wasn't part of the family. That George had never told anybody he had a kid, and that Rudy had grown up without a dad because apparently George never even met him. I think she was just doing the right thing when she deeded over the property."

Now, that did not sound like Sadie.

"I see," I said quietly. "Well, we're having the deed authenticated. I find it interesting that it was recorded mere hours before I purchased the property from Sadie."

"I don't know anything about that," Marilyn said. "Rudy took care of it."

Right. This woman didn't seem to be the type to remain in the dark. About anything. "If she gave the property to him six months ago, why did he wait 'til just the other day to record it?"

Marilyn rolled her eyes. "Because he was Rudy. He did things on his own time, and he never worried about anything. He was charming, though." She sighed. "If you can't buy the property, I'm going to put it back on the market."

"I don't think you own it," I said honestly. "Sadie wasn't a liar, and she would never have taken advantage of me like that." In my heart, I believed that.

Marilyn lifted her chin and chuckled. "You are a naïve one, aren't you?"

I didn't like her tone, but I also wasn't about to get into another fistfight.

She sighed. "I have several attorneys who could make your life a living hell, so why don't we just do it the nice way? You go away, try to find Sadie and your money, and stay out of my way."

"Do you think anybody else will buy that building?" I asked. "It's in a small town where everybody knows everybody." I shook my head. "I can make sure nobody buys it." I wasn't entirely certain I could do that, but if word got out on the street, maybe some of the residents would back me up and refuse to buy it.

She laughed. "You don't think I can handle you and a small town? Give me a break. That building's mine, and you're on notice. You've got two days to get your crap out of there."

"Why do you want it so badly?"

"Apparently, it's worth one hundred and fifty grand," Marilyn said.

Okay. That was a fair point.

"Listen," she said, "I spoke to my attorneys today. I understand the recording rules in Idaho, and since Rudy recorded first, he owned the building. He's dead. Now, I own it. That's a fact. Any legal recourse you have is against Sadie, so you need to go that route."

Unfortunately, that was my understanding, as well—*if* the quitclaim deed to Rudy was genuine. "I'm going to challenge the deed. There is no way Sadie would've double-crossed me like that."

"Then where is she?" Marilyn asked, lifting her hands. "She's nowhere to be seen."

I couldn't explain that one, so I didn't try. "If you'll excuse me," I said, "I need to get back to work."

The door opened, and I looked up, only to have my stomach sink. The hits just kept on coming, didn't they? Louise Transkei stomped over to my table.

"I thought you were in jail," I said.

She shook her head. "I got out on bond. You know I didn't mean to fire at the fish, right?"

I just looked at her. "Marilyn, meet Louise. Louise, Marilyn."

"How do you do?" Marilyn said.

Louise barely cast her a glance. "Listen. I need you to at least file a witness statement that I didn't mean to fire. Apparently, that's what I'm in trouble for."

"You shot a gun in a restaurant," I argued. "You could have killed a person. At the very least, you could have killed those fish.."

"I wasn't aiming at anybody." Louise rolled her eyes. "I just wanted to scare you away from Bobbo."

The woman was responsible for her actions. I'd learned young that if you held a weapon, you were duty bound to know how to use it responsibly. "You could've hurt somebody."

Louise slammed her hand down on the table. The woman obviously had some serious anger issues. "Listen."

I shoved away from the booth. "I'm not interested in Bobbo."

"Yeah, but you set him up with somebody else, didn't you?"

I winced. "Who told you that?"

"Bobbo did," she said, her voice rising. "I talked to him this morning."

Just wonderful. That's what I got for doing a good deed. Bobbo should have kept his mouth shut.

"What is going on?" Mert Smiley shoved open the swinging door and walked out to the counter, looking from one to the other of us. "Seriously, no screaming. Is Anna around?"

"No." I shook my head.

Mert had never quite forgiven Anna for a food fight that, honestly, was not my sister's fault. "She's not here, and everybody who's screaming is leaving," I said crisply.

"I'm not leaving." Louise stomped her foot.

"Yes, you are," Mert bellowed.

I jumped. I wasn't accustomed to him yelling at anybody but me. "Mert, you okay?"

His face turned a ruddy red. "Yes, and I'm tired of this. Tired of the shouting." He clutched his chest.

"Mert," I cried, running toward the counter.

"Ah, crap." He bent over and then fell to the floor.

I looked back at Tito, who was staring, stunned. Bud was already rushing my way, his gaze taking in the entire diner.

"Call 9-1-1!" I yelled.

CHAPTER 21

*T*he snow had turned to sleet outside and slashed against the hospital windows as I sat next to Mert Smiley's bed, fighting the urge to hold his hand. He sat up, looking every minute of his seventy-plus years. His face had regained its color, but he just didn't look right hooked up to machines. "I'm fine, Tessa. I cannot believe you closed the diner," he grumbled.

I rolled my eyes. "You had a heart attack, Mert. Of course, I closed the diner." To be truthful, I'd ridden in the ambulance with him after telling Tito to close the diner, but either way, the place was closed.

I hadn't been that scared in a long time. Even though most everyone called him by his last name, right now, here in the hospital, I needed to be closer to him. To make sure he was all right. So, I used his first name, which was rare, even for me.

Mert shook his head. His thick gray hair stuck up in every direction. "Do you know how much money we'll lose? Everybody wants to eat out between Christmas and New Year's. The tips alone this week should reach the stratosphere."

Was he complaining to hide his pain and embarrassment of being human, or was he truly upset? It was difficult to tell sometimes with him, and I wanted to both soothe and smack him. "Mert, this is serious. You need your heart in good working order."

"I'm fine." He waved a beefy hand. "According to the doctor, it was a minor one."

"I know, but you need to take it easy." I had worked with Mert since I was a teenager, and even though he was grouchy, I absolutely adored him.

I'd been in a complete panic in the ambulance, and I had to admit, I'd said more than one prayer. Then I'd listened to his doctor tell him that he had to slow down and take better care of himself, and I wanted to kick myself for not making him eat better. I should've been watching him closer.

Mert sighed. "I know." He looked at me, his brown gaze soft. "I'm sorry I get so grumpy."

"I like you grumpy," I said honestly. "It's one of my favorite parts of your personality. It's like the weather. You always know what it's going to be."

"You never know what the weather's going to be around here," he countered.

I shrugged. "I do." And, frankly, I did. I could feel the snow coming. I could feel the rain about to swoop in, and I knew when summer was near. Chances were I'd inherited that gift from Nana O'Shea. Also, I knew that Mert, no matter what the day, would be slightly grumpy. Sometimes, it was nice to have a constant in life.

I lowered my chin but could barely meet his eyes as guilt wandered through me. "Is this because I was leaving?"

He snorted. "You think I had a heart attack because you chose to open your own restaurant? I always knew you would."

"I know." But the truth was, I had helped Mert more and more throughout the years, and I hadn't really had time to train somebody new. We were a pretty good team, and I hoped he hadn't felt deserted by me. I'd never do anything to hurt Mert.

He plucked at the thin blanket and looked away before looking back at me, his forehead crinkling. "So, I've been thinking."

"Uh-oh," I murmured.

His grin was quick. "Shut up."

"You shut up," I returned. The smell of bleach and cleanser clogged my nose, but I tried to keep a cheerful countenance for him. Later, I'd have a good cry over the entire day.

He shook his head. "I guess I'm not as young as I used to be."

"None of us are," I said. "I think you almost gave *me* a heart attack today." The idea that anything could happen to Mert felt like a kick to the stomach.

"I've been thinking for a while about talking to you about this. And then you came up with these great plans with Sadie, so I didn't want to interfere, but..."

I sat back, my chest hurting. What had he wanted to discuss? "But what?"

He chewed on his lip and then scratched the weathered skin on his chin. His hand was no longer shaking, thank goodness. "You know I don't have any kin."

"Sure, you do. You have me, and you have my whole family." If somebody didn't have family around, they automatically did with us. I'd taken Mert home for the holidays many times when he didn't go to one of his friend's homes. My family liked him as much as I did, and he was always welcome.

"Well, that's kind of what I'm saying," Mert said. "I know you just bought Sadie's, but I also know you. You're an ambitious little thing."

I blinked. "I am?"

"Of course. You always have been."

Once again, it was nice to be seen. "What are you saying?"

"I'm saying I know you plan to build some restaurant empire. How about you start now?"

I stiffened. "I need more information than that."

He swallowed. "I want to leave Smiley's to you. You can put it in your portfolio with Sadie's."

I jolted. I figured he'd sell someday and then retire. Maybe. Or not. He wasn't the kind to retire. Like the old oak tree outside my parents' home, he was a solid and comforting presence that would always be there. Period. "Are you kidding me?"

"I know the timing isn't great," he said. "I was going to talk to you about it in a couple of years after you got Silver Sadie's up and running. But according to the doctor, I've got to slow down. And you know what? There are some things I want to see before I die. I've never been to the Caribbean."

"You want to go to the Caribbean?"

"Yeah," he said. "You know, on one of those singles' cruises."

If my jaw could hit the floor, it would have. Not in a million years would I have thought Mert Smiley would want to go on a singles' cruise to the Caribbean. It just wasn't him. "I gave all my money to Sadie," I said. "I can't buy you out." Panic coated my throat.

"No, you don't have to. I was thinking that you could work three days a week at Smiley's and contribute to ownership that way. I know you'll need to be four days over the pass at Sadie's once you get the deed problem cleared up. But if you do both, you could start your little empire now. What do you say?"

My heart swelled and thumped. "I say that's a pretty good offer," I murmured. I would have to find somebody to help me out with Sadie's, but I had a few people in mind already. And that was if I actually owned Sadie's, which was up in the air at the moment. If I didn't, and if I'd just somehow lost all my savings, this was a good avenue. Well, frankly, it was my only alternate avenue.

He held up a beefy hand and then patted mine awkwardly. "Just think about it. We could come up with something that works for us both. I'm willing to just give you half, but I know you won't take it."

"No, I wouldn't," I said honestly. I wanted to earn every bit of success I found in this life.

"Tessa, you've worked there since you were fourteen years old. Don't you think you've earned half of it already? Come on. You were the one who got me to update all the decor. You've changed the menu. You pretty much own half the place now." He looked away and then back. "And you should probably know I've left it to you in my will."

I gulped, my body chilling. Will? Mert could never die. "You did what?"

"Yeah, I left it to you in my will. I left you everything." His eyebrows rose. "I mean, don't go killing me or anything."

I snorted. He had the worst sense of humor sometimes. "You're not funny."

"I think I am. I think I'm hilarious," he said. "But I know it would just piss you off if I died and you found out you owned everything. So, how about I tell you now, and then you keep working for it? Then we're both happy."

The truth hit me then. This offer wasn't just about the restaurant, and it wasn't only about the future. Mert didn't want me to go. I'd worked for him since he gave me a job as a scrawny fourteen-year-old when I'd needed my cousin to drive me over the pass just to work there. But the tips were better than they were in Silverville, so I had made it work. Heck, he'd practically helped raise me along with the rest of my family. "I don't want to leave you either," I said softly.

"Oh, knock it off," he grumbled. "Don't get all emotional on me. Why do you do that?"

"I can't help it." Tears filled my eyes. Sometimes, his sweet side caught me by surprise. "I don't want to leave you. I never did. I just wanted my own restaurant."

He took a deep breath as if thrilled he could do so again. "I'm proud of you, Contessa Albertini. It would be a great honor to partner with you in a business venture."

A couple of tears slid down my face.

He groaned. "When we draw up the contract, there will be a no-crying clause. Period."

I sniffed. "Sometimes, crying is good for the soul."

"Sweetheart, my soul has been in your hands since you walked in my door. I know you pray for me."

Of course, I did. "I'm sorry I left you to build my own restaurant."

"It was a necessary step, and one I'd always hoped you would take. I'm sorry I can't give you longer to just work on Sadie's. But you're a hard worker, and you can handle it. So now you own two restaurants," he said. "We're going to have to figure out a way to make it work. Deal?" He held out his hand this time.

I thought about it. It was a lot to take on and much more than I had anticipated. That wasn't counting the court fight I might have ahead of me. But Mert was family, and family always came first. "It's a deal." I shook his hand.

"Good." He released me and leaned back. "Did you know you have a hickey beneath your left ear?"

CHAPTER 22

$\mathcal{A}$t just after four in the afternoon, I tried to cover the hickey as I fixed my makeup in the police department's bathroom. Unfortunately, Mert would have to stay in the hospital for another day or two, so I promised him I would handle the diner for the next couple of days.

My phone, which had dried out nicely after being turned off for so long, kept blowing up with texts from friends and family asking about Mert, and I had no doubt he'd have more company than he could ever want in a few more minutes.

For now, I had hustled to the police station to meet Nick. I couldn't believe he'd left a hickey behind my ear or that I hadn't noticed it all day. Had anybody else seen it? I figured Donna would've mentioned it earlier if she had, and I'd worn my hair down, but seriously, it wasn't the only mark Nick had left on my body.

I had to admit, I'd left a few on his, too. It was a night I would never forget and one I wanted to repeat. What in the world was I going to do about Nick Basanelli?

I figured both of us eventually wanted a calm and steady relationship in our lives, and I just couldn't see how we'd accomplish that together. It wasn't only our locations that hindered our happily ever after. Plus, I liked to work, and I worked hard. I'd had more than one boyfriend complain that I wasn't around enough, and with Nick's job being so demanding, we'd probably never see each other.

Yeah, I was reaching for reasons not to get hurt.

My phone dinged, and I lifted it to my ear. "Hello."

"Hey, Tessa. It's Hank Brando." His voice was low and slightly raspy. Probably from being in the cold all the time. "I promised my aunt Sadie we'd go on a date this week. I didn't know you were interested in me."

"When did you last speak with Sadie?" I asked instantly, pivoting to put my butt to the sink.

He cleared his throat. "Sometime last week. Why?"

"Do you know where she is now?"

"No. The police called, and I've looked out at her place, but nobody can find her." He didn't sound worried. "I figure she and Jonathan went on a trip to spend some of that money or scout new locations. If I know her, she's already looking to invest in new businesses like she did in my racing career. I honestly wouldn't worry about her, Tessa."

"A dead body was found in our building," I reminded him.

The sound of a snowmobile firing to life came from the background. "I have to go, but we can talk about this later," Hank said. "How about The Clumsy Penguin at six?"

"I'll be there." Good. Hank was the closest person to Sadie, at least from what I could tell. I really needed to talk to him.

"Excellent. Let's have a nice, mellow evening, all right? I'm not all for the drama." With those parting words, he hung up.

I wanted to take exception to his last statement, but I also had to be fair. Trouble did seem to follow my family, and so far this morning, I'd avoided looking at the newspaper or going online.

Jolene had taken quite a few pictures after the fish fiasco, and if history proved anything, she liked to embellish when it came to my family. However, she and Nick seemed to have a détente situation happening, so maybe she'd pass on making me look ridiculous.

Somehow, I didn't think I'd be that lucky.

Steeling my shoulders, I walked out of the bathroom and up the stairs to Detective Pierce's office. I poked my head in. "Hi. Nick said I should come and talk with Ozzie Morrison."

"Morrison has agreed to speak with you." Pierce looked up from reading something on a pile of folders, his green eyes tired. Today, he wore a dark green shirt with faded jeans, so he must be just handling paperwork and not heading out for interviews. The guy was usually dressed up a bit more. "I'm not sure it's a good idea, but so far, the guy hasn't given us anything, and he hasn't asked for a lawyer. We might as well give it a shot."

"Okay," I said. "Tell me about him." I felt like I should know something about the man before I sat down and tried to question him—as if I had any idea what I was doing.

Pierce leaned back and stretched his neck. "He's in his mid-thirties and grew up over in Montana. He and his brother, as far as I can tell, pretty much live off the land. His brother was caught poaching three times and had to go to jail after refusing to pay fines or show up for court dates."

I swallowed. "When will he be out?"

"In a month or so."

"That's odd. Why would Ozzie shoot at Nick because of that?"

Pierce shrugged. "Apparently, the brothers were pretty pissed at Nick and alleged they had the right to hunt anywhere they wanted."

"So this was a fish and wildlife violation?" I asked.

"Yep."

I'd never really heard of anybody going to jail for that, but I guessed it was possible if somebody didn't pay fines and kept breaking the law.

"If the brother's only going away for a month or so, why did Ozzie shoot at us?" I asked.

"I don't know," Pierce said. "I mean, they're both hotheads from what I understand. I know there have been different assault and battery arrests, so it could be he was just ticked and wanted to shoot at Nick."

The guys sounded like decent hunters. "Did he miss on purpose?"

Pierce cracked his knuckles. "I think so. My guess is he just wanted to scare or tick Nick off, but either way, it's attempted murder, and the prosecuting attorney's office will take him down."

That seemed fair to me. "So, he'll be going away for a lot longer than a month," I muttered.

"Absolutely," Pierce said. "Are you sure you want to talk to him?"

No. Not at all. "I *am* curious why he had my picture," I murmured.

"Okay." Pierce stood and walked around his desk. It struck me again how good-looking he was. I couldn't tell if he was in his late thirties or early forties because his eyes had that weary look that whispered he'd seen too much.

According to my sister, he'd been dating somebody and had some sort of dustup in the office about it. I wondered if he was seeing anybody now. I was getting pretty good at this match-making thing, so I tried to think who'd be a good fit for the hottie detective. Nobody came to mind, but I would still keep thinking.

"Why are you looking at me like that?" Pierce asked.

It seemed wise to level with him. "I don't know. I seem to have a penchant for matchmaking."

"Oh, God. No," he said. "No, no, no." He walked out in front of me. "Come on. We'll use interrogation room one."

"Are you going to be in there with me?"

"I think it'd be better if I wasn't," he said. "I have him waiting for you right now."

I stumbled when I followed him, surprised he'd leave me alone in an interrogation room with a suspect. He opened the door, and when I walked inside, I realized why.

Morrison was shackled to a table and, from what I could tell, his feet were tethered to the floor. He couldn't get to me if he wanted.

The interrogation room was small, with a wooden table and blank, dingy green walls. A wide mirror was situated behind Morrison, and I didn't doubt Pierce was behind there, watching. I could almost feel Nick, as well, but that could be the hickey pounding in my neck.

"Hi," I said softly.

Morrison looked up. He wore an orange jumpsuit that contrasted with his bright red face. He had sandy-blond hair and a much darker beard, was probably about five foot nine, and approximately two hundred and fifty pounds. Some of it had gone to fat, but he looked pretty tough. "Hi," he repeated, no expression on his broad face.

I pulled out a chair and sat, careful to keep a significant distance between the table and me, even though he couldn't get to me. "I've never been in an interrogation room like this," I murmured. The ones I'd been in before were much nicer, but I didn't tell him that.

"Oh, I have." He looked around. "The walls are always ugly. Why do you think they're ugly?"

I looked at the dingy walls. "I don't know. It seems like they should be cheerful. Like a bright yellow or maybe a lighter purple."

"Purple?" Morrison asked. "I don't think purple. I was thinking like an aqua."

"Aqua would be pretty," I admitted. I looked down at the stained and scratched linoleum. "Also, a wood floor or something a little homier. This floor is terrible."

He looked down. "Yeah, I noticed that, too. It's like they want you to be depressed in here."

"I'm sorry about that," I said, meaning it. "Nobody should get depressed from their environment."

"I guess that's what jail's like," Morrison said.

"Yeah, I heard about your brother. Sorry about that."

Anger filled his eyes. "We have the right to hunt wherever we want."

The laws didn't seem to work that way. "I'm not a hunter, so I never really thought about it. A lot of my family hunts, though they get their licenses first," I said.

"We shouldn't have to get licenses, the nature is there for us."

I'd never really heard it put like that. I didn't think that was true, though. I thought the population had to be managed carefully to ensure their safety. "So, they said I could come and ask you why you had my picture." And then I stared at him.

He stared back. "I'm not admitting that I had your picture."

"I didn't ask you to admit you shot at us, but you did have my picture. It was in your possession."

"Says who?"

I blinked. "Says the police."

"Maybe they're lying."

I chewed my lip and tried to think how an expert would handle this. "All right. Well, hypothetically, why would somebody like you want a printed out picture of me?"

He shrugged.

I wasn't very good at this questioning thing. "Rumor had it I was dating Nick Basanelli. Did you figure I'd be with him?"

"Oh, that jerk? I'd love five minutes in a ring with him," Morrison said. "Hypothetically, if I ever shot at him, it wouldn't be to hit him—I'd just want to make a statement, you know?"

"That's what I figured," I said. "You don't seem like a killer."

"I'm not." Morrison's eyes got wide. "The guy put my brother in jail, and penance had to be paid."

I scratched my chin, careful to keep my hair covering the

hickey below my ear. "So, hypothetically, you just shot at Basanelli to scare him? You weren't trying to kill anybody?"

"Of course, not. I'd never kill anybody," Morrison said. "That's stupid."

Okay, so this was interesting. "But why did you have my picture?"

Morrison shifted his weight slightly on the seat. "Hypothetically, if somebody gave me your picture, then they wanted you to be scared, too."

I perked up. "Somebody wanted to frighten me?"

He scratched his chin. "Let's just say if I were going to scare somebody by shooting toward them, it would either be as payback for my brother or because somebody paid me to scare them."

Who would pay him to frighten me, and why? I shook my head. "I don't understand."

"Me either. Life is hypothetical, you know?"

I sat for a moment and tried to think of the best way to ask this, but I knew he wouldn't answer me. "So, if Nick and I hadn't been together, would a hypothetical shooter have fired upon us at separate times?"

"Sure. But I have to tell you, I'm sure it would be very convenient for said hypothetical shooter if you were in the same place at the same time." He smiled, and I swore it was almost charming.

"What if he had hit us?"

He sat back as if stunned. "You think I don't know where I'm shooting? Not that I *was* shooting," he hastened to add. "But, hypothetically, I knew exactly how to fire. I've never hit anything by accident."

Well, I guessed there was that. "Who tried to scare me, Ozzie?" I asked softly.

He shook his head.

"How much did they pay you to do it?"

He stared at the dismal walls.

"Okay, hypothetically, how much would it cost for somebody

who's an experienced shooter like you to try to scare somebody like me?"

"Hypothetically?"

I rolled my eyes since this was getting ridiculous. "Absolutely."

"About two thousand dollars."

"Wow, somebody really wanted me scared," I murmured.

He gave one short nod and then refused to say another word.

CHAPTER 23

*D*etective Pierce met me outside the interrogation room and escorted me back to his office. "You did a good job," he murmured.

"I did? I felt like a total idiot." I took one of his two guest chairs and sat, my hands shaking. I hadn't realized I was scared until I left the room. "Ozzie Morrison doesn't seem like a horrible guy."

"He probably isn't. He's just a moron." Pierce crossed around his desk and sat. "He did shoot in the vicinity of people, and I don't care if he's a crack shot, he could have hurt somebody. I have no doubt he'll be prosecuted."

"Oh, he deserves it," I said. "Does that mean I'm a witness in that case?"

"Yep."

Just wonderful. I'd about had it with the judicial system for the year. Pierce wasn't quite meeting my eyes and I didn't know why. "What's going on?" I asked.

He sighed, typed something onto his laptop, and flipped the screen around. "You might want to read the article Jolene Sullivan just filed," he muttered. "It's online now and will be in print tomorrow."

"Do people still read print? I mean, newspapers?"

"Apparently."

I looked at the screen and blanched. The headline was pretty good. It read: *Murder Suspect Rescues Fish*. I snorted. "You know that's a silly title, but it would make me read the article."

"Oh, I'm sure," Pierce said.

I looked at the small headline beneath that read: *Another Troubled Albertini Sleeps With the Local Prosecutor*. The blood drained from my face. I could feel it happen, and I wavered. "Oh, no."

Pierce sighed. "You had to know when Basanelli carried you out of the police station that everybody would find out."

"I did figure," I burst out. "What I didn't think was that this wench would follow me to Donna's house. How did she even know where we were going?"

"She was probably close by, heard what happened, and followed you," Pierce said reasonably. "Or she took a guess. Everyone knows you moved out of the apartment above the diner, and where else would you stay? Jolene's pretty plugged into this community."

"And she hates my family," I muttered.

"Nah, I don't know if it's hate." Pierce lifted a shoulder. "Y'all do make good copy."

I cut a look at him. "You'd better watch it, Pierce. You're around us a lot, and my family seems to adore you for some reason. I'm sure some copy could be written about you, as well."

He didn't pale, and he didn't waver, but his eyes narrowed a little bit as he considered it. "Good point."

"Thanks." I scanned the rest of the article, noting that Jolene made a big deal of my purchasing the building in Silverville and then finding a dead body. She also somehow knew about the matching knife found in my fridge.

"You know, as I read this," I muttered, "I feel guilty. I was upset about everything going on, but I hadn't really stopped to consider...am I really a suspect?"

"Of course, you're a suspect," Pierce said. "The guy had a competing claim to your building."

Should I appreciate his directness? I did not. "Then why haven't you arrested me?"

"I don't have enough evidence," he admitted. "Nothing ties you to either knife, and there's no evidence that you actually killed Rudy Brando, or at least there's not enough to take you to trial. There's no evidence that you even knew about the competing claim to the building. In fact, if you did, I seriously doubt you would've given Sadie Brando all that money."

I warmed. It was nice that Pierce believed me, especially since he was an excellent cop. If he didn't think I was innocent, I'd probably be crying and sitting in a jail cell awaiting trial right now. Sure, it'd be over in Silverville, but he seemed more than happy to help Sheriff Franco.

Pierce sighed. "However, there's also no proof you gave the money to Sadie."

I bit my lip. "That's true. I hadn't really thought about that. So, there's a theory in the case that I didn't pay Sadie, killed Brando, and what? Made Sadie disappear?"

"It's a theory," Pierce said. "It's not one I believe or that makes any sense because I don't know how you'd make both Sadie and Jonathan disappear, but at the moment, we have absolutely no idea where they are."

I hoped they were all right and somebody hadn't hurt them just because I'd paid them in cash. "You're still no closer to finding those two?" I asked, my heart sinking. "I thought it would be easy. Isn't CCTV pretty much everywhere now? I mean, even on I-90, aren't there cameras everywhere?"

"Yeah," Pierce answered. "We've checked airlines, we've checked buses, we've checked traffic cams. We can't find anything."

That just didn't make any sense. "I gave Sheriff Franco the keys to the building and full access to search," I said. "I hadn't wanted him to get a search warrant because it wasn't necessary, so I take it he hasn't found anything there either?"

"No," Pierce said. "I've been in daily contact with Franco. Heck, hourly, because we both want to solve this as soon as possible. It was nice of you to grant him access, and I'm sure that'll go a long way in him seeing you as innocent. But we have to find Sadie."

I chewed my lip. "It just seems so weird that two bodies were found in the same place, nine months apart, and both stabbed, right?"

Pierce shook his head. "Oh, I agree it's weird, but Lenny's death looks like a scuffle or a fight that went wrong, and Brando's death looks like a murder."

I sat back. "You've been looking into Lenny's death, as well?" This was out of Pierce's jurisdiction, and I knew he was busy.

"Of course," he offered. "It's related to the knife found in your fridge here, which is related to the murders over in Silverville. Sheriff Franco and I have agreed to work together. To be honest, I like the old guy. He's smart."

Pierce shook his head again as if he just couldn't believe he was in another mess with the Albertini family. "For some reason, I'm caught up in your family. Your nonna brought me cookies earlier this morning."

I jerked my head. "My nonna brought you cookies?"

"Yes."

I looked around the office. "I don't see any cookies."

"They're your nonna's cookies," he said slowly. "I hid them instantly."

Yeah. Pierce was no dummy. "What did she say?"

He looked at me. "She thanked me for trying to help you and asked about my marital status or if I was dating anybody."

Oh, crap. Pierce was now on Nonna's radar. "Well, don't worry about it. I don't think there are too many single cousins around right now." There was no doubt in my mind she was trying to fix me up with Basanelli, so at least Pierce was safe from me. I blanched. "However, I don't think Donna is dating anybody currently."

Pierce's chin lowered, and his eyes blazed a wild emerald. "Let me tell you, with full assurance, that Donna could be the perfect mate to me in every possible conceivable way, our romance could be written in the stars and blessed by the gods, and I would never, *ever* date an Albertini woman."

I gulped. That was a little harsh, yet I couldn't blame the guy. Although, if Nonna had him in her sights for my sister, he was as good as gone and just didn't know it. However, I didn't really see Pierce and Donna together. But what did I know? "The good news is, it's only Nonna after you," I said cheerfully.

Pierce's head dropped. "Your Nana O'Shea came by last week and offered to sage my office to get rid of any negative energy."

I stared blankly at him. "Then you're toast," I finally said. "You might as well roll over now. Just choose if you want Irish or Italian and give in." I sadly shook my head. "You're in whether you like it or not, Pierce. I have no idea how or why, but we're going to be family soon." Clucking my tongue, I stood and barreled out of his office.

The guy had turned a little pale, but not as much as I would've expected. Well, he was a decent person. He'd survive whatever my grandmothers had in store for him.

He instantly ran to the doorway. "Wait a minute. You're not going to help me?"

I started. "Not in a million years." I was neither reckless nor stupid, and I knew better than to take on either of my grandmothers. I had a hard enough time handling Nonna's plans for Nick Basanelli and me. In fact, I didn't even know what I was doing.

Almost as if she'd been conjured by Pierce and me talking about her, my phone buzzed. I glanced at the screen and then lifted it to my ear. "Hi, Nana."

"I saw the news article. I am so sorry about that Jolene." Nana O'Shea's Irish lilt was stronger than my mom's. Nana was a stunning redhead who looked closer to fifty than seventy and believed in magic all the way. "I'll put a hex on her as soon as I can."

"Nana, I appreciate it, but don't hex Jolene. She didn't say anything that wasn't true."

My nana clicked her tongue. "Yes, but she's forcing you into something, and while I truly do like Nick Basanelli, and I think he's a wonderful man, he's not Irish, sweetheart. You belong with an Irishman."

I didn't see why, and I didn't see how, but she was determined, so I kept my tone gentle. "Anna has fallen in love with an Irishman, so things are good." Aiden was all Irish and even had the accent to prove it.

She cleared her throat. "Did you know that Detective Pierce Grant is Irish?"

I looked guiltily around. How did she know where I was? "Um, no." I truly hadn't known that.

"I traced his genealogy after a quiet conversation with him, and guess what? His people come from Cork—at least some of them do."

That explained the offer of saging his office. "Does he have any Italian in him?" I asked.

"Maybe a little," she said grudgingly—and that explained Nonna Albertini's interest in poor Detective Grant Pierce.

"Did you tell Nonna?"

"I may have mentioned it."

The two rarely spoke, so there must be a plan in motion for them to have done so.

Pierce watched me from his doorway. I smiled, waved, and then turned, noting Bud waiting for me at the front door.

"Nana, I should probably get going, but I have to tell you, I really don't see Pierce and Donna together." I whispered the last so nobody could hear.

"Who says I'm looking for him to be with Donna?" she asked smoothly.

All right. I didn't want to know. Sometimes, it was better just to cut your losses. "Alrighty, Nana, thanks for calling."

"Wait, wait, wait a minute," she said. "The paper said you spent the night with Nick. Is that true?"

Embarrassment clacked through me. "Nana, we don't really need to talk about that," I said, blushing so hard and fast my ears rang.

She sighed. "I'll take that as a yes. All right, you have a good day, sweetheart. Love you."

"Love you, too." I disconnected. I didn't know if she was more disappointed that I'd been with an Italian man or that I'd been caught having a sleepover outside of marriage. My grandmothers were both rather old-fashioned. However, I had noticed they were more than willing to toss their morals to the wind to get what they wanted. I didn't regret a moment of my night with Nick, although I felt as confused as ever now.

Bud stood like a massive bulwark near the doorway. His hair was in a buzz cut, and his face was broad like a boxer's. "Where to now?" he asked.

"I want to run over to the courthouse and talk to Nick really quick."

Bud nodded. He could have made a slight remark or wink, but he didn't. He was all business, which was something I admired about him.

"Thanks for watching over me," I said. "You were a great help in getting Mert Smiley to the hospital." In fact, Bud had known exactly what to do to position Mert on the floor and make sure his airway was clear as we waited for the paramedics to arrive.

"Glad to help," Bud mumbled.

There was a time we were trying to fix Bud up with my sister Donna until we found out he was married with an estranged wife. I wanted to ask him about his personal life, but he was keeping things professional, so I should probably do the same.

He opened the door. "I'm only on you for a few more minutes, and then I'm off. We don't have a night officer who can cover you. We're just too short-staffed."

"Oh, that's okay." I waved a hand. "I really don't think I'm in danger."

"Huh," he said. "Your sister always says that, and then somebody shoots at us."

Somebody had already shot at me, but that person was in a jail cell. "I'll be okay, Bud. You don't have to worry."

He rolled his eyes, which was more emotion than I'd ever seen from him. Then we walked across the gravel-covered ice to the courthouse.

Bud looked at his watch. "It's five o'clock. I have to get going. You sure you're covered?"

"I'm good. Don't worry about me," I said.

I had to leave my weapon in the car because I knew I'd go through the metal detector, but there were bailiffs and guards around, as well as police officers. The justice area of town took up two corners of the city park, with the lake at the south end and the local college to the west. This was probably one of the safest places in all of Idaho at the moment. "All right, have a good night, Bud."

"You, too." He gave the bailiff across the room a short nod and took off.

I went through the metal detector and then meandered down to the courtrooms on the lower level. I knew from watching Anna in action that the misdemeanor courtrooms were downstairs, and that's where Nick had said he'd be. The first two were empty, and I reached the third just as he walked out.

"Hey," he said.

"Hi," I murmured.

Basanelli looked good in courtroom gear. His suit was a dark charcoal, and his tie gray and green striped. It was a lighter look on him than I'd seen in other courtrooms, but since this was a misdemeanor and not a felony, that made sense to me.

"Have you read Jolene's article yet?" I asked without preamble.

He nodded. "Saw it on my phone a few minutes ago. Makes us both look bad."

People filed out of the courtroom, pretty much ignoring us. I didn't know any of them, so I did the same. I swallowed. "Is it going to hurt your career?"

He lifted one dark eyebrow, looking like a panther about to strike. "Sleeping with you?"

I blushed. At this point, my cheeks might as well just stay bright red. "Well, yeah, considering she makes out a pretty good case, and I'm a murder suspect."

Nick shook his head. "No, it's fine. She comes across as rather vindictive, if you ask me."

Well, since he was talking freely, I continued. "Why were you at dinner with her last night anyway?" It was a fair question to ask, considering the mess we were now in.

He sighed. "She asked me to grab a quick meal to talk about a different case, and since she was being so understanding in following the rules at the condo, I figured...why not? I was hungry and thought she might have valuable information."

"What case?" I asked.

"It's a burglary ring going on near 10th Street," he said. "She has some decent sources. I have one guy in custody, but I want the ringleader. It was a business dinner, Tessa."

He didn't have to explain it to me, but I appreciated that he did. "Oh, okay." I looked around. "I just wanted to make sure I didn't hurt your career too badly."

"You didn't," he said. "You couldn't."

Well, I probably could, and I definitely didn't want to. "All right, so you have a good night." I turned to leave.

"Oh, no." He instantly grabbed my shoulder. "We're not done talking."

CHAPTER 24

I was saved from having to answer because Nick's phone buzzed. He pulled it from his back pocket to read the screen. "Oh, I have to go," he said, his eyebrows rising.

"Is everything okay?" I couldn't help but ask.

He nodded. "Yeah. There's been another burglary out near 11th Street, and I want to view the scene. It helps to actually see the scene when going to trial." He looked around. "Where's Bud?"

"He had to go, but I'm fine, Nick. Ozzie Morrison is in jail, and whoever hired him only wanted to frighten me. I just wish I could figure out who that was. Unless they're messing with you because people think we're dating."

"If so, they succeeded. I'm pissed anybody put you in danger." Nick opened the door.

Snow and wind instantly blew inside, and I lowered my chin to fight the chill as I walked outside. It was only December, and memories of sunshine and the lake were far away. I loved winter and enjoyed having a snowy Christmas, but I could sure use some beach time right now.

Nick brushed snow off my forehead. "How about I drop you off at Donna's on my way to the scene?"

"Actually, my car's here," I said. "I appreciate the offer, but I'm fine. Don't worry about it."

He cleared his throat. "Everyone thinks we're dating."

"I'm aware," I said drily. "I saw the newspaper article, remember?"

He blanched. "I'm sorry about that. I didn't think Jolene would stoop to that level."

"Then you're a moron," I said honestly. "She's been stooping to that level since she started working for the Timber City Gazette."

He didn't answer, probably because there wasn't one. "I don't have any real high-profile cases right now," he murmured, "but be careful anyway. You've been tied to me, and you have enough going on."

Parts of me warmed inappropriately. "Don't worry about me. I've got this."

I turned to walk away. He grasped my arm and drew me around, and before I could blink, he planted a hard kiss on my lips. "We're not done with this, Albertini."

Desire flashed through me faster than any oncoming wind. Then he took my hand and walked me right up to my Rogue. My hand felt small and warmly protected in his, and I so didn't need those feelings. He opened my door, and I hopped inside, still not finding any words.

"I mean it. Watch your back," he said, and shut the door.

Almost in a daze, I fastened my seat belt and then locked the doors. Of course, I'd be careful.

But he was the one going to some burglary scene in an effort to take down a whole ring of criminals. He should be cautious. Unfortunately, he was already in his truck and driving away before I thought to say anything.

I dropped by Donna's house to change into dark jeans and a winter-white sweater before borrowing gold earrings and a pretty necklace from her. One cool thing about Donna was that she was willing to share.

She wasn't home yet, but she'd left a note that she'd gone into the office and would see me later that night. Donna was a very successful realtor and worked as many hours as I did. Catching sight of the time, I made sure my hickey was covered by more makeup and then dashed out to my car to drive to The Clumsy Penguin around Lilac Lake.

The Clumsy Penguin was actually one of my favorite bars. It was out on a twisty road past the lake, so only locals knew about it—at least in the wintertime. The floors were uneven wood, and the expansive windows overlooked the blistery cold water of the lake. Even though it was after Christmas, lights still sparkled around every window, and the air had a festive feeling.

I walked inside, and heat instantly rushed me, warming me. A quick glance around showed that Hank had secured one of the few tables over by the window, away from the dartboards and pool tables. I was somewhat bemused and a little delighted to see that he had brought his own red-and-white-checked tablecloth to cover the scarred wooden table. He stood as I entered. I smiled and shed my coat to drape over my seat.

"Hi, Hank," I said.

"Hi." He waited until I sat before doing the same. He put his back to the window, which meant I could look out at the vast and mysterious lake.

"The tablecloth is a nice touch," I said honestly.

He straightened his sweater. "Thanks." For our evening, he'd worn dark jeans and a green sweater that brought out the very pretty green hues in his eyes. They were green and brown with hints of gold. He was definitely the best-looking of the three Brando brothers, and it was odd that they shared the same gene pool. His hair was a light brown, and his bone structure rugged. He had the body of an athlete. I supposed competing professionally as a snowmobiler forced him to keep in shape. His skin was smooth but burned by the weather, giving him that outdoorsy hot look some guys got naturally.

Smiling, he reached to the side and dug into a backpack to bring out two candlesticks, which he planted on the table. Scrambling for a match, he lit them both. "There we go," he said. "Now, it's a date."

I grinned. I couldn't help it. Something about Hank was intriguing. He was a couple of years younger than me, which meant he was probably in his mid-twenties. I didn't know much about him. "How did you get into snowmobiling?"

"I've been snowmobiling since I was about four years old. It's a passion for me," he said. "I was lucky enough to turn it into a career, and hopefully the endorsements will keep coming for a while. I've won a couple of good pots, and my aunt Sadie is teaching me how to invest."

It was the perfect segue. I was almost sorry to move from the date portion to the business bit of the evening. However, considering I was still wearing Nick's marks on my body from the previous night, it was the appropriate thing to do. "Speaking of Sadie..." I started.

Hank smiled. "How about we have a regular date and talk about murder, theft, and espionage later?" His grin flashed a dimple in his left cheek.

I smiled. "That's fine, but I'm kind of, maybe, sort of almost seeing somebody."

His laugh was a low chuckle, and several patrons, all women, turned our way to admire it. I could see them from the corner of my eye. "Yeah, I read the newspaper article," he said.

I ducked my head. "Oh, it's so embarrassing. I swear I didn't murder anybody."

He laughed. "I didn't think you did, or I wouldn't be here. But based on your description, I take it you and Basanelli haven't made it official?"

"No. Our lives are too different. I honestly have no idea what I'm doing," I admitted.

"Well, then, let's see if we can figure that out together."

Oh, yeah, Hank Brando was charming. There was no doubt about it. I stared at him and wondered what exactly he was looking for in life. We ordered pizza with a pitcher of beer and drank it happily. Our conversation was free-flowing, and I enjoyed it. He had ambitions to own real estate and invest wisely, which he had been learning from his Aunt Sadie.

"You need to talk to my sister Donna. She's an excellent realtor." I dug into my purse for one of her cards to hand over.

"I remember Donna," he said. "I always thought she was as glamorous as any movie star. I was in junior high when she was in high school, but she really made a statement."

I smiled. "I know, right? She's still like that."

Where our grandmother looked a little like Sophia Loren, I'd always thought Donna looked like Isabella Rossellini, or to be fairer, perhaps Rossellini looked like Donna. Donna was unique, all herself, and she was pretty cool. The door opened, and I looked over my shoulder to see Bobbo and Kelsey Walker enter.

"Your brother's here," I murmured.

Hank nodded. "Yeah. I told him we were coming on a date, and he wanted to provide backup; you know, in case anything were to happen."

My jaw dropped open. "Like what?"

Hank's eyes twinkled. "Like somebody shooting at fish."

I wrinkled my eyes and fought the urge to smack my head. "You know, I can't really blame you," I said honestly. "Weird things happen sometimes."

Bobbo waved, as did Kelsey, and then they walked over to the dartboards and started playing.

"I told them to keep their distance," Hank admitted. "It was nice of you to set them up."

I smiled. "Are things going well?"

"Well, it's only been a couple of days," Hank said drily, "but I heard them hypothetically choosing kids' names the other day. So, I think you might've done a good thing."

Hypothetically. It seemed to be the way a lot of people worked these days. I wondered if I should *hypothetically* try to plan my life? Our pizza arrived, and we started eating happily. The candles were a nice touch, and I admired them. "I have to ask you, aren't you worried about Sadie at all?"

Hank shrugged. "Not really. She's been known to take off before. Considering Jonathan's with her, I'm really not concerned." He frowned. "Maybe I should be, but I don't know, Sadie's always seemed invincible to me. She's such a free spirit."

"Yeah, but she has a hundred and fifty thousand dollars in cash with her," I murmured. "That's dangerous."

"Oh, I'm sure she stashed that almost instantly. There's probably a super-secret vault somewhere that nobody can find." Hank shook his head. "The woman's brilliant. I mean, she's invested in properties all over the Pacific Northwest. She flips them and makes tons of money. I think she does it just for fun."

"I didn't know that." Sadie was pretty quiet unless she was in her bar talking to people or running gambling dens, but it made sense. She'd probably earned a lot of money through the years to invest.

I reached for my phone. "Excuse me." Thinking rapidly, I sent off a quick text to Pierce. I was sure he regretted giving me his number a while back when he was trying to protect Anna, but it was too late now. I asked him if he'd done property searches in the area.

His return text was quick and fiery.

Det. Pierce: *Of course, I've conducted property searches, as has Sheriff Franco. We have a list, and we've checked out each one. Stop bugging me. I'm at a crime scene.*

I gulped. Well, that made sense. "From what I can tell, the police searched for property records, at least in the surrounding states. Nobody has found Sadie."

Hank snorted. "Those are the recorded properties, correct?"

I nodded. "That's a good point." I had recently learned, unfortunately, that many properties weren't recorded. "Yeah, but if she's such a smart businesswoman, she would've recorded, right?" I'd learned that the hard way, as well.

"Maybe. Sadie is more a handshake type of gal, you know?"

"Yeah, I know. I shook her hand. You don't think she would've double-crossed me, do you?"

"Of course not," Hank shook his head. "Not in a million years. That isn't Sadie."

I gulped. "What about this Rudy Brando? He's supposedly a distant cousin to you."

"I met him a couple of times. The guy seemed kind of lost and clueless and looking for a family, but he also set my teeth on edge. I can't explain why."

I appreciated Hank's honesty. He seemed to have no problem discussing everything that had gone on. "Who do you think killed him?" I asked straight out.

Hank studied me. "You seem to have the best motive, but I can tell you're not a killer."

"You can?" I asked, interested.

"Sure. I read people pretty well. It's interesting. I think the more time you spend in the outdoors and the real world, the better you are with people. It should be the opposite, but it isn't."

Man, my Nana O'Shea would love this guy. "So, you didn't really get to know Rudy very well?"

"Oh, no. I just met up with him a couple of times. I know he had a few ex-wives, and he didn't speak very kindly of them." Hank glanced at the tablecloth. "I figure even if a gal is your ex, you shouldn't call her names to other people."

I totally agreed. "Did you know he had a current wife?"

"Oh, yeah. They were getting divorced, though. I guess it hadn't gone through." Hank shook his head. "He was an unhappy person, and as far as I could tell, he'd been in trouble before. Maybe it just followed him to Silverville."

That was my guess, as well, and Franco had mentioned a criminal past. "Yeah, but it just seems odd that both he and Lenny Johnson were found dead in the same place. Did Sadie ever say anything about Lenny to you?" I mostly asked out of curiosity and not a need to solve the crime. I'd promised to try in the contract, and I figured I'd done my job.

"She thought somebody had come into the business to rob it because she was still working it at that time, and that Lenny was inside, staying the night. He often broke into buildings to avoid the cold, so that was her best guess." Hank finished another piece of pizza. "Other than that, she had no idea and felt pretty terrible that somebody had died in her building."

I could understand. I definitely needed to have my Nana O'Shea sage the entire place once we figured out who'd killed both Lenny and Rudy. "They were killed in a different way," I said softly. It was entirely possible there were two different killers.

"Isn't that weird?" He shook his head. "Two murders in Silverville? I mean, we never have murders in Silverville."

"I know." And now I was connected to both of them. The door opened again, and Hank waved. I turned to see Eddie Brando sauntering inside with Roxy next to him. He had his arm around her, and she was snuggled up into his neck. "You called your other brother?" I asked.

Hank grinned. "I'm on a date with an Albertini." He left it at that, as if the statement explained everything. Unfortunately, it did.

I shook my head as the couple went over to the pool table and started playing. "It's sweet that you brought your brothers for backup." I often did the same with my sisters.

Hank straightened. "I'm the young one. They look out for me. You did a good thing with Eddie, too. I don't know Roxy well, but I had a drink with them the other night, and she's a hoot."

"Perhaps I have a future as a matchmaker," I said.

"Maybe you do." The door opened again, and I turned, wondering what other Brando relative had arrived. The only two left were Sadie and Jonathan as far as I knew. And, man, I hoped it was them. Instead, it was Sheriff Franco. "What in the world is Sheriff Franco doing over the pass?" Hank asked quietly.

"I don't know."

Franco looked around and then moved directly toward me. "Hi, Tessa."

Ah, crap. A fist lodged in my gut. "Sheriff Franco, how did you know I was here?"

"I asked your sister, Donna. You left her a note," he offered. "I dropped by her house first." He looked more like Sam Elliott than ever and even wore a weathered brown leather cowboy hat. "You need to come with me, honey."

I blinked. "What?"

He nodded. "I'm out of my jurisdiction, and you have every right to refuse, but we have additional information on both murders in Silverville, and you need to come with me."

Hank looked from me to the sheriff. "I really didn't think the date would end this way," he murmured.

"Neither did I." I stood. "Sheriff, what's going on?"

"I'll explain when we get to the station." He nodded at my purse. "You're going to want to call your lawyer."

CHAPTER 25

*T*he sheriff let me ride in the front of his Bronco with him as he drove across the pass instead of in the back like some perp. Another winter storm was coming in, or to be more accurate, the one that had been blasting us for three days hadn't stopped. Franco was quiet on the way.

"What did you mean I didn't have to come with you?" I asked softly.

He flicked me a glance and then looked back at the dark road. "You were outside my jurisdiction, so you had every right to refuse and make me go through the extradition process of having the local police pick you up."

"I wouldn't do that," I protested.

"I know," he said. "That's why I came to get you myself. I wanted to do this with as little fuss as possible."

My stomach cramped. "Are you charging me with something?"

"I don't know," he admitted. "Honestly, that's up to the county prosecutor, who's reviewing the case right now."

It was probably a good thing that Timber City and Silverville were located in different counties. At least Nick would be kept out of this problem. "So, there's a chance I could actually be charged tonight?" I couldn't breathe.

"New evidence has stacked up. We can't discuss it since you have a lawyer, right?"

"Yes. I texted Anna," I said.

Sheriff Franco pulled off I-90 at the Silverville exit. "Good. Is she going to meet us at the station?"

"Of course." I nodded.

"Good," he said again curtly. "Stop talking now."

Even though the words were brusque, there was a kindness and concern behind them that actually ratcheted up my tension even more. The sheriff was a friend, and he'd do anything to protect me, except break the law. I appreciated that because I wouldn't break it either. We reached the station and walked inside. Deputy McCracken looked up and blanched, his eyes concerned.

"Hi," I said.

"Hi," he replied. "The conference room is ready, Sheriff."

The sheriff nodded. "This way, Tess."

I followed him through the station to the comfortable conference room, which even held a nice coffee pot already brimming with warm dark roast. He poured us each a cup and then nodded toward the nearest seat.

"Get comfortable. As soon as Anna gets here, we'll start."

With that, he turned and left. I took a seat and noticed my hands were shaking. This was so strange. I sipped the coffee, surprised at how delicious it was. There was a hint of cinnamon in it. Even the conference room was cozy and comfortable with leather chairs, a handcrafted wooden table, and beautiful blown-up photographs of the surrounding mountains on each wall. I didn't know if there was another interrogation room in the station, but I appreciated being put into this one.

The door opened, and Anna walked in. Relief filled me so fast I nearly fell off the chair. "Hey," I said.

"Hi," she said, and then my gaze caught on the man behind her. "You brought Clark?" I asked. The seriousness of the situation slammed into me. Anna wouldn't have brought her law partner if she weren't concerned.

"Absolutely," Anna said. She wore a black skirt with a matching jacket and a white shell. Her jewelry was understated, and her pretty reddish-auburn hair was held back with a gold clip. She looked like an official, badass lawyer. The fact that she had changed into this outfit alarmed me even more.

"Hi, Clark," I said weakly.

"Hey." Clark Bunne was probably one of the smartest people I'd ever met. He was around six feet tall with burnished brown skin and extremely intelligent, dark eyes. He stood straight, and his handsome features were set into intense lines. Sometimes, he shaved his head. Other times, he let his hair grow. Right now, it was short and curly around his head. He was probably one of the best-looking men I'd ever seen, and his earnestness only added to that.

For this late-evening jaunt over the pass, Clark had worn dark gray dress slacks, a white button-down shirt, and a red power tie.

It was the power tie that got me. Was I actually in enough trouble that these two had to come to my rescue? As if answering my silent question, they both crossed around the table and drew up chairs on either side of me, effectively flanking me.

I wanted to throw up. "What is going on?"

Anna leaned over and slid her arm around me, tugging me into her shoulder. She then moved her head 'til her mouth was near my ear. "You need to not talk now. Okay?"

I gulped and nodded.

We all faced Sheriff Franco, who walked inside with a worn and battered leather folder that he flopped onto the table.

I jumped, even though I tried not to react. He then drew out his chair very slowly and sat. The tension in the room was palpable, but neither Anna nor Clark reacted, so I followed their lead. It was weird to be relying on my younger sister. Even though she was smart, capable, and reliable, I was her older sister, and I was supposed to protect her.

But I had to admit that it felt good to have a lawyer in the room, because I had absolutely zero idea what was going on. As if they'd agreed beforehand, Anna slightly sat back, and Clark leaned forward.

"Sheriff, why are we here after hours?" he asked calmly.

"It's not even nine." The sheriff looked at Clark. "It's good to see you again, Bunne. I'm looking forward to the spring fling up at the golf course. You think you and Sean can win again this year?"

Clark was silent for a moment. He and my Uncle Sean had bonded quickly and became golfing partners. They were more different than anybody I'd ever met, yet they made perfect partners. Sean was basically trying to draw Clark into the family and had high hopes for the man doing something other than practicing law. For some reason, Uncle Sean didn't like lawyers. He figured Anna would grow out of it, and he was determined to help Clark get on a better path. Unfortunately for Sean, both Clark and Anna were excellent lawyers and had no intention of pursuing any other careers.

"Sheriff, I asked you a question," Clark said firmly.

I kept my expression stoic, but I was impressed. Not many people could face down Sheriff Franco when he was trying to be congenial. Or perhaps he was trying to throw Clark off. If that had been the intent, he'd failed.

The sheriff tapped his round fingers on the file folder. "All right. We'll stick to business."

"Considering you brought my client over the pass in a storm at night," Clark said smoothly, "yeah, we're going to stick with business, Sheriff."

For the first time, I started to relax. Well, somewhat. I gripped my hands tightly in my lap, but who wouldn't? The sheriff turned his attention to me, no longer with the worried look in his eyes. Now, they were flat and business-like.

"Tessa, would you please run me through the day of Rudy Brando's murder again?"

Anna shifted her weight slightly. "No."

I jolted and looked at her.

Anna kept her gaze on the sheriff. "Tessa has provided a statement to you already, and she sticks to everything that's in it. She left nothing out."

I gulped. I had no problem going over the day again, but apparently, that wasn't what my lawyer wanted me to do.

"Come on, Anna," Franco said. "I just need to get through this."

Anna didn't answer. I'd never really seen Anna or Clark in court, but, man, I bet they were good. So, when she didn't answer, neither did I.

"Fine." Sheriff Franco flipped open the top of the battered folder. "According to your client, she arrived at Sadie's, went over the contract, and then waited for both you and Jonathan Brando to show up to sign as witnesses. True?"

Anna didn't answer. Neither did Clark.

The sheriff continued. "At some point, everyone left, and Tessa cleaned up the interior of the main floor without going into the basement. She then went to speed dating, whatever the hell that is, at McCloskey's before returning and noticing that the light was on. At that point, she was accompanied by the Elk County prosecuting attorney. Correct?"

Again, nobody answered.

"Subsequently, noticing the light in the basement, they walked downstairs and found the body of Rudy Brando with the deed stabbed into him. True?"

This was getting really uncomfortable. My throat was dry, so I reached out and lifted my cup to drink my coffee. The mug was thick and handmade, and I appreciated its sturdiness.

"How many times did you speak with Rudy Brando before that day?" the sheriff asked.

"I never..." I began.

Anna lifted a hand. "Why are you asking?"

The sheriff said, "Just answer the question."

"I never met nor spoke with Rudy Brando before that day," I said, ignoring my lawyers. It was the truth.

"Have any correspondence with Rudy Brando before that day?" the sheriff asked.

"No. I didn't know the guy existed." My voice rose. "Come on, Sheriff. I'd never even heard of him."

Clark shifted his weight, reminding me to be quiet. "Why?" he asked.

The sheriff pushed a couple of pieces of paper across the table. "These are emails between Tessa and Rudy Brando where she admits to knowing about the earlier deed of sale from Sadie to Rudy."

I frowned. "I never emailed..."

"Be quiet," Clark said, not looking at me.

I instantly shut up.

"Where did you get these?" Clark asked.

The sheriff concentrated on watching me. "The widow supplied them."

"I didn't send these." I stared at the sheriff. "You have to believe me."

Clark slightly turned his head. "Please, let me handle this."

"I'm trying." It was weird being represented by lawyers. I could defend myself, but they did know a lot more than I did. However, I was getting annoyed. "I didn't do anything wrong," I burst out.

The sheriff looked at me directly and cut me one hard look. "Listen to your lawyers."

"Fine." I crossed my arms.

This sucked. Clark and Anna asked a bunch of questions about the chain of evidence for the emails, and Sheriff Franco admitted that he had requested help from the crime lab in Boise as well as a forensic lab in Seattle to trace the messages. I could tell from looking at the top that one came from tessaalbertini@yahoo.com. I didn't have a yahoo.com email address. The emails were obviously fake.

"Is this all you have, Sheriff?" Clark asked. "Because I could create an email address using your name right now and shoot off a bunch of threats."

"I'm aware of that," Franco said. "That's why I haven't arrested anybody."

"What else do you have?" Anna said.

How did they know he had something else? The sheriff lifted an eyebrow.

"Come on, Sheriff," Clark said calmly. "You wouldn't have dragged us all over here unless you had more."

The sheriff rubbed his jaw. "I have more."

"What is it?" Anna asked.

The sheriff flicked his gaze toward me. "Tessa gave us permission to search Silver Sadie's anytime we wanted."

I nodded. "I did. I don't have anything to hide."

"Did you or did you not move boxes into the top floor, which should be a residence?" he asked.

"Don't answer," Clark said.

I didn't see why I couldn't answer. Everybody knew my cousins had brought my belongings over from Timber City. "Hypothetically," I said, "my family did move my belongings, at least the ones that weren't ruined, into the residence. Why?"

The sheriff pushed a picture of what looked like several pieces of a contract across the table.

"What is this?" Clark asked.

The papers looked dirty and perhaps slightly burned.

"It's a contract between Sadie Brando and the now-deceased Lenny Johnson," the sheriff drawled. "Before he was murdered, Sadie was planning to gift half of Silver Sadie's to

Lenny in exchange for him working the gambling den in the back."

I gasped. "Are you kidding me?"

The sheriff shook his head. "Yep. Nine months ago. When exactly did you and Sadie start negotiating?"

I bit my lip. "We've been hinting at each other for years, but we got serious just a few months ago." It had taken me that long to figure out if I could make it work and also talk Sadie into it. She'd never told me she planned to sell to Lenny.

"I want a copy of the contract," Clark said instantly.

"I'll get you one," the sheriff agreed.

This was unbelievable. I wanted Silver Sadie's, but not enough to kill for it. "I didn't even know Lenny and Sadie were that close."

"Oh, they've been sweethearts since high school. I think it was an on-again, off-again thing through the decades," the sheriff said.

Sadie didn't seem like a woman who combined business and pleasure, but what did I know?

"So, your theory is that my client found out that Sadie was going to give up half of her business to Lenny, so she brutally killed him? Before there was even a hint of negotiation between Tessa and Sadie? That's weak," Anna muttered.

"Well, it's stronger than normal when you figure Rudy Brando was killed next. And I have to wonder if Sadie was willing to bring in Lenny as a partner. Perhaps she really did execute that quitclaim deed to her nephew," the sheriff countered.

"She wouldn't have taken my money," I uttered. I had to believe that. I had to believe in Sadie. "We should all be worried that she's missing."

"I am," Sheriff Franco said. "I'm looking everywhere for that woman."

"So that contract was found in my boxes?" I asked slowly.

Franco nodded. "Not only that..." He pushed another picture across, revealing a six-inch serrated hunting knife with dried blood on it. It had already been bagged.

My stomach sank. "Don't tell me."

"Yeah," he said. "We think this matches the murder weapon for Lenny Johnson. I've sent it to the crime lab to find out."

I cut a look at my sister. She'd gone pale.

Even Clark had stiffened. He shook his head. "You don't have enough to charge her. She didn't bring those boxes over, and anybody could have broken into Sadie's to plant both of these things."

The sheriff's eyebrows rose. "But you had the locks changed, didn't you, Tessa?"

The room swirled around me, and I nodded. I'd definitely had the locks changed.

A timid knock sounded on the door, and it opened. "Hi, Sheriff." Stuart Nerden poked his head in.

I gulped. "Hi, Stuey."

"Hi, Tessa." Stuart straightened his too-thin purple tie and walked inside. We had graduated school together, and we'd always gotten along. His last name was unfortunate, but I'd never teased him.

He was about my height with curly blond hair, a very red face, and light blue eyes that, at the moment, were bloodshot. His suit was corduroy, his shirt a faded denim, and his lips thin. Besides the wild hair, the most noticeable thing about Stuey were his long and dark eyelashes...and the fact that his name actually fit him.

"Congrats on being hired by the new prosecutor," Anna drawled.

Stuey looked like he'd rather be shot. "Thanks." He hovered in the doorway.

The sheriff looked over his shoulder. "Well? Are we charging her or not?"

Stuey faltered. "My boss does want to charge her."

"Then where is he?" Sheriff Franco snarled.

"He's spending the holidays with family in California," Stuey said, somehow paling beneath his ruddy cheeks.

The sheriff shook his head, and I recognized the look. Somehow, Brad Backleboff, a guy who'd only moved to town a couple of years ago, had won the election in November to be the prosecuting attorney for Gem County. In other words, nobody had been paying attention.

Stuey gulped and looked directly at me. "I can hold off until he returns to Idaho New Year's Day, but I think he'll press charges, Tessa. For now, if you, um, surrender your passport, I'll try to appease him. Maybe some exonerating evidence will be found soon." He sounded like he *really* wanted to find that evidence.

My passport? "Sure." If I wanted to flee, I'd head to the mountains in Montana.

CHAPTER 26

*I*t was after ten that night when I rode in the back seat of Clark's truck. The wonderful scent of new-car hung in the air, making the ride feel luxurious. "I like the new rig," I said.

"Thanks." Clark carefully took the icy ramp to I-90.

Anna sat in the passenger side, typing on her phone.

"What are you doing?" I asked.

"I'm calling in reinforcements," she said.

Oh, no. I shook my head and tapped her shoulder. "It's too late. Everyone's in bed."

"Ha." She pressed a button.

"Hello, Anna." A cheerful voice came through the speakers immediately.

Clark cut her a look. "You already connected to my new truck via Bluetooth?"

Anna laughed. "Of course I did. Hi, Nonna," she said. "I need some details."

"Well, of course, dear. What can I do for you?"

I leaned forward between the two seats. "Nonna, I'm sorry we woke you up. I didn't want Anna to call."

"Oh, I wasn't asleep, dear. I was planning the menu for next week's family get-together. What's going on?"

I bit back a wince but let my sister tell her the full story, worrying that she would only agitate our grandmother. I had to hold back a protest when Anna alleged that the assistant prosecuting attorney browbeat me.

"Are you kidding me?" Nonna asked. "That idiot Backleboff actually wants to charge you?"

"The evidence is okay," Clark murmured. "There is enough to charge her, but we'll combat all of it."

Anna reached forward and turned up the heat in the vehicle. "What do you know about Brad Backelboff?"

"Well," Nonna said, her voice warming with the gossip, "he moved up here from San Francisco a couple of years ago, as you know. He's married—or rather, he was."

I hadn't paid attention to the guy, to be honest. Until this week, I'd lived in Timber City and voted there. "What do you mean?"

"His wife divorced him within a year of moving here and returned to the golden state," Nonna said. "I don't know why he stayed, but he ran for office, and we weren't paying any attention —which is common knowledge—and the idiot won. He hasn't even lived in Idaho for more than a couple of years. It's just a travesty."

I thought maybe that was a little strong, but considering the guy wanted to charge me for murder…all right.

"What do you know about him?" Anna asked. "Anything else?"

"Nothing. He likes to fish on the weekends. He's been fairly consistent in prosecuting cases, but he's only been on the job since November, so I really don't have much to tell you. I could contact the ex-wife, but—"

"No, no, no," Anna said. "We don't have to go that far. I just wondered if you had any details."

Nonna hummed for a moment as she obviously thought it all

through. "Well, he clearly has higher aspirations than being a prosecutor in our small town. My guess is he's been waiting for a high-profile case."

"I don't think I'm very high-profile," I argued.

"You would be if you committed two murders," Nonna said reasonably.

Well, that was true. I sat back against the comfortable leather, feeling defeated all of a sudden.

"I think we need to find Sadie," Nonna asserted. "The girls and I are on it. Don't worry."

Anna cast a worried look over her shoulder. "Nonna," she said gingerly, "you, Thelma, and Georgiana haven't really created a detective agency, have you?"

"Of course, we have, dear. I told you we were going to. We even filed for an LLC with the state. We named it Three Hens Investigations."

"Three Hens," I said weakly. "Nonna."

Clark's shoulders shook, and it took me a second to realize he was laughing silently.

"Yes, we kind of like it, and we have the best logo. You should see it. Thelma drew it and combined all the first letters of the agency's name. It's quite impressive. We're having T-shirts made. I'll make sure you get one."

Anna dropped her head into her hands, and Clark just shook his head.

"All right, Nonna," Anna said. "If you come up with anything, let us know."

"Thanks, Nonna," I whispered before she ended the call.

Clark snorted and then stopped laughing. "Calling her was a mistake."

"I'm aware," Anna replied.

I wasn't so sure. If anybody could find Sadie, I thought it was my grandmother, especially since Sadie seemed to have her share of secrets. Somebody in Silverville had to know where she might've gone.

We were all quiet the rest of the way home, and Clark drove me to The Clumsy Penguin to pick up my SUV. It was now around eleven, and most people had left.

"How was your date?" Anna asked.

"It was fine until the sheriff showed up," I admitted.

"Are you going to see Hank again?" Clark asked.

One thing I always liked about Clark was that he enjoyed gossiping as much as Anna did. I thought it was kind of cute. He was a good partner for her and seemed to be an even better friend.

"No," I murmured. I hadn't had a chance to tell Anna about my wild night with Nick, and I wasn't going to do it in front of Clark. "I'll see you guys later. Thanks for coming over. Definitely send me a bill for your services."

Clark snorted, and Anna rolled her eyes. "We are not going to bill you."

"Yes, you are. I charged you for food at Smiley's," I said.

"You don't own Smiley's," Anna contested.

That's what she thought. Yet another thing I'd go into detail about the next time I saw her. "You guys have a good night."

I shut the back door and hurried over to my snow-covered Rogue. Jumping inside, I ignited the engine, turned on the heat, and let it take care of all the snow on the windows. As I sat there, I thought through my options. They weren't good. I would be arrested on New Year's Day if I didn't figure out who killed Rudy Brando. Oh, I figured the sheriff would get there. But perhaps with Nonna's help, I could at least find out where Sadie had gone. Biting my lip and trying to think of the best avenue, I drove slowly toward Timber City around the lake, taking a detour to the hospital.

I was sure visiting hours were over hours ago, but I stopped and jumped out of my vehicle, sliding across the icy parking lot to reach the emergency room and the reception desk. I paused at seeing Kelsey Walker behind the desk.

"Hey, Kelsey," I greeted. "What are you doing here?"

She looked up and stacked a neat pile of papers in the corner. "After the funeral home closed down, or rather after my sister went to jail and my family kicked me out, I got a job here. I guess they figured I wouldn't mind seeing bloody messes since I had worked at the funeral home."

"I didn't know that."

She looked pretty in green scrubs that somehow brought out the blue in her eyes. She leaned forward. "I saw Sheriff Franco take you out of The Clumsy Penguin. Were you arrested?"

"No," I said. "He just had more questions for me about Rudy Brando's death." I cocked my head to the side. "Did you and Bobbo have a good date?"

"We did," she affirmed. "I wanted to get the night off work, but I couldn't, so he brought me here after. We played darts and had dinner. He's the nicest guy. I owe you big time for setting us up."

Her blond hair was up in a ponytail, and she looked younger and brighter than I'd seen her in a long time. We'd both had the misfortune of dating Danny Pucci, and I was glad to see her happy.

"I'm glad it's working out. Just go slow, okay?"

"Oh, I know. I learned that the hard way," she said, tapping her nails on the desk.

I studied her for a moment. "Kelsey, what were you doing over in Silverville the other night?"

She lived in Timber City and had, I thought, for her entire life. I remembered playing volleyball against her and a couple of her sisters in high school, but they'd never lived across the mountain pass.

A pretty peach wandered across her cheekbones. "I went over for the speed dating?" She made it sound like a question.

My jaw dropped. "Are you kidding?"

Her blush intensified. "Okay. No, I'm not kidding. I've been really lonely, and there's nothing going on here. I read about the speed dating happening over in Silverville and figured, why not go over there for the night?" She looked down at the ground. "I know. It's pathetic."

"I was there, too," I reminded her. "Sure, I ended up on a date first, but—"

"Yeah, Bobbo made you."

It figured that Bobbo had told her the whole story.

"Nevertheless, we were all there, and it's okay to want to date somebody," I said gently. I couldn't imagine my family turning their backs on me. Once again, I felt sorry for Kelsey. She had been there for Anna when my sister needed help, and that wasn't something I'd ever forget. "Besides, look how well it turned out."

She twirled a lock of her hair. "That's true. Bobbo and I are really getting along. I know it's only been a short time, but we talk almost every hour." She looked around. "I mean, when we can. When work doesn't get in the way. Did you know he raises alpacas?"

"Yes." I smiled as happiness lit up her face.

Her grin widened. "It's cool, right?"

"I think so," I admitted. "Have you been over to Silverville a lot?

"No," she answered. "I mean, my sisters and I went over there once in a while in the summers to pick huckleberries, and I guess I've been through a few times on the way to Montana. But that was the first time I'd really been in town."

"Maybe it was fate," I murmured.

She brightened. "Maybe it was. I did meet Bobbo. Again, I owe you."

"Speaking of which," I started, "do you mind if I pop in and see Mert Smiley?" I had to see for myself that he was still okay.

"Sure." She gestured down the hallway. "Visiting hours are way over, but I don't think anybody will care. He has his own room so you won't wake anybody else up."

"Thanks." I turned and walked down the quiet hallway to his door and nudged it open. Lights from the machines illuminated the area and showed him sleeping quietly. Even so, he looked pale and wan and not nearly like the blustering cook I was used to. Tears gathered in my eyes. He would be okay, but sometimes I forgot that he was in his seventies. My heart hurt, and all of a sudden, my head ached. I didn't want to wake him, so I just took another look, made sure his breathing was even, and then turned to head back toward the reception area.

"Hey, are you okay?" Kelsey asked.

"I am. It's just been a long day," I said. "Excuse me." I made a beeline for the bathroom. Her phone rang, so hopefully, she would be distracted. I looked at myself in the mirror. I looked pale, too. I walked over, set my back to the wall, and crouched down, trying to stay in control, but it was too late.

Seeing Mert like that, having almost been arrested, and being stone-cold broke, was just too much. Tears started sliding down my face, and I let them. I had planned to wait until I got home or at least to Donna's home to cry, but it looked like the day was ready to hit me now.

I buried my face against my knees and let the tears flow.

CHAPTER 27

After a good fifteen minutes—maybe thirty—of crying, I heard the door open, but I didn't look up. My face was still pressed to my jeans, and I just didn't care. I figured people cried in hospitals all the time, so whoever it was would use the facilities and then go away.

Instead, the scent of musk hit me and then hands descended onto my knees. I knew those hands.

I slowly lifted my head to look into Nick Basanelli's soft brown eyes. "What are you doing here?"

"What are *you* doing here?" he returned.

I wished I could look away, because I was not a pretty crier. I knew this as a fact. Donna could cry and look like a heroine from any movie made in the fifties. Not me. My nose turned red, my eyes puffed up, and with my complexion, I looked horrendous. At the moment, I couldn't even care. "Go away, Nick."

"That's not very nice." In one smooth motion, he leaned in, slid an arm beneath my knees and the other around my back, and lifted me away from the wall.

"What are you doing?"

"I'm getting you out of the bathroom," he said. Okay, that was fair. He walked out of the room, nodded at Kelsey, and took me directly out the front door. "This is becoming a habit," he murmured.

I tried incredibly hard not to snuggle into his impressive body. "You carrying me out of buildings?"

"Yeah," he said. "I kind of like it."

I couldn't help myself, so I laid my cheek against his chest and cuddled into his neck. The air was freezing, the snow bombarded us, and he was a safe and warm haven in a tumultuous world. "How did you find me?"

"Kelsey Walker called," he told me. "To be more exact, she called my service, and they called me."

"How did you get here so fast?"

His strides were sure and strong. "I was at the office."

"Why were you at the office this late?"

"Doesn't matter," he said. I lifted my head and bumped his chin. "Ouch," he murmured.

I tried to see his eyes. "That didn't hurt. Why were you at the office?"

"I was talking to contacts I have in various places," he said. "I need to figure out where Sadie and Jonathan are."

"Oh," I said lamely. He'd been working on my case, which was incredibly sweet of him, considering I was causing him nothing but political problems. "Did you hear that Sheriff Franco took me across the pass?"

"I did, but only because your sister called and told me."

I blinked. "Anna called you?"

"Yeah. She thought I might have some insight into the prosecutorial process in Gem County. She thought I might know the prosecutor."

"Do you?" I asked softly.

He shifted me a little in his arms. "No, not really. I've met him a couple of times, but the guy's only been in office since November. Don't worry. I'll handle him."

I swallowed. "You don't have any jurisdiction."

Nick was silent. Interesting. Was he talking legally, or acting like the alpha male I'd accused him of being?

"I'm in trouble here, Nick, and you can't help." I patted his chest. "That's okay. I don't expect you to fix everything."

We reached his truck, and he opened the door, setting me gently inside. "Oh, I'm going to fix everything, whether you want me to or not." He shut the door before I could answer.

Confusion clouded my mind, so I remained silent as he slid into the driver's side and drove away from the hospital. I didn't even argue when he turned away from Timber City and headed toward Tamarack Lake, the smaller body of water that fronted his condo. I didn't feel like talking tonight, so I shot Donna a quick text saying I'd see her in the morning. We'd have to figure out a way to get my car from the hospital parking lot later.

"Do you think they have a good case against me?" I finally asked.

Nick drove around the smaller lake road, his gaze intense on the storm outside. "I think it's an interesting one. Nothing ties you very well to Rudy Brando's murder," he murmured. "The knife found in your fridge? I mean, that's just weird."

"I agree," I said.

"The stronger case is the one against you for Lenny's death," he continued.

Yet I barely knew Lenny. "You know about that evidence?"

"I do. Anna told me everything."

That figured. Anna wanted to get Nick all riled up. But hey, I could use all the help I could get. "Because they found the murder weapon?"

"Yeah, because they found the murder weapon in your possessions. However, again, it's weird because you weren't in possession of those boxes. Right now, the sheriff is going through and trying to track who had which box in their truck. He's talking to all your cousins, but nobody can find Rory."

I stiffened. I'd forgotten all about Rory. "You know he takes off once in a while."

"I do know that. I also know that nobody's found Serenity."

I winced. "Hey, he gave her until New Year's Day to decide what she wanted in life." That wasn't exactly how Rory had put it, but I wouldn't throw my cousin under the bus.

"Hmm," Nick said. "He'd better make himself available to the sheriff."

"It doesn't matter—at least not with my case. Rory was long gone before we moved any boxes, and Bobbo helped clean rather than pack. You'll have to speak with Bosco, Vince, and Quint. They packed and moved the boxes."

"Franco's talking to all of them tomorrow," Nick relayed.

They wouldn't know anything interesting. "It doesn't matter. None of my cousins put that knife in the box. It must have happened after they dropped them off at Silver Sadie's. Nick, you have to know those emails are fake."

"I know," he said. "I'm not so worried about the emails. Those will be easy to prove. It's the bloody knife that bothers me. Please, tell me you haven't touched any knives lately."

I wasn't stupid. "Of course, I haven't touched any knives. My fingerprints won't be on it."

"That's something, at least." He pulled to a stop outside his condo.

I wearily jumped out, my body feeling like it was a thousand years old as I followed him up the stairs and stopped short at seeing Jolene Sullivan in a bright red parka leaning against his door, waiting.

"I can't deal with this," I murmured.

"I've got it. Jolene, leave," Nick said.

She eyed Nick and then focused on me. "Actually, I heard you were taken out of The Clumsy Penguin tonight and arrested." Her smile was catlike. There were absolutely no secrets in Timber City. I shook my head. I was used to it over in Silverville because it was so much smaller, but now Timber City was a hub of gossip, too?

"I wasn't arrested," I countered. "So, if you print that, I'll sue your ass so fast it'll make your head spin." I'd had it. My temper was close to the surface, and I didn't mind if that wench knew it.

As if knowing how close to the edge I was, Nick stepped between us. "Stick to our agreement, Jolene, or you'll never get another interview with the prosecuting attorney's office."

"I don't need an interview right now." She contemplated me. "If the sheriff didn't arrest you, why was he there? Why did you leave with him?"

"No comment," I said.

Nick opened his door. "See you later, Jolene." Grabbing my hand, he tugged me inside. I was big enough to admit that I enjoyed him shutting the door in her face way too much.

"Can she print that the sheriff came and got me?" I asked.

"Sure, but what kind of a story is that?" he asked. "Unless she has a source in Silverville, she won't know about any of the evidence against you."

I wouldn't put it past Jolene to have a source, but I also knew Sheriff Franco would lose his mind if any of his deputies spoke to the press about an active case. At the moment, I was feeling pretty safe.

"How was your date with Hank Brando?" Nick asked, shrugging out of his coat.

I unzipped mine and handed it to him to hang in the closet. "Actually, it was pretty good. He brought candles and a tablecloth to The Clumsy Penguin. I thought it was sweet."

"Sweet, huh?" Nick turned and looked at me. "Is that what you want? Sweet?"

I studied him. While sweet might not be Nick's default setting, he definitely had it in him once in a while. "Maybe sometimes." Then I shuffled my feet. "I'm sorry I lost it at the hospital. You didn't have to come get me."

Nick brushed my hair away from my face. "Everyone needs a good cry once in a while."

I couldn't imagine him crying, but it was kind of him to say. "I'm not a pretty crier." My nose still felt stuffy and swollen.

His upper lip quirked. "I think you're adorable."

Uh-oh. Trouble. Red light. Turn away. "You do?" I asked, almost batting my eyelashes.

"Yeah." He cupped my face and pulled me toward him, his touch gentle, and his eyes heated. "I almost lost my mind when I found out Franco jerked you out of The Clumsy Penguin and drove you over the pass."

My lungs stuttered. "How did you find out?"

"Seriously?"

Good point. The town thought we were dating. "How many people called you?"

"Three rang, and five texted." He cocked his head. "A quick call to Deputy McCracken confirmed that the sheriff was bringing you in for questioning, and that Nerden didn't want to charge you."

My eyebrows rose as my gaze dropped to his firm lips. "I'm surprised McCracken talked to you. The sheriff will kill him."

"I fixed McCracken up with his wife back in college during summer break. She's a cousin on the Basanelli side." He leaned in and kissed the tip of my heated nose. "The guy owes me, and he knows it."

I swallowed. "Nick? I'm kind of a mess."

He leaned back. "What kind of a mess?"

My mouth opened, and then I closed it. "I don't understand the question." His hard body so close to mine was short-circuiting my brain.

He rubbed the rough pads of his thumbs over my cheekbones. "The kind of mess that needs to go to sleep and be alone? The kind that needs me to go kick some ass—which I would? Or the kind that wants me to take away the world for a while?"

I liked that about him. He wasn't the type of guy to take advantage, and he laid it on the line. Basanelli was a straight shooter. My eyes filled again, and tears started dropping down my face.

Panic filled his expression, and then his shoulders settled. "Ah. That kind." He swept me up again.

"What are you doing?" I sniffled.

He walked over to the sofa and dropped down, extending his legs to his coffee table. He cuddled me close, cupped my head, and pressed my face to his upper chest. Then he massaged the nape of my neck, his body feeling solid and strong around me. "I've got you, Contessa." His words were a rumble against my cheek, and something inside me broke.

I cried out all my fear and anger, sobbing for Mert Smiley and even Sadie Brando. I felt secure and protected in Nick's arms, and he gently rubbed my neck, quietly holding me, his heartbeat steady in my ear. I finally wound down and just stayed there, warm and spent, until I fell asleep. I vaguely noticed when he carried me to bed, and then he was spooned around me, and I felt safe.

My dreams were peaceful until my internal alarm clock woke me around four. I stretched against his hard form, knowing full well my heart was as engaged as my body. I could handle Basanelli as a sexy Italian who wanted to get me naked, but dealing with the guy who'd held me for hours while I cried? That side of him tore right inside me where I wanted to stay Teflon-strong.

My butt was flush against his hardened groin.

"You feel better?" His breath was heated on my ear, and his voice was lazy. Sleepy.

Desire flowed through me, slamming hard into my abdomen. "Yes. Sorry about last night."

He pulled me over and rolled on top of me, holding most of his weight on his elbows. "No apologies." In the morning light, his eyes were a darker topaz. "I like that you wake up early."

Apparently, so did he. As in *all* of him was wide awake. "So do you," I whispered, my voice hoarse, taking inventory. I was dressed in one of his soft T-shirts and panties...and nothing else. He wore boxers that did nothing to hide the fact that he was aroused. His chest was bare and muscled, and I wanted to take a bite right out of his pec.

His grin was dangerous. "In or out, Albertini?"

It was a fair question. "In," I breathed, throwing all common sense to the storm outside.

"Good answer." Then he kissed me, his body warm and hard, his mouth magical and inquisitive. I'd learned the other night that Nick liked to play...until he didn't. He was soft and teasing, hard and demanding, and overwhelming the entire time. I cried out his name three times that morning, and he made sure it was louder each time.

Finally, I glanced at the clock, panting heavily, my body satiated, and my mind blown. "I have to go open the diner," I murmured.

"Sure." He slid from the bed and easily tossed me over his shoulder. "Let's hit the shower first."

Make that four times.

CHAPTER 28

"Stop calling me," I snapped into the phone as I delivered the breakfast special to a couple of ice fishermen who were itching to get out on the lake.

"I have to make sure it's going fine," Mert Smiley grumbled through the phone.

I walked back to the kitchen. "Everything's great. I opened on time. I have two servers working the floor with me, and I called in both of your backup cooks. They're all doing a good job. Mert, you need to be quiet. Take a deep breath, and watch some TV."

"Watch TV? I should be at my diner," he snarled.

"I swear to God, Mert, if you don't get off this phone and rest, I'm shutting the diner down." I meant it. I really would do it. "Not only that, I'll string crime scene tape all along the outside, so even if you show up and ignore your doctor, nobody will come in. I'll plaster pictures of rats all over." I strode into the kitchen, warming to my subject. "In addition, I'll call the Timber City Gazette and tell them there's been a code violation."

Mert sighed. "We don't have rats in Timber City."

"All right. Mice, then. Big, huge field mice that carry diseases."

"Fine. Geez, man. You make a person your partner, and they get all bossy."

I softened. "I'll be by later to check on you. For now, don't worry about the diner. I have it covered."

"All right," he said. "Ooh, the nurse is coming back. She has Jello. Got to go." He hung up.

I sighed. It had been a long morning, but everything was going smoothly now. I was still sore from playing mattress hockey with Nick, but I was more worried about my heart. I had tried to be smart about getting involved with him, but Nick Basanelli was a force of nature—one I was unable to resist.

Besides being harassed by Mert Smiley all morning, both of my sisters had called and demanded a recap of what was going on between Nick and me. I told them what I could between bussing tables before promising them we'd meet for a girls' night soon.

Right now, I had to find Sadie. It was time to take things into my own hands. My phone buzzed just as the lunch crowd dispersed, and I lifted it to my ear. If it was Mert again, I was going to lose my mind. "Hello?"

"Hey, it's Nonna. Can you come over the pass?"

I looked outside. The storm had abated somewhat, and flakes were falling slowly. "Yes, I can. Do you have something for me?"

"I do. Meet me at Sunshine, and be quiet about it." She disconnected.

I sighed. She was definitely taking this whole private investigation thing a little too seriously.

I checked in with the cooks and the servers, telling them all to give me a call if they needed anything. They were doing a good job, so I felt somewhat okay leaving. I also informed them all not to tell Mert if he called. We needed his heart to mend, and that meant no stress. I carefully drove over the pass, noting the sun finally peeking through the thick grayish-white cloud cover. I would love to see it.

I reached Sunshine Eats but didn't see my grandmother's car

anywhere. Frowning, I ran across the parking lot to get inside before the snow covered me completely. Nonna sat with Georgiana, Gerty, Larraina, and Bernadette, who was a retired county commissioner, over in the corner. I walked over, shaking snow off my shoulders. "Nonna, where's your car?" I asked.

"It's around the corner, honey." A trench coat was draped over her seat. "Sit down," she whispered.

I sat and nodded to the ladies. This all looked like trouble, yet I somehow settled into the moment. There was something fun about these women, and even though my life seemed to be spiraling out of control, I'd learned a long time ago to enjoy the good moments. This was about to be one, I could tell.

"What do you have for me?" I leaned forward.

Georgiana spoke up first. "Larraina here was telling us that Sadie liked to invest in properties."

"I'd heard that," I said. "I also heard that Sadie might not record deeds, so not everybody knows where her properties are."

"Exactly," Nonna said. "Apparently, which likely won't surprise you, Sadie liked to keep track of all of her business in a ledger."

I thought about when I'd gone through Sadie's house. There wasn't a ledger.

"She also liked sticky notes." Bernadette waved a hand. "Sticky notes were everywhere."

That was interesting. I didn't see a bunch of sticky notes at Sadie's house. "What do you mean?"

"Well, honestly, I saw her do a contract on a sticky note. I'm telling you, it's all about the sticky notes," Bernadette said.

Georgiana rolled her eyes. "Maybe we can have Thelma do a search for sticky notes all through the town."

"How is Thelma?" I asked.

"Still has a cold. She's manning headquarters," Nonna said.

Should I be frightened that they had a headquarters? I wasn't certain, so I didn't say anything.

"So." Nonna pushed away from the table. "We need to go search Sadie's house again."

"Wait a minute." I stopped her. "We can't go out there, Nonna. We don't have a right." I looked at the assembled group. "Did any of you know that Sadie was dating Lenny Johnson?"

Larraina shrugged. "They were a couple in high school, and I think they had an on-again, off-again thing throughout the years, but nobody really thought anything of it. Sadie was all about work and her business, and Lenny was, well…" Her voice trailed off. "About partying and nothing else."

Nonna finished for her. "It was just sex."

I coughed and turned to the side. I so did not want to talk to my nonna about sex.

Gerty cleared her throat. "Speaking of which."

"No," I said.

"Come on, Tessa, tell us what's going on between you and Nicolo. He promised me you'll be his date for the New Year's Eve ball. Is it true?" Gerty's faded blue eyes glimmered.

I hadn't exactly said yes, but I also hadn't said no to anything from Nick this last week. "We haven't really talked about it," I admitted. "He did ask me, and I would like to attend the Elks Lodge ball with him for New Year's."

Absolute delight lit Gerty's face.

"But I haven't told him," I hastened to say.

"What are you going to wear?" Georgiana asked.

I hadn't really thought about it.

"You should get a new dress," Nonna said. "Something pretty and sparkly. Maybe something green that brings out your eyes."

I probably should get a new dress. It'd been a while since I'd been on a fancy date, yet I was pretty much broke.

"Oh, you'll make such a handsome couple," Gerty said, clapping her hands. She looked small and delicate next to my nonna, who I also didn't consider very tough. They were formidable together, though.

Nonna motioned. "Come on, Tessa, let's go check out Sadie's house. We're going with or without you."

I wanted to drop my head into my hands, but they were trying to help me. "No more breaking windows," I pleaded.

"We don't need to break a window," Gerty said cheerfully. "I heard one is already broken."

"Whoa, wait a minute. Gerty, no, you can't come." The last thing in the world I wanted to do was get Nick's grandma in trouble.

"Oh, we're all going," Georgiana said.

Bernadette shook her head. "I can't go. I have a doctor's appointment, and Larraina is driving me."

Larraina looked absolutely crestfallen. "It's true, we can't go, but will you text us as soon as you find anything?"

"Of course, we will," Nonna said. "We're trying to build our business and our reputation. We'll text you the second we find the sticky notes."

* * *

THIS WAS A MISTAKE, and a big one. I knew it, yet I couldn't think of any way around it. The idea of finding a ledger showing all the locations of Sadie's properties was intriguing, and I hoped we could actually find her.

I didn't love the idea of Gerty holding out on me until we got to the cabin, but there wasn't much I could do about it. The elderly lady seemed delighted as we pulled up to the darkened building. The carpet from Nick's truck still covered the broken window, so at least one thing was going right. We exited my Rogue since I had driven, and all four of us walked gingerly up the snowy walk to the icy porch.

"Here you go," Nonna said, pulling out a stack of blue plastic gloves from her pocket.

"What in the world?" I asked.

Her chest puffed out proudly beneath her heavy winter wool coat. "I got them from Dr. Lewinsky. The new dentist in town?"

Lewinsky wasn't a new dentist. He'd lived in Silverville for twenty years. But to my nonna, that was new. She handed me a pair. I slipped on the gloves, wondering where exactly I'd gone wrong in life.

"Okay." Gerty clapped her hands together. "I'll go through first."

"No." I put both of my now-blue-covered hands up. "I'll go through and then unlock the front door, okay? Nobody else is going through that window."

Without waiting for an argument, I pulled part of the carpet aside and hefted myself up and into the window, falling over just like last time. This time, however, I landed on my shoulder with a muffled, "oof." Pain ricocheted up to my neck. I rolled over, panting, making sure I wasn't dead. Okay. That had hurt more than last time.

"You okay?" Gerty called out.

"I'm fine. Just hold on." I forced myself to my feet. I looked around, and the place seemed undisturbed. It looked exactly like it had last time, only with maybe a little more dust.

Wincing at my aching body, I stumbled to the front door and unlocked it, pulling it open. The three ladies instantly barreled inside.

Nonna flipped on the lights, and this time, they actually illuminated. "See, it was the storm last time," she said, smugly.

"You were right." Man, my arm ached.

Gerty clapped her covered hands together. "Okay. So, let's each take a spot."

I paused. "Gerty, what do you know?"

She shuffled her feet. "Well, I don't know that much, except Sadie once told me if you ever wanted to hide something, you should put it where nobody will find it."

My mouth gaped. "Well, yeah. Do you know anything more than that?"

"Sure. Sadie said people never look in the kitchen. Let's go through her entire kitchen."

"All right," Georgiana said, her voice low with authority. "Here's the deal. I will go through the kitchen. Tessa, investigate in the bedroom. Gerty, you search the living room. And Elda, you pick carefully through the bathroom. Be very thorough. People hide items in the backs of toilets, and there are often false doors."

I rolled my eyes. There was no way the small cabin had a false door. But I did as I was told and headed to the bedroom. We searched for a good hour, and then another, not finding a darn thing.

I still couldn't tell if Sadie had meant to leave or not. There were no suitcases, but most of her clothes were still in place. We did not find a ledger, and we sure as heck didn't find any sticky notes.

Dejected, we all sat in the living room, still wearing the bright blue gloves.

Gerty shook her head sadly. "I can't believe we didn't find anything."

"It's all right," I murmured. "At least we tried."

She sighed. "Yes, but you don't understand. Sadie loved a good hiding place. She talked about where she hid some of her money after good gambling parties. It was always somewhere interesting. I can't believe we just couldn't find anything here at her home."

Nonna looked at me. "What about at Silver Sadie's?"

I shook my head. "She cleared everything out, except for a bunch of junk that I went through."

"Yes, but did you look in possible hiding places?" Nonna asked.

"There weren't any," I said, although my mind started to spin. It wasn't like I'd tapped on all the walls or anything.

A truck echoed outside, and we all stiffened. What in the world? Then a police siren chirped twice.

"Oh, crap," Georgiana cried out, jumping to her feet. "Everybody run." She bustled for the sliding back door and opened it. "Come on. We have to get out of here."

"But my car's out front." Panic lashed through me.

"It doesn't matter. Just because your car's here doesn't mean you are," Gerty pointed out wisely. "We'll say it was stolen."

The woman had a point. The seniors scrambled off the sofa. My tall nonna, bulky Georgiana, and petite little Gerty all made a mad dash out to the back deck. I followed them, looking around to make sure we hadn't left a mess.

"Everybody run," Gerty bellowed.

And then things happened too fast to track. Nonna slipped on the deck, Georgiana tried to catch her, and they both smashed into me. I tried to wrap my arms around them and landed hard on my back, the wind blowing from my lungs. Pain rippled down my spine.

"Come on," Gerty said, frantically trying to lift Georgiana off me. Georgiana rolled and groaned, and then just kept rolling across the snow.

"Stop her!" Nonna yelled.

Gerty tried to put her small body in the path but got flattened, and then they both fell off the deck onto the snowy ground toward the lake, sinking instantly.

Gasping for breath, I stumbled to my knees.

"Get up," Nonna said, pulling wildly on my arm.

"I'm okay." I stood, worried about Gerty.

We hurried over to the edge of the deck and looked down. It was only a few feet, and the snow had cushioned their fall, but they lay in a perfect imprint of two bodies, at least three feet down in the snow.

"Oh, my," Nonna said.

"Stop right there!" Deputy McCracken bellowed, turning the corner with his gun pointed at us.

Nonna yelled and dug into her purse, bringing out the wooden spoon.

"No." I yanked it away from her, threw it to the ground, and held my hands up in the air.

"You put that gun down right now, young man," Gerty yelled, standing up in the snow, which reached nearly to her armpits. She leaned down and helped Georgiana up.

Snow fell off Georgiana's head, and she looked a little dazed, but she stood a good seven inches taller than Gerty. "Yeah, no guns," she said.

I swear to all the saints, McCracken looked as if he might pass out. He holstered his weapon and looked at the three elderly women, and then at me. His jaw slackened. Oh, I bet he would've done anything to have called in sick today.

I brushed snow off my jeans as calmly as I could. "So." I didn't know what else to say.

Nonna straightened next to me, her chin up as snow fell lightly onto her dark hair. She was covered from head to toe, and she still wore the blue gloves, as did the rest of us. "I don't suppose you'd believe we heard a noise from inside and went in to rescue Sadie?"

Georgiana nodded. "Yeah. It turned out to be the wind."

"Who could've figured?" Gerty murmured, shaking her head and dropping clumps of snow onto her thin shoulders.

CHAPTER 29

After giving us blankets and coffee, Sheriff Franco questioned the four of us in the comfortable conference room.

I had to give it to my cohorts in crime. They stuck to their story. They insisted they'd just wanted to drop by and see if they could find Sadie and heard a noise from inside. I didn't contradict them, but I also didn't add much to the conversation because I wasn't nearly as good at lying as the ladies. Finally, Franco shook his head and made sure everybody had a safe ride home.

"Tessa, I need you to remain here," he said.

My chin dropped to my chest. Of course, he needed me to stay back. I hugged my nonna and then the other two women as a much-relieved Deputy McCracken escorted them out of the police station.

I waited. The sheriff waited. We looked at each other across the conference table. I crossed my arms.

He lowered his chin. "Do you have anything else you'd like to add?" He finally ended the silence.

"I absolutely do not," I said, quite honestly. As I mentioned, my lying skills were nowhere near those of the elderly ladies, so I didn't even try. "I'm sorry, Sheriff. I know we've been adding to your duties a lot lately."

He snorted. "Do you think this is new? I've been dealing with Albertinis and O'Sheas my entire life, and that's not even mentioning the Basanellis. I am a little taken aback that your grandma conscripted wild women from Timber City to come and make my day more difficult, but I suppose it was bound to happen at some point."

I sipped my coffee. It was just as good as it had been last time, but I could taste hints of nutmeg in this batch. "I should probably get going."

"Wait a minute." He yelled for McCracken. "Bring me the blue file, would you?"

Within seconds, McCracken was back with a blue folder that he handed over. He patted my shoulder. "I'm glad you weren't arrested. I did not want to face your nonna if I had to put her in cuffs." He shivered and quickly exited the room.

Franco shook his head.

"Well, you can't blame him," I murmured. "The woman's terrifying."

"Yeah, I heard you grabbed the wooden spoon from her before she could smack him. I appreciate that."

The file beckoned me, and I didn't like it. "Anytime," I said, meaning it. "What's in the folder?"

I knew if he had been planning to arrest me for either of the murders, he would've made sure my attorneys were present. Since he hadn't, I was more curious than worried.

He sighed and pushed over a folded piece of paper. "Consider yourself served."

"Huh?" I unfolded the paper to see an Action for Quiet Title. "Ah, crap."

He nodded. "Yeah. As the sheriff, I'm tasked with process serving in our sweet little town. Marilyn Brando, Rudy's widow, has sued you for possession of the building and wants you to vacate and get your, as she put it, crap out."

I sighed. This was the least worrying of my legal problems. "I'll take this to Anna." I really didn't have time to deal with it right now. "Have we heard any news about the accuracy of the deed or from the handwriting experts in Boise?"

"No. They're way backed up." Franco shook his head. "We won't know about the authenticity for quite a while. I will tell you that I compared the signature on the deed to a couple of other things Sadie has filed through the years, and it looked similar. But I couldn't tell you if someone traced it or not. It's just not my expertise."

"Okay," I murmured.

His gaze turned sober. "Tessa, you have to know I'm working around the clock to figure out who killed Brando before that nutjob prosecutor gets back to town."

I was fairly certain a town's sheriff was not supposed to refer to a prosecuting attorney as a nutjob, but even so, Franco's bloodline in Silverville ran deep.

"I appreciate that," I said. "I really don't want to be arrested for murder, because I didn't kill anybody."

"I believe you," Sheriff Franco told me. "Unfortunately, it's not up to me whether you're charged. I'll just keep gathering evidence. And don't worry. We'll find out who killed him."

That was my fervent hope, but right now, it was hard to see the bright side. "Thanks," I said, standing. "I need to get back over the pass and check on Smiley's Diner."

"How is Mert?" Franco asked. It was no surprise the two knew each other since they had both lived in Idaho for decades upon decades.

"I think he's going to be okay, but he needs to slow down."

Franco's cheek creased. "Is that task on you?"

"I think I'm the only one who can stand up to the guy." It was beyond me that everyone didn't see the real Mert Smiley. "I don't know why. He's a marshmallow."

"If he's a marshmallow, then I'm as hard as a leather saddle." Franco shook his head. Actually, Sheriff Franco *was* as hard as a leather saddle to most people.

I smiled. "Keep me informed if you hear anything, will you?" I needed to get on with my life.

"Ditto. And stay out of other people's homes. No more breaking and entering, Tessa. I'm done."

That was more than fair. "I understand."

I stopped and chatted with McCracken for a few moments about his family before I walked out into the December day.

My stomach growled. I hadn't eaten all day, and apparently, breaking and entering really burned some calories. I figured I should get back to Smiley's and then eat something, considering it was almost dinnertime. It'd be good to see how everybody had handled the rush without me.

I had almost reached my car when Marilyn Brando emerged from the tea shop across the road. She looked at me, and I looked at her. Wow, the woman really could dress. She wore what appeared to be designer jeans and very cool black combat boots that I swore were Louboutins. Her jacket was Chanel. I didn't even know they made winter jackets. She had on the same jewelry as the day before.

"You really dressed to go to town," I murmured.

Taking that as an invitation, she crossed the street and reached me. "Sorry I had to sue you."

I shrugged. "I think your deed's fake. I'm going to fight it." It was only fair to let her know.

"That's fine. I just want to get out of this Podunk town." She looked around, her gaze sad. "There is absolutely no shopping."

Not for Chanel, that was for sure. "Are you staying over here?"

"I'm staying at the resort in Timber City," she said.

Of course. Yeah. Silverville only had one small hotel, and it definitely wasn't this woman's style. A thought occurred to me. "Where was your husband staying? Did he spend time at the hotel here?"

"Oh, no. He rented some cabin, I have no idea where, and I don't really care. I have to get out of this place." She brightened. "But then again, who knows? Maybe I'll stick around as we go to trial."

"Oh, we're not going to trial," I said. "That deed was fake." Except the longer Sadie was gone, the more I started to wonder. Had she double-crossed me and just taken my money and run? It was a theory, and one I wasn't much liking.

Marilyn smiled wider. "It looks like we have a fight on our hands." Truth be told, the woman looked way too excited about that.

"Why?" I took in her stunning earrings.

She blanched. "Rudy might've taken some of my money, too. Oh, I have plenty left, but the sale of that building will make me whole again. I can't stand losing to anybody." She glanced at my Rogue. "Cute car. I'll probably own that, too." With that last parting shot, she turned and strolled back down the sidewalk, somehow not slipping on the ice. Those fancy shoes must have decent traction.

My body feeling tired and old again, I lumbered into my vehicle and then just sat there. I was cold, tired, and hungry, yet I knew exactly where I had to go.

I had no choice.

* * *

I SAT in my car for several moments, trying to figure out my next move. I really needed to get back over the pass and make sure the diner was okay. However, I had just been almost arrested with Nonna Albertini, and that gossip would hit the local grapevine within minutes, so there really was only one place to go.

I drove out of Silverville and through a mountain pass to reach my grandparents' house. Nana O'Shea was already opening the door as I maneuvered up the walk.

"Hi, honey." She leaned in and gave me a hug.

I was about three inches taller than Nana, but she was strong. While Nonna Albertini looked a little bit like Sophia Loren, Nana O'Shea was all Maureen O'Hara. Blondish-red hair, incredible green eyes, and Irish skin. I took after her somewhat, which was a fact that had always pleased me.

"Come on in," she said, ushering me inside their log cabin home.

It sprawled over steady ground with mountains all around. In the summer, the flowers bloomed wildly because she had that touch. Her kitchen smelled like Irish stew, and my stomach grumbled. Without being asked, she dished me a bowl and set it on the bar that fronted her stove.

"You need to eat something."

"Gladly." I hopped up onto a stool and dug in.

"I'm not going to ask how you ended up almost getting arrested," she murmured.

The food was delicious. "I'm not going to ask how you already found out."

She rolled her eyes and walked around behind me, instantly digging her fingers into my neck. "Oh, my goodness. You're stiff," she said.

I let my chin drop to my chest as she went to work. Her fingers were magic. She had knots out of knots within no time. "You're amazing."

"I'm aware." She giggled.

I straightened and finished my soup.

She gestured toward the breakfast nook with its view of the pounding storm outside. "All right. Come over here. Do you need energy work?"

"I don't think I have time today," I said. "But maybe next week after New Year's?"

"That sounds good," she agreed. "It's been a while since we worked your chakras. However, why don't you have a cup of tea with me?"

I had known this visit would involve tea, and I was more than ready. So I sat at the round table that overlooked her endless backyard. Even though the snow was piling high, I could still make out her row of holly with its berries alongside the forest.

She pulled open a drawer in her antique hutch and removed several decks of tarot carts. Shuffling them, she started to pull cards and flip them over, working between the beautiful decks. "Hmm, interesting."

I sipped the tea. It was a wild huckleberry blend that she'd made herself. She had never given any of us the recipe, but I knew it would someday be mine. She'd all but promised me.

"So, I can see a romance," she said.

"Nana, you already know that." I gestured to the cards. "I'm seeing Nick Basanelli. Well, kind of. I mean maybe. Sort of."

She chuckled. "You're holding yourself back." She pointed to a tarot card with an owl facing the other way. "Your priorities are all screwed up."

"It's okay that he's Italian," I said. "Besides, we're not going anywhere. I mean, this is temporary." Even as I said the words, they kind of hurt.

She snorted. "That's not the point."

"What's the point?" I took another sip.

She turned over several more cards, revealing what looked like a moon, a princess in a green dress, and a clock. I could read tarot cards, but I would let her interpret them. Her interpretations were often much more on point than mine.

"Well?" I asked.

"What are you doing with your life?" She looked up at me, her green eyes intense.

So I told her everything. I detailed my plans for Silver Sadie's and my new agreement with Mert Smiley. "I'm going to own two restaurants. I always knew I would, just not this quickly," I admitted. "That doesn't fit with Nick's life. We all know he'll run for office and end up in DC." Who knew? The guy might actually wind up in the White House.

She shook her head. "No. You are creating this life, and you're trying to fit somebody into it."

I sat back, looking at the myriad of cards. "Well, sure."

"Honey, that's not how you do it," she said softly.

I blinked, trying to understand. "What do you mean, Nana?"

She shook her head. "You find the person, the one for you, and then you build both of your lives around the two of you as a unit."

My mouth went dry, so I took another drink of the magical brew. I'd never thought about my future like that. I knew I'd end up married with a couple of kids someday because that's the life I wanted, but I'd thought to build my little empire first.

She smiled. "Life is about people, not work or things. You know that. Stop protecting your heart and open it."

I could only stare at her. Nana believed in magic, soulmates, and karma, as well as a good curse every once in a while. I believed she had power, but right now, she seemed to hold more than that. She was speaking wisdom, and it hit me hard.

"Nick is as much of a force of nature as you are, Nana," I said softly, meaning it.

She rolled her eyes. I swore it was a look I had seen very few times in my life, but she did it anyway. "Oh, please, Contessa Carmelina Albertini. You're as strong as they come. Give it a chance. Even if one of you ends up with a broken heart, you'll both survive and find what you should anyway. However, not taking a chance is not my girl. Right?"

I bit my lip. Sometimes, it was difficult to have things put so plainly.

"Tell me you understand," she said.

"I do," I murmured. "You know he's Italian and not Irish, right?"

She chuckled. "Oh, come on. Those Basanellis have some Irish somewhere in their background. I'm sure of it."

I wasn't, but I also wouldn't argue with her. "All right. Your point was made," I said. "I'll think about it."

"That's all I'm asking." She slowly put away the cards.

I stood and refilled both of our teacups. "I need a favor."

"Sure. Anything," she murmured. "Would you like dessert? I have some cookies."

"No, thanks. I'm full." I wanted to lay off the cookies for a while. Apparently, I needed to be in some sort of ballgown for the Elks party coming up, and I would really like to knock Basanelli off his feet, whether we had a future or not. "It's my understanding that Sadie Brando invested in properties all over but rarely recorded them."

Nana tapped her finger against her pink lips. "I wasn't really a business acquaintance of Sadie's, so I don't know much more than that. I do know that she and Lenny were doing the nasty quite a bit."

"I heard that," I said. "I didn't realize it."

"Oh, you know, older people like to be discreet about that kind of thing. I wouldn't know anything about her businesses."

I didn't want to imagine Sadie and Lenny in the buff doing the nasty. "Do you think she would've let Rudy Brando stay in one of her properties?" I asked.

"I don't know. I could find out where he was staying while he was in town," she mused.

Anticipation licked through me. "Would you?"

"Of course." And then she proceeded to make several phone calls.

I listened and wondered if I should have accepted the cookie. A little sugar sounded nice, but the tea was wonderful, so I'd made the right decision. Finally, after her third phone call, she smiled.

"Rudy Brando was renting one of the Frisky cabins out past Bear Creek."

I sat back. "Really? In the winter?"

She shrugged. "Yeah. Apparently, he needed somewhere cheap, and they were willing to let him rent a place so long as he plowed the road."

"Huh. Well, that's interesting." The Frisky Trust was a series of cabins left to the city from Ralph Frisky when he passed away. The city kept the cabins, and all proceeds from the rentals went to the library and the park. It was a good arrangement, and it had been kind of Frisky to leave the property.

"Interesting," I said.

Nana patted my hand. "I'm sure Sheriff Franco knew that already."

"Yeah. He's not sharing all his information," I murmured.

She reared. "Are you kidding me? I will call him immediately."

"No, please don't." I held up a hand. "I appreciate it, Nana, but I think the sheriff has had enough of me for today."

Her chin firmed. "We'll just see about that."

CHAPTER 30

❦

I called Anna on the way out to the old Frisky Trust land to let her know about the lawsuit Marilyn Brando had filed.

Anna sighed over the phone. "If she thinks she has a valid claim, I'm not surprised. I have Aiden doing a deep dive on her. So far, she's come up pretty clean. She's wealthy and from Louisville, Kentucky. Somehow, Rudy Brando charmed his way into her million-dollar life. We're trying to get a warrant for her bank records to see if he perhaps robbed her like he did other women. But so far, we don't have enough evidence."

"She already admitted that Rudy took some of her money, but she still seems to have plenty. I think she's bored and looking for a fight," I said. "Don't let Aiden get in trouble investigating her."

He was an ATF agent and probably didn't have a valid reason to go poking around in Marilyn Brando's finances.

"Don't worry about it," Anna said. "I've got you."

"Thanks."

Then she chuckled. "I cannot believe you took those three ladies to commit a B&E."

My temples started to ache. "I didn't take them. They took me," I protested. "I couldn't let them go by themselves."

"Oh, I know. Nonna's become involved in more than one of my cases before, and Georgiana loves to commit mild crimes. We have to do something about that private investigation company."

"I know. But that's a worry for another day," I said. "If they would stick to gossip and talking to people, they'd actually be quite helpful. It's the breaking the law that concerns me."

"Ditto," Anna said.

I glanced at the dash. "Hey, would you do me a huge favor? Are you busy today?"

"Usual busy. Not much."

"Have you eaten?" I asked.

She shuffled papers in the background. "Not really."

"Perfect. Would you run down to Smiley's Diner and just make sure the place is still standing?"

"Sure," she said slowly. "What are you doing?"

It didn't occur to me to keep the truth from her. "I'm going to check out the place where Rudy Brando was staying. Apparently, he rented one of the cabins from the Frisky Trust."

"I didn't know that," Anna said. "That's a good idea. There's a chance the sheriff has already cordoned off the area as a crime scene since Rudy died, though. You know that, right?"

Actually, I didn't know that. I figured Sheriff Franco had searched the place. But I didn't know that automatically made it a crime scene, especially since Rudy had been killed elsewhere.

Considering it was the dead of winter and the area really wasn't in the best location to either go snowmobiling or skiing, the three cabins usually sat vacant all winter. I didn't think I'd run into any problems.

"You should really be careful," Anna said. "Believe me, every time I go on a journey like that, I end up falling out of a tree."

As I'd never been good at climbing trees, I wasn't too worried.

"I'll call you when I finish. I just want to see the place and get a feel for who he was and what he was doing," I offered.

I also hoped there'd be a big clue on the front door. But considering Sheriff Franco hadn't said anything, it was doubtful. Although I had also learned that Franco kept plenty of facts to himself, which I guessed was his job.

"I wish I could be there," Anna said.

Nope. This was my mess, and I would clean it up without getting my younger sister involved any further. "No, no, no," I argued. "I don't need help. I just want you to go by the diner and make sure all is well. It'd ease my mind."

"Sure," she agreed. "Please, be careful."

"I will. Love you." I clicked off. The three cabins were about twenty miles past the turnoff for Bear Creek, and I was happy the local construction companies plowed this far out in the winter. Finally, I reached an unplowed drive with a beautiful, hand-crafted, and snow-covered wooden sign on a pole that read Frisky Trust Land. I thought that was sweet.

The town had commissioned the piece after Frisky died, and I thought it was good to leave the tribute to him. It was unthinkable to me that somebody could die without any relatives or progeny, considering how many relatives I had. The idea saddened me. But it was kind that he had donated the land to the city and would always be remembered.

I changed the gear in my Rogue so I could make it down the road. Oh, it had definitely been plowed recently—no doubt, for the police—so it was easier going than it would have been. From the details my nana had been able to uncover, Rudy Brando had rented the second cabin from the road.

How she knew this, I had absolutely no idea. But I trusted her sources implicitly.

So, I bypassed the first dark and quiet cabin, noting that the snow had piled up all around it. It definitely hadn't been used. I then reached the second cabin and turned, winding through white-covered trees to reach it. There was indeed yellow crime scene tape covering the door.

I turned off my engine and sat in the silence for several moments. The trees around me were thick with snow, and huge berms filled the spaces between them. There was no way anybody could come at me from the forest.

Boot prints were visible beneath a new layer of snow, and the walkway to the cabin was partially shoveled. The police had definitely done their job.

The oncoming storm had darkened the day, and it would be pitch-dark soon. I kept my headlights pointed at the cabin. It was a small, one-story, probably one-bedroom structure and used for tourists who came to town to fish or float the river in the summer. It was surprising that Brando had been out here during the winter. Maybe the man had needed privacy.

For what, I wasn't sure. But considering he'd ended up dead, I couldn't help but wonder. I steeled my shoulders to get out of my vehicle just as my phone buzzed.

"Hello?" I answered, hoping it was Anna with good news about the diner.

"Did you almost get my grandma arrested?" Nick asked without preamble.

I winced even as the low rumble of his voice licked across my skin. I shivered. "I kept her from getting arrested. Those women were going to Sadie's cabin with or without me." How often would I have to say that statement in the next few days?

He groaned. "Our grandmothers need to be separated."

"Well, that's on you, buddy," I retorted instantly. "I'm not taking either of them on."

He sighed. "Did you petit criminals find anything?"

"Not a darn thing," I admitted. "It was a waste of time, and it ticked off Sheriff Franco."

"When I talked to him, he was laughing," Nick said.

That one little statement relieved me greatly.

"Where are you now?" he asked. "We should grab dinner."

I warmed. I shouldn't have. But I did. I would love to grab dinner with Nick. "Um, I'm still over the pass," I muttered. "I have a quick legal question for you."

"All right." He sounded wary.

"Does crime scene tape bar entry to a residence?" I asked. "I mean, is it like some sort of law that you can't cross it?"

His silence held weight before he spoke. "What exactly are you doing right now?"

"I'm at Rudy Brando's rented cabin," I murmured. "I thought I'd take a look around."

"Franco's not going to let you get away with a second B&E in one day. He's a nice guy, and he likes you, Tessa, but come on. At some point, he'll have to do his job."

The world was silent around me, save for the light dropping of snowflakes. "Nobody knows I'm out here."

"I love that idea, considering people keep shooting at you."

"They actually shoot at *you*," I retorted, not forgetting that the last shooter had wanted to scare me, as well. We still hadn't figured that one out. "Seriously, Nick. I just want to look around."

"I'd tell you not to, but I know you wouldn't listen to me. Keep me on the phone."

"All right." I kept the cell with me as I jumped out of the car and sank about a foot into the snow. It was amazing how much the powder piled up in just a couple of days since the police had no doubt searched the place. I cautiously crept up the stairs to the front door and tugged the crime scene tape out of the way. The knob turned easily.

"They didn't lock it," I said.

"There's probably nothing in there to steal. Most of those cabins aren't locked in the winter. If somebody needs shelter, they take it, and if they really need it, they'll just break in."

True. That made sense. Cold and darkness instantly assailed me when I walked inside. It was still light enough outside that I could see clearly. The cabin held one bedroom, a comfy living room, and a small kitchenette. The furniture was log-made and comfortable-looking, fronting a wide fireplace. Mountains rose high and white in the distance, framed perfectly by the back sliding glass door.

There was dust everywhere—the black kind, as if they'd dusted for prints.

"You see anything?" Nick asked.

"Just finger-printing dust." Even though I was alone, I tiptoed quietly to look through both the bedroom and the bathroom. Everything was empty. They must have taken out anything that was Rudy's and filed it for evidence. "There's nothing here," I said.

"I'm sure the police took everything. So, how about you get out of there and come back over the pass? We can go to dinner and try to figure out this case."

I wanted that dinner more than I should, and I couldn't stop thinking about Nana's words. "Are we working together now?"

"We've always been working together," he retorted.

Now that was just sweet. "Fair enough." I started toward the doorway just as one of the wooden floorboards caught my eye. The color was lighter than the other planks. I wouldn't have even noticed if a shadow from the nearest chair hadn't slid across it as the sun went down. "Huh," I said.

"What?"

"Something is off with a floorboard." I moved toward the odd patch, which was closer to the kitchen than the living room.

"What about the floor?" Nick asked.

"I don't know." I tried to keep the frustration out of my voice as I bent down and felt along the smooth wood. "There's just a slight discoloration that I wouldn't have noticed at a different time. The shadows were dancing across it."

He made a low sound of frustration. "Forget the dancing shadows and get out of there."

"I will." Yet something about that floorboard bugged me. I

tugged at it and felt a slight indent at the end of the board. "Hmm. There's something here." Standing, I went to the kitchen and searched through the drawers to find a butter knife.

"What are you doing?" Nick's voice now held a bite.

"I'm not sure what the technical term is." I returned to the odd area and dropped to my knees. "I think it might be destruction of property."

With that, I inserted the butter knife between two of the boards and lifted. It creaked slightly. I did it again. It creaked more. Finally, I used all my strength, twisted, and lifted it. The board sprang up. "Oh, my."

"What?"

"There's something under the floorboards."

The narrow opening led to a dark and square space. I reached in, hoping there wasn't anything waiting that would bite me. My hand touched a small, metal box. I lifted it out, noting it had a combination lock. "Oh, man. I bet I can get this thing open."

"What is it?"

I told him, and he hummed. "You need to take that to Sheriff Franco."

"Sure," I said, having no intention of doing that—at least not right now.

As if Nick could read my mind, he groaned. "Fine. Get your ass back over the pass and bring that thing. Leave the cabin. Now."

The wind whistled an eerie and mournful tune outside. I shivered. "Yeah, good idea."

CHAPTER 31

⚜

When I swung into Smiley's Diner after a hairy drive over the pass, I could instantly tell the late afternoon had gone awry. Grabbing my new metal box off my passenger seat, I parked at the curb and hustled inside, slipping across the icy walk. Nobody had put down gravel or salt all day. I hurried inside, and chaos ensued.

Tito looked up. "Oh, thank God you're here." She dropped three plates at a table with a shrieking toddler.

I looked around for the other server. "Where's Bertra?"

"Crying in the bathroom." Tito threw up her hands. "Customer got angry with her because we screwed up the order, and the chick just lost it."

"Okay," I said. "I've got this." First, I hurried toward the counter and around to the kitchen, where smoke lightly filtered out. "What is happening?" I bellowed when I ran inside.

Lewis, one of the two cooks, looked up. "I don't know. Jack was trying to cook something new. He wanted to be creative and started the second grill on fire."

I looked over at the mangled grill. "Where is Jack?"

"His girlfriend called. They got in a fight, and he left." Lewis ducked his head.

"All right. Stick to the easy stuff. We'll push people to order burgers and salads. We'll worry about the grill later." Yanking on an apron, I shoved the metal box onto a shelf near the stove and ran back outside. Within ten minutes, I'd taken orders from four tables and handed them back to Lewis. Tito was handling her side of the diner well, so I hustled into the bathroom to find Bertra wiping her face.

"You can't go crying every time somebody gets irritated," I said. "You wish bad things upon them."

She looked up. She was about eighteen years old with wide brown eyes and blond hair tipped with pink. "But they yelled at me."

"We'll take care of that. Nobody has a right to treat you poorly. But you can't just give up. We need you out there, and we need you working."

"I just can't." She shook her head. "I just can't talk to people right now."

I kept myself from pointing out that I was a person and shoved down my irritation. I had been eighteen at one time. "Fine, go bus tables. Anything empty, do it. You can also refill drinks. Tito and I will handle the actual people." That was about as good as I could give.

"All right," she said, sniffing.

I hustled outside, surprised by how many people were there, considering it was after dinnertime. Or perhaps they'd been here so long they'd started at dinner. We were efficient from that point, taking orders and delivering food. After, I made sure to give everybody a free dessert. It eased things quickly.

Mert called right as things were calming down, and I lied my ass off, telling him everything was fine. When I clicked off, Tito shook her head. "Man, you're not a bad liar."

"Thanks. I don't usually get that a lot."

The bell over the door rang, and a woman walked inside. It was Louise Transkei. She took a seat at a center booth, her red coat matching the leather. She slowly shed the heavy material, and her shoulders hunched.

I sighed and walked over to her, still irritated that she'd shot the fish tank. "Why are you here?"

"Didn't know where else to go." Her sadness was palpable. "Please tell me that you understand I didn't mean to shoot the fish."

I placed a glass of water in front of her. "We all make mistakes." Considering I'd broken and entered two different places today, I could kind of relate. But I hadn't fired a gun in the vicinity of people, and I hadn't risked tropical fish.

"I really screwed up." She shook her head. "I love Bobbo, and it hurt when he dumped me. Then I heard he liked you and, well, I mean, look at you."

At the moment, I looked like a complete mess. My hair was all over, and I had stains down my jeans. "Right," I said. "Sometimes, things don't work out."

"All I did was spend a little of his money. I've never had any, and I wanted some is all. I just bought a new couch," she blurted.

That wasn't exactly what Bobbo had said. But then again, he did seem a little odd. "Maybe you're better off," I murmured.

"Maybe," she said. "I would have given anything to be with him and be happy out at that farm. That's all I've ever really wanted." She plucked at a napkin. "Don't you want to be happy and not alone?"

I was still trying to figure out what I wanted. "There are a lot of fish in the sea." The pun reached her, and she gave me a small smile. Good. "Can I get you something to eat?"

"Yeah. What do you have for three dollars?"

"The burger special." Sure, I'd have to give her a discount. But the woman needed to eat. She looked pretty thin, and there were dark circles beneath her eyes.

She sighed. "Have you ever been so in love you got lost in a guy?"

"Oh, yeah." I scratched on the notepad. "Biggest mistake of my life."

Danny Pucci had ended up dead on my floor, and it had almost put me in jail, even though I hadn't been the one to kill him. In fact, was I still mad at Nick for charging me? I wasn't sure. It seemed like he had only been doing his job, and I did appreciate that he didn't really think I'd done it, even then.

"Sometimes, guys really screw you up," I murmured.

"Exactly," Louise said, her eyes wide. "I would have done anything for Bobbo, and he tossed me aside like I was nothing."

We all hated to get dumped. "You can do better, Louise." I wasn't sure if she could or not, but it seemed the right thing to say.

She swallowed. "Will you testify on my behalf about the shooting at the restaurant? I'm pleading not guilty so we can at least have a trial."

"I'll tell the truth," I said.

"You know I didn't aim at you, right?"

I nodded. "Oh, you definitely aimed above me, and I don't even think you meant to hit the aquarium."

"I didn't." Her eyes widened. "I actually like fish. I helped save a few. Remember?"

I thought back. She had started throwing fish into the tank alongside me. "Yeah, I'll tell the truth at your trial. Maybe you'll be able to plea out. It was your first offense, right?"

She nodded and took a big drink of her water. "Of course, it was my first offense. I've only been in love once."

I didn't quite understand the connection between her first offense and being in love. But she apparently did. "I'm sure it's going to be okay, Louise."

"I hope so," she said. "Rumor is you might be going to jail, too. Did you really murder those two guys?"

"You know I didn't."

She looked me over. "I don't know that. But if you're willing to believe me, I'm willing to believe you."

"Fair enough," I said. "Your dinner is on the house. This time."

* * *

THE DOOR OPENED, and the bell jingled behind me. I caught sight of who entered before Louise could. There was no way to ward off what was about to happen, so I lowered my voice instead. "Listen, Bobbo is here. Stay cool."

She did *not* stay cool. She instantly turned in the booth, her eyes lighting up, only to see Bobbo and Kelsey Walker moving toward us. Louise paled until she matched the clouds outside.

Bobbo faltered, wearing deep green overalls and a crisp white shirt today. His boots had to be a good size sixteen and were well-worn. Kelsey looked petite and wary at his side as she took in Louise. She instantly slid her arm through Bobbo's and leaned against his side, not coming close to reaching his shoulder.

"Hi, Louise," Bobbo said.

"Hi, Bobbo." Louise flicked a glance at Kelsey and then looked up at Bobbo's face, her eyes wide. "Thanks again for bailing me out."

Bobbo blanched and scratched his beard.

Kelsey frowned and slowly withdrew her arm. "You paid her bail?"

I took two steps away from the table because, honestly, if this thing went south, I was just getting out of the way.

Louise smiled, her eyes sparkling. "Of course, he paid my bail. No matter what happens, we'll always be there for each other. Right, Bobbo?"

Bobbo scratched his head and looked down at Kelsey. "I couldn't just leave her in jail. I'm sure she didn't mean to shoot those fish."

"I didn't hit any fish," Louise protested.

Kelsey looked at me and then at Louise before crossing her arms. "You should have told me you paid her bail. She went in and shot at my friend."

Well, it was nice that Kelsey considered us friends.

"Do you want to get back together with Louise? Because if you do, I need to know right now," Kelsey finished.

I liked that she called Bobbo out and laid it all on the line. "Good for you," I said.

"Thanks." She smiled.

Bobbo vehemently shook his head. "Absolutely not. Louise and I are never getting back together."

Louise's expression fell. A couple of ladies at the far end of my section waved at me, and I gave them the hand signal that I'd be right there.

At the moment, I was trying to keep everybody from detonating. "Okay, so I don't know what's happening here, but we need to keep things calm. Smiley is in the hospital, and I can't have word about a fight reaching him," I said quietly, hoping they'd all work with me.

Bobbo's eyes widened. "No one's going to get into a fight."

"Yeah." Louise's shoulders hunched. "Believe me, taking out that aquarium was the most dangerous thing I'll ever do. I'll never get in a fight."

Kelsey bit her lip, looking young and adorable with her blond hair up in a ponytail and a bright red scarf around her neck. Her puffer jacket had snow on it, adding to her look of fragility. She lifted her chin. "I'm not going to play second fiddle to anybody. So, if something is going on with you two, have at it."

I wanted to clap for her, but I also wanted to at least appear neutral.

Bobbo flopped his beefy arm over her shoulders. "Kelsey, I just helped Louise out for old times' sake. We are never getting back together."

"You don't know that." Louise reared up. "We were meant to be together, Bobbo. So I spent a little bit of your money. So what? It was there to be spent."

Bobbo's eyes widened. "Are you kidding me? You spent nearly twenty-five thousand dollars in a week."

Even I gasped. That was crazy.

"Wow." Kelsey looked at Bobbo again. "How did that happen?"

He shook his head. "Don't ask. It involved credit cards, fancy furniture, and a little too much trust."

Once again, Kelsey slid her arm through his, looking way up at his face. "I don't want your money, Bobbo. I like you. I like your lifestyle, and I really like your alpacas. If you just want to be friends, that's fine with me, but I'm not going to do this back-and-forth game any longer."

Man, I was really starting to like Kelsey Walker.

Louise reared up again.

"No," I said. "We're not doing this. You just stay calm." Maybe I wasn't as forgiving about shooting the aquarium as I'd thought. Something could have ricocheted and hit me or anybody else in that restaurant. "Louise, you've been given a second chance here. You should take it."

She swallowed and looked down at the table. "Fine. I'm sorry I spent all your money, Bobbo."

"Oh, it wasn't all of it." He grinned. "I'm glad you're out of jail, and I'm sure if you get a good lawyer, you'll probably get probation and not do any jail time. You've never done anything else wrong." He looked down at Kelsey. "Don't worry, I'm not paying for the lawyer."

Kelsey's smile was radiant. "How about we go to The Clumsy Penguin for dinner? That was really good the other night."

I nodded slightly. That was a phenomenal idea.

"Okay," Bobbo said. He patted me on the shoulder, and I nearly fell. Man, he had heavy mitts for hands. "Thanks again for helping us out, Tessa. You're a sweetheart. Is there any chance you and Hank are going out again?"

Considering I'd nearly been arrested during our first date, I didn't think so. Besides, Nick Basanelli was in my heart, whether I liked it or not. I just had to figure out what to do with him. "I don't think so. He's a great guy. Maybe we can find him somebody else."

"All right." Kelsey chucked me on the arm. "You're a pretty good matchmaker. I'll give you a call next week, and we'll see what we can come up with."

"That might be fun." Perhaps I should open a matchmaking service. I felt I had a gift.

The two left, and Louise wiped away a tear. "What about me? Could you hook me up with somebody?"

"You should probably wait until your legal troubles are over," I offered.

"Huh," she said. "Look who's talking."

CHAPTER 32

After closing up the diner around nine that evening, I drove around town and toward the smaller Tamarack Lake, parking at Nick's condo.

At this point, I felt we were in this mess together, so I might as well include him.

I carried the metal box and two roast beef sandwiches from Smiley's to his front door and knocked. After the first few hectic minutes at the diner, things had gone smoothly. It gave me hope that I'd be able to run both restaurants and give Smiley a break.

He was still in the hospital, and I wanted to see him, but I needed to figure out what was in the box first. It was probably nothing, or maybe it held cash. Plus, I didn't even know if it was Rudy Brando's. The box might have been hidden beneath that board for eons, though it felt fairly new. Although, what did I know?

The door opened, and Nick stood there in faded jeans, a ratty Marines T-shirt, and no socks. He let me in and shut the door behind me. "Are you done with breaking the law today?"

"Not even close." I handed him the bag with the food.

He padded over to his kitchen to fetch plates for the sandwiches, his chiseled face looking serious. I carried the metal safe over to his table.

He shook his head. "You're tampering with evidence?"

"Maybe. We don't know that it's evidence. This thing looks older than the first Sadie Brando," I retorted. "Plus, the police didn't find it. I did." I lifted a shoulder. There was definite luck and timing involved. "If they had been there at the same time of day I was, they would've likely seen the shadow. But, Nick, there's something in here, and we have to figure out what it is."

"Or we could give it to the police and let them figure it out. But even so..." His stunning brown gaze cut to the box and back.

Hope filled me. He was as curious as I was right now. "Come on, Nick. There's probably nothing in there."

That was a lie. There had to be something important in the little safe. What? I had no idea. Maybe a confession from Rudy that he'd falsified the deed. Yeah, that'd be fantastic. My luck had been fairly good recently, but it wasn't *that* good.

"Fine," Nick said. "I'll be right back." He went somewhere in the condo and then returned with a bunch of tools. "This is actually a pretty flimsy lock."

He took a screwdriver, inserted it where the numbers were, grabbed a hammer and started beating on the screwdriver. It was impressive how quickly Basanelli could go from law enforcer to lawbreaker. I found it incredibly sexy, which was probably something I shouldn't admit to anybody, maybe even myself. But I should probably examine it at some point in my life.

He worked for about fifteen minutes, grunting. I was surprised it took that long. But then the container suddenly flipped open. I rushed forward.

"Huh," Nick said.

"Well, that's weird," I murmured.

There were tons of different-colored sticky notes, all smashed together.

"Those are Sadie's." I reached for them. The first one I read held a grocery list. Disappointment washed through me. "What's this?" I lifted a purple note with numbers scrawled across it.

"I don't know. Longitude and latitude, maybe?"

There were so many, and we'd have to go through them all.

"This was her record-keeping system?" he asked.

"I heard she also had a ledger, but that was more for gambling debts," I murmured, excited for the first time. "Nick, the truth of where she might be hiding could be on one of these sticky notes."

"Maybe, but why in the world would Rudy Brando have these?"

Perhaps he planned to create false deeds for all her properties. But in that case, his plans for Sadie wouldn't have been good. Had he planned to kill her? If so, I was glad someone had killed him first. Yet what if he had a partner? My mind flashed to Rudy's widow. Had Marilyn hurt Sadie? The woman didn't seem the type, but looks were often deceiving.

My stomach roiled. "We have to find Sadie." Shoving the box to the side, I paused. It rattled oddly.

Nick cocked his head. "That's weird." He reached in and removed the rest of the sticky notes, placing them on the table. Then he tapped the bottom of the box. It really wasn't big enough to hold much else. "There's a false bottom."

I snorted. "A false bottom in a hidden metal box? This guy was paranoid."

"Yeah, Rudy obviously had a few skeletons." Nick reached for the screwdriver he'd used earlier and pried up the bottom of the metal box. It flipped out easily, revealing several folded pieces of paper. He grasped them and pulled them out. "Aha."

"What's that?" I leaned closer to him, trying not to notice the warmth that cascaded off Basanelli.

"It's a deed for another of Sadie's properties."

All in all, there were five deeds, and the last was a duplicate of my building. The one that held Silver Sadie's.

I gasped. "There's another one?"

Nick peered closer. "Yeah, but look, the signature isn't the same. Obviously, he was practicing."

Oh, this was good evidence. I clapped my hands together. Nick looked up, one eyebrow rising. "Don't get too excited. You obtained this illegally."

I gulped. "Well, yeah, but no. What does that mean? Does it mean it can't be used in court?"

He sighed. "No. It can be used in court since you found it. If the police had found it illegally without a search warrant, then it couldn't be used."

"So it was good that I broke and entered?"

His hard gaze dried the spit in my mouth. It was both sexy and slightly unnerving. "No, it was *not* good. I'm sure Franco had a valid warrant, and if he had found this, it would've been good. Right now, there's a question as to how you got it."

I didn't really care. The point was, I had it. "It's proof that Rudy Brando had plans to steal from Sadie."

Nick nodded grudgingly, looking beyond mouthwatering, but I had more important things to worry about than his sinewed body.

I pushed the box out of the way, put the probably fake deeds on the chair, and slowly began unsticking all the notes from each other to place in rows on Nick's table.

He sighed and walked over to pick up his sandwich, taking a big bite. "Well, at least I know what we're doing for the evening," he drawled.

I grinned. "That all you got, Basanelli?" I was joking.

He dropped his sandwich onto the counter and was on me instantly, taking me to the floor. I chuckled and kissed him, letting him take over. He was hot and wild, and I loved every minute of it. It was quite a while before either of us was hungry for food.

* * *

AFTER A COUPLE of rounds with Nick, where I saw stars and might've whimpered his name, we returned to the kitchen to eat our sandwiches and figure out some sort of organizational system for Sadie's sticky notes. There were at least four hundred of them, and they were all smooshed together.

First, I tried to create a place for each color: purple, red, yellow, blue, and green. Then I realized that Sadie hadn't bothered doing the same. There were lists of groceries on different colors. There were notes and reminders. There were even, I believed, lines of poetry scattered throughout. Several of the pieces of paper showed numbers jotted down with dollar signs. I put those in one section, having no idea what they meant. Then we found another couple of what appeared to be contracts.

"Is this Lenny's signature?" I asked.

Nick frowned and peered closer. I noticed scratches on his arm from me gripping him while he'd driven me wild earlier. "Maybe."

I tried to make out the writing. "Half interest in Sadie's bar." Huh, maybe this was the contract.

"Well, only he signed it." Nick shook his head. "That's not a valid contract."

Good. I didn't think Lenny had any living relatives, but if so, I didn't want to have to fight them for the building, as well. I found several pieces of paper with lipstick as if she had dabbed her mouth with those. I put those on the far side of the table. We didn't need them.

"Hey, here's a land description." Nick handed over a light blue piece of paper. I read it.

"It's up in Boundary County," I said.

"Hmm, all right. You keep going through these. Give me a sec." He stalked over to his briefcase by the door and tugged out a laptop. After our energetic sessions, he had dragged on faded sweats but wore nothing else. My mouth watered. Basanelli's chest was something to look at. I thought he looked amazing in a suit. He was even better out of it. There was no question.

"What?" he asked.

"Nothing." I shuffled more sticky notes in my hand, glue sticking to my fingers.

Nick's grin was hungry. "Keep looking at me like that, and we're going for round three right now instead of a little bit later."

Parts of me sparked wide awake and ready. I liked that there would be a round three. "Go back to work," I muttered, finding a note with song lyrics. I think it was from a Florida Georgia Line song if I remembered right. I put that in the song stack.

Nick opened his laptop on the counter and typed quickly.

"What are you doing?" I asked.

"I have a list of the properties Sadie owns that we know about. Sheriff Franco sent them to me. Some of these are unrecorded."

I looked over. "How did you find the unrecorded parcels? Or rather, how did the sheriff?"

"The gossip mill. He just asked around, and people who had sold, gifted, or bargained property to Sadie came forward." He lifted one powerful shoulder. "Or, let's be honest, those who lost property to Sadie in the gambling den. Please, tell me you're not going to reopen that."

I laughed. "I am not going to reopen the gambling section of Silver Sadie's. If I end up owning the building, which I think I will, I'm creating a small party area back there."

"That's a good idea," Nick said. "You've been thinking about this for a long time."

"I have," I admitted. The wind scattered ice against the windows, lending an intimacy to the condo. It was too dark outside to see the lake, but the mere emptiness that led to the lights on the other side made me feel like we were the only two people around. I was surprised by how much I enjoyed the thought of being alone with Nick with the world at bay.

"All right, here. Let me print this out." He pushed a button, and a printer echoed from the other room. Basanelli had an office right off the entryway. He padded in there and then walked out with stacks of paper. "Give me that description."

I squinted to better see and then rattled off the numbers.

"Hmm," he said. "Oh, here it is." He dug into a drawer for a pen and crossed out a line on the paper. "Okay. Let's go through all of these we find, as well as any possible contracts. Several people that Sheriff Franco spoke with admitted they'd signed things away on a sticky note, and then, of course, Sadie created a quitclaim deed."

"She seemed to be pretty good at that," I muttered.

"Yeah, but based on the one you found over there, we know the one left with Rudy Brando was a fake." He pointed to the one with the practice signatures.

Was that enough to make this whole thing go away? I didn't think so. "Yeah, but I'll have to go to court to prove it, won't I?"

He looked at me, his tawny eyes serious. "Yes, unless you can get the widow to dismiss her case."

I threw up my hands, sending one sticky note swishing to the floor. "Can't we get an early dismissal or something?"

He nodded. "It's a civil case, and you could make a motion for summary judgment, but you probably wouldn't win it. There's a dispute of fact, which means you'd have to go to trial. I think you'd win, and I think it's silly that the widow wants to take you to trial to begin with."

"Can I get attorney's fees paid back?" I asked.

"Yes," he said. "But it'll be a process and take a couple of years."

My heart sank. "So, I wouldn't be able to open the restaurant during that time?"

"No, not while the property is in litigation."

Well, I guessed there was always a chance I could take the falsified deed to Marilyn Brando and maybe get her to see reason. I mean, I didn't have anything to lose. "Fine." I pulled apart two orange pieces of paper and tried to read one.

We spent a few more hours organizing all of Sadie's notes and found at least forty-five property descriptions, all on different colors. Nick only had thirty of them on his list. Most were in Gem County, on the outskirts of Silverville, and all the way to Montana, but some were in Washington state as well as northern Idaho.

"Do you think maybe she's at one of these places?" I asked softly.

"I hope so," he murmured. "The fact that we haven't heard anything from her concerns me. People shouldn't walk around with that much cash."

I couldn't agree more, and the guilt almost swamped me.

"Hey." He tossed his pen onto the table. "We've been at this for long enough. Let's get some sleep."

"Don't you still have a trial tomorrow?" I asked.

He shook his head. "Since it's the day of New Year's Eve, we're all taking it off, but I do need to run into the office for just a couple of hours to handle some paperwork. Speaking of tomorrow night, are we going to the ball?" He lifted me easily, and my stomach rolled over once again.

I'd already told our grandmothers that I was going out with him. I might as well tell him. "Yes, I've decided to accept your invitation. I wouldn't want you disappointing your grandmother."

"I appreciate that." He cupped my ass and strode toward his bedroom. "I'll reward you greatly."

And he did. Three times.

CHAPTER 33

*A*fter he left for the office, I stretched lazily in Nick's bed. The night had been phenomenal, and I might just wear Nick beneath my skin for the rest of my life. What was I going to do about that?

When he joked that he'd ruin me for other men...it turned out he hadn't been joking.

I so didn't want to leave his condo. The scent of him was all around me, and I liked it. Tito had wanted to see if she could open the diner this morning, and I was all for it, so long as she kept Bertra on track. Lewis thought he could save the grill, and I figured I'd give him the morning to do so.

Yawning, I slipped from the bed, noting a hickey on my left hip. Who knew Basanelli liked to leave hickeys? It was kind of cute that I knew that about him and nobody else did. I wandered into the kitchen and dining room, where we had left all the stacks of sticky notes. Nick had sent off the list to Sheriff Franco, who was supposed to follow up. I certainly hoped he found Sadie. My phone buzzed, and I picked it up.

"Hello?"

"Hey, Tess, it's Kelsey Walker."

I smelled coffee, and my head swiveled toward the pot on the counter. "Hey, Kels. What's up?" It felt like we were becoming friends.

"I wanted to call you because Mert Smiley is being released around two this afternoon, and he's being a grouch about it."

I smiled and poured myself a cup of coffee. "If Smiley isn't being a grouch, then something's wrong with him."

She laughed. "I know, but we can't release him on his own, and he won't call anybody to pick him up."

"I'll pick him up," I said. "You said you think he'll be done around two o'clock?"

"I was hoping you'd say that, and yeah." The sound of a printer whirring came across the line. "I'll make sure we have all his discharge papers ready because I know he won't want to wait, and he'll be grumbling because you came."

"That's okay. I'm used to it." I wondered if I should bring him back to Donna's house. He should probably be watched. "Does he need somebody to stay with him?" I asked.

"No. He just needs to do his follow-up checkups and start on the physical therapy regimen. He has a new heart doctor he has to see." She was quiet for a couple of beats. "If you want, I can accidentally put all that together in a file that you can kind of slip into your purse."

"I would really appreciate that." Smiley wouldn't go on his own, so I would have to nag him. But I would because I needed my partner around for a long time. "Thank you, Kelsey."

"Anytime. I still owe you one." She hung up.

I figured we were about even, but she was kind to say that. Yawning more because Basanelli hadn't let me get much sleep the night before, I walked over to the now neatly arranged sticky notes on the table and counter before saying a quick prayer for Sadie because I hoped she was still alive.

My phone buzzed again. "Hello," I answered.

"Hey, it's Deputy McCracken."

"Hi there," I said, surprised. "What's up?"

He coughed. "I'm calling you and giving you a heads-up. Brad Backelboff is back from California, and he wants us to issue an arrest warrant for you." McCracken spoke low as if he were trying to whisper. "Stay over in Elk County, and don't come back. Okay?"

It was incredibly sweet that he'd phoned to warn me. "You shouldn't be calling me, McCracken," I said softly.

"I am well aware of that. Call your sister. You need a lawyer."

"Thank you." I hung up. This was incredible. I had never so much as purposely killed a spider. I was one of those dorks who put them on a piece of paper and slid them outside. The idea that I had killed two men was unfathomable, but the new prosecutor over in Gem County didn't know me, and he obviously didn't care.

Every instinct I had told me that Sheriff Franco would fight against arresting me, so I figured I still had a day or so, but I sent a quick text to Anna, letting her know what was happening. She answered instantly, saying she would bring donuts. Apparently, she was taking the day off work.

The doorbell rang, and I stilled before looking down at my outfit. I wore one of Nick's dress shirts and nothing else, but it covered me to my knees. So I shrugged and walked over to the door. No doubt Nick was receiving a package or something. Not being a dummy, I looked through the peephole and then stilled. Oh, come on. What in the world? I opened the door. "Louise, what are you doing here?"

Her face looked ravished, as if she'd been crying all night, and she shivered as if she were freezing. "I'm sorry." She gulped. "I needed to talk to somebody, and you've been so nice to me."

I frowned. "How did you know where I was?"

She gulped. "Everybody knows you're dating Nick Basanelli. How do you get a guy like that?"

Why couldn't there be any secrets in my life? I pushed my

wayward hair out of my face. "Louise, I really can't help you. You need a lawyer, and I'm a waitress." I might be an owner of a couple of diners, but really, I didn't know anything about the law. "I promise I will tell the absolute truth, and say that it's my belief you didn't mean to harm anybody or even the fish."

It truly was the best I could do for her.

"Thank you." She sniffed. "All right, I guess I'll go." Her eyes rolled back in her head, and she started to fall.

"Louise," I cried out, catching her. She stumbled and started to go down. "Whoa. When was the last time you ate?" I asked.

"I had the burger." More tears gathered in her eyes.

The woman might need more help than I could offer. We did have a psychologist in the family. "Maybe you should see my cousin, Wanda," I said. "She's been a great help to a lot of us. I think you really need to talk to somebody, Louise."

I helped her inside and shut the door. She was way too cold. "Did you stay the night in your car?" I led her to the kitchen to get her some coffee.

"I just drove around all night," she admitted. "Just thinking about the good times with Bobbo and what we could have had."

Yes. I definitely thought she should call Cousin Wanda. "I tell you what, why don't we call my cousin right now and get you some help, okay?"

Louise sniffed. "You're too kind. After everything I've done to you, I can't believe you're being this nice to me."

I actually did want to help her.

She looked over at all the sticky notes. "Well, that's weird. Is that what was in that silver box you had yesterday?"

I paused. "You know about the box?"

She wiped tears off her cheeks. "Yeah, I saw you walk into the diner. Remember? I figured there was something important in it. Was there?"

"Not really," I lied. "Just a bunch of sticky notes."

She chewed on her lip. "You know who used sticky notes all the time, don't you?"

"Who?" I asked cautiously.

"Sadie Brando." Louise looked from the sticky notes to me and then back. "You know where she is, don't you?"

Warning ticked down my spine. "I actually have no idea," I said, honestly. "I hope she's still alive."

"Oh, she's still alive." Louise pulled a gun out of her pocket and pointed it at me.

I took several steps away from her. "What in the world are you doing?"

She gestured me toward one of the chairs, still trembling from the cold. "It took forever for Basanelli to leave this morning, and I'm freezing my ass off. Sit down so I can think."

I sat, my gaze on the gun. Had I ever looked down a barrel before? Not really. "You followed us home."

"Of course. The second I saw that safe in your hand, I knew what it was."

I frowned, my chest chilling and my lungs seizing. "How?"

She shrugged. "I owed Sadie some money for gambling debts, and she kept track on those stupid sticky notes. That small safe was always near her."

How many other people knew about the box? "Were you working with Rudy Brando?"

"Nope. Never met the guy."

I tried to keep track of the conversation. "Yet you paid Sadie off somehow?"

"Yeah. Did you really think I purchased twenty-five grand in furniture? I spent about two and tried to pay off Sadie with the rest. Bobbo didn't know the difference." Tears gathered in her eyes again. "I really do love that moron."

My phone buzzed on the counter, and we both ignored it. "Did you kill Rudy Brando?" I gasped.

She jerked her head. "Of course not. Why would I have killed him?"

I didn't know, but considering she was holding a gun on me for the second time, why not ask? Or maybe it was better not to know. "You're confusing me, Louise. Why are you here holding a gun on me?"

"I need money," she said softly. "Sadie was the nicest of the people I owed for gambling. It isn't my fault." Her tone turned cajoling. "I just need a little more seed money, and I can win it all back."

I glanced at the knife block on the counter. It was too far away. "You've come to the wrong place. I don't have any money."

"No, but Sadie does. A shit ton of it." She picked up Nick's paper and noted all the crossed-out parts. "So, there are two properties up in Boundary County, one in Washington state, one here in Timber City, and one in Montana that haven't been searched?"

Could I tackle her? If so, I'd have to swipe her gun arm out and then take her down. My legs shook, and I wished I'd borrowed sweats from Nick, even though they would've been way too long.

Louise looked up, her eyes gleaming. "I know Sadie. She'd never leave the state with all that money. She has to be at the place nearest here."

I didn't agree. That place was all the way around Tamarack Lake toward the mountains and would be difficult to reach in the winter. "If Sadie is hiding or on the run, she'd want to be somewhere she could escape from quickly. The winter is too harsh for anybody to go that far out."

"Oh, I know her a lot better than you do. She'd want to stay close, and we're going to find her." Louise gestured with the gun. "Get up and move. There are no fish here right now, Tessa. If I shoot, it won't be at an aquarium this time. You're going to want to work with me."

CHAPTER 34

y legs were freezing as I sat in the driver's side of my Rogue, wearing only Nick's shirt and boots. I was lucky she'd let me slip my feet into those before shoving me outside into the cold. "I can't believe you're doing this," I said. "I was trying to help you."

She squinted at her phone. "Go left here," she muttered.

I had been following her directions for nearly an hour around the lake. Hopefully, Anna would reach Nick's with donuts and get worried when I wasn't there...especially since my phone was still on the counter. Louise had kept the weapon pointed at me pretty steadily. Still, considering she'd accidentally taken out an aquarium the other night, I didn't have a lot of faith in her ability. "Could you please put the safety back on that thing? I'll take you wherever you want to go."

She shook her head. "I don't think so. In fact, I guess you should know that I did mean to shoot the aquarium the other night."

My jaw dropped. "You did?" I turned my head and then quickly looked back at the snowy road. We were far beyond the other side of Tamarack Lake, and the roads were icy. A deer made to jump in front of my car, and I slowed down.

"What are you doing?" she snapped.

"Watching out for deer," I said slowly.

I had my seat belt on, and so did she. Ramming a tree wouldn't do any good and would probably get me shot. I could go for the gun, but that would also likely get me shot. "Louise, I think you have problems, and I want to help you. Why did you shoot at the aquarium?"

She shrugged. "I was trying to make a statement, and then once I realized it didn't work, I helped you pick up the fish. Okay, I did feel bad about the fish."

At least that was something. "How about we pile onto that feeling bad?" I murmured, slowing as more deer popped up on the side of the road. "You haven't hurt anybody yet. You can still get out of this."

"I just want to find Sadie and get the money," she said. "We both know she's hiding out."

There had to be a way out of this situation. "I think she went to Vegas." I half-meant it. "That's what I would've done."

"If she were in Vegas, enough cameras would've captured her that we'd know it by now. Believe me, I understand the reach Nick Basanelli has, even if you don't."

I understood that Nick had contacts I couldn't even imagine. Even so, this seemed like a silly waste of time that would probably end in my death. "What makes you think she is even remotely in this direction?"

"It's the only place close to Timber City. You know Sheriff Franco checked out everything in Gem County. Sadie wouldn't want to go too far from home. You have to know that this is the only place near Timber City."

My legs knocked together. "Why would she hide out at all?"

"I haven't figured that out yet. My best guess is she double-crossed you and wanted to get out of town for a while to figure out her best options."

I reached over and clicked the button to heat my seat.

"What are you doing?" she asked, focusing on me.

"Trying to warm myself up," I muttered. "I'm freezing. You could have at least let me put some pants on."

"Yeah, well, you could have at least not fixed my ex-fiancé up with Kelsey Walker."

That might be a fair point. "Don't you want him to be happy?" I tried another tack with her.

"No," she burst out. "Unless it's with me. I mean, seriously. The guy has money. He has a farm. He could share it a little bit."

I was starting to think maybe Louise didn't care about Bobbo as much as she claimed. "Why is it just about money with you?"

"Shut up, or I'll shoot you."

Okay. Time to be quiet. I took another corner onto a barely-there road. "Are you sure this is the right way?"

She looked down at her phone. "Yes. You go about two miles, and then we'll turn right."

We were truly at the far end of Tamarack Lake in the middle of nowhere. It probably was a good hiding place, but it was also a great place to hide a body. I shivered. "Did you kill Rudy Brando?" I asked again. The woman seemed capable of it.

She snorted. "No, of course not."

I looked at her. "Really?"

"Honestly. I didn't kill him. It wasn't me. I figured you killed him."

I jolted. Now, she was messing with my head. She seemed more than capable of killing Rudy, especially now that I could see the anger in her eyes. Had she killed Rudy to keep him away from Sadie? Had she planned to marry Bobbo and somehow end up with all his great-aunt's money? "You already know I didn't kill him."

"You had the most to gain," she said.

Said who? Sadie had more secrets than I realized. I had no clue she was still acting as a loan shark. "Maybe, but his deed is fraudulent."

"Maybe, maybe not." Louise shrugged. "But he still had a deed. I bet you just stabbed him right in the chest. You're tougher than you look, Tessa Albertini."

"Thanks," I muttered, slowing down. Now, she was definitely messing with me. What a liar. "Shouldn't the turnoff be soon?"

She looked at her phone. "Not yet." She kept the gun pointed steady at me. I had to think of a plan, but my hands were chilled, and my brain felt frozen. I'd never really had a gun pulled on me before, and it was much more terrifying than I realized.

"Would you *please* put the safety on that thing?" It was a Smith & Wesson Ladysmith—a weapon I knew well because I had one.

"No," she muttered. "If you ask me again, I'm going to shoot you in the leg."

"You can't shoot me in the leg. If you do, I can't drive," I retorted, instantly regretting it. But she chuckled. Yeah, Louise was way off. She needed more than Cousin Wanda could do for her.

"Turn left by the oak tree," she said.

"I thought you said to turn right."

"Well, now it says to turn left."

I rolled my eyes. "That's a tamarack tree." Even so, I took the turn.

The snow was heavy, and it didn't look like any vehicles had been this way in a while, but the massive overhang of tree branches protected the ground somewhat so my Rogue didn't get stuck.

"Since you're out on bail, aren't you supposed to stay away from guns?" I asked.

"I *am* out on bail," she said. "But there's no requirement for not having a gun. Besides, I think we're past that, don't you?"

"Yes," I muttered. "I think we are."

"Okay," she said. "Stop here."

I looked around. There was nothing. "What?"

"Stop the car!" she yelled.

I hit the brakes, and we slid several feet, stopping rapidly.

"Okay. Pull over into those trees."

I looked at her. "Are you going to shoot me?"

"No, I'm not going to shoot you. Just pull over." Her eyes were a little wild, so I did as she said. "Okay, turn off the car."

I did, my hands shaking. She looked again at her phone and the map. "The cabin should be just around that bend right there. We're going to walk."

I looked out at the snow. "Louise, it's at least three feet high out there."

"I'm aware of that," she said. "I guess you should have put on pants."

I'd never make it with my bare skin. "I'm not going out there."

"Yeah, you are." She undid her belt and pointed the gun at me.

My head ached, and my chest hurt. I could not believe I was in this situation. What would Anna do? I didn't know how my sister had survived the scrapes she'd gotten into. Fine. At least if I got Louise outside, maybe I could take her. I undid my seat belt.

"Come this way." She opened her door and motioned for me to climb over the console, holding the gun on me the entire time.

I shook my head and followed her. She fell back a little bit, and I went for the gun, grabbing it and shoving it out of the way. She yelped, grabbed my hair, and yanked me out of the vehicle. We fell onto the snow, rolling around, grunting and punching. It was freezing cold, and I didn't have any pants on, but I slapped her ears and then headbutted her. Panic gave me strength. She rolled over, shrieking, and yanked a knife from her pocket to slice into my arm.

Blood spurted, and I cried out. The cold snow dulled the sharp pain.

We kept rolling, and she landed on top of me, straddling me

with a knife in her hand. I scrambled for it, but she pressed it to my neck. I stilled. The snow and ice stung against my back and bare legs, but I could only focus on the blade.

She slowly levered off me and scrambled around, grabbing the gun off the floor of the Rogue to point it at me. "Get up," she said.

I rolled over and stood, looking down at my sliced arm.

"That looks bad." She gestured at my wound.

"It feels bad," I snapped, wavering. I was bleeding, but I didn't think she'd hit an artery. My gaze caught on the bloody knife. "Well, that's a six-inch serrated hunting knife now, isn't it, Louise?" I asked dully.

She looked down and nodded. "Yeah. I used to work over on the St. Joe with my family. These are the knives I used."

I slowly lifted my gaze to face her. It was exactly the kind of knife used to kill Lenny Johnson and then left in my box at Silver Sadie's. I'd looked carefully at the picture of it. "I bet a lot of people use those kinds of knives," I said slowly, the blood rushing through my ears and making my head ring.

"Yeah, they do." She stuck it into her back pocket.

I couldn't breathe. The snow burned the skin on my legs, and my arm pounded with pain, dripping blood everywhere. "You killed Lenny."

She sighed. "Yeah."

I shivered. "Why?"

She motioned toward the trees. "Head that way. I'm right behind you."

Almost on autopilot, I turned, wincing as more snow fell down my shirt. "Why Lenny?" The old guy had never physically hurt anybody.

"Shut up and move."

I carefully picked my way, trying to keep as much snow off my body as possible, but it wasn't easy. My legs were going numb, and my arm was starting to hurt even more. At least the cold had stemmed the flow of blood a little bit. My mind spun.

"Go left," she said, her teeth chattering.

My arms were turning blue. I moved between two blue spruce trees and saw a cabin just ahead. Smoke rolled from the chimney.

The gun pressed against my back. "Here's the plan," she murmured.

I was too cold to move and take her by surprise. Hopefully, whoever was inside would be able to help. Thoughts scattered through my head like falling ice. "Lenny was going to be Sadie's partner," I said, my lips barely moving.

"Yep." She moved to my side, keeping the gun against my ribs.

I looked at her, somehow able to feel shocked. "You killed Lenny because of Bobbo?" Was I way off base? That seemed insane.

She sighed and brushed snow off her heavy jacket. "Yes. I took out Lenny and was going to get Sadie next. Bobbo would've inherited everything."

So she had broken into my new building and planted the murder weapon. My jaw slackened, and I quickly closed my mouth as freezing air wound down my esophagus. "Why in the world did you leave the knife in my stuff?"

"Duh. You're the strongest suspect in Rudy Brando's killing, so it made sense that you probably killed Lenny as well. It was entirely too easy to get into the vacant place, you know. Even after you had the locks changed." She sounded pretty proud.

I wanted to puke. "So you *did* kill Rudy Brando."

"Pay attention, would you? Now,"—she gestured toward the cabin—"you're going to lead very quietly, and if you make any sound, I'm going to shoot you right in the head."

CHAPTER 35

I couldn't make a sound if I wanted to because my vocal cords had frozen. I wasn't feeling the chill in my feet anymore, which was a bad sign. So I kicked through the snow, careful to keep low, conscious of the gun at my back.

The cabin was a one-story structure with a tipped roof that allowed snow to fall. The blinds were drawn, and I couldn't see inside. No doubt the door was locked.

Apparently, Louise had the same thought.

She nudged me over to the side of the building, and I walked through the heavy snow to the rear of the dwelling. It hit me that I was done with cabins, and I was so fucking finished with snow. This was getting ridiculous. My teeth started chattering so hard my jaw hurt, but I couldn't stop it.

"Up the stairs," she whispered tersely behind me. I could barely make out any stairs. When I planted my boot on the lowest one, it sank so far I nearly pitched forward.

Grabbing the railing, I quietly hitched my way up, my feet and legs protesting every time I shoved them back into the snow. Unable to help myself, I pushed as fast as I could toward the wooden siding on the top of the deck, which was at least a little bit protected by the eaves.

Oh, the snow still reached my knees, but at least my thighs were free for the moment. The wind picked up, slashing into us, and I wanted to cry. Instead, I waited. Louise emerged at my side and peered around me. "Try the door," she ordered.

I reached out and attempted to open the slider. "It's locked," I whispered.

"Fair enough," she said, stepping back. Then, before I could comprehend what was happening, she moved to the side and fired three times into the glass. Huge shards dropped, and I yelled, jumping back. She pressed the gun to my hip again, and this time, it burned me. "Inside. Now," she snapped.

I coughed and stumbled inside just as Sadie and Jonathan emerged from either side of the living room, their jaws slack. Louise pointed the gun at both of them. "Everyone on the sofa," she yelled.

Sadie's jaw dropped, and she didn't look nearly as terrified as I felt. "What in the hell is going on?"

Jonathan's hair stood up straight, and he wore an old, ratty green jogging outfit. He looked at the gun. "What are you doing, young woman?"

"Louise." Sadie put her hands on her hips. She wore too-big jeans and a red Christmas sweater. "We're square. You drove out to my place twice and paid me off. Remember?"

"Oh, yeah, I know. But we are not square," Louise said. "Sit, or I will shoot you."

Sadie, the skin on her neck sagging, looked wide-eyed at the broken glass door. "What is wrong with you?" she muttered, stomping over to sit on what appeared to be an eighties-style gold sofa.

Jonathan, his face set in a perpetual scowl, stumbled over to her, grabbed a knitted blanket on the way, and tossed it onto his sister. "It's freezing in here now," he whined.

Louise pointed the gun at his face. "Shut up. I need to shoot somebody, and you're a good prospect."

I was shivering so hard, Sadie beckoned me over. "Come here, Tessa. Come sit here."

"Go ahead," Louise said. My lips ached from the cold, and I stumbled across the snow now scattering over the wooden floor to sit next to Sadie. She immediately threw the blanket over me.

"Oh, my goodness. You're freezing." Then she glanced at my arm. "You're bleeding. She needs help."

I'd forgotten about my arm. I looked down to see a lot of blood. Oh, God. My head swam.

Jonathan stood. "Let me get her something."

"No," Louise said. "Move, and I'll shoot you."

"It's okay. You still have us," Sadie said. "There's a wrap in the bathroom, Jonathan," she said.

He nodded and scurried out of the room.

Louise fired into the ceiling, and I jumped.

"I'm coming." Jonathan hustled back. There hadn't been time for him to get a phone or a weapon. He returned with an ACE bandage and tossed it to Sadie. She immediately wrapped my arm, and it didn't hurt. I figured that was bad. My whole body felt like a block of ice.

Louise still stood by the shattered door, gun pointed at the three of us. "Where's the money, Sadie?"

Sadie looked at me and then at her. "How did you find me?"

"It wasn't easy," I admitted. "We found your sticky notes."

She frowned. "That damn Rudy. The jerk told me he'd stolen my little safe." She looked over at Louise. "What's your plan here, Louise?"

"My plan is to take your money," Louise said, her gaze darting around. "Where is it?"

Sadie shook her head. "It isn't here. You don't think I'd bring all that cash with me, do you?"

I snuggled closer to Sadie, and she let me. As soon as the

feeling returned to my legs, I was going to charge Louise. It was the only way to save Sadie and her brother. The cabin looked nice enough, but it was definitely utilitarian. It didn't make sense that Sadie would take a hundred and fifty grand in cash and then hide out here.

"Are you in danger?" I just couldn't make sense of it.

"I don't think so," she murmured. "Not really. Well, maybe."

I tried to keep my brain working, but my body was trying to shut down. Fast. "Who's after you?"

"At the moment, I am," Louise snarled. "Where's the money, Sadie?"

"It's in my safe back in Silverville," Sadie said calmly. "Seriously, do you honestly think I brought that much cash here?" She snorted and looked at her brother. "Honestly. Amateurs."

As my body began to warm, my brain finally kicked in. I turned and looked at Sadie. "You know, there's one thing I just can't figure out."

"What's that?" Sadie asked, the lines around her eyes showing she'd smiled a lot during her many years of life.

"Why would you hide out?" I mumbled.

Sadie grinned. "For you, sweetheart."

What? Wait a minute. My jaw finally dropped open, and my teeth stopped chattering. There was only one reason she'd stayed that had to do with me. She wanted to protect me? "You killed Rudy?" I smacked myself on the forehead. "*That's* why you're hiding out." It was the only thing that made sense. She'd mentioned that Rudy had stolen her safe...how did she know that? The guy must've told her.

"No, I killed Rudy," Jonathan admitted. He lifted a hand. "It was an accident. Well, sort of. He came at me, and I stabbed him."

"No, brother, it's okay. You can tell the truth," Sadie said. "After you paid me, Tessa," she said clearly, "I was going to go on a nice long vacation a couple of days later, but I remembered that some of my mother's letters were still back at the bar. So I returned, and

Rudy was there, rifling through all of the garbage looking for gold. Dumbass. I'd taken everything of value that I wanted."

Louise stepped closer, her gun swinging from Jonathan to Sadie. "Keep talking," she ordered.

"Sure thing," Sadie cackled.

I wanted to put my arm around Sadie, but it was still bleeding. Should I even move it? "Did Rudy attack you?"

"Yes," she said. "The asshole had a fake deed and told me he was actually going to tell people I gave him the property. Can you believe that?"

I looked at Jonathan, then back to Sadie. She looked so frail, but I knew she was a tough woman. "What happened?"

"He said he was going to kill me, and the moron pulled out a gun, so I stabbed him. We fell over, and I kept shoving in with a knife." She shook her head. "Honestly, it was the first time I've ever stabbed anybody." Her eyes widened. "It was easier than you would think."

I hope I never found out. "What about the deed?"

"Well, I called Jonathan, and he came immediately."

"I've disliked that guy since high school when he stole my prom date," Jonathon admitted. "But I didn't want him murdered. It really was an accident."

Sadie shivered in the cold. "Then, of course, our problem was that you would be the prime suspect, and we couldn't let you take the fall. Rudy said he had recorded his fake deed earlier, so even if we had taken it after he died, there was still a record."

I lowered my head. "Sadie, what did you do?"

She gulped. "We took that deed and left it in Frisky's cabin, right where the sheriff could find it. We tried to make it so obvious that it was a setup, even leaving it dead center in the table with nothing else there." She pushed her hair back with a trembling hand. "We were too freaked out to think clearly and left the knife in his chest, darn it. Should've taken it, but by the time I figured that out, it was too late."

"Why didn't you just tell the truth?" I asked.

Sadie patted my hand, careful to stay away from the wound in my arm. "Rudy stole my safe from my cabin, which had records of gambling payoffs. I mean, they're hard to decipher, but I figured the sheriff would find them. Also, I wasn't sure I could prove self-defense. Don't worry. I would've turned myself in after we figured out the best way to do it. Probably."

I frowned. "Wait a minute. What about the matching bloody knife found in my fridge?"

"Oh, that was me," Jonathan said. "We decided if we made it look like somebody was trying to set you up, it would help you."

My stomach revolted. "Whose blood was on that knife?"

"It was deer blood. No worries." Jonathan waved it away.

My frozen brain reeled. "Why did you tear apart my entire place? You ruined my furniture."

Jonathon nodded. "I needed to make sure you called the police."

Sadie grinned. "You said you wanted new furniture, remember? So now insurance will have to get you new stuff. I thought we were doing you a favor."

I frowned. "I don't have insurance on the furniture."

Her expression sobered. "Oh. Well. Then I guess I'll take some of that cash you paid me and buy you all new furniture. It's the least I could do."

Louise stepped even closer, her boots crunching on both ice and glass. "Why did you have a knife on you in the first place?"

"I always carry one," Sadie said. "I mean, come on. I run, or at least I used to run, an illegal gambling den. Guns aren't my thing, so I always had a knife with me." She leaned over. "A kitchen knife will do just as good as any other."

"I did not know that." I looked up at Louise. "Louise, you still haven't hurt anybody." I chose to forget the fact that she had killed Lenny Johnson.

"I killed Lenny," she spat.

Sadie gasped. "You did what?"

Louise had the grace to blush. "Yes. I thought Bobbo and I were going to get married…" She let her voice trail off.

"So you thought Bobbo would inherit my fortune?" Sadie said, rearing up. "What was your plan…to kill all of us?"

"I hadn't thought that far ahead," Louise said in a rush. "I just knew that Lenny couldn't have half of the building. It was that simple."

This was such a fiasco, I didn't even know what to think.

Louise set her stance. "I am tired of all of you. Go get the money, or I'll shoot your brother."

Sadie stiffened. "I told you. I don't have the money. I left it in Silverville."

"You're a liar. I know you better than that." Louise's jaw tightened. "There is no way you would leave that much money and go on the run."

"Are you on the run?" I asked.

"Not really. We were just waiting until we made sure you were safe before we left town. I figured we'd come back in about six months and they would've given up on finding Rudy's murderer," Sadie said quietly. "I don't have the money."

Louise fired a shot, and it hit the refrigerator. "Last one," she snapped. "Next one's in your brother's head."

Sadie sighed. "Fine."

Even freezing cold, shock still rumbled through me. The woman had the money and she'd been bluffing? This was way out of my league. "Louise, don't do this." There was no doubt she'd shoot the three of us once she had the money. She had no choice. I couldn't let that happen.

"Too late," Louise said. "I'm sorry. There's no way out of this."

Sadie stood. "All right, I'll get it." She walked by her brother, and I saw my chance as Louise followed her with the weapon. I threw the blanket at her and then rushed forward in a tackle, hitting her center mass and throwing us both out onto the snowy deck. The gun fired, and pain exploded in my abdomen, and then all hell broke loose.

Nick Basanelli leaped over the deck, grabbing me and tumbling us back inside. Aiden Devlin burst through the front door while Anna ran around the back with her gun pointed at Louise. Sirens echoed in the distance. We rolled over, and Nick put me on my back, running his hands over my body.

"Are you okay? Were you hit?" he asked.

Everything hurt. I looked at my arm. "My arm and my stomach hurt."

He flipped up the shirt and ran his warm hands over my abs. I groaned.

He pulled a chunk of ice away from my skin. "It's just ice."

I gasped and looked down. "I wasn't shot?"

"No." He grabbed my face and pulled me up, cradling me and looking around. Aiden and Anna rushed in from the rear, and Aiden had Louise in front of him with her arms behind her back.

"Are you okay?" Anna ran toward me, panic in her grayish eyes.

"Yeah, I'm great," I said, and then I passed out.

CHAPTER 36

Ten hours after being stabbed—well, *sliced*—for the first time in my life, I danced beneath a sparkling disco ball with Nick Basanelli holding me close. His body was hard and warm against mine, and I couldn't forget the way he'd leaped over a deck to take down somebody with a gun.

It turned out I ended up at the hospital right when Mert Smiley was being released, so he waited until my arm was stitched. Of course, that meant he had to deal with all my family because the minute everyone found out I'd been injured, they arrived en masse. We were accustomed to showing up at the hospital for Anna, so it was a different experience for me to be the one in the bed. I could sympathize with her a lot more than I thought.

Tonight, my dress was green and sparkly, and Nana O'Shea had added flimsy sleeves within one hour to partially cover the bandage on my left arm. Nick wore a tux and looked like a dangerous animal on the prowl. I liked it. It was a good look on him.

He brushed my hair back from my face, his hand heavy on my

waist as he moved us to the soft music. "Are you sure your arm's okay?" he asked. "We don't have to dance."

"My arm is fine." My legs were still a little shaky, but I didn't have frostbite, and I would be okay.

"Good," he murmured, leaning in. "Our families are watching us."

"I know." I felt eyes on us from every direction, as well as hope. I was supposed to take it easy, but I was thrilled to be alive and wanted to have some fun. We could leave early...and have more fun together just the two of us. "They really want us together."

He leaned down and kissed my nose. "I want us together, too."

It was our third dance, and he was driving me crazy—like usual. The music stopped, and he took my hand, walking over to the bar. "You want anything?"

"Champagne," I said.

He ordered some and a scotch for himself.

Sheriff Franco sauntered up. "How's the arm?"

"It's fine," I told him. "I'm going to be okay."

"Good, good. I heard they're holding Louise without bond this time."

That was definitely the right thing to do. I nodded. "What about Sadie and Jonathan?"

Sheriff Franco shrugged. "The prosecuting attorney is looking at the evidence now, but I think she can prove self-defense. If not, she'll hire your sister and win at trial. I'm not worried about Sadie. She's as tough as they come."

I nodded.

"Also, I have good news for you," the sheriff said, smiling.

That sounded wonderful. Finally, good news. "You do?"

"Yes. I took all the proof to Marilyn Brando, and she finally agreed that Sadie did not transfer the property to Rudy."

Nick narrowed his gaze. "You went to her?"

The sheriff smiled wider. "Yes, I did, and although she seemed reluctant to believe me, I believe Sadie then paid her a visit. So, anyway, the woman has dropped her case against you. You should be receiving the paperwork later this week."

I couldn't believe it. I now owned two restaurants—or was at least part-owner of the second. "Thank you, Sheriff." I was happy about that, but I couldn't help but look at Nick. My dream had been to own restaurants…yet dreams could change.

"Come on." He held out his arm.

I slipped my hand through it and waved at my sister, Anna, who was dancing with Aiden. They made a perfect couple. It turned out she and Aiden had seen Louise force me from Nick's condo and then followed us all the way to the cabin.

Apparently, she called Nick the second it happened, and he had been close by, having decided to return home and work with me that day since his trial got canceled. They'd also called the police but reached me first. I caught a glimpse of my cousin, Rory, and his girlfriend, Serenity, over by my parents.

"Oh, there's Rory. Have you heard anything?" I asked the sheriff.

"Oh, no, that's a story for another day," the sheriff said, his eyes twinkling. "You two have fun." With that, he turned and walked away.

I couldn't wait to hear about Rory and Serenity. From my vantage point, I couldn't tell if they were getting along or not. Darn it.

"We'll talk to them in a while," Nick said. "For now, let's go for a walk."

"I'm not going outside," I said.

He laughed. "No, just this way."

"All right," I agreed, trusting him.

We walked down the stairs of the Elks Lodge over to a quiet booth by the bar. The festivities were all upstairs, but some people had filtered down here. I sat and scooted in. It felt good to sit. I still had a pretty decent bruise on my ribs, but I didn't care. "Yes, Basanelli?" I asked.

"I want you to give us a shot," he said, his gaze serious.

"I am."

He leaned in and kissed me, making my head spin. Then he sat back. "No, I mean it. You and me. I don't date a lot," he murmured.

"Yes, you do. You date everybody."

He shook his head. "No, I go on dates. I don't get serious, and now I am. You're completely in me, and I'm not letting you go, Contessa."

They were sweet words, and I liked them, but I didn't know how to answer. "Our lives are different."

"But we want the same things. I'm fine with you building a restaurant empire."

I was just getting started, but there was no question he had my heart. "But you're going to run for office. You're not going to live in Idaho."

"I'm not running for governor, which would put me in Boise, which is way too far from Silverville," he muttered. "I'll either run for Senate or Congress and split time between DC and home. We can make it work. You and I can do anything."

"What are you saying?"

In answer, he took a box out of his pocket and put it on the table, flipping it open. It was probably the most gorgeous diamond I had ever seen.

"It was my great-grandmother's," he said. "I changed the setting."

I looked at him, my entire body going numb.

His smile was a combination of hunger and amusement. "I'm not asking you tonight, but I'm telling you, we're going to date, we're going to plan our future, and then you're going to wear my ring."

I swallowed, my entire body swelling and heating. So this was what real love felt like. It was both exhilarating and slightly terrifying. "You really think we can make it work?"

"I know we can, Tessa. I've loved you for years," he admitted.

"I've watched you from afar. I've been around when I could be. You and I fit. You know that."

Did Nick Basanelli just say the l-word? I gulped. "Nick, we've only been dating a short time." My protest sounded weak, even to my ears. He was overwhelming me...but in a good way.

"I don't care," he said. "I know what I want. I always have. And when I want something, I get it."

"And now you want me?" I asked, looking at his tawny brown eyes.

"I definitely want you. Forever," he said.

Forever sounded good to me. I leaned in and kissed him, not surprised when he took over and dragged us both under. Finally, he let me breathe.

"When are you going to ask me?" I asked.

His grin held a wicked promise. "I don't know, but definitely by Valentine's Day."

That was only a month and a half away. "I can't wait," I said. "And by the way, I know this is crazy, and it's too early, but I love you, too."

* * *

It's time for new Anna and Aiden adventure in HABEAS CORPUS, available for preorder now!

And if you're enjoying the Anna Albertini series, take a look at the Deep Ops series, which features a group of outsiders who go after dangerous criminals...along with their slightly alcoholic dog and very demanding cat:

HIDDEN - Chapter 1

The day he moved in next door, dark clouds covered the sky with the promise of a powerful storm. Pippa watched from her window, the one over the kitchen sink, partially hidden by the cheerful polka-dotted curtains. Yellow dots over crisp white background—what she figured happy people would use.

He moved box after box after box through the two-stall garage, all by himself, cut muscles bunching in his arms.

Angles and shadows made up his face, more shadows than angles. He didn't smile, and although he didn't frown, his expression had settled into harsh lines.

A guy like him, dangerously handsome, should probably have friends helping.

Yet he didn't. His black truck, dusty yet seemingly well kept, sat alone in the driveway as he removed the crates.

She swallowed several times, instinctively knowing he wasn't a man to cross, even if she had been a person who crossed others. She was not.

For a while, she tried to amuse herself with counting the boxes, and then guessing the weight, and then just studying the man. He appeared to be in his early thirties, maybe just a few years older than her.

Thick black hair fell to his collar in unruly waves, giving him an unkempt appearance that hinted nobody took care of him. His shoulders were tense yet his body language fluid. She couldn't see his eyes.

The question, the damn wondering, would keep her up at night.

But no way, there was absolutely *no way*, she would venture outside to appease the beast of curiosity.

The new neighbor stood well over six feet tall, his shoulders broad, his long legs encased in worn and frayed jeans. If a man could be hard all over, head to toe, even in movement, then he was.

A scar curved in a half-moon shape over his left eye, and some sort of tattoo, a crest or something, decorated his muscled left bicep. She tilted her head, reaching for the curtains to push them aside a little more.

He paused and turned, much like an animal going on alert, an overlarge box held easily in his arms. Green. Those eyes, narrow and suspicious, alert and dangerous, focused directly on her.

She gasped. Her heart thundered. She fell to the floor below the counter. Not to the side, not even in a crouch, she fell flat on her butt on the well-scrubbed tiles. Her heart ticking, she wrapped her arms around her shins and rested her chin on her knees.

She bit her lip and held her breath, shutting her eyes.

Nothing.

No sound, no hint of an approaching person, no rap on the door. Her throat closed, making it nearly impossible to breathe.

After about ten minutes of holding perfectly still, she lifted her head. Another five and she released her legs. Then she rolled up onto her knees and reached for the counter, her fingers curling over.

Taking a deep breath, she pulled herself to stand, angling to the side of the counter.

He stood at the window, facing her, his chest taking up most of the panes.

Her heart exploded. She screamed, turned, and ran. She cleared the kitchen in three steps and plowed through the living room, smashing into an antique table that had sat in the same place since the day she'd moved in.

Pain ratcheted up her leg, and she dropped, making panicked grunting noises as she crawled past the sofa toward her bedroom. Her hands slapped the polished wooden floor, and she sobbed out, reaching the room and slamming the door.

She yanked her legs up to her chest again, her back to the door, and reached up to engage the lock. She rocked back and forth, careful not to make a sound.

The doorbell rang.

Her chest tightened, and her vision fuzzed. Tremors started from her shoulders down to her waist and back up. *Not now. Not now. God, not now.* She took several deep breaths and acknowledged the oncoming panic attack much as Dr. Valentine had taught her. Sometimes letting the panic in actually abated it.

Not this time.

The attack took her full force, pricking sweat along her body. Her arms shook and her legs went numb. Her breathing panted out, her vision fuzzed, and her heart blasted into motion.

Maybe it really was a heart attack this time.

No. It was only a panic attack.

But it could be a heart attack. Maybe the doctors had missed something in her tests. Or maybe it was a stroke.

She couldn't make it to the phone to dial for help.

Her heart hurt. Her chest really ached. Glancing up at the lock, a flimsy golden thing, she inched away from the door to the bed table on her hands and knees. Jerking open the drawer, she fumbled for a Xanax.

She popped the pill beneath her tongue, letting it quickly absorb. The bitter chalkiness made her gag, but she didn't move until it had dissolved.

A hard, rapping sound echoed from the living room.

No, no, no. He was knocking on the door. Was it locked? Of course it was locked. She always kept it locked. But would a lock, even a really good one, keep a guy like that out?

Definitely no.

She'd been watching him, and he knew it. Maybe he wasn't a guy who wanted to be watched, which was why he was moving his stuff all alone. Worse yet, had he been sent to find her? He had looked so furious. Was he angry?

If so, what could she do?

The online martial arts lessons she'd taken lately ran through her head, but once again, she wondered if one could really learn self-defense by watching videos. Something told her that all the self-defense lessons in the world wouldn't help against that guy.

Oh, why had Mrs. Maloni moved to Florida? Sure, the elderly

lady wanted to be closer to her grandchildren, but Cottage Grove was a much better place to live.

Her house had sold in less than a week.

Pippa had hoped to watch young children play and frolic in the large treed backyard, but this guy didn't seem to have a family.

Perhaps he'd bring one in, yet there was something chillingly solitary about him.

Of course, she hadn't set foot outside her house for nearly five years, so maybe family men had changed.

Probably not, though.

He knocked again, the sound somehow stronger and more insistent this time.

She opened the bedroom door and peered around the corner. The front door was visible above the sofa.

He knocked again. "Lady?" Deep and rich, his voice easily carried into her home.

She might have squawked.

"Listen, lady. I, ah, saw you fall and just wanna make sure you're all right. You don't have to answer the door." His tone didn't rise and remained perfectly calm.

She sucked in a deep breath and tried to answer him, but only air came out. Man, she was pathetic. She tapped her head against the doorframe in a sad attempt to self-soothe.

"Um, are you okay?" he asked, hidden by the big front door. "I can call for help."

No. Oh, no. She swallowed several times. "I'm all right." Finally, her voice worked. "Honest. It's okay. Don't call for anybody." If she didn't let them in, the authorities would probably break down the door, right? She couldn't have that.

Silence came from the front porch, but no steps echoed. He remained in place.

Her heart continued to thunder against her ribs. She wiped her sweaty palms down her yoga pants. Why wasn't he leaving? "Okay?" she whispered.

"You sure you don't need help?" he called, his voice rich and deep. Definitely sexy, with a whole male edge that went with that spectacular body. "I promise I can be all sorts of helpful to damsels in distress."

Was that a line? Was he trying to flirt with her or put her at ease? What could she say back? Something equally flirty so he'd be at ease and not curious about her? Nothing came to her fuzzing mind. "I'm sure." *Go away.* Please, he had to go away.

"Okay." Heavy bootsteps clomped across her front porch, and then silence.

He was gone.

***

Hours later, Malcolm West kept moving boxes into his house, wondering about the pretty lady next door. She hadn't reappeared in the window for hours.

He knew the sound of terror, and he knew it well. The woman, whoever she was, had been beyond frightened at seeing him in the window. Damn it. What the hell had he been thinking to approach her house like that?

A fence enclosed their backyards together, and he'd wondered why. Had a family once shared the two homes?

He grabbed the last box of stuff from the truck and hefted it toward the house. Maybe this had been a mistake. He'd purchased the little one-story home sight unseen because of the white clapboard siding, the blue shutters, and the damn name of the town— Cottage Grove. It sounded peaceful.

He'd never truly see peace again, and he knew it.

All the homes the real estate agent had emailed him about had been sad and run-down...until this one. It had been on the market only a few days, and the agent had insisted it wouldn't be for long. After a month of searching desperately for a place to call home, he'd jumped on the sale.

It had been so convenient, it seemed like a stroke of fate.

If he believed in fate, which he did not.

He walked through the simple one-story home and dropped another box in the kitchen, looking out at the pine trees beyond the wooden fence. The area had been subdivided into twenty-acre lots, with tons and tons of trees, so he'd figured he wouldn't see any other houses, which had suited him just fine.

Yet his house was next to another, and one fence enclosed their backyards together.

No other homes were even visible.

He sighed and started to turn for the living room when a sound caught his attention. His body automatically went on full alert, and he reached for the SIG hidden at the back of his waist. Had they found him? Somebody had just come in the front door.

"Detective West? Don't shoot. I'm a friendly," came a deep male voice.

Malcolm pulled the gun free, the weight of it in his hand more familiar than his own voice. "Friendlies don't show up uninvited," he said calmly, eyeing the two main exits from the room in case he needed to run.

A guy strode into the kitchen, hands loose at his sides. Probably in his thirties, he had bloodshot eyes, short, mussed-up brown hair, and graceful movements. His gaze showed he'd seen some shit, and there was a slight tremble in his right arm. Trying to kick a habit, was he?

Malcolm pointed the weapon at the guy's head. "Two seconds."

The man looked at the few boxes set around the room, not seeming to notice the gun. Even with the tremor, he moved like he could fight. "There's nowhere to sit."

"You're not staying." Malcolm could get to the vehicle hidden a mile away within minutes and then take off again. The pretty cottage was a useless dream, and he'd known it the second he'd signed the papers. "I'd hate to ruin the minty-green wallpaper." It had flowers on it, and he'd planned to change it anyway.

"Then don't." The guy leaned against the wall and shook out his arm.

"What are you kicking?" Malcolm asked, his voice going low.

The guy winced. "I'm losing some friends."

"Jack, Jose, and Bud?" Mal guessed easily.

"Mainly Jack Daniel's." Now he eyed the weapon. "Mind putting that down?"

Mal didn't flinch. "Who are you?"

Broad shoulders heaved in an exaggerated sigh. "My name is Angus Force, and I'm here to offer you an opportunity."

"Is that a fact? I don't need a new toaster." Mal slid the gun back into place. "Go away."

"Detective—"

"I'm not a detective any longer. Get out of my house." Mal could use a good fight, and he was about to give himself what he needed.

"Whoa." Force held up a hand. "Just hear me out. I'm with a new unit attached to the Homeland Defense Department, and we need a guy with your skills."

Heat rushed up Mal's chest. His main skill these days was keeping himself from going ballistic on assholes, and he was about to fail in that. "I'm not interested, Force. Now get the hell out of my house."

Force shook his head. "I understand you're struggling with the aftereffects of a difficult assignment, but you won. You got the bad guys."

Yeah, but how many people had died? In front of him? Mal's vision started to narrow with darkness from the corners of his eyes. "You don't want to be here any longer, Force."

"You think you're the only one with PTSD, dickhead?" Force spat, losing his casual façade.

"No, but I ain't lookin' to bond over it." Sweat rolled down Mal's back. "How'd you find me anyway?"

Force visibly settled himself. "It's not exactly a coincidence that you bought this house. The only one that came close to what you were looking for." He looked around the old-lady cheerful kitchen. "Though it is sweet."

Mal's fingers closed into a fist. "You set me up."

"Yeah, we did. We need you here." Force gestured around.

Mal's lungs compressed. "Why?"

"Because you're the best undercover cop we've ever seen, and we need that right now. Bad." Force ran a shaking hand through his hair.

"Why?" Mal asked, already fearing the answer.

"The shut-in next door. She's the key to one of the biggest homegrown threats to our entire country. And here you are." Force's eyes gleamed with the hit.

Well, fuck.

***Read HIDDEN today!

WOLF - CHAPTER 1

Also, if you're interested in a fun, sexy, and suspenseful paranormal romance, take a look at WOLF:

Chapter 1

A predator stared back at her.

Mia Stone set her face into calm lines, her hand inching to where her weapon used to sit on her hip. Only a leather belt existed there now. She shook off the unease. Jail bars. Many bars, evenly spaced, stood between her and the man currently meeting her gaze without expression.

She'd faced evil, good people who'd committed evil...yet she'd never really faced someone truly unreadable. She swallowed.

His gaze dropped to her throat.

An odd quaver wandered down her spine. What in the world was wrong with her? Maybe she'd been out of the game for too long. Focusing, she did her job and studied him.

Near the end of a cot, he lounged against the far wall of the cell. Most prisoners automatically sat when doing time in jail. Not this guy. He had to be, what? Early thirties? At least six and a half feet tall, he leaned his shoulders against the worn brick. His hair was a pure black and his features masculine and solid. Though his eyes were a mix of different blues—light to dark.

A scar ran down the right side of his jaw to disappear into thick hair that almost reached his shoulders. Too rough to be called handsome, there was no doubt he was compelling.

Many killers were.

Mia cut her eyes to the quilt. Pink and homemade, the bed cover belonged in a jail cell as much as the diamond earrings she wore belonged in the small-town sheriff's office. But she'd promised her mother, and there hadn't been time for a fight before driving to the middle of nowhere. Still, she'd left her hair down to camouflage the sparkle.

She squared her shoulders and stepped up to the bars. "Mr. Volk, my name is Mia."

Upon arriving at the station, she'd asked to talk to the prisoner alone and had promised to stay in the hall. The sheriff had merely shaken his head and shut the door separating the main office from the two cells. Seeing the man in the cell, gratitude filled her that she hadn't pushed to go inside with Volk.

She tried to appear in control. "I was hoping we could talk."

Slowly, one dark eyebrow rose. "You're a cop."

"No, I'm not." She kept her face in pleasant lines, showing honesty.

"You reached for your weapon," he said softly.

Surprise had her stilling. "Yes. I used to be a cop. FBI, actually."

Volk straightened. "That makes you sad." Intense, he studied her.

The breath caught in her throat. She forced herself to exhale. This wasn't the first subject who'd tried to get inside her head. "Are *you* sad, Mr. Volk?"

"My father is Mr. Volk." Two long strides, and he stood much closer on the other side of the bars. The scent of wild sage came with him. "Call me Seth."

Courage had her lifting her chin and refusing to retreat. He could easily reach through and grab her. The last time she'd messed with a psychopath, she'd lost. "Seth."

He cocked his head to the side. Slowly. "I like how you say my name."

A warning trilled in the back of her mind. "So, you'll talk to me?"

"I am talking to you." Low, rough, his voice wrapped around the silence.

"Thank you." She'd learned early on that respect went a long way with killers and sociopaths. "As I said, I'm not a cop, but they've asked me to speak with you. If you're okay with that, we can talk."

He quirked his upper lip, making him seem approachable. Almost. "I want to talk to you."

She frowned. "Why?"

"Your voice is pretty." He rubbed the stubble on his chin. "Kind of like Ingrid Bergman's in *Casablanca*. Soft and classy with a hint of sass."

Warmth messed with caution in her chest. Bogie embodied everything she'd ever wanted in a man. Plus, that was her favorite movie.

"But your eyes are sad. Haunted." Seth's large hands wrapped around the bars. "Who hurt you, Mia?"

She jerked her head to the side. Instinct told her to run. "I'm asking the questions."

His expression went blank again. "You said you wanted to talk. Talking goes both ways."

This was no stupid country hick. She stared deeper into his eyes, seeing intelligence and...what else simmered in those dark depths? An emotion deep down. Anger. The guy was pissed. "Do you have a temper, Seth?"

"Yes." His knuckles whitened on the steel. "Did somebody hurt you?"

"Yes." She kept her arms loose at her sides, just in case he reached for her. "Do you harm women?"

"No." His jaw firmed. "Is the person who hurt you still alive?"

"No." She shoved emotion into a box. "Did you kill Ruby Redbird?"

His head cocked. "No. Why did you just lie to me?"

"I didn't."

Exhaling, he released the bars and turned his broad back to her. "Yes, you did." Faded jeans covered a hard butt and led up to a dark T-shirt. Those shoulders spread wider than a linebacker wearing pads. The flak boots on his feet were probably size fourteen, yet he moved with masculine grace. "You can go now."

Panic threatened to cut off her air. She needed to prove that she could still do the job. "I shot and killed the man who wanted to hurt me." When had she lost control of the conversation?

"And?"

Seth should've been the profiler. "I believe that man had a partner. If so, he's still alive." She could do this. Reveal her past pain to get to the truth.

Seth turned around. "I'm sorry."

"Doesn't matter—and most people think I'm wrong." The world centered again. "If you didn't kill Ruby, who did?"

"I don't know. But I will find out."

Now, *he* was lying. She didn't know how she knew that, but she did. What she didn't know was *the lie*. Had he killed Ruby? Or was he protecting the person who did? "I thought you disliked lying. That goes both ways, too."

His eyes darkened as his gaze traced every contour of her face.

Nerves sprang to life as if his fingers caressed her skin. She stepped even closer to the bars. "Have you killed before?"

"Yes." Thick boots clanged against metal as he took the final step toward her. Warmth from his massive body brushed her silk shirt. Only metal bars separated them...no air. "Besides the man you just mentioned, have you killed before?"

Her head jerked back. "No."

"Now, who's lying?" he asked softly, curiosity and an odd gentleness curving his bottom lip.

She blinked twice. Something about his voice was mesmerizing. A killer who hinted at safety right before murdering. His mouth caught her attention. Full, sexy, male. "I will find out who killed Ruby."

The moment stretched until her heartbeat echoed in her head.

"Step away from the cell," Seth said, taking a large stride back from the bars.

Keys rattled outside the exit door.

Startled, Mia shuffled across the rough concrete until her shoulders rested against worn brick on the opposite wall. There was no logical reason for her to obey his command.

Yet there she stood.

His gaze remained on her, dark and thoughtful, as the door opened.

Then a metamorphosis occurred. His expression went blank with boredom and a fierce insolence. He glanced at the two men striding toward them.

"Sheriff, you'd better have a decent reason for arresting Seth this time." A tall man in a sleek gray Armani suit led the way, his hair a perfect salt and pepper, his skin bronzed from sun obviously enjoyed away from Washington state.

The sheriff sighed. His hair was *more* salt than pepper, and grooves cut lines into the sides of his mouth. Apparently, Sheriff Pete Maxwell had spent some time at the local diner over the last year if the strain on his brown uniform was any indication. "Your client is a killer," he said shortly.

"That's slander," the tall guy said, stopping in front of Mia. "Who the hell are you?"

Seth stepped toward the bars.

Mia had the strangest urge to wave him back. She focused on the well-dressed man and extended her hand. "Mia Stone."

He took her hand, gripping tightly as they shook. "Prat Lenessee, Mr. Volk's attorney. I do hope you didn't question my client outside of my presence, Stone."

Mia slid her cop face into place, biting back a wince at the hard pressure. This wasn't the first asshole lawyer she'd dealt with. "I'm not a cop."

Lenessee released her. "If the police invited you here, then you're an agent of the police, so you're as good as a cop."

Yet she wasn't. She might not ever be a cop again. In any case, instead of wallowing, she allowed a slightly pissed-off smile to curve her lips with the unintimidating pink lipstick she'd chosen. "I've shaken a lot of men's hands, Mr. Lenessee. The ones with obvious insecurities,"—she dropped her gaze to his pressed pants and then traveled back up to his face—"always grip too hard."

Surprise opened his mouth, which he quickly snapped shut.

Her smirk widened just enough to let him know she saw the surprise. "*You* grip too hard."

In her peripheral vision, she caught a flash of Seth's grin.

The sheriff chortled, not even trying to hide his amusement.

Yeah. No doubt the lawyer thought she'd shake off the purposeful show of strength. She hadn't been the best profiler in DC for nothing...well, until they determined she'd grown crazier than the bastards she hunted. Throwing an attorney off track was half the fun of her former job.

He leaned over her in an obvious intimidation tactic. "Perhaps you're too soft to play with the big boys."

Seth hissed out a breath. "Lenessee, get me the hell out of here." His voice rumbled low with threat and danger.

The attorney straightened to stare at Seth. "Of course. Your bail has been posted, Mr. Volk." The lawyer's tone hinted at no deference, no affection, and no respect. If anything, he seemed indifferent to the point of condescension.

The sheriff exhaled loudly and unlocked the door, sliding it open.

Seth stepped out.

Lenessee retreated.

Interesting.

Mia glanced from Seth to the lawyer. The attorney was on guard. Just how dangerous was Seth that even his lawyer feared him?

He brushed by the attorney, heading down the hallway without another word.

Lenessee turned to the sheriff. "You had no basis to arrest him, and you know it. You might want to contact the county attorneys, because there will be a civil rights violation filed by the end of the day."

"No, there won't." Seth's low voice rumbled back before he shoved open the exit door and disappeared.

Lenessee inhaled, both nostrils flaring. Pivoting on Italian loafers, he strode after his client.

The sheriff raised an eyebrow. "Well?"

Mia shrugged. "I don't know. But I want to find out." Turning, she hustled away from the cells, moved through the small interior of the police station, and out to the waiting room.

The space held several worn leather chairs around a large coffee table displaying magazines about hunting, farming, and football. A wide wall of windows looked out onto the deserted Main Street.

Mia skirted the table and stared out the window.

Seth and his attorney spoke on the sidewalk, the lawyer keeping his distance. Well, the lawyer talked while Seth glanced around the quiet street. He stood next to a *No Parking* sign, his head nearly as tall as the placard.

His shoulders straightened, and he shifted his attention to her.

Finally, the lawyer wound down, turned on his heel, and headed for a Cadillac parked across the street.

Seth cocked his head to the side, his expression full of dare.

Mia shoved open the glass door. She should get a weapons

permit if she continued to work in the state—not that she hadn't already stuck a small Glock 43 into her ankle holster. Several steps across a rough sidewalk had her close enough to smell wild sage. Her shoulders went back.

"You're very pretty, Mia."

Not what she'd expected. She frowned. "Who killed Ruby Redbird?"

Seth slowly shook his head, wrapping a hand around her biceps. "That's a mystery you're no longer involved in." His grip was warm and unbelievably strong.

He moved into a stride.

She tried to yank free.

His hold slid smoothly to the back of her elbow, effectively putting her in a position where she had to move, much like a parent with a wayward toddler. For the briefest of moments, she felt vulnerable—like a civilian and not a trained law enforcement officer. Confusion had her biting back an expletive. They'd traveled halfway down the block before she dug in her heels and turned to face him.

She swallowed, angling her head. Up close, he was even bigger than he'd seemed in the station. Heat cascaded off the man. "Stop manhandling me."

"Where's your car?" His harsh features held no expression.

She shook her head. "None of your business."

Sighing, he glanced toward the parking lot that served the entire block and pointed to her older Toyota. "That's the only one I don't recognize. You need to take your sweet butt over there and go home, wherever that might be."

Small chunks of concrete scattered when she settled her stance. "I'm trained, Volk."

His smile was instant and almost charming. "You're half my size, darlin'. And your training won't do you any good."

Something in his tone suggested she believe him. But she'd faced killers before, and she'd solved murders before. This was her chance to get back into the life she'd loved. "I'm not going anywhere until you tell me the truth."

He released her. Almost in slow motion, he reached out to run a thumb along her cheekbone. It was a whisper of a touch that swept a flash of heat through her body.

Shock kept her immobile.

His features were strong and somehow ruthless, but he dropped his hand and released her from his spell. "Please, leave."

"No."

Those blue eyes darkened to almost black. "Leave, or you'll be as dead as Ruby."

Mia retreated a step, her heart shooting into a gallop. "Is that a threat?"

"No." A veil dropped over his eyes. "That's a fact, Mia Stone."

**READ WOLF today!

ABOUT THE AUTHOR

New York Times and *USA Today bestselling* author Rebecca Zanetti has published more than seventy novels, which have been translated into several languages, with millions of copies sold worldwide. Her books have received Kirkus and Publisher's Weekly starred reviews, been featured in Entertainment Weekly, Woman's World and Women's Day Magazines, have been included in retailer's best books of the year.They have also have been favorably reviewed in both the Washington Post and the New York Times Book Reviews. Rebecca has ridden in a locked Chevy trunk, has asked the unfortunate delivery guy to release her from a set of handcuffs, and has discovered the best silver mine shafts in which to bury a body...all in the name of research. Honest. Find Rebecca at: www.RebeccaZanetti.com

ALSO BY & READING ORDER OF THE SERIES'

I know a lot of you like the exact reading order for a series, so here's the exact reading order as of the release of this book, although if you read most novels out of order, it's okay.

THE ANNA ALBERTINI FILES

1. Disorderly Conduct (Book 1)
2. Bailed Out (Book 2)
3. Adverse Possession (Book 3)
4. Holiday Rescue novella (Novella 3.5)
5. Santa's Subpoena (Book 4)
6. Holiday Rogue (Novella 4.5)
7. Tessa's Trust (Book 5)
8. Holiday Rebel (Novella 5.5)
9. Habeas Corpus (Book 6)
10. 2025 Book (Book 7) TBA

* * *

LAUREL SNOW SERIES

1. You Can Run (Book 1)
2. You Can Hide (Book 2)
3. You Can Die (Book 3)
4. You Can Kill (Book 4) - 2024

* * *

DEEP OPS SERIES

1. Hidden (Book 1)
2. Taken Novella (Book 1.5)
3. Fallen (Book 2)
4. Shaken (in Pivot Anthology) (2.5)
5. Broken (Book 3)
6. Driven (Book 4)
7. Unforgiven (Book 5)
8. Frostbitten (Book 6)
9. Unforgotten (Book 7) - TBA
10. Deep Ops # 8 - TBA

* * *

REDEMPTION, WY SERIES

1. Rescue Cowboy Style (Novella in the Lone Wolf Anthology)
2. Rescue Hero Style (Novella in the Peril Anthology)
3. Rescue Rancher Style (Novella in the Cowboy Anthology)
4. Book # 1 launch - subscribe to my newsletter for more information about the new series.

* * *

Dark Protectors / Realm Enforcers / 1001 Dark Nights novellas

1. Fated (Dark Protectors Book 1)
2. Claimed (Dark Protectors Book 2)
3. Tempted Novella (Dark Protectors 2.5)
4. Hunted (Dark Protectors Book 3)
5. Consumed (Dark Protectors Book 4)
6. Provoked (Dark Protectors Book 5)
7. Twisted Novella (Dark Protectors 5.5)
8. Shadowed (Dark Protectors Book 6)
9. Tamed Novella (Dark Protectors 6.5)
10. Marked (Dark Protectors Book 7)
11. Wicked Ride (Realm Enforcers 1)
12. Wicked Edge (Realm Enforcers 2)
13. Wicked Burn (Realm Enforcers 3)
14. Talen Novella (Dark Protectors 7.5)
15. Wicked Kiss (Realm Enforcers 4)
16. Wicked Bite (Realm Enforcers 5)
17. Teased (Reese -1001 DN Novella)
18. Tricked (Reese-1001 DN Novella)
19. Tangled (Reese-1001 DN Novella)
20. Vampire's Faith (Dark Protectors 8) *****A great entry point for series, if you want to start here*****
21. Demon's Mercy (Dark Protectors 9)
22. Vengeance (Rebels 1001 DN Novella)
23. Alpha's Promise (Dark Protectors 10)
24. Hero's Haven (Dark Protectors 11)
25. Vixen (Rebels 1001 DN Novella)
26. Guardian's Grace (Dark Protectors 12)
27. Vampire (Rebels-1001 DN)
28. Rebel's Karma (Dark Protectors 13)
29. Immortal's Honor (Dark Protector 14)
30. A Vampire's Kiss (Rebels-1000 DN)

31. Garrett's Destiny (Dark Protectors 15)
32. Warrior's Hope (Dark Protectors 16)
33. A Vampire's Mate (Rebels-1000 DN)
34. New Dark Protectors (DP 17) 2024
35. New Dark Protectors (DP 18) 2024

* * *

STOPE PACKS (wolf shifters)

1. Wolf
2. Alpha
3. Shifter

SIN BROTHERS/BLOOD BROTHERS spinoff

1. Forgotten Sins (Sin Brothers 1)
2. Sweet Revenge (Sin Brothers 2)
3. Blind Faith (Sin Brothers 3)
4. Total Surrender (Sin Brothers 4)
5. Deadly Silence (Blood Brothers 1)
6. Lethal Lies (Blood Brothers 2)
7. Twisted Truths (Blood Brothers 3)

* * *

SCORPIUS SYNDROME SERIES

**This is technically the right timeline, but I'd always meant for the series to start with Mercury Striking.

Scorpius Syndrome/The Brigade Novellas

1. Scorpius Rising
2. Blaze Erupting
3. Power Surging - TBA

4. Hunter Advancing - TBA

Scorpius Syndrome NOVELS

1. Mercury Striking (Scorpius 1)
2. Shadow Falling (Scorpius 2)
3. Justice Ascending (Scorpius 3)
4. Storm Gathering (Scorpius 4)
5. Winter Igniting (Scorpius 5)
6. Knight Awakening (Scorpius 6)

* * *

Printed in Poland
by Amazon Fulfillment
Poland Sp. z o.o., Wrocław